Praise for *Six Reasons to Stay a Virgin*

'A light, funny read about playing Cupid'
Hot Stars

'Refreshing, light-hearted and emotionally intelligent,
Six Reasons says that it's more than OK to stand
apart from the crowd and follow your heart'
The Times

and for *Calling On Lily*

'Fresh and young with a rural setting and lots of fun'
Sarah Broadhurst, *Bookseller*

'Insightful'
Daily Mirror

'A warm, witty debut'
Heat

'Written with a confident, light touch, humour and realism'
Shrewsbury Chronicle

As well as the bestselling *Six Reasons to Stay a Virgin* and *Calling On Lily*, Louise Harwood is also the author of *Lucy Blue, Where Are You?*. An ex-publishing editor, she is now a full-time writer. She is married to a literary agent, and lives in Oxfordshire with her husband and two sons. Her new novel, *Hippy Chick*, will be published by Pan in August 2007.

Also by Louise Harwood

Lucy Blue, Where Are You?

LOUISE HARWOOD

six reasons
to stay a virgin
&
calling on Lily

PAN BOOKS

Six Reasons to Stay a Virgin first published 2003 by Pan Books.
Calling on Lily first published 2002 by Pan Books.

This omnibus first published 2007 by Pan Books
an imprint of Pan Macmillan Ltd
Pan Macmillan, 20 New Wharf Road, London N1 9RR
Basingstoke and Oxford
Associated companies throughout the world
www.panmacmillan.com

ISBN 978-0-330-45229-8

1 3 5 7 9 8 6 4 2

A CIP catalogue record for this book is available from
the British Library.

Typeset by SetSystems Ltd, Saffron Walden, Essex
Printed and bound in Great Britain by
Mackays of Chatham plc, Chatham, Kent

six reasons to stay a virgin

For Charlotte

1

If the ugly man with the beard and the bacon sandwich had looked where he was going, Emily wouldn't have been trying on a white shirt in Ruffles Department Store, wouldn't have trodden on a sleepy spring wasp and wouldn't have run out of her cubicle wearing only a pair of pink knickers, straight into the arms of Sam Finch.

Sam had been looking for a birthday present for his sister. When Emily suddenly joined him, he took a heavy step backwards and closed his arms around her, a skirt in one hand, and for a few seconds he held her there, hot breath against his chest. He looked down at her bare shoulders and at the golden brown head tucked half inside his coat and knew he should give her up again, any longer and she'd think she'd thrown herself at the wrong sort of man.

'I'm sorry. There's a wasp in the changing room,' she told him, keeping her arms tight around his waist.

'It won't buy anything. They never have any money.'

'I'm not joking. It stung me. It hurts.'

'I'm sorry.'

'Hurts a lot.'

'I'm *really* sorry. Shall I find you some ice?' Ice? What was he thinking of? Where was he going to find ice?

She shook her head and let go of him and made a

quick dive back towards her cubicle, but as she opened the door the wasp flew out at her and she had to duck away towards the open shop floor.

The wasp went too, hovering in wait as she slipped behind a rail of coats, then zooming in on her the instant she re-emerged. It was like watching film from a police helicopter of a stolen car, Sam thought, one that bumped across ploughed fields, forged across rivers, demolished gates but was never going to get away.

Still holding the skirt, he went after her, followed at a trot by a fat, breathless sales assistant and a few grinning shoppers. Pinned against a range of tartan shirts, Emily was keeping one hand across her front and swiping wildly at the wasp with the other.

'Help me,' she hissed at the sales girl, who rifled hurriedly through the shirts, selected one, held it out to Emily and leapt back quickly.

'No, I meant kill it, stamp on it!' Emily cried. 'Stamp on it!'

As Emily pulled the shirt against her Sam stepped in, slapped the wasp against the wall behind her with his hand and then ground it into the floor with his boot.

The sales assistant glowed at him admiringly and smoothed back her hair.

Emily gave him a shy smile. 'Thank you. Again.' She turned quickly away and pulled the shirt over her head, stopped, hair tumbled around her face, and looked back at him.

'I thought so,' she said. 'It's even worse! I *know* you . . . It's Sam!'

He smiled. 'Hello, Emily.'

They looked at each other, neither knowing quite what else to say.

'This season, I shall mostly be wearing pink pants,' Emily said.

He laughed, thinking how those pants were going to be etched upon his brain for evermore.

'You can wear this if you want to.' He held out the skirt and she looked at it dubiously.

'Do you still want ice? There'll be a cafe somewhere. Or I could find a first-aid box?'

'I think I'd better go and get dressed. I'm going to be late for an interview.'

'For a job?'

'Yes, sort of. I hope so. I've a feeling it's more of a chat.'

'Then don't go. Come and have a coffee with me instead.'

She thought about it for half a second. 'I'd love to but I can't. It's the first chance I've had for ages.' She shifted restlessly from bare foot to bare foot and glared back at her still-fascinated audience of shoppers. 'I can't stand it. Talking out here like this. I have to go and get dressed.'

He nodded.

'But thanks so much, Sam. You were fantastic.'

She was back in control, wanting to be dressed, thinking about the interview, turning away from him, moving smoothly out of his life. But Sam still had the feeling of her in his arms. He desperately tried to think of something to make her stop, to keep her next to him for just a few moments more.

And then she did stop and turned back to him.

'Do you ever hear from Oliver?' she asked.

Not what he wanted her to say. He saw the interest in her face and felt old, familiar frustration rising inside him.

Sam nodded. 'Did you hear he's back from the States? For good this time, he says.' Why had he told her that? 'That's why I'm here. I came up from Cornwall to see him.'

'He's come back early?' She sounded thrown by the news.

Sam shook his head. 'No, he's done the year. Like he planned.'

'But it's gone so fast.' She still couldn't take it in.

'Well. Time flies. He's back again.'

'I had no idea. I can't believe it. And if I hadn't been stung, I'd never have come out. And then I'd never have seen you.'

And it's a good trade-off, is it? Sam thought sourly. A wasp sting in exchange for some news of Oliver.

She came back to him and touched the skirt bunched up in his hand.

'Say hi to him for me.' He shrugged and nodded, sure he wouldn't. 'And Sam – ' she was looking curiously at the skirt – 'tell him that I left my job.'

He gritted his teeth. 'OK.'

'And Sam – ' now she was smiling again as she tugged the skirt out of his hand – 'satin. Mmm.' She held it up in front of her. 'And with pleats too!'

4

'I could have got it in green and white, but then I thought the brown and yellow—' He saw the look on her face. 'But you don't like it, do you?' he groaned. 'It's horrible, isn't it?'

'Who are you buying it for?'

'My sister. For her birthday.'

He waited and Emily shook her head.

'Damn. Give me some advice, then.'

'Go across the road to Jigsaw. It'll be open now.'

'But I'm sure I could find something here. If you helped me.'

'There is nothing nice here. Trust me.'

'But you're here . . .' Sam said, unable to stop himself, cringing even as he said it.

She smiled up at him. 'I'm here because this was the only shop that opened at nine.'

Sam lost. Emily left him, running back to the safety of her cubicle. He put the rejected skirt back on a nearby rail and slowly looked around. Where before sales assistants had been thin on the ground, now it seemed as if they were all around him with dewy eyes and soft smiles of appreciation, watching the brave wasp assassin and his beautiful girl.

Sorry to spoil your enjoyment, he wanted to tell them, but we are not talking *Brief Encounter* here. Didn't you hear? She doesn't like my skirt and I don't think she likes me much either. But, until he'd seen her again, Sam had forgotten how it felt to have her glance at him, to be, for just a few seconds, the object of her complete attention. He looked across the floor to where she had gone and thought how lovely she was and how she looked no different to when she was sixteen, when he'd first met her, in Cornwall with Oliver.

He eyed her cubicle, thinking, this is too good a chance. I don't have to give up so easily. I am not going to give up so easily. Not again. He slowly circled the shop, wanting to put some distance between himself and the sales assistants, then strode over to the cubicle and put his head close to the door.

'You have got to help me,' he insisted. 'If you don't, it'll be my sister who pays the price.'

There was a pause, then a quiet 'OK'.

'I'll wait for you at the door.'

He turned away, delighted. But then an unfamiliar voice asked, 'Has she been taken hostage?'

'Oh, God.' He laughed, knifed with disappointment. 'Wrong changing room.'

When had she left? How could he not have noticed?

He moved away, aiming for the door, but even before he'd reached it he could see that it was too late. The streets outside were empty. She had gone.

In ten more minutes she'd be late. Twenty and they'd wonder if she was showing up. Thirty and they'd have their answer. It wasn't ideal but the wasp sting had been the final straw, that and running around the shop in her knickers – she who hated coming out of the changing room with new clothes *on* – and admitting to herself that she was wasting her time going to the interview anyway. And seeing Sam again. And hearing Oliver was home.

Emily stood on the street looking for a taxi but when one pulled up she mouthed an apology. She wasn't in a rush any more. She could walk to work in fifteen minutes and be at her desk for nine thirty. No excuses necessary.

She walked, thinking the same thing over and over again. *Oliver's home. I don't believe it, Oliver's back.* Every step she took he was with her, jostling her, making it impossible to think about anything else. And at first it wasn't the Oliver who had left England a year ago who was there at her shoulder, but the Oliver of eight years earlier. Oliver as she'd first met him, one late afternoon on a wide, empty, sun-streaked beach in Cornwall. She'd seen his shadow first, had watched it moving across the flat hard sand towards hers until it had taken over and become hers, and she had looked up, her heart already beating with anticipation. It was a vivid enough memory to make her falter and then stop in the middle of the street.

She imagined what he would say if he was standing in front of her now, his surprise and outrage when he realized where she was heading. *So you told Sam a lie! You haven't left your job at all! And you promised me you'd leave. How can you still be there when you promised me you would leave a year ago?*

Because I am too much of a wimp to leave without something to go to, Emily would tell him. And bloody hell, I didn't realize you were about to turn up again, did I? I didn't realize I'd run out of time. Because, you see, the longer I survive there, the more I have to make all those miserable days count for something. Yes, I want to throw

7

up every time I see the front door, but I fought off hundreds of other people for that job and I'd be crazy to walk away from it just because of *her*.

And yet hearing that Oliver was home again threw everything into the air. There was no ignoring the fact that one whole year had gone by since she'd joined Carrie Piper's theatrical agency. When Oliver had left for the States she'd only just started. She remembered Oliver arriving to take her out one lunchtime in her first week, how he had shuddered at the cold, stagnant atmosphere, had listened to how miserable she was and had angrily sworn to send the boys around if only she gave the word. But she hadn't and those awful minutes and hours and days and weeks and months had now clocked up to a whole massive year, and nothing at all had changed apart from her, each day a little more dented and knocked and miserable than the one before.

She walked faster down the grey streets, stamping down on the pavement in her long leather boots, pulling her coat tightly around her, head down, teeth clenched, clamping down on the flashes of panic and frustration, consumed with the need to put things right. It was as if that wasp had stung her awake at last.

For the first few weeks working with Carrie Piper, her boss, she'd still managed to believe it would get better, that once Carrie Piper got to know her, she would drop the hostility, that the two of them would get on. When, instead, the hostility had got worse, Emily had spent the next few months sure that something new was just a week away. That she was about to be tipped off about a great new job in another agency, or she'd see one advertised, something that she would only have a chance of landing if she were applying from inside the business. But as the months went by and nothing came to save her, her optimism inevitably dimmed. She'd gradually stopped following up every contact she'd ever made because, despite all the effort, nothing ever materialized. But now Oliver was home again and suddenly it was as if a little light of determination had been re-fired.

I am handing in my notice, she decided. Today. And as she thought about it, she realized there would be nothing she missed. That she didn't care if she never read another script or screenplay in her life, didn't care if she never saw another play. She was getting out. And that was why she'd told Sam a lie, a little lie that was so white it was almost true. She was leaving because on measured, mature consideration she could see that a year was long enough. Absolutely nothing to do with the fact that she'd been taken by surprise and didn't want Oliver to think badly of her.

Perhaps she was wrong, she told herself, and a year on Oliver wouldn't care anyway. Perhaps he'd be confused when Sam passed on her news. *Emily? Do I know an Emily?* But of course it wasn't so. She knew that even if they hadn't ever met again after Cornwall, Oliver wouldn't have forgotten her. As it was, they *had* met again years later, working together at a production company called Black Box, when they'd been brought together on the same production. It had been a surprise to see him again, an even greater surprise to realize she would be working with him, every day, breakfast, lunch and tea, for at least three months. But then, no surprise at all to hear that in the intervening years he'd not only built himself a dazzling career but also of course found himself a dazzling live-in girlfriend.

By now she'd walked far enough for the streets to have become decidedly downmarket. Gone were the pretty flower shops, the delis and boutiques and in their place were the cheap burger bars, two second-hand office furniture shops, a pawnbrokers and a launderette that took up the first fifty yards of Robbins Road. As she turned the corner an empty Budweiser can rolled towards her in welcome.

She thought about how it would feel at last to tell Carrie Piper that she was leaving. The wonderful satisfaction as her carefully selected words of resignation, honed and sharpened for so many months, were finally released. How the relief would feel, how it would get to work inside her, unfreezing her brain, lifting the weight off her shoulders, allowing all the new ideas to unfold and shake themselves out, excitement like soft warm rain, giving life to plans that she'd long given up on.

She wanted to walk around for a bit; rehearse her words one final time. But it was too late. She knew she would already have been seen from the upstairs windows.

Emily stopped outside the front door and searched her bag for her keys. A dead pigeon was lying in the doorway of the launderette next door, a frail little pigeon. She concentrated on what she was doing but in the corner of her eye its downy breast kept moving, blown first one way then another by the wind.

She found her keys and took them out of her bag, imagining herself walking in, the door slamming behind her, picking up the post and placing it on the stairs for Carrie Piper to take up with her, then going into the dark cave that was her office, sitting down at her desk. But she didn't move.

Why did you leave my post on the wrong stair? Carrie Piper, with fiery red hair and livid electric rage, trembling yet elated, relishing the confrontation. Carrie Piper, whose anger bent coffee spoons, burned holes in mouse mats, fused lights and shattered glass.

I'm not going to go in, Emily decided.

Why did you do that? What are you trying to tell me?

She would stand behind Emily's chair, waiting for Emily to turn to look at her.

Emily, I need to understand why you hate me.

Slowly Emily looked up to the first-floor window. She was there, staring down at Emily, hunched over the window sill.

Emily looked down at her keys, hating the weight of them in her hand, and then she pushed them, one at a time, through the brass letter box, feeling the heavy springs bite greedily at her fingers each time she pulled them clear.

Chubb first, Banham second. One after the other, her keys hit the cold stone floor on the other side of the door and at the sound Emily felt a wonderful exuberance lift

her up and spin her away. She turned, looked up one last
time and waved a quick, cheeky goodbye before she was
off down the street, so light-footed she was nearly dancing. She paused for a cat, tickled him quickly under the
chin and then she was gone. Leaving the squalid, rubbish-
strewn, infested, dirty street for ever, she turned to the
bus stop and the number 29 and freedom.

2

It was a celebration cake for Emily, and it looked great for about thirty seconds until Holly tried to get it out of the cake tin and only half of it came away.

'This is good,' Holly told her friend Caitlin, trying to shake and scrape at the same time. 'It proves it's homemade.'

'Which counts for so much more,' said Caitlin, taking the knife from her, sliding it around the inside of the tin and loosening the cake expertly. 'Now Emily will know who is her kindest, most talented, most *caring* friend.'

'Stop it!' Holly cried. 'And wait until you see what I've got for her birthday!'

'Given it's Emily, I doubt that it's a blow-up Robert Downey Jr.'

There was a familiar edge to Caitlin's voice. Holly heard it and stopped shaking the cake tin and stopped smiling, on the brink of warning Caitlin that as she was gatecrashing Emily's evening, she should watch her step.

They'd met a couple of hours earlier at Holly's front door, Holly just off the tube and weighed down with food, Caitlin fresh from an afternoon buying a new pair of boots and sleeping through a facial. Caitlin had walked into the kitchen with a bag of Holly's shopping swinging from a finger and had then jumped onto one of the high silver bar stools where she had stayed for the next hour, swinging her feet and admiring her new brown pony-skin boots, while Holly made her some toast and poured her a glass of wine, cleared the table of newspapers and dead flowers, emptied the dishwasher, hung up her coat, whipped cream, marinated prawns and tossed a salad. And yet, as always, Caitlin was so funny, so disarmingly rude about her terrible boyfriends and everyone else, that Holly didn't mind. Not until she began on Emily.

Holly gripped the tin hard so that Caitlin could again run the knife around the inside, and they watched as, at last, the rest of the cake slowly gave up the struggle and fell out.

'There,' Caitlin said, watching Holly shove it all together, 'you clever thing. It looks perfect.' She picked up a stray crumb and dropped it into her mouth. 'Tastes perfect too.'

Caitlin slid off her stool and went over to Holly's huge stainless-steel fridge, opened it and peered inside. Then she held up another bottle of wine. 'Do you mind?'

In answer Holly flung the corkscrew to her, a bit too quickly, and Caitlin gave her a glance of alarm. Hands on hips, Holly watched while Caitlin twisted it in.

'What?' Caitlin asked, looking up, the wine bottle between her knees. 'I only said I liked your cake.'

'Please don't give Emily a hard time tonight,' Holly begged. 'She's left her job. Let's concentrate on that.'

'She can handle me. Anyway, I'll be nice!'

'But she upsets you. And you always let it show and I don't want you to.'

'She doesn't upset me, condescending person. She confuses me,' Caitlin said. 'And I'm not the only one.'

Without replying, Holly carried the last of the dirty bowls over to the sink and squirted an arc of washing-up liquid over them. Behind her, Caitlin waited for a few seconds more, then stalked out of the room, flicking off the light switch and leaving Holly in darkness.

Holly washed up by the light thrown in from the hall. Caitlin's walking out of the room made her smile because Caitlin was the most self-assured, opinionated person she knew and yet Emily got to her, made her tongue-tied and awkward like no one else could.

She dried and put away the last of the bowls and then looked around for the bottle of wine, guessing that it had probably left with Caitlin. She went over to the fridge and took out another one, jumped up onto a stool and poured out a glass, knowing that Caitlin would soon be back.

Free of all the usual clutter, her kitchen looked and felt as it had when it had first been fitted, all stainless steel and chrome and spare clean lines, with a reinforced glass floor, pale lilac walls and wonderful hand-painted tiles. Holly loved it. And she loved it best as it was now, immaculate, expectant, ready for a party, bowls of food taking up every spare inch of the fridge, the floor swept, the dishwasher empty. Around the house she knew she'd made some bad mistakes but she was confident that she'd got her kitchen right.

Behind her, Caitlin shuffled back in apologetically, pulled out another stool and sat down next to her. 'Sorry.'

Holly looked over at her.

'Very, very sorry,' Caitlin pleaded. 'Please don't expel me. Please let me stay.'

Holly laughed. 'Of course you can stay.'

'I can't believe Emily stayed at that office so long,' Caitlin said in a normal voice, hands gripping the sides of her stool. 'That she found it so hard to admit she'd made a mistake.'

Holly shrugged.

'Sad that she'd rather spend a whole year being miserable than admit to it? Don't you think so?'

'Yes. And she'd be the first to agree that she's wasted her time. She can't believe she took so long to go.' Holly glanced across at her. 'Why does that irritate you so much?'

'It doesn't irritate me. It troubles me. It makes me think. Perhaps she should ask herself if she's right about other things, too. Whether there are other parts of her life that are making her unhappy, attitudes that she won't let go of.'

There was a mutinous silence from Holly.

'Holly, I like her!' Caitlin insisted. 'I do. I just don't want her to say in ten years' time, "*Oh, my God! Made a huge mistake about that too!*"'

'She's not making a mistake. And I don't think it's any business of yours if she is.'

'Oh, why can't I ever talk about her to you?' Caitlin pleaded. 'Why do we all have to step around her so carefully? Why is her love life such a taboo subject? We talk about everybody else's! Why do you always have to shut me up about Emily? You don't even know what I'm going to say.'

'I don't need to know what you're going to say. I know what you want to do. You want to get me to agree with you that Emily's got it wrong. That she's making another *huge mistake*. And I won't.'

Caitlin shook her head. 'I hope you're this protective about me.'

'No one needs to be this protective about you.'

Holly slipped off her stool and turned the lights on, then went to the fridge, opened the door and brought out the bowl of whipped cream, moved to the cutlery drawer and found a knife and a spoon and pulled the cake towards her. Next to her, Caitlin dipped a finger in the bowl of whipped cream and licked it.

'Self-denial is not a virtue,' she said quietly. 'Emily is wrong about that.'

'She might move to Cornwall,' Holly said, ignoring her. 'Go and live near her brother and open a shop.'

'Then that'll be the end of her. She'll never meet anyone. Mr Wrong or Mr Right.'

Holly lifted out a spoonful of whipped cream and flicked it at the top of the cake. 'She'd call her shop "Saltwater". I think it's a great idea. You know she'd be brilliant at it. She's not in love with the theatre any more and she's certainly not in love with London. She was thinking of paintings and sculptures and things to do with the sea.'

'Emily left university with a first,' Caitlin said, full of

frustration. 'Why would she want to go and work in some shop in Cornwall? Why is she so determined to miss out on everything? And I'm saying that because I do like her.'

Holly smeared the whipped cream all over the cake and then reached for a punnet of raspberries. 'You've got her so wrong. You're presuming she's unhappy, living as she is, but she's not. She knows what she wants, she knows what she's aiming for. She's happier than any of us is.'

'You should have got her a cherry,' Caitlin said flippantly, pinching one of the raspberries between her finger and thumb before biting it in half.

Emily walked up the flight of old York stone steps, knocked gently with the polished knocker and waited. Every time she arrived on Holly's doorstep, she thought the same thing. She would look up at the glossy black front door and think how incredible it was that Holly was going to open it. That Holly could possibly own such a house, a house that must be worth millions. Big enough for huge families to get lost in, let alone one twenty-five-year-old woman.

It was on Richmond Hill, a take-your-breath-away Georgian house, leaning out towards the water meadows. Holly had been the only grandchild of an extremely rich grandmother who had left her the house, figuring rightly that her only child, Holly's mother, didn't need it. In the basement was a two-bedroom, self-contained flat that Holly rented out, using the income to pay for the running of the rest of the house. Grand, flamboyant, extravagant things had happened to Holly ever since Emily had first met her at university. The house was merely the best and most extravagant.

Hearing Emily's knock, Holly opened the door, exclaiming at the blast of freezing night air that greeted her. She shut the door firmly against the cold and led Emily in, whispering that she hoped Emily wouldn't mind but that Caitlin was in the drawing room.

'Why should I mind?' Emily asked, less interested in Caitlin's presence in the drawing room than in a new painting taking up most of one wall in the hallway.

She handed Holly a bottle of wine and went over to look at it. 'Tell me this wasn't here last time I came.'

'No, it wasn't.'

Holly came and stood beside her.

'What's it called?'

'It's called *Naked lady blowing bubbles*,' Holly said, a look of wonderment on her face. 'What do you think? Do you like it?'

Emily nodded and grinned. 'Indescribable.'

'Fuck off, Emily!' Holly protested. 'You clearly know nothing.'

'When did you get it?'

'In the summer. I saw it in this fantastic exhibition in Piccadilly.'

'Not the Royal Academy?'

'No, on the street! It carried on all the way down the road from Green Park. All the way down.'

Given how the hall had already suffered at Holly's hands, Emily mused that perhaps it was no bad thing that a joyous, fleshy lady and a cloud of iridescent bubbles now covered most of it. Painted an inoffensive cream when Holly had moved in, the hall had been one of the first areas she had tackled, choosing a purple and gold shiny striped wallpaper that went all the way up the stairs, from the ground to the cathedral-high ceiling, and clashed badly with the old black and white checked floor that fortunately was listed and therefore safe from Holly's unpredictable taste.

'But I don't want to talk about my picture,' Holly said, turning to her and giving her a great beaming smile. 'I want to talk about you. Brilliant to walk out like that. Fantastic. I'm so proud of you!'

'I pity my replacement,' Emily said, taking off her coat. 'I'm going to have to write and warn her. But thank you for saying so and thank you for organizing this. You're very sweet.'

Holly took Emily's coat and hung it up on a rail beside the front door. 'It's only the five of us: you, me, Rachel and Jo-Jo, and now Caitlin. It's not as if I've made a huge effort.'

'It's lovely of you.' Emily lowered her voice. 'I'm surprised Caitlin wanted to stay. She must be spoiling for a fight.'

'Don't say that,' Holly protested. 'It's not like that. She was really upset when she realized that this was happening and that I hadn't invited her.'

'Oh, great,' said Emily sarcastically. She nodded towards the drawing-room door. 'She's probably selecting her spell as we speak.'

'No! She's realized that we're getting together, wanting

20

to celebrate what you've finally done – ' Holly squeezed Emily's arm – 'and she wanted to celebrate too.' Holly raised her eyebrows. 'So, how does is it feel to be gone? To be free at last? Actually, I don't know why I'm asking. It must be fantastic. You're free! You must be so happy.'

But Emily shook her head. 'No, it was wonderful for about the first ten minutes but since then it's not felt so good . . . It's not felt good at all.'

Holly stopped, one arm already stretched to open the drawing-room door, knowing that if she did, that would be the end of the conversation. In all the years of knowing Emily, Holly had never been so taken aback. Emily didn't say things like that, had never admitted to anything being less than good before.

'I left because I had no choice. But that doesn't mean I'm not scared of tomorrow, scared of the next day. I knew I'd feel like this, too. It was what kept me there so long. At least I had something to do when I worked for Carrie Piper, somewhere to go to, even if it was grim when I got there. Now, I have a dump of a flat that needs the rent paying on it but no money. I don't think I want to go to another theatrical agency but I don't know what else to do. I have a vague idea that I might set up a shop in Cornwall, because I don't think I want to live in London any more, but I don't know if I want to do that, and nobody would want to come and buy anything anyway. I have two parents but I haven't spoken to either of them for eleven months—'

'Don't say that.' It was such a shock to hear Emily speaking like this. Holly had to stop her. 'You haven't got used to the change, that's all. You need time to adjust. Have a holiday. I am – I'm having a couple of weeks here in London, and then I'm going skiing.'

Emily laughed. 'Good for you. But how do I pay the rent?'

'By spending a few of the thousands of pounds that I know you have stashed away in the Alliance & Leicester. Don't pretend you're so broke.'

Emily shook her head. 'I'm not pretending.'

Holly went on, 'You only left the place *yesterday*. Please give yourself a break. And don't, please don't, go straight into the first job you're offered or it will be another disaster. Don't do that!'

'What about Saltwater? Do you think I should go for it?'

'If you have to.'

'Glad you think it's such a good idea.'

'Don't you think Saltwater comes up when you don't know what else to do?'

'But I need to do something . . .'

'Emily,' Holly insisted, coming back to her, squeezing her shoulder affectionately, 'you don't have to have your life all organized by tomorrow. Why don't you have a holiday? I could ask Jo-Jo to come and Rachel. We can ask them tonight. It would be fun. Don't even think about Saltwater just yet. And please don't go and live in Cornwall,' she beseeched her. 'Have holidays with your brother there, but don't go and live there. We'd all miss you too much.'

Emily smiled. 'I'm sorry. And thank you. Believe it or not I was in quite a good mood when I walked in just now. I don't know what happened. Why I did I tell you all that?'

Holly had been more taken aback by Emily's outburst than she was going to let on.

'We'll talk about it later. We shouldn't leave Caitlin on her own for too long. She'll be wondering what's wrong and you don't want to get her involved. But tell me quickly. Might you come skiing? In two weeks' time.'

'Thank you, of course I will. I'd love to come. I've got a couple of interviews lined up. I rang around a few recruitment agencies this afternoon. Nothing very exciting. But I can't believe any of them would want me to start before Easter.' For a second Emily let herself lean in against Holly. 'I know, what am I doing? Have a break, take my time, you're right, but it's hard. I need to know where I'm going next.'

Holly thought how this was the girl who'd always seemed to know where she was going, far better than any of her other friends did. Who'd always seemed so strong, so sure of what she believed in and, as a result, invincible. And she kicked herself for ever thinking it could be so simple. And she wondered how much more was going on, wondered if she could have missed danger signals over the past few months, thought how the departure from Carrie Piper wouldn't alone have provoked such a wobble. Had Emily been less buoyant and optimistic for a while now? Had Holly not noticed? And Holly kicked herself for not knowing the answer, for not thinking about it until now.

As she opened the door to the drawing room she pushed Emily inside. 'Talk to her while I check the food.'

But I don't want to talk to Caitlin, Emily thought, walking reluctantly in. She looked across the room. As far away as was possible, Caitlin was waiting for her, sitting in the corner of a lime green velvet sofa, the size of a double bed, with her knees up. She was dressed in black, which seemed to emphasize how tiny she was, and the contrast between the green sofa, the black clothes and the striking silvery blonde of her curly hair was dramatic. Emily caught her eye and smiled and thought how Caitlin looked like a little pixie, untrustworthy and enchanting, and she felt a familiar wariness prickle down her spine.

'Hi!' Caitlin pushed herself off the sofa and came across the long, purple-painted wooden floor to Emily, to greet her and kiss her lightly on each cheek, and Emily breathed in the warm scent of orange blossom, just as Holly popped her head around the door. 'I'm going upstairs to change.'

'No, please. We love you as you are!' Caitlin called after her. And Emily imagined that what she was really calling was, *Please, don't leave me alone with her*.

She guessed it was a deliberate ploy on Holly's part. A ploy to give her and Caitlin a chance to talk, break the ice before the others arrived. But Holly had missed the point that Caitlin didn't want to be left alone with her, hadn't taken it in that in eight years – three years of university and five years in London – Caitlin and Emily only had conversations when somebody else arranged them.

Emily had guessed right. From the beginning, Caitlin had told herself and anyone else who'd listen that Emily's looks and style disguised a personality that was too good to be true and, as a result, had never got close enough to get to know her. Yet, in most respects, Emily was exactly the sort of person Caitlin loved to have as a friend. She looked great, had a glamorous job (until that morning anyway) and was witty and fun. But having a conversation with her always left Caitlin calling out for a drink. Emily made her feel as if she shouldn't even mention rock and roll, let alone the sex and the drugs.

Occasionally Holly or one of the others might be coerced into acknowledging that Emily was a bit of a control freak, and, yes, perhaps a bit unworldly, but that was as far as it would ever go. The others loved Emily and wanted to look after her. Emily made them laugh, held their attention and enjoyed their respect in a way Caitlin never could. And in return they could tease Emily about her lifestyle and attitudes with a lightness of touch that Caitlin knew she'd never be able to achieve herself.

Having kissed her hello, Caitlin went over to the window, pulled aside a heavy curtain and stood for a few moments, staring out into the street. To Emily it was obvious that Caitlin was looking out for Jo-Jo and Rachel, clearly hoping that they might already be approaching the front door. Then Caitlin dropped the curtain, turned back to the sofa and sat down.

Emily followed her across the room and felt Caitlin start as she sat down beside her.

'You haven't got any wine,' Caitlin said, immediately jumping up.

But Emily got up too and walked away in front of her, leading the way to the kitchen.

'I was in Ruffles in Hammersmith yesterday morning,' Emily said, attempting to kick-start the conversation.

'What were you doing there?' Caitlin lived in Hammersmith and passed Ruffles almost every day.

'Do you mean in Hammersmith, or what was I doing in Ruffles?' Emily fetched herself a glass and handed it to Caitlin who refilled her own and poured some wine for Emily.

'In Ruffles. It's where all the old ladies get their twinsets and their trouser suits. It's ten per cent off on a Monday.'

'I was running around in my knickers actually,' Emily said.

'Are you joking?'

'No, you should try it. I find it's a great way of meeting new people.' She took her glass from Caitlin and turned towards the door, back to the drawing room. 'Come in here. I'll tell you about it.'

Emily told her.

'But *Emily*! Wait!' Caitlin said melodramatically, putting a concerned hand on hers. 'I cannot believe that you came out without any clothes on. Not *you*!'

'I can't believe I did either.' Emily flinched from Caitlin's hand. 'But you have no idea how much that wasp hurt. I wasn't exactly thinking about what I was wearing. You'd have done the same.'

Caitlin sat down on the sofa and this time patted for

Emily to join her. 'Let's face it, Emily. I'm out of my clothes rather more often than you are. For *you* to do that . . . you must have been so embarrassed.'

'I didn't look that bad,' Emily insisted, deliberately misunderstanding her. 'It was no worse than being on the beach. I don't think anyone saw me properly, anyway.'

'Don't tell me you go topless on the beach.'

'Sometimes I do,' Emily retorted, wanting to slap Caitlin's incredulous face. 'If it's a hot day and my dad isn't around.'

'Oh, my God! I would never have had you down for topless sunbathing.'

'Why do you have me down for anything at all?'

Caitlin didn't know what to say to that. Looking up into Emily's cool, clear eyes, she went quiet, feeling out of her depth, floundering, kicking feebly in some vast ocean as she searched in vain for a way to save herself. How was it Emily always managed to do this to her?

'It's only a turn of phrase,' Caitlin said, standing up again, now pacing the room so her heels rapped out hard on the wooden floor. 'I don't . . . have you down for anything.'

She could feel herself blushing, which was all the more humiliating, and she lowered her eyes and found herself staring awkwardly at Emily's thighs in their faded button-flyed jeans. Little Mother Superior, she thought, turning longingly towards the door, towards the distant stairs. Come back Holly . . . R. E. S. C. U. E. M. E. Tell me what one says to a virgin. What to talk about? Seashells? Puppies? Alice bands? Apple blossom?

There was a pale blue leather armchair at a right angle to Caitlin's sofa and Emily moved across to it, sat on its soft squashy arm and leaned towards Caitlin.

'You mustn't worry so much about me,' she said quietly. 'I was covered up in no time.'

Caitlin nodded, scrabbling for an excuse to leave Emily alone in the room or at least for something to say, something that would change the subject fast and for sure. And she managed to come up with something sufficiently bizarre that also happened to be true.

'You know I have a boyfriend called Leon?'

Emily nodded.

'He took me out for tea with a chimp last week.' Caitlin made it sound rather casual, as if it was the sort of thing that could happen any time.

'Fantastic!' Emily laughed in appreciation and Caitlin surprised herself by cautiously smiling back.

'He was called Bert and apparently he's especially popular with the under-fives, which, I suppose, says rather a lot about me.'

'I'd like to have done that too,' Emily reassured her.

'I didn't think I would. But I fell in love with him,' Caitlin smiled again. 'He was gorgeous. And as Leon said to Holly, what do you give the girl who will dissolve if she has another spa treatment? After tea I washed his face and he cleaned his teeth . . . And then I put him to bed.'

'And he was good, was he? Good in bed?' Emily asked, remembering suddenly that she'd been supposed to follow up a call about another job at seven thirty and she'd forgotten all about it. She looked at her watch, wondering whether it was too late to call now.

'He was so good. And once you've had a chimp . . .'

But Emily had leapt up and was out of the door before Caitlin had finished the sentence.

Typical bloody Emily, Caitlin thought, left alone in the room. Let down your guard for just a second, think you're getting on, think she's fun, that she has a sense of humour after all. Then you say something you shouldn't and immediately she's stomping out of the room in disgust. Nervously she wondered what Holly would do when she found out. But then, seconds later, Emily came back. She stood in the doorway, pressing buttons on her mobile, not even looking at Caitlin, then held the phone up to her ear. Caitlin saw a look of frustration flash across her face and then Emily put the phone down on a bookshelf and sat back down.

'Sorry.'

'No problem.' Caitlin shrugged.

Emily beamed at her

'Why did you run out of the room?'

'I was meant to have called someone about a job. I forgot about it. I forget everything all the time. But I can ring him in the morning. Please tell me more about Bert.'

Caitlin nodded slowly, looked back at her. 'If your memory's that bad,' she said, 'perhaps you *have* slept with someone after all, and forgotten about it?' *Don't let me have said that out loud.*

'Oh God! That's true!' Emily laughed. 'Perhaps I've had sex loads of times.'

Had sex? It sounded so wrong when Emily said it. 'I thought you'd left the room in disgust. I was wondering how I'd explain it to Holly.'

'Why would I do that?'

Caitlin shook her head. 'No reason at all. I just thought . . .' She picked up her glass of wine and took a huge swallow.

'We've often got it wrong, haven't we?' Emily said gently. 'You and me.'

Caitlin nodded.

'I don't think there is anything you could say that would make me leave a room.'

'And I wouldn't want to.' Caitlin got up and walked over to the doorway, looking up the stairs for Holly.

No, she thought stubbornly, not willing after so many years to admit she'd misjudged her. *You and I* don't get it wrong, *you* get it wrong. I'm not the weirdo, you are. Everyone else can think you're on to something, that you're a happy, harmless twenty-first-century hippy, but I don't. 'Where is that girl?' she exploded instead.

'Don't hurry her,' Emily said, 'she'll be down soon. We can manage without her.'

Caitlin turned back to her.

'What do you think of *Naked lady blowing bubbles*?' Emily asked.

'That she shouldn't be allowed.'

'Did you tell Holly?'

'I told her she has less taste than chamomile tea. What did *you* say to Holly?'

'That I liked it. I didn't want to hurt her feelings.'

'How come?' Caitlin asked, still standing in the doorway. 'I thought you believed in honesty, in being true to yourself, standing by your principles?'

'How about you change the habit of a lifetime and give me a break?' Emily retorted. 'For this one evening, how about you try to forget that I haven't ever had sex?'

Had sex. She'd said it again.

They both heard the creak of footsteps on the stairs, and then Holly was walking across the hall towards them, coming through the open doorway, joining Caitlin, and although they both smiled at her, they couldn't disguise the tension still crackling in the air.

'She started it!' Caitlin insisted, finally starting to laugh.

Holly shook her head in despair. 'I'm going back upstairs.'

'Don't, don't,' Emily reassured her. 'Everything's fine. Caitlin was saying how much she liked your new haircut.'

Holly combed her fingers through her hair and looked at Emily uncertainly. 'Why don't I believe you?'

'I agree,' Caitlin insisted. 'It looks great.'

Holly's hair was the outcome of a reckless trip to the hairdressers at the end of the road that had, against the odds, worked brilliantly well. It was cut short, sliced back behind her ears, and dyed a dark fox red which looked great against her wonderful creamy skin.

'It's perfect,' Emily said again, meaning it. Long hair

hadn't flattered Holly, disguising the angle of her jaw line, making her face look heavy and round, whereas the new cut seemed to lift weight away, and emphasize her cheekbones and huge brown eyes.

'And we were just wondering where those other two tarts could have got to.' Again Caitlin walked over to the window and checked the street outside.

'OK?' Holly asked Emily, keeping her voice low.

Caitlin heard her and turned. 'Stop fussing.'

Ignoring her, Holly went over to the other side of the room to put on some music and Caitlin kicked off her shoes and sat down on the floor beside Emily's chair.

'Did anyone tell you how she ran around Ruffles stark naked?' Caitlin asked Holly.

'Caitlin's very worried about the damage it's done to my reputation,' said Emily.

'I heard,' Holly replied, still searching through CDs.

'And she ran slap bang into Sam Finch!' Caitlin went on. 'Do you remember him?'

'We met him once with Oliver Mills, didn't we?' Holly asked.

'That's right,' said Caitlin. 'And he always fancied you, Emily. He must have thought today was his lucky day.'

Emily opened her mouth to deny it, but decided there was no point and closed it again.

'So how did he react when you threw yourself at him?' Caitlin asked Emily. 'Did he offer to suck out the sting?'

'No, of course not. He shielded me. From the wasp and from all the nosy people standing around watching me.'

'How nice.'

'He was . . . surprisingly nice.' Emily remembered Sam wrapping her up in his coat. 'And so relaxed about it too. He acted like it happened all the time.'

'Surprisingly nice because you thought it would be nasty but actually it was nice?' Caitlin asked. 'Or surprisingly nice because nothing like that had happened to you before?'

'No,' said Emily. 'Surprisingly nice because he was surprising and nice.'

'But what was he doing in Ruffles?' Caitlin persisted. 'I thought he lived in Cornwall?'

'He does. But when I saw him he was buying a present for his sister.'

There's so much more I want to know. All those things she's never going to tell me, thought Caitlin. She sat back on the sofa and studied Emily. What had it felt like to be Emily then, she wondered, standing naked and close up against a man perhaps for the very first time? How had it been to feel his heartbeat, the warmth of his body against her bare skin? How much had she liked it? Had it tempted her at all? Made her want to do it again? Do some more? But Caitlin couldn't ask, and Holly wouldn't ask, so Caitlin could only guess that of course Emily had liked it. Of course she had been tempted.

'So did you buy the white shirt?' Caitlin asked instead.

Emily shook her head. 'I should have done. But I was late and I wanted to get away.' Emily stopped, remembering the sense of futility that had hit her outside the shop. 'Anyway, I didn't make it to the interview, so I'm glad I saved the money.'

'What happened? Why didn't you go?' Caitlin demanded. 'I don't understand.'

'Because I knew I was wasting my time. There was no job there anyway.'

'And then you chucked it in at Carrie Piper's! Why?'

Emily pulled her top lip between her teeth, not sure what to say. She was sure that she shouldn't be confiding in Caitlin about anything, long used to hiding any vulnerability from her, and yet at the same time she felt certain that it couldn't do any harm. And, more than that, she wanted to tell them both, to say his name aloud again.

'Because Oliver Mills has come home,' she said.

3

Rachel Croft and Jo-Jo Beecher met in the dark at the pedestrian crossing at the bottom of Richmond Hill. Rachel had been walking fast, her eyes stinging from the bitter cold, her chin tucked deep inside her coat. When she'd caught sight of Jo-Jo moving through a knot of people fifty yards ahead she had pushed on even faster, but as she'd found herself getting close something – shyness – made her slow down, held her back from making contact. She'd followed Jo-Jo, watching the way she strode through the crowd, head up, shoulders thrown back, seemingly oblivious to the cold. She was wearing a bottle-green corduroy coat with the belt tied tightly around her narrow waist, and her shiny, slippery-looking hair was lifted up off her long neck and spilling out of a clip on the back of her head. The only concession to the cold was a long stripy scarf.

Then Rachel had felt like a stalker and she'd broken into a run, ducking and diving between people, reaching Jo-Jo as she went to cross at the lights, grabbing hold of her arm just as the man went green.

'Hi there!' she said breathlessly. 'Are you on your way to Holly's?'

'Sure am,' Jo-Jo said, turning to Rachel and giving her a big, wide smile. Her teeth were very white and slightly crooked at the front, Rachel noticed. In the street lights and icy cold air, everything about Jo-Jo seemed to sparkle and shine. 'It's celebration time for Emily, isn't it? She said you were coming. Great to see you again!'

'You too!'

Now Rachel felt rather awkward, and wished that she hadn't caught Jo-Jo up, that she was still walking alone, without the pressure of having to think up things to say.

'I'm so pleased for Emily,' she began tentatively, as they strode up the hill. 'I mean I know she's got nothing else lined up, but so what? I'm sure she'll walk into a new job.' Jo-Jo didn't answer. Rachel went on, 'And did you hear about her last day?'

'Holly called me at work and told me – asked me around tonight to celebrate.'

Rachel pictured Jo-Jo at work, colleagues all around her, everyone vying for her attention. 'She was fantastic, wasn't she?'

Jo-Jo nodded non-committally.

'Don't you think?'

'Depends how ambitious Emily is. It was a good job on paper.'

At twenty-eight Jo-Jo had already proved how ambitious she was. She had worked as a second assistant director on two major television dramas and was currently in pre-production on her first feature film, for which in a couple of months she'd be off for eighteen weeks' shooting in Tuscany and North Africa. It would be very hard work, she insisted, exhausting seven-day weeks, late nights and crack-of-dawn starts to catch the early Tuscan light . . . Her friends heaved great sighs of pity on her behalf. Jo-Jo would make a show of denying any such thing but there was no doubt that she was on the fast track.

Jo-Jo had met Emily on a low-budget television drama when they had both been runners. But Emily had not been quite as quick to leap up the career ladder, which was exactly why Carrie Piper's job had seemed such a golden opportunity: a chance to stay in the world of television – and theatre – but come at it from a different angle, with no secretarial work and the long-term chance to develop her own list of clients. When Emily got down to the last four applicants, it was Jo-Jo who'd primed her and pumped her with information, worked out what she was going to be asked, made sure she had the answers ready.

Neither of them knew then that the tiny Carrie Piper Agency was on its knees, or that within six months of Emily's arrival the one surviving co-director would leave, taking the last of the five major-earning clients with him.

Rachel, on the other hand, had first met Emily at school and, although they'd lost touch soon after they left, some years later they had found themselves living one above the other in a rented house in Clapham. Supper once every few months had developed into time out together every week. But despite the fact that Jo-Jo and her both counted Emily as one of their closest friends, they hadn't got to know each other. Rachel, shy and insecure, found that being with Jo-Jo always tied her tongue up in knots, while Jo-Jo was unaware of the effect she had and didn't think much about Rachel at all.

'When I spoke to Emily,' Rachel told Jo-Jo now, her breath coming faster with the effort of matching strides with her, 'she told me how she'd stood outside her office yesterday morning, knowing she couldn't face another day of work, and so she posted her keys through the letter box and ran for it! Didn't bother with saying goodbye or the fact that she should have given three months' notice.'

But Jo-Jo didn't react as she was meant to. 'It's a shame she let it get to her. It was a great break for Emily.'

'Oh, come on, it was terrible! You have to be pleased she's gone.'

Jo-Jo let out a long sigh, then laughed. 'You're right, of course. Why am I doubting whether she was right to leave? Of course she was! Emily always knows what she's doing.' She smiled again to show there was no malice in her words. 'Emily knows exactly what's best for her. Knows what she wants better than anyone. If it's time to leave she's not bothered about some silly little convention like handing in her notice first.'

'Wasn't that great?' Rachel agreed. 'Whereas if it had been me, I'd have stuck my keys through the letter box and then realized I'd left my handbag inside and I'd have to ring the bell and be let in.'

Jo-Jo laughed. 'Absolutely,' she said. 'Me too.'

'Oh, no. I don't think so.' Glancing across to Jo-Jo, seeing the grin on her face, Rachel felt warm bubbles of pleasure popping inside her. She'd never made Jo-Jo laugh before, never had a conversation that flowed so easily. 'And yet the strange thing is, I still feel far more protective of her than I would of you or Caitlin or Holly,' she went on, and glanced again across at Jo-Jo, expecting another nod of agreement. It wasn't there. 'I'm not feeling protective of her,' she backtracked instantly. 'Not really. And not protective of you or Caitlin either.' Now there was definite disagreement on Jo-Jo's face. 'I'd say I was *concerned* about Emily, that's all. You said it yourself,' Rachel reminded Jo-Jo hastily. 'She hasn't seemed so happy recently.'

'Do you think Emily needs your concern?'

Rachel tried to laugh it off. 'Of course she does, everyone needs my concern.'

'Why?'

'Because she's so funny.'

'You think Emily's funny?'

'No! Yes. Funny and odd and all sorts of other things too. Unconventional, courageous, stubborn, wonderful . . .' Rachel searched. 'And also fragile. I think she's more vulnerable than the rest of us, because of the way she's chosen to live her life. And that makes me want to look out for her in a way I don't for other people. That time when her boss refused to speak to her for four days, I wanted to kill that woman. I wouldn't have felt like that if it was you or Holly. I'd think, "Put up with it." But with Emily . . .' Rachel searched again for the right words. 'And now I'm worried it's actually about something else altogether. And I'm looking out for her all over again.'

'You make it sound like we're all protected against something that Emily's not. Like she's missed an important vaccination. '

In a way that was what she meant, but Rachel couldn't think how to explain herself, wished that a few precise, insightful words might fall – just for once – from her lips.

'You know, it bothers me that even you – someone who's been her friend since school – can't seem to put it aside,' Jo-Jo challenged her. 'It's as if every time you think about her you see this big *handle with care* sign flashing above her head.'

'Oh, no,' Rachel exclaimed. 'Is that how it seems? That's not how it is at all.'

'Tell me how it is, then.'

But Rachel couldn't go on. Why, when she needed to think on her feet, did her brain always grind immediately to a halt? Why, when she had a perfectly good point to make, did she always lose it somewhere in mid sentence and then say something she hadn't been meaning to say at all? It didn't happen with her close friends. With Emily, whom she'd known so long, she knew she could be quite funny but with Jo-Jo and Caitlin it was a nightmare, like she was being controlled by a ventriloquist, hell-bent on getting her to speak the most clumsy, embarrassing lines.

'Emily does not need us to look after her,' Jo-Jo said more gently, seeing her troubled face. 'Emily has not got a problem. She has not got a disorder.'

'I know that. I don't mean that she has.' All Rachel wanted now was to shut up, but Jo-Jo was still pressing her to explain. She took a breath and thought about what she wanted to say. 'It's not just seeing the men trying it on all the time, thinking Emily's this wonderful challenge, or the bitchy comments she has to put up with, or people thinking she's a bit freaky, because we're used to that. It's wanting to make sure Emily is happy, that she's not lonely, that she's not beginning to shut herself away.'

'You think there's a danger of that? I don't. I don't think it's like that at all. Emily's not struggling to keep hold of this big idea. It isn't an ideal that Emily's holding on to. It's just happened that way: she's an accidental virgin, not a deliberate one.'

'I don't know how you can say that!'

'She's come this far, she's damn well going to make sure it happens with someone worthwhile. If I was in Emily's position I'm sure I'd feel exactly the same.'

Rachel had never heard anyone talk like this about Emily before and couldn't imagine how Jo-Jo had got it so wrong. She believed Emily's virginity was absolutely deliberate, that Emily was a pillar of conviction and wisdom, not the accidental virgin at all but the victorious virgin, the triumphant virgin, holding out against a culture that glorified cheap thrills and instant gratification. Someone she thought was absolutely wonderful. Now Rachel felt terrible because Emily deserved her to stand up and defend her and explain how it really was, but she couldn't do it. I'm twenty-five years old, Rachel thought. But this person makes me feel about ten.

'Don't worry about Emily, worry about us,' Jo-Jo argued. 'We're the ones getting into trouble all the time. Getting hurt. Getting dumped. If Emily's looking to us to show her the way, I can see why she's still waiting.'

When were you ever hurt or dumped? Rachel wondered, looking at Jo-Jo striding up the hill as she talked, shining with confidence.

'We sit there panicking that some guy hasn't called or miserable because we got drunk and had some grim one-night stand or because we've been dumped for some personal fitness coach,' Jo-Jo went on.

'Don't pretend any of that stuff has ever happened to you.' Jo-Jo turned to her, surprised. 'I know what you're talking about, but I don't think *you* do.'

'You'd be surprised.'

'Yes,' Rachel agreed. 'I would.'

Five more houses and they'd be at Holly's.

'The problem for Emily,' Jo-Jo said, changing the subject, 'is that she has tuned men out of her world. She doesn't smell, see, hear, taste them, and she certainly doesn't touch. Otherwise, surely, somewhere along the way, there'd have been a starry night and an attractive guy and she'd have ended up going for it. But there hasn't been anyone, and I can't see how it will ever change. Unless she lets herself go a little, it never will happen, with Mr Right or Mr Wrong or anybody else.'

'You're so unromantic.'

Jo-Jo ran lightly up the steps and banged on the knocker and then turned and grinned back at Rachel, a hand resting on one of the two white pillars that flanked the front door. 'And you think her prince is out there somewhere, do you? Hacking down the forest. You think someone will manage to wake her up?'

Jo-Jo could hear Holly coming to the front door and she turned away from Rachel and slowly unwound her scarf from around her long, elegant neck. It was striped in pinks, turquoises and a soft oatmeal brown, a scarf Rachel would have walked past in a shop without a second thought but which looked beautiful on Jo-Jo.

'One day I want you to tell me what Emily was like at school,' Jo-Jo said, folding the scarf over in her hand. 'Was she head-girl? I bet she was.'

'She's just the same as she was then,' Rachel said slowly, thinking about it and not liking what she was saying. 'Exactly the same. She hasn't changed at all.'

Holly's conservatory was a golden spotlight in the pitch dark of her garden and beyond her garden wall lay the huge presence of Richmond Park. Somewhere close by the house a fox barked and there was an answering crackle in the bracken as sleeping deer shifted warily in response.

Inside, the small, warm conservatory was smothered in luscious plants, so well fed and watered that they looked ready to burst. Sweet-smelling stephanotis twined with winter jasmine and tiny butter yellow orchids. And in each of the four corners of the conservatory, a little orange tree grew in a beautiful pale terracotta pot, their scented, waxy flowers pinpricks of white among dark green oval glossy leaves. It wasn't down to Holly that they flourished so beautifully but thanks to a housekeeper she had inherited with the house from her grandmother, who, for over twenty years, had watered and pruned and cherished, so that the conservatory was as lush and well established as a mini rainforest.

'Sautéed in lemon and garlic and chilli oil, wrapped in petals of rocket and watercress ... It's just a simple supper,' Caitlin teased Holly as she came down the two shallow steps that linked the conservatory to the kitchen and joined them at the round oak table. Holly leaned over Caitlin and placed a large blue terracotta bowl in the middle. Thirty or forty tiger prawns hid between leaves of salad.

'Who said anything about simple?' Holly replied. 'This took me hours.'

Across the table, Emily leapt to Holly's defence. 'They look delicious,' she said, wishing Caitlin could be drugged and locked in a faraway bedroom until the rest of them were ready to go home.

Jo-Jo leaned across to Caitlin and touched her arm. 'How is Leon, by the way? Still being sued?'

'Don't joke about Leon.'

'Why, what's he done now?'

'Nothing.' Caitlin lifted her glass of wine to her lips. 'And Leon is very thoughtful, very kind . . .'

Jo-Jo nodded seriously.

'And he gave me tea with a chimp for my birthday!'

'That's downright weird.' Jo-Jo stabbed together a forkful of salad and then skewered her last prawn on the end of it. 'You should watch out.'

Caitlin stood up and reached across the table for the breadboard. 'Why don't you like Leon?'

And she cared, Emily realized, surprised. She really cared.

'I like him,' said Holly unexpectedly. 'I think he's good for you, Caitlin, he's softening you up.'

'And I don't *not* like him,' Jo-Jo insisted. 'I've hardly even met him.'

Caitlin nodded. 'He's a good guy.' Then she turned purposefully to Emily and Emily felt herself stiffen in response. 'Now, I want to know something.' She paused, knowing she'd got everyone's attention. 'And I hope you won't mind me asking. But how come we spend a year telling you to get out of that job, and you take no notice whatsoever, but Oliver doesn't even need to make an appearance, you just hear mention of his name, and you leave the place immediately?'

Emily hadn't known what she might say and for a moment she sat still, looking up at Caitlin, thinking about it. 'You're right to ask,' she agreed eventually, tipping back her chair. 'The fact is, I'd stopped noticing how long I'd been there. I needed a jump-start, a reason to get myself back in gear. And Oliver was it.'

'Do you mean Oliver Mills?' Jo-Jo interrupted. 'Beautiful Oliver from *Breaking Free*? Oliver who snogged you in the sand dunes when you were sixteen? Oliver who highlights his hair?'

'That's not true.' Emily laughed. 'Yes, he's back from New York.'

Breaking Free was the film that Jo-Jo and Emily had worked on together – where they'd met each other, and where, a couple of months after they had started, Oliver had joined them. Hearing a lot about him before he'd arrived, Emily had guessed it would be the same Oliver Mills she'd known in Cornwall so many years ago and anticipation and hope had sent her heart knocking against her ribs at the thought of seeing him again. And then the hope had flickered and died within an hour of meeting him, because while Oliver was as big and golden and attractive as ever, and was so pleased to see her again – instantly regaling the whole cast and crew with the story of how they'd snogged in the sand dunes within half an hour of meeting each other – he also told them all about his girlfriend, Nessa O'Neill. Not deliberately, in a warning-Emily-off kind of way, but casually, so that she slipped into all his conversations in such a way that everyone, but especially Emily, couldn't fail to understand that she was the only woman in his life; he adored her. There was so clearly no chance of anything more happening between them, no point in falling for him, that all Emily could do was switch her excitement off again, her pride intact, and do it so successfully that she hardly ever remembered that she'd wished for something else. She managed it. She might still have felt the occasional flutter in the stomach when he came too close, but it was so feather light she could easily ignore it. And when he pulled her into a hug, and told her how adorable she was, she didn't let herself relax in his arms or remember how it had felt to kiss him.

She and Oliver worked together only once more, on a short film where they had crossed over for just two weeks, but they still saw each other most months, often with others – Holly, Jo-Jo and Nessa especially – but sometimes out on their own. The last occasion was when she had promised him she would leave her job.

'I saw Oliver at the weekend.' Holly surprised them all. She walked out of the conservatory still speaking. 'He had a party. Sam Finch was there too . . . He'd come up from Cornwall.'

'Oliver had a party!' Jo-Jo cried, 'and he didn't ask me or Emily?'

'He wanted to,' Holly comforted her. 'He couldn't get hold of either of you.'

'But we were around. He can't have made much effort,' Jo-Jo grumbled.

'He only called me on Saturday. It was a last-minute party. He told me to bring you both but neither of you was around.'

'You only know Oliver because of me and Emily!' Jo-Jo was used to being the party queen. 'Who else was there? Was Nessa there?'

'No.' Holly took a breath, poised to explain, and in that split second Caitlin glanced across at Emily and so happened to catch the look of wide-eyed disbelief that crossed her face when Holly said again, No. Explained that Nessa had stayed in New York. Nessa and Oliver had split up a few weeks before he came home.

'She always said she'd done her bit in England,' Holly went on, unaware of the effect she'd just had on Emily, 'that if she and Oliver were going to last, it was going to be in New York.'

'But they were perfect for each other. I can't believe it,' Jo-Jo exclaimed. 'Oliver must be devastated.'

'I don't think so. He was having a great time at the party.'

Caitlin quickly looked around at the others but nobody else had noticed Emily's reaction. She turned back to Emily and saw shock, alarm and hope all still battling it out in her face.

Then Emily pulled herself together. 'I should see him sometime,' she said light-heartedly. 'Maybe he can find me a job. Oh, I didn't tell you all,' she went on, and Caitlin thought how chattery and strained she sounded. 'I might have found something. I'm having an interview next Thursday with the Williams Office, in Bloomsbury. They called me this afternoon.'

Caitlin had heard and seen enough. She watched as Emily regained her composure, as the faint flush in her cheeks subsided. She took in how she even managed to laugh at herself for finding the interviews so quickly. And Caitlin carefully clicked together all the facts and impressions, the frustrations and presumptions, everything she'd ever known about Emily over the years, and realized at last what she'd got. That in Emily and Oliver's case, one and one made a perfect two. That here was the man who could refresh the parts the other guys couldn't reach. It wasn't Sam, Caitlin saw in sudden absolute clarity. It wasn't Sam Finch she was interested in. She was completely in love with Oliver.

All of a sudden, Emily was restless and keen to go home. Refusing to acknowledge why, she told herself she was fed up with them all: with Jo-Jo always having to be the girl everyone wanted or wanted to be; with Caitlin's sniping and her horrible boyfriends, Leon being just the latest in a pinstriped, slimy snail-trail of others; with Rachel's gushy clumsiness; and with their collective fascination with Oliver Mills and Sam Finch. But truly she knew it wasn't her friends who were the problem. She loved them all, had even enjoyed sparring with Caitlin and listening to her talk about the horrible boyfriends. If she felt as if they were all suddenly rasping away at her good humour, it was because something else had got to her.

She would go home, Emily decided, as soon as she could. She would eat a slice of her raspberry cake, wait for a pause in the conversation and slip away. She picked up a piece, stuffed it into her dry mouth and found she couldn't swallow. She took a sip of coffee and burned the roof of her mouth, so she coughed and spluttered and had to wipe away tears. She knew that when she opened her eyes again Holly would be watching her, wise brown eyes full of concern, Holly, from whom she could never hide anything. And when she did and looked around the table she saw that they were all looking at her.

'What?' She made herself laugh.

'Emily, you sounded as if you were dying,' Holly told her. Emily shrugged and determinedly swallowed the mouthful of cake.

When she did finally push back her chair and stand up to go, Rachel leapt up to join her.

'I'm sorry we're breaking things up,' she said, going over to Holly and kissing her goodbye.

Jo-Jo yawned and stretched back her arms. 'I'm coming too. I've got to be up again at four.'

At the front door, Emily turned to Holly and hugged her. 'Thank you,' she whispered, 'it was great. I'm sorry I'm leaving so early.'

'Did something happen? Something I missed?'

Emily shook her head. 'Of course not. I'm tired. You know I'm always the first to go home.'

'Call me tomorrow?'

Emily nodded and went through the doorway, down the steps and out onto the street, wanting to put a bit of distance between herself and the rest of them. Then she waited for Rachel to join her.

4

Holly, Jo-Jo and Caitlin stood in the doorway and watched Emily and Rachel walk away down the street.

'I should be off too,' Jo-Jo said, breaking the silence. She picked her coat and scarf off the rack by the front door and slid her coat around her shoulders, then turned back to Holly. 'Was Emily OK?'

Caitlin pounced, taking hold of her arm. 'I'm so glad you noticed.'

'What are *you* talking about?' Jo-Jo asked.

'I'll tell you. It's nothing awful, don't worry,' Caitlin reassured them both, noticing Holly's sudden look of panic. 'But there is something the matter with Emily. And I think I know what.'

Caitlin said nothing while Jo-Jo took off her coat again and then led her and Holly into the drawing room, still waiting while Jo-Jo and Holly sat together on the sofa. Then she dimmed the main light, switched on a couple of lamps, then turned to face them both. And Holly was struck by the thought that it was as if the three of them were on a stage at the start of a play, that there was Caitlin – hero or villain? – preparing to win them over with her words.

'What is it,' she said, worried. 'I knew something was wrong. Poor Emily.'

'There's nothing wrong.' Caitlin prepared the ground

in her mind, aware that she was deliberately softening her voice, switching on all her persuasive charm. 'There's an idea I have about Emily,' she said. 'It's something I've known for a long time, but tonight it was so obvious it kind of jumped at me. And I want you to forget it's me telling you this, because I know you think I have a problem with her. And maybe I do, but it's got nothing to do with what I'm going to say.'

'Wait,' Holly said, 'I need a drink.' She leapt off the sofa, and ran out of the room, returning at lightning speed with three glasses and another bottle of wine. 'Now talk,' she said, pulling the cork.

Caitlin smiled, liking the way they both leaned in towards her.

'You know Oliver's come home without Nessa?'

'Yes,' they both replied at the same time.

'Did you see what hearing that news did to Emily? She didn't know.'

'Yes, she knew. That's why she left her job,' Holly cried, impatient with Caitlin.

'That's not what I meant.'

'Then what did you mean?' Jo-Jo asked suspiciously. 'What are you trying to suggest about Emily?'

Off we go again, thought Caitlin. Attack of the giant mother hens.

'He's come home *without Nessa*. Don't you see that changes everything for Emily? Oliver's free. He could get together with Emily now.'

There was a pause. Then Holly asked incredulously, 'Are you suggesting we try to set her up?'

'Don't be ridiculous.' Jo-Jo laughed at the thought. 'Why would Oliver fancy Emily?'

'Why not?' Caitlin challenged.

'Because there's no point in fancying Emily!'

'No point! Of course there's a point. I can think of three, four, ten men who would tell you just what the point is. And Oliver too. Oliver's not oblivious to her charms. Think about how she met him. It couldn't have been more romantic. Hot sun, swimming in the sea, snogging in the sand dunes. All that wonderful long hair and those amazing legs. Sweet sixteen and probably never been kissed. He probably wishes he'd got in there and finished the job when he had the chance.'

'It wasn't like that,' Holly insisted, putting down the wine bottle and throwing herself back into the sofa. 'It really wasn't. Emily would have told me. They barely kissed and they didn't even keep in touch afterwards. When Oliver walked into *Breaking Free* it was the first time Emily had seen him for over five years.'

'Maybe,' Caitlin said quietly. 'But you didn't see her face when she heard Nessa's not come back. Emily's in love with Oliver and she has been ever since she first met him. After that holiday she never forgot him. Sixteen, seventeen, eighteen, nineteen, twenty . . . I know she had a few boyfriends, but none of them came close to those memories of Oliver. No one else ever made her feel like he did. All the things you do in those vital years, going out with guys for the first time, losing your virginity, falling in love – letting all the most important, life-changing things happen to you – Emily didn't do any of them. And it's because of Oliver. And look what happened. Look where she is now.'

'What happened to her?' Holly said, but half-heartedly, because neither she nor Jo-Jo was fighting now and Caitlin could tell from the silence that she had them listening, that they understood, that they were halfway to agreeing with her.

She bent to the floor and poured more wine to give them a moment to think about it. 'Maybe that brief time with Oliver wouldn't have mattered. Emily would probably have met someone else, eventually. But then she leaves university, she gets her first job and who walks onto the set of *Breaking Free* and back into her life again? It was the worst thing that could have happened to her because this time, right from the start, he was with Nessa. You tell us all the time about how intense it gets on location,' Caitlin reminded Jo-Jo, 'how you get to know a crew better in twelve weeks than other people in twelve years. Breakfast, lunch, evenings, early mornings, every second he's there, reminding her how there really is nobody else as perfect as him. And he is perfect. Big, strong, sexy, scruffy, charming when he wants to be, bolshie enough to be interesting, fantastic at his job. God, we *all* fell in love with him, didn't we?' She went on before the others could agree or disagree. 'But he's got Nessa. And so there's no way Emily can take it further. No need to put herself on the line, no chance of being rejected. She can love him from afar, she doesn't have to deal with any realities.' Caitlin hadn't thought about it like this before, but the more she talked the more she was sure that she was getting it right, because it all made such sense, explained so much about Emily.

'And do you see how Oliver is never going to get the chance to let her down? He's never going to mess up – he'll never get pissed with the lads or shag some other girl, or call his friends on his mobile from the bus to tell them what she's like in bed.'

'But Oliver wouldn't do that anyway, would he? Because he's a lovely guy,' said Holly, hopelessly sentimental, and her eyes filled with tears. She blinked, stretched her arm down for the glass on the floor and automatically gulped down the wine. 'Has she really been waiting for him all this time?'

Caitlin nodded. 'I think she has.'

'I always wondered at the way she could turn everyone down,' Jo-Jo admitted. 'I sometimes wondered why it wasn't more difficult for her.'

Caitlin nodded. 'I've wondered too. And believe it or not, I've been there too. I know what I'm talking about,' she went on, turning away from them and walking across the room to the windows.

'*You* were never a virgin!' Jo-Jo asked, mockingly.

'I know how it feels to be Emily,' Caitlin insisted. 'Getting into work at seven thirty because he does, convincing yourself it's your *job* you love, not *him*. And I remember how I felt and I multiply it maybe one hundred times for Emily, because for Emily there's never been anyone else!'

'But does she realize? Has she admitted to herself how she feels?' Holly asked.

'I don't think so.' Caitlin said. 'She's never acknowl-edged he's the reason why.'

'Why what?'

'Why she's still an Extra Strong Mint, not a Polo. But, yes, I think she must know she fancies him. And now that he's free again, she'll crucify herself about what to do about him and end up doing nothing at all. She'll be paralysed with fear. Poor Emily. Holding out for Mr Right might be wonderful in theory, but in practice it must be a nightmare. Don't you think she's having a far harder time *not* having sex than we are having it?' She challenged Holly and Jo-Jo.

'Don't look at me,' Holly countered. 'I haven't had sex for so long I wonder if I am a virgin again.'

Caitlin grinned. 'What I think I'm trying to say is that we're happy. Aren't we? Generally happy?' She looked at them both. 'But Emily is *miserable*. Even I can see it and I hardly know her. And don't think protecting her, not challenging her, not making her talk about whether she's doing the right thing is being a good friend to her. You may believe you're supporting a good cause, but you're not. You think I don't like her, but I do,' Caitlin said quietly as if reading Holly's mind. 'It's just all the time I've known her I've wanted to shake her, because she's missing out on so much. But now it's different. We can't let her go through the next ten years waiting for some fairy-tale ending that's never going to happen.

'We have an opportunity that we didn't have before,' Caitlin continued. 'We have a chance to get involved here and now. Oliver is available for action.' She pulled apart the curtains and looked out through the glass. 'He is two miles away! Either he's the one or he's not, but it's time Emily found out. And she's not going to find out if we don't help her.' Caitlin turned back to them, waiting for a reply.

'Yes, Emily admits that Oliver is her perfect man. She's told me as much already,' Jo-Jo said, clearly treading carefully. 'And, yes, I can see that Oliver's pedestal can't be knocked over unless she gets much closer to him, and that meanwhile Emily is getting older and older and it's becoming a bigger and bigger issue that she's not sleeping with anyone. She's almost *famous*. She's a phenomenon. It's ridiculous! Other people, people she doesn't even know, discuss her sex life around the supper table and they have no idea what she's really like. And I can see that if she was forced to confront Oliver and even if it all went wrong, then still his spell would be broken . . .'

'So you agree that I'm right?' Caitlin asked, coming back eagerly, sitting down again. 'Do you agree that we should try to do something to help her?'

Jo-Jo glanced quickly to Holly but Holly had her eyes to the floor. 'Yes, I think I do,' she admitted. 'I think you're right. If we can find a way to do it. I think we should step in.'

Caitlin hurried on. 'All I'm suggesting is that we set up some dates for the two of them. Make sure they get some chances to be alone together over the next few months, that's all. The rest we leave up to them. Or we leave it to Emily to decide what she really wants to do. I don't think it's likely that Oliver would turn her down.'

Then, just when she thought she had them both, Holly interrupted. 'It makes great sense,' she said, 'as long as we forget we're talking about Emily. You know her – ' she turned to Jo-Jo – 'you've listened to her, you've been won over just like I have, and Rachel has too. How can you now agree that everything she has said and done – or not done – is simply the result of an infatuation with Oliver? Aren't you belittling her? And is that, perhaps, because you don't want to believe in what she says? Maybe we're talking about our own motives, not Emily's, because she makes us judge ourselves as well as her and maybe it's making us uncomfortable.' She turned her attention to Caitlin. 'Forgive me, but I wonder if you're envious. Maybe you wish you could wipe the slate clean of some of your encounters and whenever you see Emily she reminds you of them.'

'Oh, no.' Caitlin laughed to soften her words. 'Don't start on me. I'm not the issue here. And I'm not wanting to trick her into anything. I'm not even trying to get her to admit that, yes, she's living in the nineteen fifties. And, if we leave her alone, yes, maybe she will eventually run around a few cornfields holding hands with some suitably patient man, get married, finally have sex and live happily ever after. But before that can happen, she needs to get Oliver out of her system. And if it is him, if it turns out that he *is* the one, the one and only Mr Right, then she may as well find out now.' Then she added, challenging them for an answer, 'Either way, tell me the harm in putting the two of them together?'

'Perhaps we should ask her about it?' Holly said instead.

'Completely pointless. If you do that,' said Caitlin, 'she'll deny it. Firstly, because she's absolutely terrified of the idea of getting close to Oliver, so she'll probably hare off to Cornwall, to her brother's to hide, and secondly because she has had her radar trained on all of us for years. She knows we'd love to fix her up with someone. It's why she never tells us anything. We cannot let her know we have any interest whatsoever in her and Oliver.'

Holly nodded and sighed. She thought how surprising it was to hear Caitlin, of all her friends, talking and thinking about Emily in this way.

'And we thought all you ever cared about was sex and shopping.' Jo-Jo laughed, echoing Holly's thoughts.

Caitlin smiled back. 'I think you'll find this is all about sex, Jo-Jo, don't you think? It was the expression on her face when she heard Nessa had stayed in the States. It was so sweet and sad. I liked seeing her like that. It was good to see that she's not so completely in control of herself after all.'

'I've known Emily for so long,' Jo-Jo said, 'and I can't believe I've never thought about Oliver like this before. Surely we'd have picked it up if she was in love with him. Wouldn't we have noticed something?'

'No, because Emily is a queen of deception,' Caitlin said. 'She's even deceived herself.'

'But if you put them together and Oliver doesn't fancy Emily . . . What happens then?' Jo-Jo asked.

'I know she won't die. She won't throw herself off a bridge or under a bus. If Oliver doesn't fancy her, tough. It's happened to all of us. We survive.'

Caitlin got up and walked away, circling the room, and again Holly was reminded of an actor on stage, trying to win over her partners in crime. Caitlin turned to her. 'Don't you think it's important to get hurt, to *feel* things and take risks with our emotions, even if it sometimes means getting kicked in the teeth by some bastard? Of course it's horrible at the time but you get over it. It's what makes us who we are. Emily needs to know those feelings,' Caitlin went on, into her stride, certain now. 'She is not happy living her bland, uneventful life. She's searching around for something more. So she chucks in her job, talks of going to live in Cornwall, but we all know it's not that. She's frustrated! She's lonely! She's worried she's never going to have sex, she's starved herself of physical contact of any sort. When was the last time we heard about Emily kissing someone, let alone sleeping with them?'

'Come and sit down,' Holly insisted. 'Stop throwing yourself around the room and tell us what to do.'

Caitlin sat back down. 'Get them together before he meets someone else.'

The thought that Oliver might meet someone else galvanized Holly and Jo-Jo.

'We need candlelight and log fires and soft feather beds,' Jo-Jo started enthusiastically.

Caitlin nodded. 'I'll start. I'll invite her to supper in the next few days and I'll have Oliver there, waiting for her, all very casual, very last minute.'

'And I'll invite everyone to the chalet,' Holly said generously. 'I've already asked Emily.'

'Oh, darlings, do let's all go to Holly's chalet,' Jo-Jo teased. 'Holly, I always forget you're from a different planet.'

'I know, I'm sorry.' Holly looked embarrassed. 'Feel free to take advantage of me.'

'We do!' Caitlin grinned. 'That's a great idea. Take Emily out of her natural environment. Nothing matters so much when you're on holiday. Skiing would loosen her up, help her forget her inhibitions . . . Skiing would be perfect.'

'If we can persuade Oliver to come,' Holly said doubtfully. 'Will he come? He might know Emily and Jo-Jo, but he hardly knows me!'

'Of course he'll come. What are you worried about? That he'll be a bit shy? Ask a friend for him if you're worried. Get Sam Finch along.'

'And anyone else? Who else can we think of?' Holly asked, and because this was how she always was, keen to fill her house, or houses, with friends, Jo-Jo and Caitlin took her at her word.

'How about Leon?' Caitlin said.

'I thought you were getting rid of him.'

She shook her head. 'I can't. And I think it would be good if he came, not just for me but because he's fun and he's someone we all know and because I think we'd be more likely to persuade Oliver if he thought he had a few allies, if he didn't think he was coming along with just a bunch of girls.'

'Really? Isn't that just the sort of holiday Oliver loves?' said Holly.

'Sam would be great,' Caitlin went on. 'But if we can't persuade him we need Leon as a back-up, because we can be certain that he'll come.'

'Sure, of course, ask Leon.' Holly turned to Jo-Jo's groan. 'I know, I know. Tell me I didn't just say that.'

'No, I'm groaning because I can't come. Not over Easter. I'll be in Siena. I leave next week. Damn!'

'But if you're not there, how do we persuade Oliver?' Holly started to panic. 'He hardly knows us.'

'I think sex with a virgin is an extremely good offer.' Caitlin grinned. 'Get Emily to ask him.'

'Find him a friend and he'll come,' Jo-Jo said confidently. 'It's a fantastic offer. Of course he'll want to.'

'And we have to invite Rachel, too,' Holly insisted. 'I'd feel terrible if we left her out.'

'Don't feel terrible,' Caitlin said. She had no time for Rachel. 'If she wasn't such a tired little mouse, she wouldn't have gone home, she could have been part of this. But she did and she's not. I don't trust her. She's Emily's self-styled protector of high morals. She certainly doesn't have her worst interests at heart, like we do.'

Much later, when Caitlin finally did up the buttons of her coat in readiness to leave, she turned to Holly one last time. 'What are we hoping to achieve here?' she asked. There was no challenge in her question but genuine concern. 'What do you see in six months' time? I hope it's not a church and Emily in a big white dress and a long aisle with Oliver waiting at the end of it. You know we're not about to make a Disney film?'

Holly shook her head.

'It's not happy-ever-after we're aiming for, is it? Or happy-later-on. It's happy-now, isn't it? She needs to have some fun. She's miserable and lonely. You can see that, can't you?'

'Virginity can fuck you up, can't it.'

'Exactly.' Caitlin smiled. 'And I'm pleased we can admit that now. Before tonight we all had opinions about Emily but we kept quiet about them . . . She's missed out on too much for too long, don't you think? And I'm not just talking about her love life. I'm talking about talking, about how we didn't feel we could get involved.'

'She talks to her brother.'

Caitlin nodded. 'I'm glad she has *someone*.'

'I know we're doing the right thing for her,' Holly said. 'I'm sure that we are. But I'm scared stiff that she'll sleep with him.'

Caitlin shrugged. 'And I'm scared stiff that she won't.'

5

Having two distracted strangers for parents – a couple
who had never got to grips with the fact that they had
children – Emily was forever thankful that she'd also been
given a brother like Arthur and her default setting was to
turn to him whenever she felt under pressure or wanted
good advice. Endlessly interested, and utterly adoring of
Emily, he was her suit of armour, her shield against the
harsher realities of life in London, against the assaults of
the Carrie Pipers and the skirmishes with the Caitlins.
Whenever she needed him, she didn't have to ask herself
whether he would be there for her. He was always there
for her, and not just in spirit – because Arthur hardly ever
left St Brides, the little town in Cornwall where he had
found the friends and environment that suited him best,
where he could look out of his office window at the sea
and could surf all weekend if he wanted to. He lived alone
– girls were always falling for him but he hadn't met
the one he wanted to pick up and hang onto – and so,
whenever Emily wanted, she could go to St Brides and
slot straight back into Arthur's life.

Emily knew that when talking about him to her friends
she'd probably made Arthur sound a bit eccentric, exag-
gerated him even, telling them how he lived alone in
Cornwall, in a converted coastguard station, on a spit of

land called Dodger Point, and had a social life that revolved around the Hen's Tooth pub in St Brides, how he hardly ever travelled and was happy to spend the weekend surfing or walking the cliffs, alone but for his dog Clara. The decidedly strange parents, and the rather unconventional sister, probably only added to his oddball credentials.

But then, one by one, Emily had brought Holly, Jo-Jo and Rachel down to stay at Dodger Point and watched their preconceptions crumble. A day at Dodger Point and even Jo-Jo, the ultimate city chick, was wondering aloud if you could hear the sound of the sea from Arthur's bedroom, was standing on the cliffs, staring out at a soft pink sea fading in the evening light, and talking about falling in love.

Dodger Point had to be one of the most ruggedly beautiful places on earth and Arthur's home one of the most perfectly romantic. It sat small and squat and secure on a rocky peninsula a couple of hundred feet above the sea, with a little windswept garden leading up to the front door and rough steps carved into the rocks winding down to the tiny beach below. And it had a tower, so that it was possible to climb up a spiral staircase to look out at the sea. A couple of years after he had bought it, Arthur had put on an extension to the back, adding two more small bedrooms and another bathroom to the single bedroom in the main house.

Having brought her to St Brides, Emily had watched Jo-Jo fall, like others before her, just a little in love with Arthur as well as with his house, but despite Emily's blatant matchmaking Arthur never obliged. He flirted enough to be flattering and was always charming and kind but never took it further, displaying an evasiveness that was never unfriendly and certainly not calculated and only served to make him all the more attractive. And when this detachment made him distant, as it sometimes did, this only served to remind Jo-Jo and the others of Emily, and then they would recall Emily and Arthur's parents, who had emigrated to New Zealand six weeks after Emily had left school. Neither Emily nor Arthur had seen them since.

Whenever Arthur made a trip to London, Emily spent most of her time fussing around him, convinced he or Clara were about to be run over or mugged or abducted. Of course she knew he could look after himself. It was only because she loved him so much, because he was all she had, that she became so neurotic. When she failed to prevent Caitlin from finally meeting Arthur – Emily had done her best to keep the two of them apart – and Caitlin immediately arranged to take him clubbing the following evening, Emily had nearly exploded with outrage. Whereupon Arthur had held her firmly by the shoulders and reminded her that he'd lived in Tooting for five years and could well cope with the pressure of ordering a round of drinks. Emily had wanted to tell him that Caitlin wasn't anything like the girls in Tooting, that she was a vampire who would sink her teeth into him and suck him dry, but Caitlin was standing there at his shoulder and even Emily didn't dare.

And now here she was thinking about joining him in

St Brides for good. She wondered whether Arthur might not want his sister to move to his town but deep down was sure he wouldn't mind. Arthur had moved to St Brides because of a good job and because of the sea, not because he was wanting to escape anything. Far from feeling she would cramp his style, Emily got the impression he would love to have her living nearby.

If anything, it wouldn't be Arthur's refuge she might be destroying but her own, because surely it was the stark contrast with London that made St Brides so idyllic. She needed the enclosed London streets in order to appreciate the vastness of the sea, needed to breathe in the city fug to appreciate the salty clean air, needed to open her bedroom window to row upon row of cramped and scrubby back gardens in order to appreciate the cliffs of Dodger Point.

And yet, Emily was filled with a terrible restlessness. It was time to do something seriously different, something bigger than merely walking out of her job. Something that would jolt her and make her feel alive again. She had been marking time for too long.

The next morning, her second day of unemployment, and even before she was fully awake, Emily stretched out an arm for the telephone and called Arthur. The longer his mobile rang the wider awake she became. Finally he picked up.

'Can I come and stay?' she demanded immediately.

'Hello, Arthur. How are you? Oh, hi there, Emily. Good to hear from you. I'm very well, thanks.'

'Hello, Arthur,' she said smiling. 'Where've you been? Why did you take so long to answer the phone?'

'None of your business.'

'I wanted to come and see you.' When he didn't say anything she went on more tentatively, 'Tonight. Is that OK? If I get in at about seven.' Surely it was OK? It was always OK.

There was a pause. 'Come for supper at the Pelican?'

'What? No fish and chips in front of the telly?'

'No, you can come out for dinner.' Emily could hear there was something else coming. She pushed herself up against her pillows. Lying down was suddenly making her feel vulnerable.

'Come and meet my girlfriend,' he said.

There was another pause.

'A desperately-in-love-with-her girlfriend or an only-just-met-her girlfriend?'

'Perhaps both.'

She could hear in his voice that he meant it too. *Why the bloody hell do you have to nd a new girlfriend now?* And she couldn't think what else to say. Her mind was leaping ahead: *What if she wants to move into Dodger Point? What if you get married? How can I come and stay then? Where will I go?*

'What's her name?'

'It's Jennifer.'

Jennifer. What kind of a person was a Jennifer? Not a Jenny or a Jen but a Jennifer. A Jennifer filled her with foreboding. She saw someone tall and serious, with long straight black hair and a pale, unsmiling face.

'When did you meet her? And where? Does she live in St Brides?'

'Only a week ago. On the beach. And yes, she does. She was looking for shells and we kind of bumped into each other.'

'That sounds so unlikely.' *Damn Jennifer.*

Arthur laughed. 'Don't be so suspicious. Weren't you looking for shells when someone bumped into you?'

'Yes, but I was sixteen and, anyway, he didn't bump.'

'She did.'

'So she has little milk-bottle-bottom glasses, does she?'

'Emily!'

'Or someone jostled her? The beach was packed full of people?'

'It was empty.'

'Then she didn't bump, did she?' Emily challenged. 'It was a cunning plan to get talking to you.'

'I hope so. She's beautiful . . .'

Emily laughed warily. 'OK. You're keen. I'm going to have to like her.'

'But if you don't?'

'Then I'll behave really badly, let you down.'

Arthur sighed theatrically. 'I think we're going to have to find someone else to come to supper. Someone to dilute you.'

'Do you have someone in mind? Some sad work colleague who never gets out?'

'Actually, I do know someone. Someone who happened to wander into my office yesterday morning. Do you remember Sam Finch?'

'I know Sam. What was he doing in your office?'

'Do you like him? Would you like him to come?' Arthur waited but Emily didn't say anything. 'We were talking and then he asked me if I had a sister called Emily and I said yes, I had, and he said he remembered meeting me years ago. He said it was with you, here one summer. And how he'd seen you again just this week.' Arthur wasn't about to tell Emily how it had taken Sam perhaps twenty seconds to bring the conversation around to Emily, nor how obvious it was that she was really the only reason why Sam was there in his office. 'He's just come back to live in Cornwall.'

'I don't need setting up just because you've got Jennifer.'

'It wouldn't be like that.'

'I met him through Oliver. Oliver Mills? Do you remember him? I worked with him on Breaking Free. He's just come back from New York.'

'You snogged him in the sand dunes. I remember Oliver. He could water-ski with bare feet.'

'That's the one.'

Emily, with time to think about it, liked the idea of Sam joining them and she didn't really mind Arthur knowing but she wanted to move the conversation on from Oliver. 'Call Sam,' she encouraged Arthur. 'Don't let him say no.' She was nervous about meeting Jennifer and it would be good to have an ally.

Afterwards she put down the telephone and lay back against the pillows. Her bed was at a right angle to the window and she lay there with her eyes closed, feeling the air from the half-open window cold on her face. She ran back over the conversation with Arthur, hearing his words again, the reverential *she's beautiful*, and in her mind Jennifer transformed into someone laughing and bewitchingly pretty, an undefined version of Jennifer Aniston. Emily saw Jennifer and Arthur striding away from her across the beach at Dodger Point, Clara at their heels, their arms round each other, a criss-cross of unity on their backs. Great that he'd found someone, she told herself bouncing up again in bed in agitation. She meant it too. She loved him. She was thrilled for him, she really was – or she knew she would be when she had got herself sorted out.

But right now the effect of Arthur's news was to make her feel distanced from him, turned and twisted and wrenched away. Not surprising that the loneliness that had been creeping around for the past few days was suddenly there, full on, harsh and unrelenting. While some might picture hordes of men beating on her bedroom door only to be turned away by a virginal Emily in a long white nightdress, the reality was that there had been no one for Emily to turn down for nearly a year. Nobody to test, nobody to miss, nobody to think about, and now, with Arthur in love and Oliver back home Nessa-less, it felt as if she had been left more alone than ever, while around her everything had turned upside down, so that all those things that had been impossible before were possible now and she found herself hating the change.

She got up and opened the curtains. She looked out of her third-floor window and down to the twelve tiny

gardens below, a messy, irregular patchwork of dilapidated garden fences dividing one set of weeds and rusty
bicycles from another. In one garden hung a row of red-
coloured washing, surely frozen to the line it had been
there so long and hung there so still.

She shut the window and sat down on her bed again,
then rose once more and left her bedroom, made her way
down the short hall to her kitchen, fed a slice of bread into
the toaster and filled the kettle, pulled out a chair and sat
at the small square wooden table. Then decided to go
running.

Before the kettle had boiled or the bread toasted she
was back in her bedroom. She didn't want breakfast. She
couldn't sit down. She didn't want to eat. She imagined
herself sprinting effortlessly though dark woods, twigs
snapping under her feet, up and down hills, like Clarice
Starling in *The Silence of the Lambs*. She wanted to do what
she knew other people did when they were so worked up
they couldn't stop themselves prowling around their flats.
She would go for a run in Richmond Park.

She dug in a drawer for a pair of socks and then
burrowed deep in her cupboard and found a pair of
trainers rolled up in some Lycra running shorts and a
fluorescent vest. She straightened up, holding them in her
hands, and for a brief moment she could hear the blood
roaring in her ears and the sound of her gasping, rasping
breathing, could look down at her thighs, mottled orange
and purple with cold, spattered with mud. She pushed the
memory away. Running was a good idea. This would be

a fun run, she would take it gently. She would walk as soon as she wanted.

The park was less than half an hour away, but if Holly hadn't taken her there for a picnic soon after she'd moved into the house in Richmond, Emily doubted she'd ever have thought to go. Now she knew it would be the place she missed most if she ever did get around to leaving London.

She parked at Sheen Gate. It was a cold, bright morning and there was hardly anybody about – only a few committed dog walkers, sitting in their cars with the doors open, pulling on wellingtons and buttoning up oilskins, or opening the boots of hatchback cars to let out eager, bouncing dogs.

Emily locked her car, re-tied her trainers, stuffed her keys and phone into her belt-bag and went to touch her toes, but quickly changed her mind. She walked at first, instantly soothed by the silent magic of the woods. There was a fallen tree ahead of her and, seeing it, she started to jog, measured it up, then leapt lightly over the trunk, only to land with a noisy splash in a puddle on the other side.

I think that's enough running a loud, persuasive voice in her head said then. *Stop now, before it gets nasty.* But she couldn't, she told the voice, not yet, not when she'd hardly begun, when she'd managed to run little more than twenty feet.

Determined to keep going, she left the woods and made herself run on into the park, her feet squelching in her now soggy trainers. Keeping the boundary wall on her right, she found that she was running easier, even able to let her mind wander a little, to think how the wall kept out so much more than it kept in, how it embraced the park and held it safe from all the concrete and glass and exhaust fumes that were crowding up behind it. Inside, the sun rested warm on her back, the sky pure and blue.

She ran along the edge of the woods, sending squirrels leaping for the safety of the oaks, and thought how Charles I hunted deer there, had maybe galloped along the very path she was running on now. How wonderful it was that the park and the deer had survived so unchanged, to be here still, centuries later.

And then the path turned and she saw her first hill. She dug deep and started to climb and immediately any ideas of this being an enjoyable experience disappeared completely. Within a few strides the hill became an assault course and benign King Charles faded away, replaced by a vicious red devil who jabbed her in the ribs with his pointed trident.

She heard herself hissing through clenched teeth. Why had she done it again? Why hadn't she remembered how much she hated running, had always hated it? She'd done this so many times before. She remembered thundering along a lane in Cornwall after Arthur, in the same trainers, shorts and vest she was wearing now, blood roaring in her ears, convinced she was about to die.

She made it to the top of the hill and left the path like a shipwreck survivor staggering from the sea. There was a bench ahead of her, bracken all around it, too tempting to ignore. She sat down and with trembling hands managed to take off her wet trainers and feebly wring out her socks. And then she lay down with her knees bent, clammy cold feet resting on the slats of the bench while her breathing slowly calmed and eventually she could see clearly again.

She pushed herself upright, keeping her knees bunched up against her chest, and looked around.

Now everywhere looked beautiful. Around her bench, baby green shoots of new bracken were just starting to uncurl, bursting through the earth at her feet, above a kestrel circled idly in the perfect blue sky. Tipping back her head she found that the sun felt warm on her face. And she wondered why she was thinking of moving to St Brides when all this was on her doorstep. She could move three miles rather than three hundred and rent a flat in Richmond if she wanted open spaces. She hadn't acknowledged before that it wasn't London she wanted to escape from. That moving away wasn't necessarily going to make her any happier.

And then she stared more closely at the branch sticking up out of a patch of bracken a gentle toss of a stone away from her bench, and realized, belatedly, that the branch was one of a pair and that where there were two branches, there were maybe a hundred others rising out of the bracken all around her. And how had she not noticed the Bambi-brown eyes staring at her from all around? Not even taken in the two huge stags facing each other aggressively less than fifty feet away?

As if they had been waiting for her attention, the two stags dropped their heads, clashed antlers and roared at each other and Emily picked up her socks and shoes and sprinted, head down and without a glance behind her, back to the path.

When she thought she had put a safe distance between her and the deer, she stopped and put her trainers back on and looked back. Maybe they hadn't bothered to chase her, but she wasn't going to tempt them a second time, which meant a wide loop around them before she could return to her car.

The path led her downhill now and her wobbly legs began to run away with themselves even as she tried to walk and with each bump and jolt another wave of self-pity rose within her until she found she was almost willing herself to trip over, wanting to hit the ground with a smack, wanting the shoot of pain from a twisted ankle to take her attention instead and allow her to burst into tears. But her feet kept her upright instinctively, balancing and springing her deftly off the tussocks of grass and sharp rocks that littered the path.

As far as self-diagnosis went, it was pretty obvious something was shifting inside her. Was it simply a recognition that she was lonely? It felt as if she was missing someone, but perhaps someone she'd never even known. She'd arrived home after supper with Holly and the others and had lain down on her little patchwork sofa, her knees pulled up almost to her chin, and it had felt as if she was waiting for someone, someone she could almost touch, smell, whose smile she could almost see. Six months ago –

even six weeks ago – it hadn't been like that. Work had been miserable, but once home she'd been able to forget about work. Having Rachel downstairs and Holly down the street and her brother on the end of the phone had been all that she'd needed, but not any more.

Oliver was home again and Nessa had been left behind. Emily finally allowed herself to confront it, to face the niggling, nagging, sleep-destroying fact that had been tormenting her ever since she'd first heard. Oliver was free. What did that mean for her?

Another great hill loomed up ahead of her. Her legs were hurting, her lungs heaving for air, in her head she was screaming every expletive she'd ever known, in her head only because she hadn't the breath to say them aloud.

She came to a second exhausted halt and stared down at her mud-spattered legs, looking so distressed that an old lady walking a West Highland terrier stopped to offer her a piece of chocolate.

She looked up at the high ornate gates open just ahead of her and saw that she'd got as far as Richmond. She was only a few hundred yards from Holly's house. And Holly was taking a few days off, she remembered, and so she might possibly be in.

Emily walked out through the gates and down Richmond Hill in her Lycra shorts and soaked vest, sweat pouring down her flaming cheeks, oblivious to all the smart boutiques and shoppers to match, thinking about being strong and following a path she had carved out for herself years ago and was not about to give up on, however much the dazzle of Oliver might tempt her. Oliver. Again, her mind skidded away from the challenge of him, ignoring the opportunity that was presenting itself – the fact that she could, right now, go after him with the same single-minded determination that she'd seen other girls use on other men.

A hundred yards from Holly's front door, her mobile rang and she turned away from the noise of the street to answer it.

'Emily. Hi, it's Caitlin.'

Sounding unusually friendly, Emily thought, instantly suspicious.

'I've left a message on your answerphone, but then I thought why not try your mobile?' Emily waited. 'I wondered if you were free for supper on Saturday night. Probably not,' Caitlin added without pausing for breath. 'I know it's not much notice, but it would be so good to see you.'

'Saturday? This Saturday?' Emily cupped her hand around her ear trying to block out the sound of the street, convinced she wasn't hearing right.

'Yes. But I can hear you don't want to. You're trying to think of a way out, aren't you?'

'No, I'm not! I'm out of breath. I've been running,' Emily protested, even as she was trying to think of an excuse. 'That would be great. I'm off to see Arthur. Catching a train in about an hour.' An hour! What was she doing in Richmond? 'But I can come back on Saturday.'

'Fantastic.'

'Caitlin,' Emily said, 'why do you want me?' She knew

she sounded confrontational but she had to ask, knew it would be bugging her all the time she was in Cornwall if she didn't.

Caitlin paused. 'Does there have to be a reason?' And from the way she said it, Emily knew there was of course a reason. Then Caitlin sighed, acknowledging what they both knew already. 'OK. You're right! There is.'

'Why?'

'I want you because . . . you're such good company.'

'Rubbish.' Emily laughed. 'Try again.'

'No, you are! I should have got you round years ago.'

Emily shook her head. 'That's not the reason.'

'No,' Caitlin admitted. She started again, 'Half because I was horrid last night and I want to apologize. Really, that's the truth . . . and also because I've got Oliver coming and I want someone I know he likes to join us.'

Oliver was coming. 'Anyone else?' Emily asked, carefully avoiding mentioning his name.

'Only Leon.'

'I'd love to come. Thank you.' *Caitlin and Oliver?* Was that the reason Caitlin wanted Oliver to come for supper? Because Caitlin was after him? The thought made Emily want to punch her. Leon being there wouldn't stop her. Probably it would make it more exciting for her. 'Caitlin, I've got to go,' she said, walking up the steps to Holly's house and leaning on the bell. She wanted to ask Holly if she was right, not talk to Caitlin any more, and so she said a hasty goodbye and put away her phone.

Holly opened the door and gave her a startled look. 'Tell me you haven't run here all the way from Clapham.'

Emily rolled her eyes at the terrible thought and didn't reply. She walked past Holly and went into the kitchen in search of a glass of orange juice.

In Holly's shower, she closed her eyes and lifted her chin to the water, letting it beat down blissfully onto her forehead. She would get to Arthur's for supper. She would meet Jennifer. She would persuade Arthur to take tomorrow morning off, and would ask him to drive her along the coast, looking out for suitable places to open Saltwater. Back to London on Saturday morning. Saturday evening, supper at Caitlin's, where she would somehow have to fix it that Oliver didn't fall for Caitlin. Caitlin. How she was going to stop him she wasn't quite sure.

'Why do you think Caitlin wants me there?' she asked Holly, sitting in the kitchen afterwards in a pair of Holly's jeans and one of her T-shirts. 'Is it because I am the most unthreatening single woman around?'

Holly put a croissant and a cup of coffee down in front of her. 'There are other single women who are far less threatening than you. No. I think Caitlin genuinely wants to begin again with you.'

Emily shook her head. She hoped Holly was right, but she knew Caitlin well enough to give it less than a ten per cent chance of being true.

'You'll find out on Saturday,' said Holly. 'It's not long to wait.'

'How did you know it was Saturday? I didn't tell you? Has Caitlin already told you about it?' Emily caught the troubled look on Holly's face. 'She has! Why? What's going on? Holly, what have you been saying about me?'

'Don't be so suspicious,' Holly said smoothly. 'Caitlin called me about half an hour ago. It must have been just a few minutes before she called you and she mentioned it then.' Which was true. The fact that Holly had already known Emily was going to be asked for supper was beside the point. 'That's how I know. And do you know something? I've booked the skiing today.'

'Don't change the subject!' Emily's eyes bore into Holly's. 'Is there anything else I might like to know?'

'Caitlin mentioned that she was asking you around on Saturday night.'

'But why would she do that? I think it's because she fancies Oliver. And do you know – ' Emily groaned – 'I couldn't stand it if that's the reason. I cannot think of anything worse than sitting in Caitlin's flat watching her moving in on him.'

Holly took in the groan and the misery on Emily's face and was pleased by what she saw. 'Go and have a good time,' she insisted. 'Don't think about Caitlin. Think about seeing Oliver again. Don't try to outguess what might happen.'

And then, later, she drove Emily back to her car, leaving enough time for Emily to get back to her flat, change and pick up her bag to catch the early afternoon train to St Brides.

6

Emily saw Arthur from her window on the train, standing in a fisherman's jersey and dark cords, tall and thin among the huddle of people waiting in the neon lights and the cold.

He let her walk right up to him before he made a move, then suddenly opened wide his arms and let a great grin break across his face. Then he caught her in a hug and she knew she'd done the right thing, that she'd come to stay with the world's best person. She took his arm and let him lead her down the steep steps of St Brides station.

'Jennifer?' she said tentatively as they reached his car, raising her eyebrows at him. 'I'm so looking forward to meeting her.'

'And she's so looking forward to meeting you.'

Emily was momentarily taken aback. Then it dawned on her that of course Arthur and Jennifer would have talked about her, she should have expected it. Even so, it was a new feeling. She wanted to know what Arthur's description would have included and what he would have left out. She had a sudden image of Jennifer, lovely eyes crinkling with surprise, Jennifer laughing, her hand over her mouth. *A virgin? You're joking! How sweet!* And she hoped she was right to trust that Arthur wouldn't have told Jennifer that. Wouldn't have revealed something so personal.

Emily opened the passenger door of Arthur's car, slid into her seat and waited for him to join her, and behind her Arthur opened a back door and swung her bag onto the seat.

'I've booked a table for eight thirty,' he told her as he started the engine. 'Sam and Jennifer are going to meet us there.' He paused. 'So you've got time to change if you want to.'

'That sounds like I need to.'

'Not at all.'

She did need to. She wanted to dress to kill. She wanted to dispel the image of the soft, gentle innocent that Arthur had perhaps planted in Jennifer's mind. The irritating thing was that soft and gentle was exactly the image she'd packed for that evening: jeans and a pale pink cotton shirt printed with roses and a minty-green angora tank top. She'd have to find something else, she thought. She'd have to adapt it.

In companionable silence they drove away from the station and followed the main road, through the austere grey-stone town of St Brides, then along the coast road which in a few months' time would be clogged with holidaymakers but now, in the early evening dusk, was tranquil and empty. And then they picked up speed and left the town behind, the road still hugging the coastline but climbing and twisting all the way. Emily knew it all so well. It felt like coming home.

They were soon at the bend in the road from where they could see the lights of Dodger Point even though it would be another ten minutes before they arrived. She told herself not to be so excited about being here again, reminded herself that it wasn't her home.

They drove on, both aware that the other had more to say, neither of them fooled by the catching-up conversations that they continued to persist with. Emily timed Arthur's change of subject almost to the second, noticing how his lips started to move before he spoke, as if he was trying out the words before he spoke them out loud.

'I'm terrified at the thought of you meeting her,' he admitted, glancing at her.

She was struck by the vulnerability showing on his face. 'You mustn't be. And watch the road.'

'You're the only person whose opinion I care about.'

'Of course I'll like her.'

He nodded.

'And I'll be diluted, remember.' She smiled. 'It'll be fine. I like Sam. We'll have a great time.'

She described to Arthur how she'd literally run into Sam the other day, and he decided not to admit that he'd already heard it all from Sam.

They turned another corner and they were running along the coast again. Emily wound down her window, closed her eyes and breathed in the sea-scented air.

'Can you still smell the salt or have you become immune?'

Arthur didn't answer. She closed up her window again because it was freezing cold, turned back to him and touched his hand holding the steering wheel.

'I'm pleased for you. Now, can you fix it for me too, please?'

He squeezed her hand back. 'You want that?'

'Of course I do!'

'Then thank God I suggested getting him along! I'm so pleased you want to give him a chance.'

'Not Sam! I don't mean fix it for me with Sam!'

'Oh, I wasn't talking about *Sam*.' Arthur backtracked. 'Whatever made you think I was talking about Sam? I meant to say *her*. I meant give *her* a big chance. I was talking about Jennifer.'

'You big liar.' She looked across at him and slowly shook her head. 'Let us be clear about this: I am not interested in Sam.'

'Who *are* you interested in, then?' he said, obviously disappointed. 'Who is it who's turned you so prickly?'

She smiled. 'Picky or prickly?'

'Both.'

'Nobody. It's how I am.'

'And you're getting worse.'

'No, I'm not. I'm the same as I've always been. Tell me more about Jennifer,' she said, looking out of the window again. 'Have you shown her Dodger Point?'

'Yes.'

'And did she like it?'

'She did. Who is he, Emily?'

They drove on, both watching the road in the car's headlights, until Emily said, 'She was with you when I rang this morning, wasn't she?'

'Why do you say that?'

'There was something in your voice.'

'Yes, she was.'

'So, I suppose you were in the middle of showing her your bedroom, were you?'

Arthur was tempted to tell Emily the truth. To say no, they hadn't bothered going up to his bedroom because they'd just had icy-cold, fantastic sex in the sand dunes instead.

'Let's talk about you,' he said instead. 'Who do you want to be fixed up with? I can't help if I don't know who it is.'

Emily said nothing. 'OK, we'll talk about something else,' he said, looking at her with concern. 'But we're going to come back to it again and again and again until you tell me. So,' he added brightly, 'have you had any interviews?'

'I've fixed up a few. Everyone's telling me to have a break.'

'What about revenge? How about dropping a scorpion through Carrie Piper's letter box?'

'She'd probably eat it alive.' Emily took a deep breath. 'I was thinking about moving here, Arthur. Would you mind?'

'You know I'd love you to do that.'

'I'm wondering about Saltwater again.' Arthur nodded. 'And I thought perhaps you and I could do some shop hunting tomorrow. I wondered whether you might be able to take a bit of time off work to show me around.'

'I could.'

'Thank you.' She smiled gratefully.

'You know I think Saltwater is a terrific idea.'

'You don't think I'd be running away?'

'Would you be?' He waited five seconds, then tried again. 'From who? Tell me who he is?'

She shook her head again. 'It's no one!' Then she sighed. 'Nothing is wrong, at least not in a big, dramatic kind of a way. But I suppose something has changed and I don't know what to do about it . . .' She shrugged. 'And it's probably making me twitchy. Distracted. Prickly, whatever.'

'Try telling me.'

But just as they'd reached the moment where Emily might have opened up to Arthur, they turned into the short bumpy drive that led to Dodger Point. Arthur pulled up beside the house, turned off the engine and waited in the moonlit darkness for her to say some more.

She heaved a giant sigh. 'I suppose we're talking about sex,' she said.

'Or no sex?'

She laughed bitterly. 'You know me.'

'And someone in particular is making it an issue?'

'No. But I wish he would!' She gave him a flicker of a smile before her face fell again. 'For the first time, I'm seriously asking myself what I'll do if I meet someone I really care about. What I'll do if he won't wait for me. I'm amazed it's never happened to me before, but it hasn't. It's always been me ending relationships, not them. And the guys I've been out with, so far they've been happy to wait, happy for us to do other things . . . It hasn't been a problem. And it's been easy for me to say if they won't wait for me, then they're not worth sleeping with.' She stopped but Arthur knew better than to interrupt her flow. 'Now I'm wondering whether I should have thrown myself at some man years ago. Got it all over and done with, stopped it becoming an issue, like everyone else did.'

'But you didn't and you can't change that.'

'But I still could, couldn't I? It doesn't take much.'

'Someone is making you talk like this. Do I know him?'

'Yes, you do,' she said simply. 'It's Oliver.'

'Oliver Mills.' And from the way he said it, she knew it was no great surprise.

Her admission made, she felt cold. She wrapped her arms around herself and pulled up her knees, lifting her feet onto the dashboard. Now that she'd said it out loud it was as if she was freed up to think about Oliver in a way she hadn't allowed herself to for years. Admit how much she liked him. How much she'd like more of those entrancing moments that she'd been given so many years earlier, but had had to forget.

Then she swore out loud with the certain knowledge that while she fretted and did nothing he would quickly find somebody else, had probably found her already.

'He's back and he's single,' Emily said. 'But I know he won't turn to me . . . And for the first time he's making me question something I've always been so sure about. And it's making me angry . . . It's making me think if I wasn't so realistic, perhaps I could have jumped into bed with lots of guys. It's only because I know they're not going to last that I don't. I never saw the point in sleeping with the wrong guy. By wrong I mean someone I knew it wasn't going to last with. But other people don't think like me, other people throw themselves into their relationships, they're optimistic about them, they don't think realistically about the future. Why do I have to?'

'Is it possible – ' Arthur chose his words carefully – 'that the reasons you had for making that promise to yourself don't hold true any more? Might it be the promise to yourself that's keeping you back, more than the reasons behind the promise? And if that's the case, you mustn't think of a promise to yourself in the same way as a promise to someone else. If you're changing your mind now, that's not wrong. What would be wrong would be to deny it or run away from it. I've sat up for too many evenings with you not to know you've thought it all through. You have more courage than anyone else I know. But you're more stubborn, too. It would be hard for you to admit to yourself that it's time to change your mind.'

'You're right, and if that was all there was to it I'd agree with you, but it's not.'

'Tell me.'

Emily swallowed, trying to gather together the right words in her mind. How to explain a certainty that had grown and taken root over so many years.

He looked at her, full of kindness and concern. 'I'm Emily and I'm a virgin because . . .' he suggested helpfully.

'Stop it.' She laughed. 'This is serious.' And it was and yet it wasn't too, because while she could give lots of good reasons for why she'd stayed a virgin, the simple truth was that nobody had made it a difficult choice, until now.

'Lots of girls – and men too – have slept with people

because they felt they should, because they wanted to be part of the crowd. Not because they really wanted to.'

'That's true,' Arthur agreed. 'And if you sleep with Oliver for the wrong reasons, you'll be more angry with yourself than if you lose him over it.'

'But the years are flying by and I'm still alone. I never thought it would take so long!' she cried. 'Dammit, I sound completely sex-starved. Do you think that's what all this is about? Is it finally getting to me?'

'No.' Arthur laughed.

'You don't think I'm mad to be holding out?'

'As I've said, it depends what you're holding out for.'

'Holding out for more than a quick shag. Holding out for someone I really love, who really loves me. Holding out because I don't have a problem with waiting.'

'And there's nothing wrong with that.'

'Isn't there? Because I wonder sometimes if I'm making it impossible for me ever to get to know anyone. Perhaps waiting went out of fashion because it was such a bad idea?'

'All you've ever said is that you don't want to have sex with someone until you know your relationship will last; that you don't see the point in sleeping with a series of Mr Wrongs, men you know are going to slip out of your life and disappear. You want to wait. You believe that sex is something that should happen between two people who really love each other and you want to wait until you've found that.'

She nodded. 'And I can't help thinking what a lovely

thing it would be, *for me*,' she interrupted him, 'to give my virginity to the right man.'

Arthur said, 'And for those reasons I don't think it's mad, or terribly old-fashioned, or pointless. I think it's great. It's a wonderful ideal to have. And I wonder why it should be so hard. Why you're not surrounded by people thinking the same way.'

'But you didn't wait,' Emily reminded him. 'I don't suppose you and Jennifer have waited.'

'No.'

'What would you have done if she'd wanted to?'

'Dumped her instantly.'

'Seriously!'

'I'd have respected her! I'd have waited for as long as she wanted too, and I've have hoped it wouldn't be too long. As it was, it was about a day and most of a night.'

'Arthur! You shouldn't have told me that.'

'She wouldn't mind.'

'And won't you be crucified now if it all goes wrong? Won't it be far worse for you than if you hadn't slept together?'

He shook his head. 'I don't think of it like that. Better to have loved and lost, perhaps. And I'm eternally optimistic too. The truth is that until *you* get into a relationship, you won't know how you want to take it further. You have to get close, you have to let yourself fall for someone before you can know where it's going next. And you've never done that, have you?' He turned to Emily, waiting for her to respond, and she gave a small nod of agreement. 'It's only then that you'll fully appreciate what it is you've been holding on to, and whether it's right to let it go. Right now, you're saying that to be in lust isn't enough, that you want to be sure of a lifelong commitment. But how do you know? You've never been there! Wait, yes. Waiting is good. But be brave, too. Don't be so wary or you will never get involved.'

'I do understand how it can be,' said Emily. 'I know it often sounds like I don't. And I want to tell you something else about Oliver Mills,' she went on. 'I am not in love with him. But I could be. I want the chance to fall in love with him and what's driving me crazy is the thought that I'm not going to get it because he won't wait around for me. In fact, he won't come near me, let alone hang around, because for Oliver, my being a virgin will mean I'm off-limits. He will never see me as anything other than a friend, or perhaps a little sister.'

'How do you know? He didn't think of you like that when you were sixteen. You don't know Oliver won't want you just as you are.'

'I do.'

'Then stop being off-limits,' Arthur encouraged. 'Let him know you fancy him.'

'I don't think I can.'

'You've done it before, with other boyfriends,' Arthur urged.

'I know I have. It's just with him I feel paralysed. Completely hopeless.'

'You can't say that. Get a grip, girl. Take hold of your destiny. And now we have to get a move on,' he told her, opening his door, 'or we will be late for Jennifer and Sam.'

Emily left Arthur in the kitchen and, although they were running out of time, she climbed the spiral staircase to the tiny round room in the tower. She'd decorated this room for Arthur, painted it with a sea green oil glaze right up to the high round ceiling, somehow carrying a chair up the spiral staircase to do the highest bits. She'd hunted through antique shops for furniture and had eventually found an old oak curved bench with an arm at each end that must have once been made for a round table and now fitted perfectly into the curve of the tower. Arthur had had to chop off the legs to get it up to the room, then glue them on again afterwards. She'd added deep velvet-covered cushions in red and burnt sienna and green to match the walls and had polished the grey stone floor and left it bare. Now one could sit back, comfortable and secure, against the cushions and look out of the large rectangular windows down to the sea below.

She sat there, warm inside her coat, looking down at the midnight blue water, at the cliffs and the dark sky . . . and wondered what to wear to meet Jennifer.

She was looking forward to the evening now, she felt rejuvenated. The conversation in the car with Arthur had changed her mood, filled her with anticipation. She was glad now that they were going out, that there was a chance to dress up and to see Sam again and to meet Jennifer.

It was a calm night and the sea was flat and reflective

like oil. To the west, Emily could see the lights of St Brides. She thought how much fun it would be to look around there tomorrow with Arthur, because of all the nearby towns St Brides was the place she was most familiar with and the place she could best imagine opening her shop.

She stretched out her fingers and touched the china animals that had been hers as a child and had found their way to St Brides, to this window sill. She picked up a galloping horse, pricking her fingertips on its spiky china mane and then tracing the line of its delicate thoroughbred legs. The horse had come with a foal, but her mother, knowing how much her daughter adored it, had given it to one of Emily's school friends, one of the times when she had stopped being just vague and had seemed deliberately cruel. Why did she have to remember that now? Emily put the horse down. Next to it was a bronze bell, green with age and without its knocker, and beside that a purple velvet gonk. She picked up the gonk and turned him so that his big, lopsided, grinning face could look out of the window.

When she'd dressed she made her way back down to the kitchen. Arthur was filleting mackerel, Clara had her head between her paws, watching him intently. He stopped when he saw her in the doorway and stared at her. 'Very nice.'

'Thanks!'

Emily pulled out a chair. 'Is that our breakfast?'

He nodded. 'I bought them on the way to the station

just after they'd been caught. I thought I'd finish preparing them before we go out.'

In the summer Arthur would have caught them himself. He had a little motor boat that he'd take out after work, dragging a line of hooks behind him.

'Do *I* look all right?' he asked her then, turning around so that she could see him properly.

She smiled at the question because she didn't think she'd ever seen him look any other way. Did he own a loud shirt, or a jumper that wasn't olive green or navy blue, or trousers that weren't denim or cord? She wondered what plans Jennifer might have for him, whether next time Arthur might be waiting for her at the station in flip-flops and a sarong.

'You look very handsome.' She walked over to him and stretched up and kissed his freshly shaved cheek. 'Holly and Jo-Jo are going to be very disappointed when they hear about Jennifer.'

Like most tourist towns, St Brides survived on its summers. For the past three years visitor numbers had been boosted by the presence of the Pelican, a seafood restaurant situated in a spectacular setting, high on the cliffs, run by a woman called Hope Maguire. Inside it was unpretentious and yet very stylish, with simple, square, bleached oak tables and chairs and walls painted a metallic greeny-gold. And although the food was notoriously slow to arrive, when it did it was so good that people had been heard to talk about it afterwards in their sleep. Waiters threaded their way between the tables, carrying huge white china platters just too high to be able to see what was on them, so it was possible to catch only tantalizing glimpses of crab claws or lobsters' legs trailing over the sides, encouraging waiting diners to frantically return to their menus to work out which dishes were which. Between May and October the Pelican was full every night and it was necessary to book weeks in advance.

If Arthur had been able to choose he would have booked them a table near the huge floor-to-ceiling windows that looked out to the sea, but, understandably, they were the first to go, and only having booked that morning, he had been lucky to get a table at all. He led Emily across the room, Emily drawing everyone's eyes as she walked. Instead of the shirt she had packed for the evening, she was wearing a cream lace vest. High necked and sleeveless, it was more than a little transparent, but as she wouldn't be getting it wet, she thought she'd get away with it.

As they were led to their table, Emily saw there was a girl in a tailored black jacket with long black hair sitting alone with her back to them.

'There she is,' Arthur muttered nervously. 'Do you see how she's plaited her hair. Isn't that great?'

It was amazing hair, a heavy, shiny curtain that had undoubtedly been washed and conditioned and brushed a hundred times before being plaited on either side in a series of tiny intricate plaits that met at the back while the rest of her hair hung loose beneath. Emily's heart sank, because all too often the effort of producing such hair seemed to destroy the sense of humour entirely. She imagined a face plain and unsmiling, bare of even the merest scrap of make-up.

As Emily and Arthur slowly made their way towards her Jennifer slowly turned and rose from her chair to greet them and Emily could see her for real and see that she had been completely wrong in her predictions. For a start Jennifer did believe in make-up. Lots of it. Black eyeliner ringed her huge eyes, emphasizing the translucent whiteness of her skin and the ruby red of her lips.

Emily greeted her with a smile and an outstretched hand, taking in battered stiletto boots and flared low cut jeans. In contrast the black jacket was made of a dull brocade and was very tight, nipped in around a tiny waist. Why hadn't Arthur warned her! Not that Emily knew what he might have said. All she knew was that she felt silly and overdressed, even though all she was wearing was a vest and velvet trousers.

Jennifer meanwhile dropped her eyelashes and gave Arthur a provocative lingering smile. *And Arthur thought this girl collected sea shells on the beach?*

'Hello,' Emily said smiling at her.

'This is Emily,' Arthur encouraged Jennifer.

Jennifer managed a faint smile back.

'Sam's late,' said Arthur.

'He'll be here,' Emily reassured him. She looked at her watch. 'We're five minutes early.'

There was another awkward pause.

'Shall we sit down?' Emily suggested then, seeing how

behind her a log-jam of waiters had quickly built up, all balancing heavy trays and impatient to serve the nearby tables. 'Jennifer? Can we sit down?'

Standing in front of Emily and blocking the way, Jennifer either didn't hear or ignored her deliberately.

Emily gave the waiters behind her an apologetic smile and Jennifer a gentle nudge in the small of her back. 'I think we should get out of the way of the waiters,' she repeated to Arthur over Jennifer's shoulder.

Arthur nodded. Then Emily saw a look of alarm widen his eyes. She turned and saw that the waiter nearest to her, carrying a heavy glass jug of water in one hand and four glasses in the other, was in trouble and, anticipating what was about to happen, she shoved Jennifer forward, trying to find some space. At Emily's push, Jennifer tipped forward into Arthur who stepped backwards, Jennifer in his arms and out of reach but there was still no room for Emily to escape to. Even so, if Emily had been able to resist looking back once again, she wouldn't have got quite so wet. As it was, she turned just in time to catch a jug of icy water full in her face. With ice cubes in her hair and down her neck and water pouring down her face and down her skimpy cream vest, she stood in the middle of the restaurant, gasping with shock.

The first thing that Sam thought, when he walked through the door and saw her standing there, with her eyes closed and her shoulders thrown back, was how she might as well have been wearing nothing at all.

Sam, who had seen it all before, became her saviour

again. Emily opened her eyes and watched, frozen to the spot, as he steadily made his way towards her, pulling off a jumper as he came, so that he could reach her and slip it around her shoulders all in one movement.

'Hello, again,' he said, coming even closer. 'Another happy coincidence, I think.'

He took a napkin off the table and gently wiped her face. She stared at him, so close, and when he had finished couldn't resist falling forward to rest her wet cheek against his shirt.

When she moved away again she saw that she'd left a large round wet patch behind. She slipped her arms into his jumper and pulled it over her head. It was warm and soft and smelled of him. 'Can I keep this?'

'For good?'

'No! For tonight.'

'Of course you can.'

She looked down at herself. Her trousers were only damp and her vest, wet through, would dry out beneath Sam's jumper. She took the napkin off him and wiped her face again and then her hair and the back of her neck, then shook the water out of her ears and reassured the horrified waiter that she was fine.

Sam pulled back her chair but she was in no rush to sit down.

It seemed that neither was Sam. 'Did you get the job?' he asked her.

Emily shook her head. 'Didn't bother going to the interview.'

'You realize that wasp made my day?'

She laughed. 'I'm so pleased. Did you find another skirt for your sister?'

'No, I bought that one I showed you and she loved it.'

'That's impossible,' Emily said, catching Arthur's eye, and finally making a move towards her chair.

Sam paused. 'I'm lying. I spent half an hour in Jigsaw choosing something else.'

He moved around to his own chair and sat down too. 'Emily helped me choose a present for my sister,' he explained to Arthur and Jennifer.

'Did she?' Arthur nodded impatiently. 'Are you all right, Emily? I'm so sorry about that. Do we need to find you some dry clothes?'

She shook her head, feeling very happy inside Sam's jumper. She leaned in to Jennifer. 'But if you'd moved sooner I'd have got out of the way.'

Around them a couple of waiters were hurriedly mopping, while others had brought dry glasses and cutlery. Surprisingly the glass jug had bounced on the wooden floor and survived.

'I didn't hear you,' Jennifer muttered. 'I didn't realize what was going on.'

A complimentary bottle of champagne was brought to their table, even though to Emily's mind the blame rested not with the waiter but entirely with Jennifer, who had twice ignored her plea to move and who should have been listening better and who wasn't apologizing.

'Perhaps I could fold you a dry outfit out of table napkins,' Jennifer offered then, with an utterly straight face.

Was it meant to be a joke? Emily had no idea. 'That's a very kind thought. But I'm fine in Sam's jumper.' Seeing Arthur's troubled face she shook her head. 'I'm fine apart from some water on the brain.'

'Your hair's certainly gone fluffy,' said Sam.

'Let's start again,' Emily said to Jennifer. 'We've hardly even said hello.'

Jennifer held out a narrow white hand and Emily took it and shook, noticing short fingernails painted dark green and a heavy silver thumb ring. 'And you know Sam?' she checked, still sounding painfully polite.

Jennifer nodded and glanced across at him and he gave her a little surreptitious wink back. Maybe it was only a wink of reassurance, but Emily was surprised to see it, and wondered if he was laughing at her. Certainly if there were sides to be on, it made her think Sam was on Jennifer's and she'd thought that he'd be on hers.

He caught her eye and she realized she'd been staring at him. 'Traitor,' she whispered, then couldn't help her face breaking into a smile realizing she hadn't taken him in before. She hadn't noticed whether he was tall or short, fat or thin, couldn't have said what colour his eyes were or his hair. Now she was looking at him properly and liking what she saw, held for a moment by his lovely wide smile and rather sad brown eyes. And he was attractive, in a rugged, messy kind of a way, with thick brown hair, spiky surely with wind and sea spray, not gel. And, in contrast to Jennifer, he was wearing reassuringly familiar clothes, faded blue jeans, and the navy shirt she had dried her face on. Fleetingly she remembered how it had felt to press up close to him, remembered his warmth and the lean hard body against her cheek.

Yet, even as she saw his charms, he left her unmoved. It was as if they'd met on an escalator, him travelling down, her travelling up. There was time to watch him as he came into view and to think idly that he looked nice, strong and attractive, lucky the girl who got him. But that was it. A few seconds later and he would be forgotten because she was on her way somewhere else, somewhere that was taking all her attention because it was her destination that was important, not whom she passed on the way.

'So how well do you two know each other?' Emily enquired politely, looking from Sam to Jennifer.

'Only a little. We've met once before, haven't we, Jennifer? Through a friend of a friend.'

Jennifer nodded her agreement.

'And you both knew the other was coming tonight?' Emily asked, taking a piece of bread and spreading it with butter.

'Yes, we did,' Jennifer said. 'Arthur certainly told me about Sam –' she took Arthur's hand – 'and I think he warned you that you'd see me here, yes?' She turned and included Sam in her little smile.

For a long moment nobody said anything. Then Sam followed Emily's example and took some bread for himself and Jennifer picked up her napkin. She sounded relaxed, her voice low but clear, and yet Emily watched the napkin tremble in her hand, then shake all the way from the table to her lap. She had to stop herself from staring at Jennifer's face, wanting to see if the tension was reflected there too. The next moment the napkin slid right off Jennifer's lap and as she bent to retrieve it Sam leaned forward and whispered so not even Arthur could hear, 'Be nice. She's worth it.'

Then a waiter came up and began loudly to run through the menu, and Jennifer leapt up in alarm, flicking her head around at the sound of his voice, so that Emily, sitting beside her, was whipped in the face with a fast-moving mouthful of hair.

Out of sisterly support for Arthur, she didn't react at all, even as she could see Sam struggling not to smile. She discreetly removed the strands stuck to her eyelids, and her top lip, and concentrated instead on her menu and on listening to the waiter. But she couldn't resist letting her eyes drift slowly over the top of the menu and back to Sam. *See?* she beamed to him, without saying anything aloud, *See what she did to me?* He returned such a deadpan stare that she quickly had to duck back behind her menu and stop herself laughing.

Emily attracted a good deal more of Jennifer's hair during that evening. Perhaps being damp made her very static. And each time she lifted a hair away, Sam would notice and would be looking at her with bright, laughing eyes.

Arthur, on the other hand, noticed nothing. Jennifer Aniston could have come to sit beside him and he wouldn't even have been aware of it. For Arthur there was nothing else but his Jennifer. It was obvious that he couldn't believe his luck.

'Do you ever come to London?' Emily asked her,

determined that Arthur wasn't going to monopolize her all evening and that they would leave at the end having had at least one proper conversation.

'London.' Jennifer stabbed at a bread roll with her knife. 'The first time I went to London I was ten years old and I got accused of shoplifting.'

'You didn't! What happened?'

'We'd come for the trooping the colour, but I got arrested in Hamleys.'

OK, it wasn't particularly funny, had probably been a horrible experience, but the complete lack of animation in Jennifer's voice and her utter refusal to smile had Emily clutching the sides of her chair in her effort to keep a straight face.

'If you look anything like you do now, I can understand why,' said Sam. 'I don't somehow imagine you were ever a pigtails-and-pinafore type of girl.'

Jennifer grinned back at him.

'You're right,' she agreed. 'Think Carrie and you're getting close.' She turned back to Emily and dropped her voice. 'Actually, I did steal something.'

As Jennifer spoke, her knife went straight through the bread roll, hit the plate on the other side with a terrible glass-shattering screech, then clattered to the floor.

There was silence around the table and way beyond. Then Arthur said, 'Boom-ching!' and Jennifer collapsed into giggles.

'It was a cuddly puffin,' said Jennifer. She reached down for her knife. 'I knew my mother would never buy him for me.'

'So what else were you to do?' Emily said, laughing too, still not knowing what to make of her but at least deciding she liked her now.

'The police eventually believed it was a mistake. I said I thought my mother had bought him.'

'So they let you keep him?'

'They would have done but my mother said she didn't want him in the house, that he was *polluted*.'

For no good reason, that made Emily laugh even more. She was just so relieved that Jennifer had a sense of humour after all, buried deep, but there in the end.

'I'll buy you another one,' Arthur interrupted, grinning delightedly at Emily and Jennifer. 'We'll go shopping tomorrow and I'll buy you one.'

Jennifer had picked up her knife again, and had her buttered roll halfway to her mouth. 'You don't think I took any notice of her? Not after all I'd been through! He's in a shoe box under my bed.'

'But you must come back to London,' Emily said eagerly. 'You should come with Arthur. He could take you to the trooping of the colour,' she joked.

'Please, no. Anything but that.'

'Jennifer is an interior designer,' Arthur interrupted with pride. 'Of course she's been back to London hundreds of times.'

Emily nodded. Of course she had. Stupid to think she wouldn't have done. She tried but couldn't quite imagine the kind of interior design Jennifer would produce.

'Jennifer's booked up for the whole of the year.'

'You should have told me!' Feeling wrong-footed once again, Emily criticized Arthur.

'It's how we met,' Sam interrupted. 'Jennifer did a friend of a friend's beach house.'

Waiters arrived with a steaming, fragrant fish soup, again compliments of the house. Emily, Sam, Jennifer and Arthur leant back from the table and waited as the bowls were passed to each of them.

The soup tasted sublime. As they ate, Sam turned back to Emily, allowing Jennifer gratefully to slide back to Arthur.

'I remember the summer I met you.'

Emily couldn't look at him. 'I do too.'

'You told me how you came to St Brides every summer with your parents.' She nodded. 'But then you never came back.'

'You're right. That was our last year.'

'Was it something I said?'

She finally met his eyes, smiled and shook her head.

'Why didn't you come back?'

'I suppose I grew out of holidays with my parents.'

He looked at her, knowing that she was thinking of Oliver.

'You know, I was so angry with him!' he admitted. 'I'd seen you first – the day before, walking through the sand dunes from the car park – and I'd told him about you. And that evening when we saw you on the beach, that was meant to be my big chance.' And he laughed in a way that told her it was all in the past, that they could joke about it now, because whatever had happened had happened so long ago, it didn't matter any more.

Even so, Emily realized how it had once been for him and she was touched. In truth, she'd been so instantly bowled over by the golden figure leaning down towards her that evening on the beach that she hadn't even seen his friend, waiting there behind him. All she ever remembered about that moment was how it had felt when Oliver pulled her to her feet, and later the feel of his arm around her shoulders, a long brown arm, with soft sun-bleached hairs, and how, later still, she had touched the hairs with her fingertips and gently rubbed away the fine grains of white sand caught between them.

'Are you going to see him again, now that he's back?' Sam asked.

There wasn't an easy question. There was now a tension in Sam's voice that hadn't been there before and yet the opportunity to talk about Oliver, when he was all that was on her mind, was irresistible.

'I think so. I hope so. I missed his party, the one you came down for. I know you saw Holly there, but I was away for it.' She was aware that she was saying too much but she couldn't stop speaking.

'You know Nessa and he . . .'

She nodded, not looking at him, waiting for him to say something more but knowing she wouldn't like what she heard.

'Watch out for him, Emily.'

She was right.

'He wouldn't make you happy.'

She looked at him in surprise, still said nothing.

'Am I overstepping the mark?'

'I think you are.'

Sam was undeterred. 'I could tell in that shop – Ruffles – that it was all the same as ever. I can see it now, in your face.'

She stared back at him. It was outrageous that he could say such a thing, when he had so little, nothing, to go on at all.

'He has just left his girlfriend of nearly five years.' Sam was speaking quietly still with a smile and yet Arthur's head shot up from the sweet nothings he was murmuring to Jennifer to check what was going on. Emily rolled her eyes at him in mock desperation and he smiled back at her, convinced all was well and turned back to Jennifer.

'I know you think he's a great guy,' Sam went on. 'Thoughtful, kind, not just to you but to everyone. And he's good-looking and charming and funny and sweet, but right now he wants to be a selfish bastard, too, and you should remember that or you might get hurt. He wants to look out for himself, he wants to have some fun. After Nessa, don't think he's going to want another relationship for a while.' He paused. 'It might be hard to believe, but he's quite good at being a selfish bastard, when he concentrates on it.'

'I want to have some fun too!' she retaliated. 'With or without Oliver . . .'

'Don't be angry.'

Emily could see that Arthur's antennae were still

twitching. He kept looking over to them, giving her little worried glances.

'It's you who's sounding angry. With me,' Emily hissed.

'The last thing I am is angry with you.'

'Whatever, you've got it wrong. I haven't even seen him.' But she was going to, on Saturday night.

He nodded. 'I'm sorry. I didn't mean to say anything to offend you.'

Abruptly, he pushed back his chair, tipped the last of the champagne into her glass and picked up the wine list. 'What shall we have now, white or red?'

And the conversation was over as quickly as it had begun, almost as if Sam had never said anything. Certainly as if it had had no effect on him, saying what he'd said. As if reading the wine list was all that was on his mind.

But Emily was wrong to think that. The reality was that the conversation had been difficult for Sam. And what had been even harder was not shouting out what he really wanted to say. *Emily! Look at me! Couldn't you have fun with me?*

Awkward as it was, Emily found she couldn't drop the subject of Oliver. 'Do you see him much?'

He shook his head. 'Cornwall and London. We live too far apart to see each other very often,' he shrugged. 'And we've grown apart, too.'

'But you still came down to his party last weekend.'

'I thought I might see you there.'

She didn't know how to take it. Was it a throwaway remark that meant nothing at all, or was Sam telling her he'd travelled three hundred miles in the vague hope of seeing her? She hoped not. She hoped it wasn't that. And why would it be true? She hardly knew him, she'd met him perhaps only three times before the time in Ruffles. He couldn't have meant that.

'Come outside with me,' Sam said, startling her. 'Come and see the sea.'

'Are you joking?'

'We can't see the sea from the table.'

'No, we can't,' she laughed.

'It's a full moon tonight, did you see it?'

She shook her head.

He looked across to Arthur and Jennifer, deep in conversation. 'Who will notice? Not those two, and the next course won't be here for at least another half an hour – if we're lucky – so come outside with me. It's too warm in here. I need some air.'

And so she found herself standing up, laying down her napkin on her chair, and when Arthur and Jennifer looked over to her, she explained where they were going and that they'd soon be back.

Outside, there was a bite in the air and Emily was very glad of Sam's jumper.

'Aren't you cold?' She rubbed her arms as he led her around the side of the restaurant and through a little gate onto the terrace.

'Not at all,' he lied, teeth clenched to stop them chattering.

She had had lunch on the terrace many times but never been out there at night, and she hadn't realized how beautiful it would be with the thousands of lights twinkling and glittering against the sea – lights from the fishing boats setting out to sea, lights from cars travelling along the coast road, lights from the town and from the houses high in the hills, and at least a thousand others that she couldn't identify.

As she looked, Sam dragged a couple of wooden chairs over to the furthest edge of the terrace. There was a low stone wall, about a foot high, that marked its end and after that nothing but the rocks that dropped away to a tiny pebbly beach a couple of hundred feet below. Sam placed their two chairs side by side and Emily sat down and then Sam sat down beside her, shifting his chair close enough for his shoulder to be touching hers, and they sat in the darkness in conspiratorial silence, listening to the waves unfurling down on the beach below.

'Listen! You hear the grating roar of pebbles which the waves draw back, and fling . . .' Emily said in a low voice. She took her time, slowly remembering the words. '. . . Begin, and cease, and then again begin, with tremulous cadence slow, and bring the eternal note of sadness in . . .' She stopped.

'You don't know any more, do you?' Sam teased.

'I do, I do,' she protested, laughing, and then she was seized by a sudden shiver of cold. 'I'm sorry.'

'Do you want to go in?'

'No.'

'Come here, then.' Sam shifted closer and put his arm around her and she let herself fall in against his warm body. 'That was lovely. What comes next?'

'I can't remember any more.'

They sat in silence, Sam fighting hard not to bend his head and kiss her.

'What do you do here?' she asked him suddenly.

'I'm working with my father,' he said. 'We grow roses together.'

It was all he said but there was something in the way that he spoke that caught her attention and made it important that she know more.

Emily knew already that Sam had been born and brought up in Cornwall. What she hadn't known was that Sam's family home was called Trevissey and that six months earlier Sam had come back to live in Cornwall to start working with his father.

'Trevissey has a lovely garden,' he told her simply, 'famous for its roses.'

If Emily had known the first thing about roses, the names Finch and Trevissey might have meant something to her, but she hadn't and they didn't. Warmed by her enthusiasm, Sam tried to explain in two minutes what it had taken him all his life to learn about roses. Then, at Emily's insistence, he stopped and, with a few better chosen words, started again.

'If you thought of a rose, what would it look like?' he asked.

Still sitting with his arm around her, Emily closed her eyes and thought about it. 'It would be long-stemmed, very straight and elegant, with one single flower,' she decided. 'A beautiful, crimson rose.'

'Would it smell?'

'Yes. Wonderful.'

'Unlikely.'

She opened her eyes and looked at him in surprise. 'Why?'

'You've described a modern rose and they don't usually have much of a scent.'

'OK,' she said cautiously, 'presumably *some* roses do. Which ones might they be?'

'Which was the right question,' he said.

'Tell me.'

'The ones that do smell are the old roses. The rose you've just described is a modern rose, probably a modern hybrid tea.'

'Who would want a modern rose that doesn't smell of anything?'

'Lots of people. They're the ones for sale in all the garden centres. People buy them because they're more likely to flower all summer rather than for just a few weeks. Most people don't realize there's any other choice.'

'But do they look the same, old and modern roses?'

'No, they don't. Modern rose bushes stick up out of the ground very tense and stiff, as if they've been bound up for so long they can't quite get the hang of being free. They can't mix and entwine with the rest of the garden like the old shrub roses do. And their colours are usually very, very bright. Lots of fluorescent oranges and lipstick pinks. You know the type – huge petals, enormous heads. They're nothing like old roses. The old roses are usually a shade of pink, but not always, some of them have the most gorgeous colours, and their flowers are the most wonderful shapes.' He cupped his hands into a bowl.

'Like this. Sometimes their heads are so heavy with petals they can barely support themselves.'

'Let me guess which sort grow at Trevissey!'

'No, it's not as straightforward as that.'

'Why not? Which ones do you grow?'

'Neither.'

She frowned at him. 'Tell me.'

'I'm explaining as fast as I can,' he insisted. 'The old roses divide into different classes, there are the Gallicas, the Damasks, the Albas, and lots of others too, they're mostly French and they've been with us for centuries. Then, about a hundred years ago, came the modern hybrid tea rose, bred to be strong and bright and to flower over and over again. It had to be there at the start of the summer, and it had to last all the way through. The fact that it wasn't as nice to look at, or smell, seemed almost irrelevant. Once it had arrived it took over so quickly that the old roses went completely out of fashion. For a while it looked as if some of the most wonderful varieties were going to die out altogether.'

'Didn't anyone want to protect them? Is *that* what you do?'

'In the twenties and thirties, some of the great English gardeners like Gertrude Jekyll and Constance Spry did start to champion them again. Vita Sackville-West grew them at Sissinghurst, and they saved the old roses for us. Wonderful roses like "Rosa Mundi", said to be named after Henry II's mistress in the twelfth century, "Belle de Crécy", "Cardinal de Richelieu", "Comtesse de Murinais".'

When Sam spoke their names, he made them sound so beautiful and precious that Emily, who'd never given a moment's thought to roses, ancient or modern, sat beside him entranced.

'Then other gardeners followed their lead and now there are wonderful collections of old roses all over the country.'

'Including Trevissey?'

'We do have some but no, that's not what we do.' He paused. 'Some of the old roses are very similar to their wild relatives, and although that means they can be utterly beautiful, they only flower for a very short time and they're not very hardy, often less able to withstand disease than the modern roses. The short flowering period doesn't matter if you have a huge garden with hundreds of different varieties but most people don't have gardens like that – it's one of the reasons the modern hybrid tea became so popular. Then, in the nineteen sixties, a solution was pioneered in Shropshire by a rose grower called David Austin and in Cornwall by my father.'

Emily was back in the crook of his arm, enjoying the rise and fall of his voice in the darkness.

'They began cross-breeding some of the best of the old roses with several modern hybrid teas, trying to persuade the resilience and repeat flowering of a modern hybrid tea rose to combine with the scent and beauty of an old rose. And, eventually, they managed it. They managed to create an entirely new but traditional rose. David Austin called his collection "English Roses", my father called his "Heritage Roses".

116

'So, today, forty years on, in the gardens at Trevissey, we are growing them together, ancient varieties alongside our Heritage Roses. They blend in together and into the landscape of the garden. Our roses look and smell as beautiful as their old French relations but they do flower repeatedly and most of them are disease resistant – they don't get black spot and powdery mildew.'

'Thousands? Hundreds? How many do you have?'

'Most years we introduce three or four. Last year it was only two. "Gabriel's Daughter" and "Song for Summer". We launched them at the Chelsea Flower Show last May.'

'So is it still very difficult to cross-breed? It must be if you're only producing one or two a year.'

'It takes years to develop a new rose. And we don't want to produce any more than one or two at a time. We're deliberately keeping our collection fairly small.'

Emily thought back to her childhood. 'Modern hybrid teas,' she said, surprised at what she could remember. She was nine years old, in a rain-drenched garden full of rose bushes and the flowers were just as Sam described them, long stemmed, huge heads, orange and lilac and cerise. She remembered trailing along behind her mother through long grass that soaked her legs, hearing her mother speaking more to herself than to Emily. 'Why are modern hybrid teas always such ghastly colours?' Emily had been convinced they were about to turn a corner and find a table piled high with orange and red and green fairy cakes and biscuits wrapped in purple foil – a modern, hybrid *tea*.

'When did you start working at Trevissey?' she asked.

'When I was six or seven. Then summer jobs when I

was a teenager. I've always been involved but I only started full-time six months ago.'

She wondered what it was like for him, working with his father.

'And we get on fine together,' he said and she could hear from his voice that he was smiling. 'He tells me what to do and I shut up and do it.'

'Really?'

'No. He's amazing. He knows intuitively what will work and what won't – helped by forty years of trial and error.'

'Presumably it's all written down somewhere? It's not all inside his head?'

'We write down every cross we make.'

'There must be so many thorns,' she said, then shook her head apologetically. 'How dumb did that sound?'

Sam laughed. 'You get the hang of where to hold them. It becomes a sixth sense. Look. No scratches.' He spread his hands.

She took hold of one and looked at it closely. 'It's so green,' she teased. 'You really do have green fingers.'

He laughed, happy to leave his hand in hers. 'Dirty brown, I think. If you'd like to see Trevissey, I could show you around tomorrow.'

'I'm spending tomorrow with Arthur. And then I go back to London the next morning.' She gently disentangled her hand from his.

'Busy all of tomorrow?'

'Arthur will have to go to work . . .'

'So give me an hour?'

She nodded. 'I'd love to.'

'Nothing will be flowering,' he warned her. 'It's completely the wrong time of year. March is much too early. June and July are the best months. You'll have to promise to come back then. At the moment the only roses you'll see will be in the greenhouses.'

'I could come after we've been to St Brides. I could get Arthur to drop me off.'

'Do that.'

By unspoken agreement they stood up together.

'Do you think we've been a very long time?' Emily asked.

'They won't have noticed. They'll have been pleased to have some time together alone.'

When they re-entered the restaurant Emily was relieved to see Arthur and Jennifer still waiting for their main courses. She caught Arthur's eye across the table and he gave her a quick encouraging smile and she guessed she was in for an inquisition the moment they got in the car. She knew, absolutely *knew*, that Arthur would think Sam one hundred times more suitable for her than Oliver.

'What about your brother and sister?' Emily asked Sam, when they'd sat back down. 'Do they work with you?'

Sam shook his head. 'My brother is a teacher in Exeter, my sister is a fund manager in the City.'

Emily pictured her arriving for work in Sam's pleated brown and yellow skirt.

Out of the corner of her eye Emily could see Arthur turning to Jennifer, taking one of her hands in his, turning it over and slowly stroking her palm with his finger. He's going to remember nothing about us leaving the room, he'll remember nothing else about this evening at all, she realized.

And afterwards, after they'd waited a further ten minutes, and had then been served with great platters of *fruits de mer*, after she and Arthur had driven home and she had said good night and got into bed, it was Trevissey that she thought about, the details of Trevissey that she could recall almost word for word. And she found she was looking forward very much to the next afternoon, when she would be able to see it for real.

8

But before Trevissey, St Brides had to be explored.

In the morning the sky was clear again but the temperature had dropped and the wind was blustery and very cold. It licked the tips of the waves far out to sea and sent Arthur and Emily huddling deep into their coats for warmth.

They left Arthur's car in a car park next to the beach and walked into the heart of St Brides and it seemed to Emily that they were almost alone there, certainly the only people with nothing to do but wander the streets.

It was a good thing to see St Brides at its quietest but it was also somewhat disheartening. Though Emily had been there so many times before, in pouring rain and snow as well as in the heat of high summer, somehow she always pictured St Brides bathed in hot sunlight and buzzing with people. It took her aback to find it like this, the one time she was hoping it would show itself off to her. She told herself that it was only early spring, not high summer, and that she shouldn't have expected to find it any other way, but somehow she hadn't ever realized how truly quiet it could be, emphasized by the bowed heads and silent treads of the few people who passed them by. Neither had she realized that at least half the shops closed down for the winter, several having signs in their windows announcing that they wouldn't be opening again until 31 May, still over two months away. In only a few minutes, the reality of opening her shop became not just difficult, risky and challenging but rather grim. Looking up and down the narrow streets she knew for sure that whatever she put inside the shop, passing trade would be non-existent, that St Brides wasn't a town already stuffed full of art galleries and craft shops that attracted browsers, apart from in the few months in high summer when holiday-makers poured in everywhere and were found happily browsing in the ironmongers and locksmiths, as well as the more obvious places. For the rest of the time, it was the full-time residents who shopped in St Brides and they came because it was a simple, working town with shops full of things they needed, rather than things they hankered after. And so she would have to be good enough to draw people, to bring them out on a special trip to see her, and her stock would have to be irresistible.

Emily wasn't put off completely. She was convinced that St Brides was moving upmarket, that more and more people were coming there for their holidays, and would be looking for opportunities to spend their money. The success of the Pelican proved it could be done. And if she had to shut up shop for a few months in the winter, that would be when she could concentrate on her suppliers, visit the trade shows and discover the wonderful artists and milliners, handbag makers and ceramicists who worked in the Cockpit or Great Western studios in London. She would be able to talk to the local artists, some of whom she'd met already through Arthur: one made wooden boats that bobbed across a painted sea at the turn of a handle and another designed gorgeous spiralling mobiles from coloured stones and shells and sticks washed up on the beach. She also had a friend from university who made beautiful birds out of driftwood, and who had already hinted that Saltwater could be her exclusive stockist.

'Let's go,' Arthur said after less than five minutes of wandering. He walked away from her, then turned so that his back was against the wind. 'If you want to come and live here,' he shouted to her, 'I'm sure I could find you a job. You don't *have* to open a shop.'

'Are you serious?' Emily moved over to him. 'Are you saying that because you really don't think I should do it? Or are you saying it because you're in a bad mood with me this morning?'

He shook his head. 'You could do it, but it would be bloody hard work.'

'Wait a second.' There was an estate agents on the other side of the road and she pulled Arthur with her towards it. Together they looked in through tiny leaded windows.

'If I found the right place,' she said to Arthur, after they'd scanned all the pictures in one window, 'you know I could do it. I have the right contacts, I know where to look for stock, I've got all the ideas, all the enthusiasm. I'm artistic-ish. Even though there's nothing for me here today, something will come up. And I'll make it work.'

'So, you are serious?'

She shrugged. 'I think I am. Don't you think I should be?'

'I thought you were serious about staying in the theatre? I thought that was why you held out with it for so long . . .'

Emily sighed. 'That's true. But I think it was more to do with being stubborn. Not wanting to be pushed out by her, leaving when I wanted to, when I was ready and had something to go for instead . . . Not that I managed that.'

'And how much money have you got?'

'Not enough. I'd have to do a business plan and get a loan from the bank.'

'I think you should open somewhere bigger than St Brides.'

'Or do you mean somewhere further away from you?'

'No!'

'Even after last night?'

'What about last night?'

'I thought perhaps I didn't behave very well . . . with Jennifer. And the way Sam and I left you . . .'

'Did you?' He smiled. 'I don't remember.'

Emily remembered Arthur kissing Jennifer's fingers, leaning in close, the two of them giggling together most of the evening, and knew it was true.

They moved away from the estate agents' window and down the high street. 'If I opened in a bigger town, then the rates and rent would be even higher.'

'I suppose so.'

They cut down an alleyway, then along another and up and down the flights of steps that linked the narrow streets, onto a street called Flass Street, which took them back to the sea.

And then, just as she sensed Arthur was about to say something more about Jennifer, a shop called simply 'Number Seventeen' caught Emily's eye, and of all the places that they had passed, she saw that this one came closest to what she wanted. She touched Arthur's sleeve, stopped him walking off in the wrong direction and they wandered down towards it.

From the outside it looked sweet. It was painted fondant pink, part of a little terrace of shops all painted in different colours, with a large bow window in the front and two small steps leading up to the half-open door. Curious, Emily looked in through the window at the items displayed for sale.

The effect was pretty, but not sufficiently enticing. Cautious rather than original. As she leaned in to get a better look, Emily caught the eye of a smart, dark-haired woman sitting alone behind a white-painted desk, hands folded in front of her, and she felt an overwhelming urge to climb the steps, go in and spend a huge amount of money, if only to wipe away the defeated look in the woman's eye.

'Go on. She could be you,' Arthur said encouragingly.

'No, she could not be me.'

Emily went up the steps, Arthur behind her, pushed open the door and they went inside.

She stood for a moment, breathing in the warm scent of lavender. A piano concerto rippled gently in the background. Emily cast an appraising eye around the room, giving the woman a bright smile.

The central feature of the room was an ornamental wooden stepladder with a card balanced on the top step, stating in neat black ink that it was 'Not For Sale'. The other steps were laden with terracotta pots of blue artificial hyacinths that presumably *were* for sale. Behind the step-ladder was a pretty wooden chest of drawers, painted antique white and distressed, on which were displayed various delicately patterned glass bottles. Emily walked over to them, lifting each one and turning it upside down to see the price. They were astoundingly expensive. She moved away again, aware that every movement she made was being watched intently.

The piano concerto finished and in the silence Emily turned slowly around, and then around again, letting tea towels, white china soap dishes, wooden bowls filled with wooden pears, brooms made out of twigs, wicker baskets, silver photo frames and floral biscuit tins blur before her eyes. Behind her, Arthur muttered that he would wait for her outside and she heard the clunk of the door shutting, leaving her alone.

She wanted to leave but couldn't empty-handed. What to buy? What to buy? Beside the till was a rack of flowery wrapping paper and a stand of boring flowery cards. To her right an open drawer was filled with napkins and napkin rings and above the drawer was a lavender collection – bottles of lavender water, egg-shaped lavender soap and bundles of dried lavender tied with raffia bows neatly laid out in a trug. What could Emily buy? She grabbed an egg soap and turned to the woman, only to remember that she'd no cash and she couldn't face writing out a cheque to this woman for just two pounds ninety-eight pence.

She looked out of the window, hoping to catch Arthur's

attention, but he'd wandered off down the road. There was nothing else to do. She turned back and guiltily replaced the soap in the drawer, feeling her face flush with embarrassment.

All she was aware of now was the door and the prospect of walking through it.

Then in the corner of her eye she saw something red and she stopped and turned towards it. It was in a half-open drawer in the little white painted chest. What it was she couldn't tell, but it did look interesting.

Curiosity beat back the need to escape. She peered at it more closely, and even as she was telling herself to *go, go, go*, she couldn't resist pulling it free of the drawer. Behind her, she heard the scrape of the woman's chair and Emily waited for her to come near.

'I bought it months ago,' she said with a sigh. 'There's not much of a market for it in St Brides but I couldn't resist.'

Emily held it out to look at, letting the material drop in front of her, still unsure what it was. It was definitely beautiful, made from gossamer-thin silk as delicate and translucent as a web, a deep pinky red top with three-quarter-length sleeves and a low scooped neck. She took it over to a Venetian-glass mirror hanging on one wall to see it against herself, but even before she looked she knew that she was going to buy it and not only to make the dreary woman happy but because it would be perfect to wear to meet Oliver the following evening.

She didn't look at the price tag or ask how much it was, just smiled and nodded and handed over her credit card, but the way the woman coloured with pleasure as she took it, and then the reverence with which she wrapped the top in tissue paper, gave Emily a good idea of the size of hole she was blasting in her bank account.

In less than a minute she was running down the steps, calling out a hasty 'Thanks, goodbye!' She caught up with Arthur and grabbed his arm.

'I hope you wouldn't end up like her,' he said straight away. 'I couldn't bear it.'

'Lonely and miserable?'

'Creepy and strange.'

'Of course I won't. Especially not if I have people like me coming in.' She swung her bag at him. 'I think I've just spent enough to keep her afloat for the next six months. Enough to send her on safari,' she added, seeing his smile.

The truth was that, apart from the brief flush of pleasure at the sale, the woman's eyes had never lost their mournful look. Emily doubted those eyes smiled even in the summer when her shop was crowded with holiday-makers itching to spend, people who would leap at the chance to buy a whole fruit bowl's worth of her expensive, wooden pears.

Her shop was so clearly pictured in her mind that every tiny detail was in focus. It would be light and white, the colour coming from the gorgeous things she had to sell, not from the room itself. And not a big room because she wanted it always to be full. Emily knew how hard it would be constantly to keep it that way.

In the middle of the room she wanted a big wrought-iron and glass table, like one she'd seen once in a gorgeous shop in Barnes. She wanted it so people were drawn to the table first, to find the items on it irresistible, impossible not to touch and pick up and buy. What those things would be she didn't yet know. Knew only that they would have to change all the time, and that her biggest challenge would be finding enough items to sell, and still to be able to run the shop. She knew that as soon as she could afford to, she would have to take on an assistant to free her up to go hunting for new stock.

Back in Arthur's car, when warm air finally came through the heater and Emily had stopped shuddering inside her coat and was ready to talk again, they returned to the subject of the evening at the Pelican.

'I liked Jennifer,' she told him as they drove along the sea front.

'Thank you. You told me so last night.'

'I know I did, and I'm telling you again. At first I wasn't sure I was going to, but I really did.' She could see sailing boats out at sea, bright sails stretched as tight as drums by the wind, and a lone windsurfer streaking along the shoreline, kicking up an impressive wake behind him. 'She wasn't at all like I expected.'

'What did you expect? What makes you have me down for a particular sort of girl?'

'Nothing. Of course I don't.' Something put her in mind of Caitlin and their conversation in Holly's drawing room. She remembered how she'd pulled up Caitlin with almost exactly the same words.

'I think I imagined someone more straightforward,' she

said carefully. 'Someone more *normal*, someone who wore jeans and watched too much television and liked fish and chips, who I knew would look after you and Dodger Point, who'd want to play with Clara and have a little garden outside the house.' She turned back to Arthur and grinned. 'I suppose I wanted you to meet someone safe ... someone I could push around a bit. Not some amazingly talented designer with a lovely face and so much hair.' Arthur laughed. 'So at first, I thought, *get her away from me* – and *get away from him*. I'm sorry, but I did. I was so taken aback. Then I looked at her again, took her in, stopped being so overprotective – of myself, not of you – and I realized I was wrong. Then I thought she was great.'

'She's better than great. Last night, while you were outside with Sam, I looked across at her and realized I was so incredibly lucky. I've known her for less than two weeks and now I can't imagine my life without her.'

Listening to him, Emily thought how lucky she was to have him as her brother. He was so expressive and so honest. She loved how his dazzling confidence in Jennifer allowed him to cast aside all his defences and speak the truth. He would be happy to tell the world how he felt, not just Emily, and she felt her heart pierced with tenderness and admiration for him. How she would love to be as comfortable with her own feelings as Arthur was with his, and how she would love to find someone the way Arthur had found Jennifer. Her own muddled, troubled feelings for Oliver felt somehow furtive and inferior in comparison.

Back at Dodger Point, Arthur pulled on the handbrake and turned off the engine and Emily looked through the windscreen towards the house and didn't move. 'She might have great taste, but I'm scared at the thought of what she'd do to this place.'

'Tear it down and start again, she says.'

'That's what I meant.'

'Of course she wouldn't!' Arthur got out. 'She loves it. She especially likes what you did to the tower.'

He slammed his door shut and left Emily still inside the car, feeling disproportionately pleased that Jennifer liked her tower. She opened her door and called after him, 'Oh, I *really* like her now.'

She got out of the car and caught him up.

'And by the way,' Arthur told her, 'she does wear jeans, and eats fish and chips and watches television. And she was only saying yesterday how she'd like to do the garden. So you can relax.'

He blocked her way into the house.

'And Emily, if those are the things that are important to you –' he counted them off on his fingers – 'if you'd like someone who ... wears jeans, enjoys gardening ... Not sure about the television but I could find out ...'

She smiled as she realized where he was heading.

'There's someone I know just like that. Someone we both know ... who you happen to be seeing this afternoon.'

'Not interested,' she insisted, pushing past him and going into the kitchen. 'Not interested at all. Don't you understand anything, Arthur? There is someone else. I have been waiting for him for nearly ten years and I will be seeing him again in approximately thirty-one hours. And the anticipation is killing me. His name is Oliver. It is not Sam. Sam is a lovely guy but all I can think about now is Oliver.'

After lunch Arthur drove her to Trevissey. It was twenty minutes inland from Dodger Point, through thick woods and steep-sided valleys, until they passed through the little village of Leswidden and then turned in through a pair of intricate and beautiful wrought-iron gates made of intertwined roses and up a short, straight gravel drive through an avenue of lime trees. Standing square in front of them was a perfectly proportioned Georgian house, built in dark grey stone.

Rather than follow the drive in its sweeping arc to the front door, Arthur turned instead to the right, taking a second, smaller drive that met the first and led them away from the house and on behind a high yew hedge, where it opened out into a car park. It was, Emily noticed, completely screened from the house and garden. There was a separate area for coaches, and signs in dark green and gold for an arboretum and herb garden as well as for the visitor centre and garden centre. Emily hadn't expected Trevissey to be on such a large, business-like scale.

She sat for a moment. Then, through an unobtrusive archway cut into a grey stone wall, came Sam.

He waved to Arthur and then opened Emily's door and leaned in to her with a rush of cold air and kissed her cheek. 'There are no wasps. No jugs of water. I promise you're safe here.'

Emily laughed and took his hand and let him pull her out of the car. His hands were cold, too.

'Isn't this wonderful,' Arthur said to Sam, turning and looking all around him.

'Join us, if you like,' Sam offered. 'I can show you both around.'

'No, I can't. I've got work to do in the village.'

'Then let me drop Emily home for you,' Sam offered.

'No, I can come and pick her up on the way home.' He got back into the car. 'Call me when you're ready,' he said to Emily, then he waved to them both and was gone.

Sam took her back through the archway and they came out in a small courtyard against one great grey wall of the house. Then they turned down a narrow gravelled path between two low box hedges and came out in another small courtyard, on the left of which was a garden centre.

She'd not expected buildings and customers and shops. She'd imagined long avenues and large empty gardens, and silence, the roses invisibly getting on with the business of growing with little help from anyone beyond a bit of pruning and perhaps a forkful of manure. When Sam had said he was joining his dad, she'd imagined it would be just the two of them with a few extra pairs of hands employed at the busiest times of year.

Now she saw how very wrong she'd been. Everywhere she turned there were young, busy-looking people, wheeling wheelbarrows, moving briskly in and out of the plant

centre, helping customers, talking and laughing, all looking incredibly healthy with shiny hair and great skin, all
wearing bottle-green hooded fleeces embroidered with a
tasteful gold rose underneath which appeared, in gold
letters, 'Thomas Finch Roses'.

Instantly Emily thought that she didn't want to open
Saltwater at all, she wanted to come to work here, learn
about roses and be part of it all.

'Shall I show you around now?' Sam asked. 'Or would
you like a cup of coffee? Or tea or a beer? Whatever you
like.'

'No. I'd like to see it now.'

'Are you warm enough?'

'Too warm,' she said, squinting up at the sun, pulling
off her hat and stuffing it into her jacket pocket. Chilled
by the trip to St Brides, she'd come to Sam's in a long-
sleeved T-shirt, polo-necked jumper and a quilted jacket.
Seeing Sam in just a shirt and jeans she realized she'd
rather overdone it.

Planned and laid out to show off the roses, the gardens
opened, one after another, like rooms in a house, pergolas
and arches inviting them through to each new space
beyond. It was all so imaginatively and beautifully
designed that even now, with not a rose in bloom, it still
took Emily's breath away.

They walked side by side. There was so much to see,
even though what buds there were were all tightly closed
and dripping with recent rain, and the new green shoots
were only just beginning to take hold of the trellises and

fences. They walked around statues and hidden benches and gazebos, past an eighteenth-century dovecote, and everywhere there were the roses waiting for the sun to shine down upon them to ripen the buds until they burst. It was a dormant garden, a green garden, and Emily knew she would have to come back.

Dipping beneath a stone archway covered in lichen and moss they came out in a perfect square of grass and Sam led Emily across it to an ornate Victorian wooden summer house. 'A revolving summer house!' he told her. 'Get up those steps and I'll show you.' She did as he said, climbed the two wooden steps and went to sit down on the rather flimsy-looking garden chair left out on the veranda and Sam put his weight behind the summerhouse and suddenly she was moving in a slow dignified swing. 'Moving to follow the sun,' Sam explained, jumping up beside her. 'Don't you think that's a good idea?'

'It's a lovely idea.' They stopped again and she looked at him. 'I wish I could see the roses. I'd like to see this garden as it's meant to be.'

'You can imagine it instead. Look. Over on that wall.' She looked, waiting for him to go on. 'Think there's magenta and red and purple. The red is a Thomas Finch rose called "Helen of Troy". It has dark foliage and crimson petals and it's huge, it will be spreading all across the back of the wall, all along to the other side. And then, beneath it, we have a velvety Gallica rose called "Tuscany Superb". It's a darker red than "Helen of Troy" and it doesn't flower for so long, but if we were here in late June, we would probably be catching them both out at the same time. And then, all around the garden – ' he swept his arm around to the right – 'the colours are changing, slowly moving from the dark reds to orange and scarlet and then, right there – ' he pointed directly opposite them to a bare grey stone wall – 'imagine that wall covered in pale frothy pink. The pink of iced buns.' He made a small circle with his finger and thumb. 'Sweet, tiny, pink roses, not a Heritage Rose, it's called "Long Goodbye" because it flowers until the first frosts.'

And she could see it all, as clearly as if she was there one hot July day when the beds were full of roses and the air sweet and full with all the scents of summer.

'Thank you,' she said, not wanting to stand up again and move on, to leave the lovely garden behind.

After they had left the summer house Sam took her to the boundary of the gardens and they looked over a fence, Emily casting her eyes over the fields beyond, and loving the fact that the crop, stretching away as far as the eye could see, was roses, not corn.

She found herself telling him how she wanted to stay, how much she wanted to move to Cornwall. How Saltwater might be the way to make it happen. Standing here, with this view, it was so much easier to be sure of herself than it had been in London. Looking out at all the space, at the beautiful rolling hills, at the sapphire sea glinting in the distance, she wondered aloud what had taken her so long.

Then Sam took her to the greenhouses where he attempted to explain, simply enough for Emily to begin to understand, how unpredictable it all was, how one couldn't set out to breed a new rose and expect to know in advance how it would turn out. Emily listened and meanwhile nearly expired with the heat, pulling off her jacket and handing it to Sam when he insisted on carrying it for her.

In the first of the greenhouses thousands upon thousands of delicate seedlings, all just a few weeks old, waited for Sam and his father to work their way through them selecting the best plants. Thousands of crosses were made each year to produce just three or four new roses. And they would be ready in six or seven years' time, Sam explained. The narrowing down happened very gradually, year by year.

The best of the seedlings in front of them would be propagated and left to grow and, after a few more years, there might be ten that they wanted to keep. These ten would then be re-propagated, perhaps producing a hundred more of each of the plants, which would then be watched for a few more years. And at the end of the line, six or seven years on from the plants that Emily was looking at now, perhaps two, perhaps three or four, would be named and patented and put on sale.

Sam led her down to the end of the greenhouse to a large cupboard and pulled open a drawer. Inside was tray upon tray of fine sable paintbrushes. 'We use these to transfer pollen from one plant to another. That's how it's *physically* done. We take the pollen from the anther of one rose, at the top of the stem, and we paint it onto the stigma of another flower. The stigma is female. The pollen is male.'

'And propagating? How do you do that?'

'By budding.'

'Of course, *budding*!'

He grinned at her, a long, slow, appreciative smile and she remembered the night before, how it had felt to be sitting beside him with his arm around her shoulders. 'Budding means we transfer the leaf bud of one rose onto the neck of a root stock.'

'I know that.' She shook her head. 'No, I don't. I know nothing about this at all.'

'We're not manipulating genes,' Sam said. 'Some other commercial gardeners do, but this is not genetic engineering. Everything we're doing here could happen in the wild. All we're doing is steering the roses in certain directions. We make the critical selections for them rather than letting the pollination happen at random. Arranged marriages, if you like.'

'What about making roses disease resistant?' Emily countered.

'It's still a natural process. Whatever scientists do to a tomato's genes to stop it bruising or softening does not happen here. We're simply taking the best of one rose and introducing it to the best of another. And we hope to make a lovely new rose at the end of it.'

In the next greenhouse, roses were already flowering, their sweet scent catching in the air. A huge area at one end was devoted to the preparation of the Thomas Finch Garden for Chelsea Flower Show. The plants would be carefully orchestrated so that all the display roses would flower at the same time and be at their peak for the five days of the event. This year, Sam told her, they would be launching three new roses.

Emily wandered over to look at them.

'Here – ' Sam took her hand – 'smell this one.' He lifted a pale pink flower towards her and Emily dipped her head and breathed it in.

'It's wonderful.'

Then he took out a pair of secateurs from a drawer under one of the tables, carefully snipped off a rose and handed it to her.

'Don't tell Dad because he would explode. But he'll have lots more to choose from.'

Emily took it. It was one of the most beautiful roses she'd ever seen, the flower was a perfect cup, its colour a soft blush pink and the petals within the cup each placed with exquisite perfection. It had a smooth stem, only one or two thorns, and the most wonderful lemony scent.

'This is "Gabriel's Daughter," Sam told her. 'We bred her from an old Portland rose called "Gabriel Delphine."'

'Do you know who Gabriel was?'

'All we know is that he lived in Paris at the beginning of the eighteenth century.'

'And now, two hundred years later, you've given him a daughter.'

'Yes,' Sam agreed. 'I hope a gold-medal-winning daughter.'

They walked back through the gardens to the house. She had loved it all so much she didn't want it to be over, didn't want to go inside. Emily twirled the rose between her fingers, looking down at it. 'I can see why you had to come back,' she said.

He looked at her speculatively, then walked away. 'Come with me.'

She followed him along a narrow, grassy path that ran between two hedges and for the first time she was acutely aware of being there alone with him, of the stillness of the air, and the silence. Then Sam stopped beside her, put his hands around her waist and, without warning, lifted her towards the branches of an old pear tree. There were places to put her feet and she pulled herself up until she found herself on a wet wooden platform a few feet above him. In the summer it would be hidden behind the leaves and would have a bird's-eye 360-degree view of the gardens.

'"Rambling Rector" climbs up there,' he told her, looking up at her.

She looked down at him. 'Disgraceful. He shouldn't be allowed.'

'Don't you think that's the perfect place to spy from?'

'You snoop on people from up here, do you?'

'I see people taking cuttings and picking roses when they think nobody is looking. Once a woman stuffed about six up her jumper.'

'Ouch!' she laughed.

He lifted her gently down again and took his time letting her go. *He likes me. He's flirting with me*, she thought. But her mind skittered away from the realization because she didn't really want to know. Yes, she was aware of Sam still standing close beside her. They were alone in his gardens, and the air seemed weighted with expectation, but how could there be any desire, any sexual tension on her part, any desire to get close to Sam, when she felt only half with him, while her other half was already on the train back to London, was putting on her make-up in her flat, then locking the front door, catching a cab to Caitlin's flat, where, after so long, she would finally, finally, see Oliver again?

She turned away from him, not meeting his eye. 'Is most of your business done here in Trevissey?' she asked, walking away.

For a long moment he neither answered her question nor followed her. She walked on, then stopped and turned back to him.

'Trevissey is our flagship,' he said, sounding all businesslike and professional, back on the script. 'It's where people come to see what we're doing, but we sell only a few roses here. The real business rests on the roses we breed and sell to nurseries and garden centres. We can copyright those.'

'And do you get a pink rose if you mix a red one and a white one?' she asked, one safe question after another.

'Sometimes. Other times you might get another red one, or a yellow one or even a purple one. Because you have little idea of what went on in the generations before, you can never be sure about what's coming next.'

'How would you get a pink one, then?'

'You'd select and select and select. And hope.'

'And would you say there's a rose for every shade of pink?'

Instead of answering, he stopped beside a door into the house.

'Come in for a while? Or will your protective brother be wondering where you are?'

He's changed, Emily noticed. He's gone cool on me.

The door opened into a scullery and boot room and Sam led them through, up stone steps into an enormous high-ceilinged kitchen. There was a long-haired black and white cat curled up asleep in the middle of a large empty fruit bowl on the table and Sam stroked it absentmindedly as he passed by. A huge honey gold oak dresser, so big it had to have been built for the house, took up the whole of one side of the room.

'You think Arthur's protective of me? He's not as bad as you!' Emily didn't know why she suddenly wanted to be so provocative. She copied Sam and stroked the cat, but obviously not with Sam's special touch, because it immediately rose up and leapt out of the fruit bowl and off the table.

She pulled out a chair and sat down as the cat stalked out of the room. Meanwhile Sam disappeared through another doorway and came back with two mugs.

'Talking about being overprotective,' he teased, 'I saw how you were with poor, defenceless Jennifer.'

'What did I do? I'm not protective of Arthur. Not in an unhealthy kind of way! And Jennifer's hardly defenceless.'

'I'm teasing you.'

He went through yet another door and reappeared with a pint of milk. Obviously, where most people had a cupboard, Sam had a whole room.

She hung her coat over the back of an old rocking chair, then balanced her rose on top of it.

But the kitchen was a very warm room and Emily wanted to take her jumper off too. She waited until Sam had his back to her and then quickly pulled her jumper up and over her head. But Sam turned back at the worst possible moment, when not only her stomach (hastily pulled in) but also her bra (old and grey) were showing. At least he couldn't see her flaming red face.

He put down the milk, leaned over to her and firmly held down her T-shirt while she pulled the jumper clear, then said from a few inches away, 'You've got to stop doing this to me.'

'I'm sorry, I will.' Surprised by the feel of his hand on her waist, she felt her heart start to bump in her chest, and colour flame again in her cheeks. She turned away and looked around the room. 'Who did these lovely pictures?' Hanging on the walls were framed watercolours, some of individual roses, others of the gardens at Trevissey.

'My mother.'

She went over to look at the one hanging furthest away from Sam. 'Does she live here too?' She asked because there'd been no mention of her and the house, lovely as it was, seemed to lack her presence.

'No. It's just me and Dad. She died.'

'I'm sorry.'

'Five years ago now. She died here.'

'How sad that she didn't see you come home to live here again.'

Sam nodded. 'But then I probably wouldn't have done if Dad hadn't been alone. It's still very strange being back here without her. But she knew I would come back to work here one day. It was always going to happen.'

'And how is it, living with your dad again?'

'We've had the last six months together and sometimes it feels much too long. Other times it's just great. I'm sure Dad would say the same. I suspect we'd get on better if we lived apart, especially with working together all day, but I guess neither of us likes the idea of living alone.'

What she couldn't deny was that she was looking at Sam clearly now and liking what she saw. Strip away the outside world and inevitably you see much more of the truth about someone. She was sitting at the table where he had breakfast every morning. There, against the wall, was a neatly folded pile of his socks and boxers and T-shirts – she presumed they were his, presumed his dad didn't own a Radiohead T-shirt. There was a book lying on a small table beside the window, *Nightwatch, a Practical Guide to Viewing the Universe*, and underneath the table a pair of muddy-soled Caterpillar boots. Hanging over the back of the chair she was sitting on was a bow tie, a proper one, untied now, and fleetingly Emily imagined Sam dressed in a dinner jacket and wondered where he'd gone. Who had he been with? Upstairs was the bed he slept in, the books that he read, in the bathroom was his toothbrush. Somewhere up there was the room where his mother had died. The cartoon hero who'd rescued the damsel in distress was gone and there was so much more in his place. He was Sam, who lived here in magical Trevissey, and she couldn't deny that she would have liked to know more.

'I should go,' she said, draining her cup and standing up.

Sam nodded. He was standing at the other end of the room, leaning back against a dark red Aga.

She didn't know where it came from but the thought was suddenly there in Emily's mind that he was waiting for her, expecting her to come to him, waiting to kiss her. While the impulsive mad side of her told her to fall into his arms, that it would be fantastic, the more powerful rational side forbade her from doing any such thing. She knew that Sam liked her and she knew that if she kissed him now, he wouldn't want to walk away afterwards. She would be entangling him in her life and she didn't want him there, not while there was so much else already waiting to be resolved. So she went to him and brushed his cheek briefly with her lips and didn't meet his eye, then turned back to the chair with her jacket hanging on its back.

'You think you've given Arthur enough time?' Sam sounded relaxed and unconcerned.

'Yes, I think so. I was wondering where my phone had got to. I'll call him.'

'Use ours,' he offered, indicating a telephone half hidden under a heap of unopened post.

She nodded her thanks. Her heart was thumping and all she was aware of was a dreadful sense of anticlimax. 'I'm going back to London tomorrow,' she told Sam while she waited for Arthur to answer the phone. Not mentioning the fact that she was going home to see Oliver.

9

Anticipation washed over her again as the train pulled out of St Brides. Speaking with Arthur the previous night had made her see everything differently, made her realize how pointless it was to try to predict how Oliver would react to her, how, in this case, worrying about the future would effectively stop anything happening in the present. And as a consequence Arthur had freed her up. Fired her up. The thought that at last she would be seeing Oliver again drove every memory of Sam clean from her mind.

Oliver is free, she thought as the train slowly gathered speed. There's no Nessa. As her carriage was pulled along the coastal track, twisting left and right, rolling from side to side as only ancient British trains do, she looked out of the window at the landscape flashing by and thought, *Here he is, here he is, all these years and here he is.* Then, when the train turned away from the sea and headed inland, running now through rich green fields full of cattle and spring lambs that skittered in fright at its sound, she thought, *It could be me, it could be me.* It felt as if, at last, the moment was upon her.

But then, halfway back to London, Emily took out Sam's rose, the lovely 'Gabriel's Daughter', which she had tried to press between the pages of her book, and held it in her lap, stroking the soft, damp, battered petals. The rose hadn't had a chance to dry out, and it lay there, not pressed so much as squashed and, inevitably, it reminded her of Sam, of standing beside him in the greenhouse as he snipped and he was there, not forgotten at all, vivid and vibrant, warning her to stay away from Oliver. She felt a flash of unease which she smothered quickly. Sam was wrong: wrong to presume he knew what Emily was looking for, wrong to think she was in danger of getting hurt, wrong to condemn Oliver. She knew Oliver, she'd spent more time with Oliver in the last few years than Sam ever had. And she knew herself too, knew how skilled she was at looking after herself, knew she could avoid being swept off her feet. She wanted to believe in Arthur's advice, not Sam's. It would be Arthur she kept in mind as she went to Caitlin's that evening, and she would arrive unhindered by any doubts or preconceptions, there to have fun, to take the moment as it came and find out which way it could take her.

Once off the train she hurried down the platform into the hurly-burly of Paddington Station, and stood for a while to regain her bearings. Ahead of her she saw the signs for the underground and she walked towards the steps, handbag and rose in her left hand, hold-all in her right.

Just as she was shifting her grip on the rose, ready to negotiate her way down, a thorn pricked the soft pad of her thumb and she cried out and dropped it. Around her, the sea of commuters separated around her and then closed again, oblivious. She picked up the rose gingerly. She could see a man in a fluorescent vest leaning on a broom beside the ticket machine, with an open wheelie bin beside him. Emily took the rose over to his bin and found, hard-hearted woman that she was, that she could drop it in with no remorse at all.

In the early evening, as Emily pulled the red top she'd bought in St Brides over her head, she heard the beat of music coming from the flat above. It was a familiar enough sound on a Saturday evening – Rachel, having partied away Friday night, would have got into bed at about nine on Saturday morning and would be rising now for a second dose. Emily was seized by the temptation to go upstairs, find her friend and spill the beans. Impulsively she grabbed her front-door keys and ran up the rickety stairs, dressed only in the new top and a pair of knickers, to find her.

It was only on the stairs that she realized she was galloping up to tell Rachel all about Oliver, about how she felt and what Arthur had said, and how she was going to see him that evening. In the past she'd never have contemplated telling Rachel anything so juicy and personal, but excitement and anticipation were making her uncharacteristically reckless. She knew that telling Rachel would lead to a fresh torrent of opinions and endless advice and interference that she really didn't need. And yet Rachel was a friend and the new Emily wanted to trust her, wanted to do as Arthur had advised and stop evaluating the consequences of every action she took and be more instinctive. If her instincts told her to tell Rachel what was on her mind, she would tell Rachel . . .

Her friendship with Rachel had crept up upon her. Emily had left school with little intention of keeping in touch and yet Rachel was now the only school friend she still saw. Hard not to when she lived only a floor above Emily, but in the years that they'd lived here Emily had been endlessly grateful that fate had worked out the way it did. She and Rachel had slowly but certainly become good friends.

But Rachel didn't answer the door. Emily stood on the stairs, thinking how she'd done this half-naked thing once too often and that she should go back downstairs. Perhaps she'd imagined the sound of Rachel's music above her. And then, just as she was turning to go, a croaky voice called out a hello.

'It's me,' Emily hissed back.

The handle slowly turned and 'Let Me Entertain You' blasted through the door. A bemused, pyjama-clad, hung-over-looking Rachel peered around it and rubbed her eyes at Emily. 'Have ... you ... brought ... me ... some ... Nurofen?'

Emily took in the tiny bloodshot eyes, the pale, shiny face and the wild hair.

'I'm ill,' Rachel groaned.

'I still haven't brought you any. I thought I heard your music.'

'I was trying to make myself feel better. Where did you lose your trousers?' Rachel squinted at Emily's bare legs.

'I haven't put them on yet. I was getting dressed and I heard you and I thought I'd come up.'

Rachel beckoned Emily into the flat, shut the door and led the way to her bedroom.

'Sit on the bed and talk to me. I'm just trying to get up.'

Emily did as she was told and sat on the end of the bed. 'It's seven in the evening . . . As good a time as any, I suppose.'

Rachel got back into bed and pulled up her duvet. She looked at Emily and was about to speak, started to cough, then bent down and held her head in her hands for a moment. 'Where have you been again?' she croaked.

'Cornwall.'

The room was dark and Emily reached over and switched on Rachel's bedside light. Lemsip and Lucozade sat convincingly on her bedside table.

Rachel winced at the light. 'You haven't asked so I'll tell you anyway. I've been in bed since the morning after Holly's, ill enough for more sympathy from you. Ill enough for flowers even, if I had anyone kind enough to bring me some. This is not a hangover.'

'I'll buy you some. I thought it was a hangover, but now I can see. You look terrible. Can I get you anything?'

Rachel shook her head. 'I'm feeling better having you here to talk to. Tell me about Cornwall. No, tell me about tonight,' Rachel said, changing her mind. 'Is that what you're wearing?'

Emily nodded.

'It's wonderful – ' Rachel nodded approvingly – 'absolutely beautiful.' Then she said provocatively, 'So what will it be like seeing Oliver again?'

What was going on? Emily stiffened. What had changed since Holly's party when Oliver's return had barely made a ripple of interest? What did Rachel *think* she knew?

'I haven't really thought about it.'

'Come on. You must have done.' Suddenly Rachel was sounding bright and alert.

'There's no big deal about Oliver.'

'But you must be excited about seeing him again?'

'Not particularly,' Emily said defiantly and the disbelief on Rachel's face made her add recklessly, 'I met someone in Cornwall.'

It produced such a wonderful look of surprise that Emily started to laugh.

'No way? You can't have done!' Rachel sat bolt upright, held her head and groaned.

'Yes . . . It's Sam Finch.' Emily gave Rachel a look with just the right mix of coyness and suggestiveness to be completely convincing. 'I couldn't believe it.' Emily hadn't realized she was going to say that either, but she was tired of Rachel, tired of the lot of them always acting like they knew her so well, with just that hint of superiority, as if their experiences had given them a wisdom Emily didn't possess. 'I can't have done what?'

'Nothing important happened between you two, did it?' Rachel asked right on cue.

Emily let out a deep sigh. 'Why is it so bloody impossible?'

Now it was Rachel's turn to laugh, making her clutch at her head again. 'You're the one who kept telling us it was. But of course it isn't impossible – you're gorgeous and it's up to you – and if it happened in Cornwall just a day after meeting someone, and if you're OK about it . . . I suppose that's fine. Join the club!' Emily nodded, encouraging her to go on, encouraging her to believe it. 'But I'm so stunned,' Rachel said. 'Remember, I saw you only a few days ago and there was no talk of going to Cornwall then, certainly not of Sam Finch and . . . I didn't think you would go and do this on the spur of the moment. So understand, seeing as it is the last thing in the world I expected you to say, I'm a little taken aback.'

'I understand.'

'I'm pleased for you, I suppose. You look very happy . . . But – ' she wrinkled up her nose – 'OK, I'll admit it, I thought you were waiting for better things. I'm gutted. I liked the way you were. I thought it was great, everything you said . . .'

Touched as she was, Emily wasn't quite ready to let her off the hook. 'But you have to admit, Sam Finch is a lovely name.'

'A lovely name,' Rachel agreed.

'And he is the one who rescued me from the wasp.'

'Oh, so *that* was the elusive combination. *That's* why it's taken you twenty-five years to find the right man. He had to rescue you from mortal danger *and* have a nice name.'

'Whereas all you had to do was find was a guy who went to the same school as you and was called John,' Emily teased, 'so it took you only sixteen years.'

'And don't I regret it.' The shock on Rachel's face made Emily falter. How had it got to this? Where had it started?

'I'm sorry. So sorry. John was lovely. I'm teasing. Don't worry,' she went on, unable to keep up the lie any longer, 'I'm still pure, I'm still innocent. I'm still there, on the side of the angels.'

Rachel failed to come up with a good reply, sank back on her pillows and closed her eyes. 'So that was just a joke? It's not true?'

'No,' Emily confirmed, 'it's not true. Nothing happened. I'm as pure and innocent and all alone as I was before I left.'

'Thank God for that.'

Because how inconvenient it would have been if Emily – Emily who had managed to go twenty-five years without a man in her life – should find one almost on the very day that all her friends were moving into action with the perfect man and a simple strategy for getting him. Holly had called the morning after her party and had filled Rachel in, cautiously at first because she knew that, of all Emily's friends, Rachel was her most ardent fan and more convinced than anyone else of the value of what Emily was holding out for. But as Rachel had listened and agreed, Holly had happily told her everything, stressing how important it was that Rachel was involved too, that she was too much a part of Emily's life not to be told what was going on (whatever Caitlin might have said to the contrary). And ever keen to please, and to say and do the right thing, Rachel had been easily persuaded. And then Holly had asked Rachel whether she'd like to come skiing too – defying Caitlin again and sighing with relief when

Rachel said that she was tied up with a huge family party and so wouldn't be able to.

Rachel kept her eyes shut, trying to force her thick head to gauge whether or not Sam was a danger to their plans for Emily and Oliver. In the midst of the joking, had she detected something genuine? Did Emily feel more for Sam than she was letting on? If there was any danger at all that Sam might divert attention away from Oliver, she would have to quickly get back to Holly before she called Sam and invited him skiing.

'I don't understand why,' Emily said in a small voice.

Rachel opened an eye and looked at her.

'You don't understand why what?'

'Why it's "thank God" that I haven't met anyone.'

'Because otherwise I'd be the only one without a boy-friend. No, Emily, I'm joking. I'm joking. Really. There's nothing I'd like better than for you to fall in love. We all want you to find someone.'

'Now it sounds as if you've been having a class discussion.'

'No. Of course we haven't.' Rachel slid out a pile of old magazines from under her duvet and dropped them on the floor. 'And you know how I feel about you. I want you to find someone, of course I do.' She paused. 'So, tell me. Did you really fancy Sam Finch?'

'Is that all that's important to you? You're not really interested in who he is, what he does, or how I met him again. You only want to know whether I fancy him or not? Whether I might have slept with him?'

'Absolutely.'

'No,' Emily said, irritated, 'I did not fancy him.'

She got off the bed and wandered over to the window. She knew she shouldn't have even thought about talking to Rachel. Rachel might support her stand, but she didn't know her as Holly did. Holly would have been different. Emily could imagine telling Holly all about Oliver and Sam and Arthur and everyone else. But not Rachel.

'So who do you want?' Rachel asked, almost as if she'd read Emily's mind. There was a stillness to her face, again as if she knew exactly who Emily would say.

'Nobody! You're obsessed! Leave me alone.'

And, seeing how wary she was, it was clear to Rachel that Emily mustn't ever be told that her friends were on to her. That if she did find out, it would only make her run a mile in the wrong direction.

'But you do want to meet someone?'

'Of course I do, in theory. I don't want to hang around for ever.' Emily's smile softened. 'How was I to know it would take me this long!'

'And is it still marriage that you're waiting for?' Rachel asked cautiously, in case Emily became even more defensive.

Emily came back at her immediately. 'You know exactly what I want. Not necessarily a ring and a cake, but lifelong commitment. You know the score.'

'I know that was how it always was for you,' Rachel said. 'I wasn't sure whether you'd changed, that's all.'

'Nothing has changed. I still don't see the point in

sleeping with the wrong guy,' Emily said, 'not if it's clear he is wrong from the start.'

'And what would make him wrong?'

'Wrong as in you know he's not the guy for you, that you won't last.'

'So if it's not going to last it must be wrong?'

'Yes – ' Emily nodded – 'surely you don't want to be with someone who you know you're going to break up with?'

'Sometimes I do,' Rachel admitted. 'Sometimes I don't think that far ahead.'

'I know that living like that would make me unhappy,' Emily said. 'I'm sure sex is fun and exhilarating and good for your skin and great exercise and I can see how it brings you closer to your partner . . . but that's not enough for me. It never has been. If that's all you want, play tennis.'

'You may not believe this, but people say sex is even better.'

'I don't believe you!'

'And much better exercise, too.'

'But sex isn't like tennis, is it?' Emily said, becoming more serious. 'You don't get something stuck inside you during tennis.'

'For God's sake, Emily,' Rachel exploded. 'Why do you have to put it like that?'

'Because it's true!'

'There speaks a true virgin.'

Now Emily was getting seriously defensive. 'I know

that if I am contemplating becoming physically joined to someone, then I want to be emotionally joined to them first.'

'And I agree with you.' Rachel rubbed her face and stared at Emily. 'You know I am not some girl who runs around screwing everything in sight. Neither are your friends. You don't have to convince us about that. But an emotional commitment at the time and everlasting love are not the same thing.'

What was bothering Rachel most wasn't the implicit criticism of herself and the others, but that Emily seemed to think it was the easiest thing in the world to *know* who would provide her with everlasting love. As if she was the only one to have thought about such things. And, for the first time, Rachel – loyal supporter that she had always been – felt rather irritated with Emily for seeing it all in such black and white terms. 'Don't you think we're all looking to be happy, too?' she asked.

'Sometimes I think you are.' Emily bit her lip and looked at Rachel as if unsure whether to go on. 'And sometimes ... I'll admit it, sometimes I look at a guy you're with and I think you must be blind not to see where it's heading. And I look at Caitlin and I think how sordid she is to take home men she hardly knows.'

Rachel had never heard Emily be so judgemental. And she was filled with misgiving. It was as if rational, worldly Emily was there one moment and gone the next, diving below the surface of some sugary, pink, romantic world that Rachel didn't know and no longer wanted to follow her to. She wondered if this was truly how Emily saw them all, the walking wounded, battle-scarred, soiled and half-defeated, while she marched past, untouched and invincible?

'Those are the extremes,' she retaliated, aware how strange it was to be provoked into defending a corner she hadn't even realized she wanted to protect. 'Most of the time it doesn't happen like that. Look at me! I'm not wrecked by the love affairs that haven't worked out, I'm having fun! And so are Jo-Jo and Holly and Caitlin. OK, maybe Caitlin enjoys herself more often than I do and, OK, sometimes I expect she does wish she could turn back the clock. And, yes, sometimes her men are gross. But I don't think it's destroying her. And neither am I being destroyed. My relationships haven't worked out so far, but I've not been left less of a person because of them.'

'I think Caitlin is miserable,' Emily replied. 'I think she feels worthless. I think her self-esteem is shot to shreds and she doesn't like me because I remind her of it. You're suggesting it's possible to sleep with someone and walk away and it doesn't matter who they are,' Emily went on, 'and I don't think that's true. I don't think you can.' She repeated it deliberately. 'I don't think *you* can. And I think you're fooling yourself when you say otherwise. You, you especially, Rachel. You get hurt! Admit it. You try on their surname after the first date and you collapse into bed when they don't call. And it's because you've *slept* with them that it gets you so hard. You wouldn't feel so vulnerable, so bad, if you hadn't slept with them. So don't pretend it's all just one long laugh. I know it's not.'

'Until you fall madly, passionately, overwhelmingly in

lust with someone, not in love, you won't know that you're wrong.'

'I will meet the right guy. I have faith that he will like me just the way I am and he will wait with me. I'm not arguing for abstinence. I'm arguing for patience. I'm saying, what's wrong with waiting? I'm saying I'm sick of instant everything. Fast food, fast tans, fast sex. I hate the way nobody is prepared to wait, *for anything*. It's as if things are only worth having if they're had now. But I say waiting is good, patience is good.'

At that moment, Emily saw it in Rachel's face, the surprise and confusion, scorn even. It made her flinch. 'I don't judge you,' she said, 'so don't judge me. I judge myself. I don't mean to suggest your attitudes are wrong.'

'But I'm suggesting yours are.'

Emily looked at her.

'It is wrong to be so afraid of getting hurt. Don't think it's an advantage to be so cautious and afraid of everything. You survive getting hurt and you learn and move on again. And you can't ward it off, you can't stop it from happening, however much you try. You might get bullied at work, or your dog might get run over, or your mother and father might abandon you and bugger off to New Zealand ... You still survive, don't you? And those events make you grow up, teach you what you want and what you don't want. What you care about, what makes you hurt terribly and what makes you happy too. And whether or not you have sex is *everything* to do with it.'

Rachel got off the bed, turned her back on Emily and started to dress.

'I'd shut the curtains,' Emily told her, with a weak smile. 'Or is that just me being a prude?'

Rachel whipped them closed and turned back to her. 'On this subject, you've always gone it alone and I still think that you're amazing for doing so, brave and so right in so many things that you say. But –' Emily looked down at the bed and waited – 'at the same time you are too afraid of making mistakes. You fear that you wouldn't be able to cope with one, you fear that if you give yourself up to someone that they will inevitably hurt you. Yet it would be no better or worse for you than it is for any of us. And coping with it when it goes wrong is what makes us strong.'

'I am not frightened of making a mistake. So far it has not been a dilemma for me. So far no guy has come close. I haven't been near anyone who's made me want him that badly.'

'And when you do?'

'When I do, I believe that everything I've said now will still hold true. Because they're good, valid reasons, Rachel, they're not easily ditched. Not when I've held on to them for so long. I will prove that my way can work. I will prove that it is possible to find someone and be sure of them, that being patient, saving the moment, making sex the last thing you do with someone rather than the first will make you happy, *happier*. Because, for me, sex will never be just another way of having fun. I know that I will never want to share the innermost part of me with someone who doesn't love me. I do not want men walking the streets who have known me in the most intimate way possible and who no longer think about me at all.'

Rachel nodded. 'I hope you find him.'

Emily took a deep breath 'I know I will.'

'Such a great top,' Rachel said.

Back to normality.

'Why is Caitlin having this little party, do you think? Is it because she fancies Oliver?' Emily asked the same question she'd asked Holly, and Rachel replied just as Holly had.

'No, I don't think so. I think she wants to make things up with you. I think that's why.'

Slipping down the stairs again, letting herself back into her flat, Emily realized that Rachel's forceful words had unsettled her, and she knew too that there'd been some truth in what she'd said. Rachel was right when she said that she was cautious, afraid of mistakes – Emily knew it was true. And she wondered how much she'd be prepared to change in order to get closer to Oliver.

10

'There's something different about you.'

'No!'

'You've met someone. I can tell by the way you're looking at me.'

'Stop it!' Emily laughed, turning away from him.

Oliver put his head to one side and considered her. 'Oh, I think so. Come and tell me who he is.' He patted the sofa beside him.

'No!' she said again.

'Emily. You have to . . .'

In the kitchen, crouching down to look through the window of her oven to check up on her four towering cheese soufflés, Caitlin felt momentarily disheartened. She could hear Oliver and Emily laughing again, imagined them sitting side by side on the little sofa and wondered, sourly, what could have possessed her to come up with such a totally great idea that involved giving Emily, of all people, a clean shot at the most attractive man she knew.

When Caitlin had opened her front door and taken her first look at Oliver in over a year, her first thought had been, *She is not going to be able to resist you.* One year on and Oliver was even more attractive. Not very tall, which Caitlin liked – when he stood beside Leon he'd seem even shorter – but bigger and broader and less clean-cut than she'd remembered, his tawny hair grown longer and streaked with gold, and there was a definitely naughty gleam in his gorgeous brown eyes.

Oliver had come forward, kissed her and handed her a huge bunch of frilly orange parrot tulips (and she was hardly ever given classy flowers) and her second thought, the thought that had repeated through her head ever since, was, *Do I really have to do this? Can't I have him instead?*

But when Emily had arrived and slipped off her coat to reveal a surprisingly see-through little red top and very low-cut jeans, Caitlin had felt quite proud of her, and resolved again to make the evening work. She had retreated to the kitchen as quickly as she decently could, dragging Leon with her and leaving Emily and Oliver alone in the sitting room.

But Leon was proving surprisingly difficult to control. From the moment that Caitlin got him into the kitchen he was fidgeting to get out again, all the time looking through the doorway to the sitting room opposite, as if he was trying to see what Emily and Oliver were up to, and she could do nothing to distract him. In the end, frustrated by all the chores Caitlin kept piling on him, he announced he was off to the bathroom, whereupon Caitlin knew that, for the time being, she'd lost him, that he had no intention of rejoining her in the kitchen afterwards.

Left alone, Caitlin reached for mustard, salt and pepper, brown sugar, olive oil and balsamic vinegar and a little brown jug, telling herself she would not look through the door and spy on Oliver and Emily herself until after she'd made a dressing. Which took all of thirty seconds. Still managing not to look, she reached into the corner of the kitchen for the two sticks of French bread propped up against the wall and slid them out of their cellophane.

Surely twenty minutes had passed since Caitlin last looked? Surely it was fair enough if she now allowed herself a little glimpse, another quick check on progress? She glanced. Emily and Oliver had moved from the sofa and were standing together at the far end of the little sitting room, Emily with her back to the wall (so Caitlin was able to see her clearly from the kitchen), Oliver with his back to Caitlin.

'Something has changed,' she heard Oliver say.

Glad that you've noticed, Caitlin thought. She watched Oliver pretend to peer carefully all over Emily's face and make Emily blush. He knows he's right, and he's not sure he likes it, and it's making him want to flirt with her. But what he can't see is that the change is because of him, that he's the one who's lit her up, that he's the one she can't take her eyes off now. And even though Caitlin would have said yes to him herself at any other time, even though it was still more bitter than sweet to see Oliver and Emily coming together, at that moment it seemed that the planning might all be about to pay off, and that felt good. Emily was glowing in his company, standing so close to him she was practically in his arms, and still she hadn't taken her eyes off his face. Caitlin felt like a fairy godmother to a god-daughter she'd never much liked but who was now turning out to be rather rewarding.

For so long Caitlin had felt like the flaky, irresponsible one of the three of them – at least she imagined that was how Holly and Jo-Jo saw her: the one without the proper job, the one who was broke all the time, the one who lived off her boyfriends, and her friends too if she had the chance, and who appeared to spend what little money she had on shoes and facials rather than on getting her life together. They might enjoy her company, but Caitlin knew that they didn't take her seriously. So it was great to have something positive to share with Holly and Jo-Jo, especially when it was something she, Caitlin, had initiated. Yet another reason to prolong the experience for as long as she could. Now she had Emily to work on, perceptions of Caitlin might be about to change.

'Hey, Emily!'

Leon was standing in the doorway of the bathroom. Caitlin watched in despair as he set off towards her, still zipping up his flies. He glanced in at Caitlin, gave her a smile that said it all, and stopped. But only for long enough to take a comb from his breast pocket and run it quickly through his hair and to grab a bottle of wine from her fridge.

Caitlin watched him walk into the sitting room, come up behind Oliver and purposefully move him out of the way. She watched him refill Emily's glass, turn and refill Oliver's, then stretch his arm behind Emily and put the bottle on the fireplace behind her, leaving his arm there. Fat, hairy fingers supported his weight. He had effectively annexed Emily for himself.

When Caitlin had first met Leon she'd been reminded

of a seal. Now as irritation burst inside her, she looked at his small flat nose, his ears pressed close to his little head, his slicked-down hair, his body bulging softly in his black suit, and she thought that he looked like a slug. A slug in a toupee. He moved even closer to Emily. What the hell was Leon doing? Damn him!

'Go and help Caitlin in the kitchen,' she heard him tell Oliver and, in disbelief, Caitlin watched Oliver do exactly as he was told. When he came into the kitchen she had to stop herself from shooing him back out again.

'Because I think it's my turn to talk to you,' she heard Leon say to a silenced Emily, 'or were you planning on ignoring me all evening?'

And then, belatedly, Caitlin understood. Leon desperately fancied Emily. And her heart sank because she knew Leon too well, knew how it would make him behave.

Caitlin turned her back on Oliver and stomped across her kitchen in disgust. Why hadn't she seen this coming, hadn't once thought about how Leon would react to Emily? Why, when Leon had asked who Emily was, what she did, where she came from, had Caitlin told him so much more than he needed to know? But Caitlin knew exactly why. She had told Leon about Emily because she knew how much it would fascinate him and she hadn't been able to resist. She had wanted to stun him, and at the same time tempt him with someone she knew he'd never have. *She's stunningly pretty, Leon. And, amazingly, she's still a virgin.*

She'd told him just half an hour ago, when it was only the two of them, still waiting for Emily and Oliver to arrive. And then, having told him, instead of regretting it, covering up, backtracking swiftly and making nothing of it, she'd made things even worse, had thrown him the challenge: *Don't look like that. She's hardly going to be interested in you.*

But he was interested in her, which meant that Emily was going to have him fawning and falling over her all evening. If it wasn't that he'd be getting in the way of Oliver, it would have been funny to watch.

'Anything I can do?' Oliver asked Caitlin.

You can go and be a man.

She passed him a large plate of toasted brown pitta cut into strips and a bowl of roughly chopped guacamole and he held it still while she gave it a squeeze of lemon juice. 'Give it some salt and pepper and then you can take it through to them,' she said instead. 'Split them up and save her from a fate worse than death.'

Oliver laughed and instead of doing as he was told he placed the plate and the bowl back on the tiny work surface and then jumped up beside it, took a piece of pitta and dipped. 'I think it's fair enough that Leon gets some quality time with Emily. And I think I'd rather stay with you.'

She shook her head because they were veering off the script – and yet, she thought, surely it couldn't harm. The night was young and there was plenty of time for Emily and Oliver to get close later on. Surely she didn't have to be rude to Oliver? Turn him out of her kitchen when he'd asked to stay? She hadn't seen him for a year, and he was her friend too. And perhaps if Leon was left alone with

Emily for ten minutes, he might see the other, rather more irritating aspects to her personality. Leaving Leon alone with Emily might be the best way of getting her out of his system.

'I love to watch a woman cook,' he told Caitlin, watching as she halved an avocado, peeled it, threw away the stone and proceeded to chop it at the speed of light. 'And you are cooking in the most minute kitchen I've ever seen.'

She glanced up at him. 'Chauvinist.'

What Oliver had said about her kitchen was true. Compared with Holly's gleaming industrial-sized space, her kitchen was barely bigger than a biscuit tin, and because there were only one or two small cupboards everything – all her pots and pans, the potato mashers and metal spoons with holes in, and garlic presses and egg whisks – hung from the ceiling, getting tangled in her hair and collecting dust every day that they weren't being used. In order to sit where he was now, Oliver had had to make a parting in the line of utensils swinging level with his head, and he was positioned between a sharp pair of scissors and a pizza cutter.

Pushed up against the wall tiles were her bottles of oils and vinegars and pots of flour and herbs, all specially selected for size as well as for flavour. She had a very small fridge and her little oven drove her crazy, needing telepathic intuition to judge its temperature, its door falling off its hinges almost every time she opened it. Having someone else in there when she cooked usually sent her into a frenzy of irritation. But it wasn't the same when the someone else was Oliver.

'Did I get it right about Emily?' Oliver asked Caitlin. 'Has she met someone?'

Say yes and she might whet his appetite ... but she might put him off. Say no and she was diluting the challenge ... but she might be encouraging him.

'Possibly.' Caitlin ran the chopping board under the tap, then wiped clean the knife, opened her fridge and brought out a cucumber. 'Rachel said she'd met someone in Cornwall,' she told him, 'but I don't think it's anything serious.'

'That'll be Sam Finch,' he said, tossing back his hair and dropping guacamole into his mouth. 'Not serious.' He agreed and licked his fingers clean.

'You know that?'

'Sam said he'd seen her. Sam's known Emily for years, as long as I have. Nothing's going on there.' He lowered his voice. 'So, she's still not slept with anyone?'

Caitlin looked at him. 'I'm not the one to ask.'

'No?'

'You should ask Emily, not me.'

'I'm going to,' Oliver said defensively. 'I'm checking with you that she's OK, that's all.'

'She's got a perfectly good brother already,' Caitlin said, sharper than she intended.

'Spiky Caitlin! I know she's got a brother.'

'So she doesn't need another one.' She started to roll the plastic wrapper off the cucumber.

'No. She doesn't need another one,' Oliver agreed, 'but I like to think I'm a friend. Someone she knows cares about her.'

'And you hope she's been good while you've been away in New York?'

'What is this?' But Oliver was laughing as he said it, distracted by the way Caitlin was loosening the plastic around the cucumber, by rubbing it vigorously up and down.

Too late Caitlin realized what she was doing. She laid the cucumber down on the chopping board and refused to look at Oliver. Then she reached into a drawer and brought out a Sabatier knife, steadied herself and chopped.

Oliver flinched.

She slid the knife under the plastic and pulled the cucumber free. 'We all like to look out for Emily.' She picked up the knife again and started to peel.

'I never realized you were such a friend.'

'She's grown on me. I want her to be happy. I think her attitudes are all wrong, of course. I hope for her sake that she starts to adapt them.'

'She's a lovely girl. She'll adapt when she finds some-one who deserves her.'

Seeing Oliver sitting there, so good-looking in a heart-breaking kind of a way, someone who really meant it when he said he cared about Emily – in short, the perfect man for her – Caitlin had to fight the urge to tell him everything, to stop herself from suggesting that even if he hadn't thought about Emily like that since he was sixteen, it was now time he did.

'Sam Finch is a good friend of yours, is he?' she asked instead.

Oliver nodded. 'Great friend. Known him all my life.'

'And do you like skiing?'

Oliver laughed. 'There's a link there somewhere but I'm damned if I can find it. Sam and snow? Sam and me . . . and snow?' He laughed, giving up. 'Yes, I like skiing.'

'It's Holly's holiday. Expect a call.'

'To say what?'

Caitlin was wandering off the script, but she carried on recklessly. 'She's going to say that she requests the pleasure of your company at her chalet in Magine, in the French Alps, over Easter,' she grinned. 'For *liaisons dangereuses*.'

Oliver raised an eyebrow. 'Interesting.'

Caitlin nodded, thinking she should have kept her mouth shut. And that Holly should have asked him, not her.

Still sitting on the kitchen unit, he suddenly hooked a leg around her and pulled her close. 'And who am I meant to be liaising with? I can resist liaising with Leon. But if you'll be there . . .'

'You know I'll be there.'

'With Leon?'

'Of course.'

'Why?'

'Because he's sweet.'

She wriggled out of Oliver's reach and decided to ignore what he had just done. *Because he's my boyfriend*, she should have added, *and I adore him. Leave me alone.*

'And Emily will be there. She'll be so pleased to know you're coming too. We should go back next door and tell her—'

172

'Caitlin, what are you doing with him?'

'There's a lot to Leon that you don't see the first time you meet him.' She went on without pausing, giving him no chance to interrupt. 'And if you're staying here, you can help me. Chop up some parsley, then we can go through.' She pointed to where a large pot was balanced precariously on a narrow window ledge.

Without getting down, he turned and tore off a handful of the parsley. She gave him the chopping board and the sharp knife and he started to chop while Caitlin ripped open a packet of lamb's lettuce and dropped it into a china salad bowl. Then she bent to the oven and lifted out, one by one, her four soufflés. Behind her, Oliver jumped off the cupboard and went through to the sitting room. Alone again, Caitlin scooped up the parsley, sprinkled some onto the top of each soufflé, placed them on a tray and carried them through.

Caitlin walked into the sitting room just in time to hear Leon tell Emily with a lascivious smile the old cliché that he'd never met anyone quite like her before.

He was sitting beside her on the sofa, and in response Emily flicked at him with her hand, batting him away like a bluebottle. But Caitlin was surprised to see that she had a grin on her face and she didn't take advantage of their arrival to escape him. If anything, Caitlin thought, Leon was so plain bad at flirting that Emily probably found him endearing. It made Caitlin feel both irritation and affection for the pair of them. Irritation at Emily for being so hopeless, for not using opportunities to talk to

Oliver, and irritation at Leon for finding a virgin irresistibly attractive. Yet through her irritation, Caitlin knew that it was Emily's vulnerability and lack of confidence that was preventing her making any move on Oliver. And she wondered if it wasn't Leon's lack of confidence speaking too. Perhaps the thought of being with someone who couldn't compare him to anyone else was very attractive? Especially in contrast to the voracious, been-there-done-everything nymphomaniacs he usually went for, herself excluded.

The problem was that Leon's infatuation meant he was in no hurry to leave Emily alone. And he'd stick even closer to her if he ever realized what Caitlin had planned for Emily and Oliver. If Caitlin didn't do something about Leon, she could see her evening becoming a farce. She imagined Jo-Jo's lecture and felt a surge of renewed determination. She would have to get Emily and Oliver alone together, somewhere Emily couldn't run away from sometime that evening. But she wasn't sure how.

In the opposite corner of the sitting room to the sofa was a small wooden table. Caitlin went over to it and put down the tray and Oliver followed her. She handed him two plates, each with a blue ramekin holding a soufflé, and he passed one to Leon and one to Emily.

As soon as Emily got hers, she slid off the sofa and sat on the floor.

'Stay where you were,' Caitlin protested. 'I'm sorry that there's not more room to sit down.'

'No, honestly, you sit on the sofa,' said Emily. 'I'm fine on the floor.'

Possibly it had been a strategic move, designed to put her out of reach of Leon, or an invitation to Oliver to join her, but if it was it misfired, because Oliver didn't move fast enough and Leon practically threw himself to the floor next to her. He ended up half lying, half sitting by her side, supporting himself eagerly on his little white hands and looking up at Oliver in triumph. Then, as Caitlin watched in horror, he took his spoon, dipped it into his soufflé, leant forwards and tried to drop it into Emily's mouth.

Catching Oliver's eye, Emily shut her mouth tight, whereupon Leon shrugged self-consciously and ate the soufflé himself. There were a few awkward seconds, until Emily put her plate on the floor and climbed back to her feet.

'Where's the bathroom?' she asked Caitlin, pink with embarrassment.

'Oliver,' Caitlin said, seeing him standing close to the door. 'Show Emily the bathroom.'

She ignored his *how should I know where your bathroom is?* shrug, and as he and Emily left the room Caitlin moved over to the sofa, gave Leon a look and patted the space beside her. He did as he was told, sat down and looked at her warily.

There were only two doors for Oliver to choose between. Caitlin heard him make the right choice and open the door to her bathroom. She wanted to run up behind them, give them both a good shove in the back and lock the bathroom door.

'Here we are,' she heard Oliver say. Caitlin imagined him standing aside to let her pass and enter the room.

It was perfect timing. There would be no shoving necessary. Oliver stepped forward to turn on the light for Emily and momentarily disappeared into the room. And Caitlin got up, moved quickly to the bathroom door and pulled it gently shut behind him. It didn't even make a sound, and she was beside Leon almost before he had realized she'd left the room.

Quick as a flash, Caitlin returned to the sitting room and poured herself and Leon another glass of wine.

As the seconds became a minute, Caitlin felt a tug of jealousy. She imagined Oliver kissing Emily's forehead, taking her in his arms. *Ssshh!* he'd whisper, covering her mouth with his. *Let's not be rescued yet.*

Caitlin looked over to Leon, blissfully eating his supper. She was dying to say something about how long Oliver and Emily were taking, but Leon still hadn't noticed their absence and she knew she shouldn't involve him. If he realized what was happening, he'd be the first to break down the door. One more minute and she'd go back to the kitchen and on her way listen at the bathroom door.

Then, from the bathroom, came the rather disconcerting sound of a flushing loo and finally, a rattling of the door and then, at last, Oliver's voice appealing for help.

'Coming, I'm coming,' Caitlin called back, leaping up and almost tripping over herself in her haste to get out of the sitting room. Forget about leaving them there for hours, forget about keeping the door shut to allow the temperature to rise, she wanted to open the door and see their faces immediately, to work out exactly what and how much had gone on between them.

'Are you stuck in there?' she shouted.

'Don't worry. Take your time,' Oliver called back.

Leon joined Caitlin at the door. 'What's going on?'

'They're stuck,' she told him.

'In there together? I'll break down the door. *I'll break down the door*,' Leon repeated loudly, mouth to the keyhole.

'No, don't you dare,' Caitlin said, pushing him out of the way.

'I'm serious, I mean it. Take your time,' Oliver insisted from the other side.

'I've got a spanner in the kitchen,' Caitlin called to him. 'What I usually do is pass it through the space at the bottom of the door, then you can use it as a door handle.'

'You're telling me you knew about this door?' Oliver shouted back incredulously. 'Other people have met the same fate?'

'Yes. I'm sorry, I'm not very good at DIY.'

She went to the kitchen and ransacked the tiny kitchen drawers, pulling out an array of napkin rings, video repair manuals, home-delivery restaurant menus, assorted keys, tea towels, the instruction manual for her fridge, paper napkins, some nasty table mats and finally the spanner. She went back to the bathroom and fed the spanner slowly under the door and waited while Oliver got to work on the other side. Eventually the door opened.

And Oliver was standing there alone.

'Where's Emily?' Caitlin cried in frustration.

'I'm here!' And there she was. Standing red-faced in the doorway of Caitlin's bedroom, watching them.

'What the hell are you doing there?' Caitlin exploded.

'I didn't think you'd mind. I've been in your room. Not snooping, just sitting on your bed.'

'She kindly offered to let me go first,' Oliver explained.

'Isn't that just so romantic?' said Caitlin, finding it hard to stop herself banging her head against the wall.

'I was sitting on your bed, waiting for him. And I found your photographs,' Emily came over to her. 'They're gorgeous. When were you in India?'

Shut up about India! Caitlin nearly spat at her.

'I truly wasn't nosing. The album was on your bed. I didn't think you'd mind. Oliver!' she said, turning to him. 'You were ages! Are you ill? What were you doing in there?'

'I don't think we need to know the answer to that, do we, Emily? Do we, Oliver?' Caitlin butted in.

'I'm sorry,' Oliver said to Emily. 'I wish you had got locked in with me. It would have been far more fun.' He turned to Caitlin. 'How about an *I'm sorry you got locked in, Oliver*. Or *I'll make sure I fix that door before you come around again, Oliver.*'

'Sorry.' Caitlin gave him a grudging smile.

'I'll just go myself,' Emily said, sidling past them, 'if you don't mind. And I'll only push the door to, so nobody's to come in.'

Ten minutes later Caitlin came back to the sitting room to find that Leon, Oliver and Emily had all decided to move to the floor to eat their supper. Emily looked relaxed for the first time that evening, and, at last, it was Oliver she was smiling at and talking to, not Leon.

Because Caitlin's flat was so tiny, this was the way she always ended up entertaining. The room was so small that there was room only for the little table at one end of the room and the two-seater sofa at the other, so if four people wanted to eat together, the only way was for all four to sit on the floor. As it was, some of the best evenings were at Caitlin's, where the intimacy of the room, the unfailingly delicious food, the candlelight and cushions, rather than chairs, easily beat the formality of a sit-down supper.

She would let them eat and then she would try again to think of some way to give Emily and Oliver quality time together. The missed opportunity in the bathroom had to be put aside. She was somehow going to remove Leon from the room and leave Oliver alone there. It wasn't going to be easy. Leon was not going to give up his place lightly – even as he saw her struggling with a heavy dish he didn't move a muscle. It was, of course, Oliver who jumped up to give her a hand.

But in the end it was simple enough. She gave them all helpings of salad, handed around the buttery hot baguettes, the salt and pepper, the napkins, knives and forks, waited until they'd eaten almost every scrap of food, then she picked up and took out the china salad bowl. Once in her kitchen, she let the bowl slip through her fingers and hit the ceramic tiled floor where it smashed satisfyingly. She'd always disliked it and getting rid of it in aid of such a good cause was doubly justified.

'Leon, please!' she ordered before Oliver could get up. 'Come and give me a hand.'

There was something in her voice that compelled Leon to do as he was told. He came in, saw what had happened and heaved a sigh. 'Clumsy girl,' he said, daring Caitlin's wrath, as he reached for some kitchen roll, bent to her feet and carefully began to clear it up. Caitlin didn't reply. She wasn't going to say anything to hasten his return to the other room. Instead, she reached over to the kitchen door and shut it.

Crawling around at her feet, Leon gingerly picked up the larger pieces of china and dropped them into the bin while she busied herself with wiping olive oil off the wall. When that was done she turned to the washing up, which made Leon look up at her in surprise. 'Why now?'

'It'll only take a second,' she explained.

Leon, having picked up the last pieces of lamb's lettuce and rocket and avocado and cucumber, swept the floor. Then, at Caitlin's instruction, he washed it while she rinsed and rubbed clean her pots and pans.

'You'll make someone a good husband some day,' Caitlin told him, as he squeezed out the mop.

'But not you.'

'I don't think you want that, do you?'

'I don't think you'd have me.'

Their words belied the fact that this was the closest they'd been to each other all evening. Caitlin slowly walked towards him, stretched up and kissed him and he pulled her to him. 'Would you?'

'No chance.'

'I'd be good for you.'

'Would you?'

He reached down and kissed her lips and she slid her arms around his reassuringly solid waist.

Then Oliver called to them from the sitting room. 'Come on, you two. What are you doing in there?'

'We're coming. In a second,' Leon called, holding her tight.

'We should go back,' Caitlin told him, kissing him again just below his right ear. Then she pushed him away and opened the door.

'About time too,' Oliver said as soon as she opened it. 'What were you two doing in there?'

And he was irritated, Caitlin realized. She could see it clearly on his face.

She looked back at Leon, who was waiting obediently for her to tell him whether he was allowed back into the sitting room or whether there were further chores expected of him, and all at once she was tired of plotting, unsure about what she was doing and unsettled by the reality of Oliver.

She turned off the overhead light as she came in, so there were now only the dimmest of lamps lit in the room and the two candles, still burning on the mantelpiece. The room was shadowy and dark. The walls, petrol blue in the daylight, were black now.

She was encouraged to see that, left alone together, Oliver and Emily had moved closer to each other. They were both sitting on the floor, their legs stretched out in front of them, side by side, their empty plates pushed to one side, and it was clear that at that moment they were close. As she watched, Oliver wiped a tiny speck of food from Emily's cheek.

He likes her, Caitlin decided. It wouldn't be too hard to move him up a gear. Perhaps he was already more than interested? Perhaps an evening alone together would be all that was necessary to set the course for the two of them?

But then, infuriatingly, as soon as Emily saw Caitlin, she picked up the two empty plates in one hand and got up off the floor.

'Sit down,' Caitlin insisted.

'No, you sit down. I want to help. I'll take these through.' And before Caitlin could say or do anything Emily had picked up the other two plates as well and had left the room.

Leon, who had only just sat down, spied an empty serving dish and hurried out of the room after her.

Caitlin heaved a sigh of frustration then sat down on the floor beside Oliver. Why was it proving so completely impossible to get the four of them in the same room at the same time?

'It's all right, leave them to it. Don't get up again,' Oliver told her.

She reluctantly stayed put, stiff, uncommunicative, waiting for Emily and Leon to come back, planning how, as soon as they did, she'd move back to the sofa and she'd damned well take Leon with her.

But Emily and Leon didn't reappear and for every minute that they stayed away, Oliver seemed to creep ever closer towards her. This was not what was meant to happen at all. She ignored Oliver's encroachment at first and then started to edge away, all the time managing to keep the conversation going with inanities while snatching glances towards the kitchen, not sure whether it would be better or worse for Emily to come back in right now.

Through the doorway into the kitchen she saw that Leon had Emily practically pinned to the wall and Emily was flicking him away with a tea towel. Caitlin felt like laughing with despair that everything could be so back to front. Holly and Jo-Jo would never understand how hard it had been, how hard she'd tried. Or how determined Oliver was.

Oliver is resistible, she reminded herself. Lust after him as she might, it was still more important to Caitlin that when it came to recounting the evening to Jo-Jo and Holly she would be able to tell the whole truth. More important that she would be seen to have behaved impeccably.

But then, she thought, what more could Holly and Jo-Jo expect from the very first date? She'd got Oliver and Emily together again – wasn't it mad of all of them to expect some wild romance to blossom so fast? And if Emily insisted on wiping clean every surface in Caitlin's kitchen – which was what she seemed to be doing now – rather than taking advantage of the chance to get close to Oliver, was there anything Caitlin could do about it? No. She had done her bit and now it was up to Holly and then Rachel to take the couple-to-be on to the next stages. But more importantly, it had to be up to Emily too. She had to help things along herself. And surely she was only imagining that Oliver had been coming on to her?

'Come here,' said Oliver.

Caitlin laughed. 'I can't exactly come any closer. Tell me about America,' she went straight on. 'Was *The Second Guess* a nightmare?'

That was what Caitlin was so good at, remembering everything anyone ever told her, in this case playing on Oliver's ego to distract him.

'*The Second Guess* was a nightmare. But then I worked on the most wonderful thriller called *Into the Noose*.'

He told her about it, now fully stretched out beside her, and Caitlin felt him there, so close, and tried to concentrate on what he was saying, but at the same time she couldn't help sneaking glances at his face, taking in the line of his throat, the long streaks of gold in his hair, the way he kept his beautiful tawny eyes focused on her face while he talked.

Standing in the kitchen, waiting to dry the ramekins as Emily washed them, Leon was at first stuck for something to say. All he could think was to tell her how sweet the Fairy Liquid bubbles looked on her smooth slender forearms, or to point out that she had been washing the same ramekin for nearly a minute.

And while she washed up, Emily was thinking about Oliver, thinking how useless and pathetic she was – that she would prefer to stand in Caitlin's kitchen, washing up with Leon, than be sitting beside Oliver. 'Prefer' was the wrong word. Of course she would prefer to be sitting beside Oliver, but something had stopped her – a paralysis that she'd never experienced before and that she certainly hadn't expected. She despised herself for it, couldn't believe that it was happening to her, that even after the pep talks from Arthur, and the genuine conviction she'd felt that she could go for it, she'd been utterly useless.

She thought back to the year before, how relaxed she'd been in Oliver's company simply because Nessa had been there in the background, her presence keeping everything nice and safe. Of course, Emily could see now that it was Nessa who had made it possible for her to laugh with Oliver, made it possible for her to rest her head on his shoulder, to turn to him for a dance at a party, to call him up to go out for lunch. Now that Nessa was out of the picture and Oliver was available again, Emily had frozen in fear. What is *wrong* with me? she asked herself.

Still, she hadn't exactly had any encouragement from Oliver this evening. She had been aware from the moment she'd walked into Caitlin's flat that he wasn't looking at her the way she wanted him to, not as a potential girl-friend, nor as someone to have a bit of fun with. Oliver had hugged her tightly to him, had kissed her hello and had been very pleased to see her again, but he was greeting the Emily he used to know. He was seeing her as he'd always done – as someone he liked very much, someone to take care of, but not someone to fancy. And that knowledge made it cripplingly hard to behave the way she wanted to. When she'd caught Oliver's eye while Leon was trying to feed her the soufflé, she'd seen that he was laughing at her. Whereas before she might have been able to laugh back, in the present circumstances she had been so embarrassed she'd had to leave the room.

Was it simply that Oliver didn't fancy her and never would? Or was it her virginity that was putting him off? If Sam was right and all he was looking for now was a bit of fun, perhaps it was reasonable of Oliver to decided she was out of bounds.

Catching Caitlin alone in the kitchen earlier on, Emily had nearly told her how she felt about Oliver. Now, standing over the sink, she felt a hot flush of embarrassment. How could she have even thought of doing that? But Caitlin had been a revelation this evening. Even-tempered, considerate, encouraging. She'd admired Emily's little red top, she'd laughed at her jokes, she'd brought her into every conversation. She'd even seemed to know what was on Emily's mind. There'd been a moment when she'd interrupted something Emily was telling her and had said, *If you know what you want, go for it.* Emily had automatically argued that that was what she always did and Caitlin had shrugged and moved the conversation on again and they hadn't said anything more. Now she wished she had.

She ended up letting Leon make coffee for her rather than face the moment when she had to return to the sitting room. She sat on one of the kitchen units next to the sink while he found mugs and milk, and every minute she was away from Oliver made it harder to get back in there.

Leon, needless to say, seemed happy to stay with her. But finally, when the coffee had been drunk, and the conversation exhausted, there was nothing left to do but go through to Oliver and Caitlin. Emily jumped down and Leon led the way with another pot of coffee and a jug of milk and two mugs on a tray. And then he suddenly stopped and turned back, nearly crashing into her, making some feeble excuse, standing in the doorway so that she couldn't even see past him, let alone squeeze past him.

Emily laughed and tried to push him aside, once more determined to spend some time with Oliver, but then Oliver himself came through the door, with bright eyes and pink flushed cheeks.

Later, when Caitlin had finished tidying, undressed, washed and climbed into bed, she was filled with remorse. Along with the awful pang of conscience with regard to Leon there was an afterglow of affection for Emily. Emily might still talk and think like a choirgirl, but she was a choirgirl Caitlin liked more and more the better she knew her, a choirgirl who provoked little of the irritation of old, who with a couple of glasses of wine inside her had almost blurted out in the kitchen that she fancied Oliver. And the memory of that tentative, hopeful look on Emily's face made Caitlin want to curl up and die.

'Are you listening?' Oliver had asked her, his smiling face six inches from hers. How had he got so close? So close that she could see the tiny pores on his nose and the rogue hair that was sticking out at a right angle from his eyebrow. She could smell his musky warm body, hear his soft, shallow breathing, so close she could have touched him with her tongue.

'You don't have to ask me about America.'

'What do you want to talk about?'

'Who says I want to talk about anything?'

And before she realized what he was about to do, he'd leaned forward and taken her chin in his hand and gently tipped it up towards him, had slowly moved closer until he was near enough to kiss her on the mouth.

For just a second or two Caitlin didn't move, but then she jerked backwards as if she'd touched her lips to an electric fence.

This couldn't happen. This mustn't happen.

With enormous will power she dropped her head so that he couldn't reach her lips again, and she stayed like that, held herself steady, gathering herself together, and then she looked up at him again.

'You shouldn't do that,' she said very quietly, their heads still very close.

'Yes, I should. You're the sexiest woman I know.'

'You shouldn't say that.'

'Why not?'

Caitlin groaned.

'Lose Leon. He's pathetic. You can't fancy him.'

'I do. I don't want to lose him.'

'Then have me too.'

Oliver was leaning forward again, reaching with his lips for hers, and she felt her stomach flip over with lust for him. 'Are you offering me a threesome?'

'Not exactly. Even with you there, I don't think I could bear that.' He came closer still. 'And I can't bear the thought of you with him either.'

'Tough,' she said smartly, pulling away from him and sitting up. 'Because, actually, Leon and I are very happy.'

'I don't believe you.'

'I don't care whether you believe me or not.' She was amused that it seemed to bother him so much.

She said nothing more and slowly he started to believe she was serious, and then when she saw that it had worked, she kissed him gently on the tip of the nose, saying goodbye. 'I'm sorry. Leon and I might seem an odd couple, but we're good together.'

He pursed his lips, thought about it, then shrugged, recovering his bravado. 'That's cool. Forget I said anything.'

'But you will still come skiing, won't you? You weren't only coming to try to pull me?'

'You've got a nerve. Of course I wasn't.'

'Emily will be there, and Holly. And Holly is going to invite Sam too, to keep you company,' she added for good measure.

'I'll think about it.' He leaned forward again and kissed her on the cheek. He pushed himself quickly to his feet and went to the door.

11

The next morning, the phone lines were hot.

When Caitlin heard her telephone start to ring she pulled her duvet up to her chin and let the answerphone click in.

'Broadsword to Danny Boy. ' It was Holly. 'Caitlin! For Christ's sake, pick up the damn phone. It's nine thirty and you should have called by now to tell me what happened last night.'

Caitlin opened her eyes.

'I know you're there . . . and I want to know –' but the tone was changing now, caution creeping in – 'unless . . . you're not there? Oh, Caitlin, you didn't! Tell me you didn't?' Caitlin's heart leapt in fear and she looked across at the answerphone in panic.

'Did you go home with Leon?'

Better than that, I kissed Oliver.

She got out of bed and stalked out of her bedroom to the kitchen, where she leaned against the door and waited for Holly to give up.

'Or are you trying to stay asleep?' Holly changed tack again. 'That won't work either. If you're lying in bed listening to me and not answering, *la la la,*' she sang down the phone. 'I am not going to let you go back to sleep. Pick up the phone now! Please! I'm going to keep ringing until you answer. It's nine thirty, it's time to get up. You will *not* go back to sleep.'

Sometimes Holly was so irritating. Caitlin wanted to pick up the phone and tell her just that and nothing more. In a few more seconds the tape would run out, and she definitely needed a little time to think before she talked to Holly. Holly, meanwhile, tried sounding more serious.

'I understand something's happened that we didn't expect. That we might have a problem ... That there's someone who might be about to cause problems.'

Was this it? How had Holly heard? Caitlin told herself it was impossible, that nobody had seen her and Oliver, and that anyway she'd done nothing wrong.

Then the answerphone exploded. 'Sam bloody Finch?' Holly's voice picked up more speed and outrage with every word. 'How come he keeps popping up everywhere? Rachel called me last night. Emily told her she'd met *this new man*! And Rachel's worried, even though Emily then said she was joking. Emily swears that there's nothing going on, but Rachel thinks there is ... There was definitely something special about the way she was talking about Sam. And if that's true, I am worried. Did you hear he gave her a rose? Only he hadn't bought it he'd *grown* it, no, even better, he'd *bred* it. Can you believe it?' There was a pause, then, 'Oh, bloody hell, Caitlin, just call me. Call me back.' And finally Holly hung up.

Caitlin opened a drawer and took out a dessertspoon, then opened the fridge door. Inside was a bowl of chocolate mousse she'd made for the night before but, after what had happened between her and Oliver, she hadn't had the stomach for chocolate mousse.

She made herself a mug of coffee and took it and the mousse back to her bedroom. She had done nothing bad – it was just a kiss – but if she told the others about it they were sure to think she had behaved true to form and that there was much more that she wasn't telling them. And then they would feel responsible for Emily, like they always did, and they would pull Emily from the scene of danger, make it clear to her that Oliver wasn't the man for her.

But whether or not Oliver was the one for Emily or not – and after last night she had to admit she'd begun to think not – Caitlin knew that what was still important was that Emily believed he *was* the one for her, and that that was the problem that needed to be resolved one way or the other. Somehow Emily was going to have to get closer to him before she could move away. And Caitlin did not want to give up on Emily just yet. Somehow she knew Oliver's eyes would soon be opened to Emily's charms. It wasn't that he *couldn't* fancy her, he'd proved he could do that eight years earlier, it was simply that he was blinded by what she represented rather than who she really was.

But if she didn't tell the others about what happened last night, she'd be keeping a secret from them and she didn't want that either.

And then she considered what in fact there was to tell. Yes, Oliver had kissed her, but so briefly that it barely counted and certainly it hadn't been a kiss she'd invited or even very much enjoyed. In which case, surely she was free to put it out of her mind, put *him* out of her mind. She was Emily's fairy godmother, after all. She was orchestrating a fine romance. The fact that she herself had briefly fancied Prince Charming wasn't the point. And briefly fancied was all that it was, because although she was a sucker for Oliver's kind of sleepy, lazy sexiness, when she'd realized she might have been seen by Leon it provoked a far greater reaction inside her. It had taken her aback, the awful fear that she might lose him, and the urge to put things right between them was still there, very strong.

She reached across for the telephone but instead of calling Holly back, she called Leon.

'Are you alone?' Leon asked pointedly.

'Of course I am. Whatever you think you saw last night didn't happen, you know. It matters to me that you believe me.'

'I do believe you. But, for what it's worth, I didn't like Oliver. Why did you invite him?'

'Complicated reasons.'

'Keep him away from Emily.'

'You're only saying that because you want her for yourself.'

'No, I don't actually,' he said mildly. 'I'd rather have you. I was looking after her.'

'It didn't look like that.'

'It didn't look like you were pushing Oliver away either.'

'I did. He kissed me. I didn't kiss him. I stopped him.'

'Actually I believe you.'

'So why didn't you tell me that last night?'

'Because I was pissed off. I wanted to go home.'

'Leon.'

'But I could come and see you now, if you want to talk about it.'

She knew how Leon hated weekends, forced to confront the fact that he had no plans. She imagined him at his breakfast table in his white and chrome kitchen, drinking coffee and reading the *FT*, sitting in pressed jeans with a belt and a stripy Thomas Pink shirt.

'Yes please.' It was what she'd wanted him to say. It was why she'd rung in the first place. 'I'll be waiting.'

Emily rang Holly as soon as she thought it was OK. Saturday morning, about ten seemed like a civilized enough hour.

'About the skiing . . .' she said nervously.

'Don't talk to me about skiing. Tell me about Caitlin's party! How was it? Did you survive?'

'She was lovely,' Emily said. Then hurried on, 'She was just as you'd said she'd be. I have to talk to you about the skiing, it's important. I can't come.' She wanted to say her bit before Holly started arguing with her. 'I've been thinking.'

'Oh yes?'

'How I've got to grab what I want and go for it. Everyone keeps telling me I should. And I want my shop, Saltwater. Now. I need to get started. I hate not working like this, not doing anything. I've got to take a risk, and Saltwater is something I've always wanted to do. So I'm going to say no to your kind and generous offer and I'm going to start setting it up right away. I'm going back to Cornwall tomorrow.'

'You *are* coming skiing.'

'I'm sorry?'

'You are coming skiing. With Oliver and me and Caitlin and Leon. I've booked the tickets, you're not getting out of it.'

'But, Holly, I can't.' Emily knew that she had to explain some more but she couldn't face telling Holly the truth, that it had all gone so badly with Oliver the night before that she couldn't face the thought of going skiing with him.

'You've got to come to keep me company. You know Rachel and Jo-Jo can't come. How will I survive Leon and Caitlin without you?'

'But I have to stop everything sliding past me,' Emily explained. 'I've got to take charge of my life. Which means I shouldn't be going on holiday. I should be in Cornwall, checking out sites, finding stock, working out how much money I need from the bank, drawing up business plans, maybe finding an investor.'

'Emily, tell me what happened last night,' Holly urged gently, knowing that Emily's change of heart was nothing to do with Saltwater at all. 'What's changed your mind?'

Emily hesitated. 'It was something Rachel said. It was before I got to Caitlin's. She told me how I had to go after what I wanted, even if it all went wrong. That it was better to have thrown myself in than stayed on the side.'

'Are you sure she was talking about Saltwater?'

'It doesn't matter. The same advice applies for everything, doesn't it?'

'I don't know about that.' Holly paused. 'But what I do know,' she went on with renewed determination, 'is that you are still coming skiing.' Emily could deal with Saltwater afterwards. She had to come skiing.

Emily had been so sure she was going to win this one, but Holly, mild and gentle as she usually was, went into four-wheel drive when she was after something she really wanted.

'It's such a short time. Only the Thursday to the Tuesday after Easter. Tell Arthur you'll see him after that.'

'Yes, Holly,' Emily said, meekly giving in because she owed it to Holly, especially if Holly had bought the tickets.

'Good. Thank you. And was it fun last night? Did you talk to Oliver? Has he changed at all?'

'No, still the same. I hardly talked to him. I spent most of the evening washing up with Leon.'

'Why? Not because Caitlin asked you to?'

'Not at all. It just ended up that way.'

Emily didn't elaborate. At that moment the evening was not one she wanted to think about.

When you've had people around for supper the night before and you've woken once and had plenty of time to remember how much you drank and smoked and how you ended the evening kissing the one guy in the world you shouldn't under any circumstances kiss like that, and then you've fallen back into bed and into guiltless sleep, the last thing you want is to be woken up again half an hour later.

Caitlin let the phone ring six times, then reached across to her bedside table and picked it up.

'Hello, Holly,' she said.

'You guessed!'

'You're like an alarm clock.'

'So you did hear me ringing earlier?'

'No, I was asleep.'

'So tell me. How did it go?'

'We all got on extremely well.'

'And?'

'And what else do you expect? We were in my flat, not in some sauna together.'

'Did he talk to her? I spoke to Emily and she sounded rather down.'

'The point was to reintroduce them to each other and that's what I did. But they didn't exactly stick together like glue.'

'She's definitely keen on him. I'm sure that's why she's miserable.'

'So you don't think we need to worry about Sam?'

'Not at all. There's nothing going on there.'

Holly could detect something vulnerable in Caitlin's voice. 'Are you OK?'

'I'm fine.'

'It was great you organized that for Emily.'

'Yes.'

'Want to come around this evening?'

'Yes, please.'

Caitlin was overcome with a mad impulse to confess, to explain how hard it had been to reject Oliver. But she didn't say it.

'I'll get Jo-Jo and Rachel around too. They're dying to hear how it went and we can plan phase two.'

'Oliver might not want to come skiing,' Caitlin blurted out.

'I didn't know you were going to ask him.'

'I didn't either. But it was the right time and it came out of my mouth and he said yes. And then later on . . . I think he might have changed his mind.'

Holly heaved a sigh. 'I can't believe I've just been on the phone making sure Emily comes. She tried to get out of it too.'

'Don't worry. We'll get him.'

'You don't sound so enthusiastic about the idea now.'

'He wasn't quite like I remembered. He's different without Nessa.'

'Are you saying we shouldn't like him any more?'

'Yes. No, no, no. And if it's yes it's more important than ever that Emily sees him for what he is and gets him out of her system. I'm just saying, I don't know him as well as I thought. And it's going to be hard. Because Oliver's oblivious to her and Emily's too shy to make herself noticed. She's so different when she's with him. She spent half the evening hiding in my bedroom and the other half hiding in the kitchen, talking to Leon, for God's sake. It made me wonder if we shouldn't be more hands-on. Maybe not spell it out for Oliver, but hint a little, make him think about her. We certainly need to set them up together with no distractions and without her suspecting what's going on. This has all got to feel natural. That's why the skiing is so perfect. You know, high up and alone on long and winding chairlifts. We need to find places where it's impossible for them to get away from each other. That was the problem last night: there's no room here where Leon and I could have left them.'

'I think you should invite Oliver again,' Holly decided. 'You're more persuasive than me and you know him better. Be as persuasive as you can. Don't take no for an answer. And if we're sure that Sam's no threat, ask him too. He's an old friend of Oliver's, it might make Oliver come.'

'How long have we got?'

'We've got ten days.'

12

There was something so dazzling about Emily that Sam was damned if he was going to let Oliver have a clear run at her for a second time. Fate had conspired to bring Emily back into his life, and he didn't want to let her go without giving himself one more decent chance . . .

And so he started to put out word that he was looking for a shop, on behalf of a friend. A small place in a town centre, ideally in St Brides. Shops came up on the estate agents' books regularly enough, but he figured that if he could find one for Emily privately and then call her about it, she would have to come back to Cornwall to see it and, if she had any feelings for him at all, she would surely take the opportunity to see him again? Particularly if it had been he who introduced her to the shop in the first place?

And if she did come back to St Brides and she did see him again, and if the shop was right for her, she would then move in somewhere nearby. And then he'd have her on his doorstep, and far enough away from Oliver to be able to take his time with her.

Within a week Bethany Nightingale, one of the employees at Trevissey, caught up with him in the staff canteen to tell him that her sister was retiring after thirty years and that she had a shop in St Brides that she was looking to lease out rather than sell because she was going to live in the flat above, and it seemed that fate was moving into action on Sam's behalf once more.

He quizzed Bethany and found out that the shop had been unofficially on the market for a month. They were both surprised nobody had snapped it up. He wondered how much rent it would be, but Bethany didn't know. Still, he presumed that Emily had an idea of what she was letting herself in for. The fact that it hadn't been snapped up meant she might be able to get it for a good price. The fact that it was in Humble Street, the prettiest shopping street in St Brides, in the oldest part of the town and close to the seafront, was bound to appeal to her.

But it was also one of the busiest weeks of the year at Trevissey. Although the gardens themselves were still quiet, March and April were the months when the trade – not just the garden centres and other nurseries that stocked Thomas Finch roses, but the town planners, the landscape gardeners, anyone developing a garden on a large scale – wanted their stock delivered. It was still early enough in the year for the plants to have time to settle into their new soil before the summer. Some would even manage to flower. Therefore hundreds of plants were leaving the Trevissey nurseries every day. Much as Sam was itching to drive into St Brides and see the shop, he had to wait until the next day before he got the chance.

He parked in St Brides and, passing an estate agents on the way to Humble Street, he stopped and glanced quickly at what else was available. There was a photograph of another shop for rent, a new instruction, only posted that day. It was only a couple of streets from where he stood, a pretty-looking shop in Flass Street. Sam went inside and grabbed the details. Surely one of the two would tempt her.

When he set eyes on 13 Humble Street, the faded black awning still carrying the shop's name, Jack and Jill, his heart sank. It was about as shabby and grim and unappealing as it was possible to be. Like the shop on Flass Street, this one also had a pink-painted front, but that was where the similarities ended. The front of number 13 was streaked with something dirty and yellow and whereas the Flass Street property had a wide, inviting front window, the windows of number 13 were divided into small rectangular panes, several of which had round impenetrable whorls in the middle of them that couldn't exactly have been good for business.

When he cupped his hand to his eyes and peered in, it didn't get any better. He could make out a gloomy, empty, brown-painted interior. Along one wall were fitted shelves from floor to ceiling, one or two of which had been pulled away from the wall, and at the back a red velvet curtain hung crookedly from a circular curtain rail. It was much wider at the front than at the back, a poky and awkward shape. As far as Sam could see, there were a few coat-hangers lying on the floor and nothing else, nothing inside of any use or salvage value, certainly nothing that was tempting in any way at all.

For a moment he thought about getting the key and giving it a good clean and a lick of paint before Emily came to see it, even considered asking Jennifer to get to work on it for him, but he knew he couldn't, that Emily would have to see it as it was.

When it came to it, he simply called her to tell her about both properties, knowing that he had to leave her to make her own decision. It was five days since he'd last seen her. She wasn't in so he left her a message.

Ten minutes after Sam called, the Williams Office also left a message on Emily's answer phone, ringing to put off her interview until the following week. Emily, however, had left the house early to be in good time for her first temping job in nearly five years so didn't hear either message until she got home.

Setting off across London for her first morning at Bunyan Graphic Design brought back all sorts of horrible temping memories. First time around, Emily had been fresh out of university and had arrived at the offices of each unlucky employer with her heart in her mouth, knowing she was horrendously ill-equipped with snail-slow typing and no office experience whatever. Of course her agency knew this too but had sent her out anyway, into the world of temperamental office machinery and nervy, aggressive employers who had less than no time to show her the ropes.

This time she turned into a tiny dead-end road off Fulham High Street and found she was almost looking forward to the day ahead. Five years on, she was experienced, efficient, cool in a crisis, could type like a concert pianist and felt that this employer was lucky to get her.

Nice Work, her recruitment agency, had thought so too and had promised her this was a *fabulous* job, with a boss who was *a great laugh*, who headed up a *superb* graphic-design team.

Even so, Emily walked into the office at ten past nine, and walked out, never to return, in time for lunch.

From the moment she sat down at her desk in the corner of the seventh floor, the tension and aggression between the three account executives who were supposed to be sharing her was loud and clear. The fact that they were too busy fighting to pay her any attention wasn't a problem – if anything, it had been quite funny at first, sitting at her empty desk with nothing to do while they ripped each other's throats out. But then it became clear that when they weren't fighting between themselves they were turning on one junior employee who cowered at her desk and reminded Emily so much of herself that she couldn't bear to stay. To sit there, in an environment that she'd made such an effort to leave, seemed too awful for words. So she called Nice Work to tell them what she was about to do. Then she left, but not before she'd spent half an hour unsuccessfully trying to persuade the poor girl to do the same.

Setting off down the High Street again, she experienced not the slightest concern for the mail-order bunk-bed brochure, *Going on Top*, that was not now going to be *put to bed* that evening as the superb design team had been demanding. Instead she defiantly swung her bag over her shoulder and ran down the steps to the underground.

*

So Sam caught her at just the right time with his message about the two shops.

She leant against the breakfast bar in her kitchen, still in her coat, and pressed play. *Hello, Emily. It's Sam.* Hearing his voice made her smile. First he told her about the shop on Flass Street, and from his description Emily recognized it straight away as the one she had been into with Arthur. The morose woman behind the till had obviously had enough. Emily felt very sorry for her and knew straight away that there was no conceivable way that she would take on *that* shop.

Then Sam mentioned the shop in Humble Street. *It used to be a children's clothes shop called Jack and Jill. It's a dump. But I think you could transform it.* But Emily wasn't listening any more. She'd switched off at the mention of the name Jack and Jill and she felt her heart squeeze as the intensity of her memories overwhelmed her.

Two stone steps, then cautiously open the door. The bell rings, warning Mrs Maddox that she has a customer and acting like a starting pistol for Emily, propelling her across the room to the depths of the shop, to the back rail, so tightly stuffed with beautiful clothes that she has to fight them free in order to look at them.

When Emily was thirteen, Jack and Jill was the best thing about coming to Cornwall. Hitting the spot at a time when she was old enough to care desperately about what she wore, yet still young enough to want to sleep the night in a new pair of Jack and Jill maroon corduroy trousers because she couldn't bear to take them off.

But now, remembering those visits to the shop, it wasn't

the clothes that Emily recalled. It was being with her mother.

She remembered the warmth in her stomach as she walked out from behind the red velvet curtain of the changing room and caught rare approval in her mother's eyes. There was an intimacy between them when they shopped together that they hadn't found at any other time. Why it was so, Emily wasn't sure, but she remembered being aware, even then, that her mother was proud of her when they shopped together, liked the way she looked in the clothes. It was through shopping and almost only through shopping that she found pleasure in the company of her tall, pretty daughter.

As Emily played Sam's message again, she could still hear her mother's voice from outside the changing room, urging her to be quick. She could feel the pressure on her fingertips as she fiddled to push buttons through stiff new buttonholes, the breathless rush to do up zips and retie her shoes. And she remembered the wonderful high as she left the shop, striding away at her mother's side, both of them happy, the weight of a shiny red Jack and Jill bag swinging from her hand.

She rang Sam back but missed him and left a gushing message of thanks on his answerphone. And then, immediately, she called Arthur in great excitement to tell him about the shop and that, as she had no reason not to come straight back to St Brides that day, she would aim to catch the seven-thirty train. And could he be there to pick her up?

Arthur sounded tentatively optimistic about the shop,

but Emily was in such a state of exhilaration and focused energy that he decided to save his concerns for when they were talking face to face. He felt he had roles to play – as cautious solicitor and steady older brother he was duty-bound not to be too enthusiastic – but the reality was that he knew she could do it, and the prospect of Emily moving to St Brides was a fantastic one.

Once on the train, Emily finally had time to think. And what she thought about was less the running of the shop than how it could be possible that she, who was so cautious, so controlled, so safe, could be so wholeheartedly embracing such a risky proposition.

Look at me! she wanted to demand of Caitlin and Holly and Jo-Jo, who laughed at her inability to take the plunge or to stick her neck out. She knew that that was how they thought of her, and how they explained why she hadn't slept with anyone. *Watch me now! When it's the right thing to do, look how I can go for it. Look how I can follow my instincts with no hesitation at all.* But she hadn't gone for it, she reminded herself, she was just thinking about going for it. So far her money was still safe and she'd made no commitment of any kind.

Her savings would not be enough to buy her opening stock. She would have to go to the bank with a business plan. And she wondered whether Mrs Maddox, who was planning on retiring to the flat upstairs, and keeping the shop on as an investment, might take the rent in arrears. She wondered too whether she might have to lease the shop from Mrs Maddox for years or whether she could play it more gradually, take it for just six months at a time.

How quickly would she have to decide? For as long as she could remember, Saltwater had been a game, like playing fantasy shopkeeping, her stock picked on a whim and discarded just as easily. Not so now.

The next morning, Emily was alone as she walked up to 13 Humble Street, ten minutes before Mrs Maddox had agreed to join her with the key. Alone, because Emily's sudden arrival hadn't left Arthur with enough time to organize a morning out of his office.

Standing there on the step, after only the briefest of looks through the window, Emily was already sure that if she possibly could afford it, and if she was going to set up the shop anywhere, she wanted it to be here.

Where Sam saw cramped, she saw cosy. Where he saw a crooked interior and too low a ceiling, she saw character. Where he saw grubby walls, she saw paintbrushes and fresh white paint. It was so sweet and so woebegone and appealed to her far more than the well-maintained shop on Flass Street which she'd looked around with Arthur the last time she was in St Brides.

So when, ten minutes late, a sweaty and flustered Mrs Maddox turned the corner into Humble Street and saw Emily standing there on the top step, she smiled. From the way that Emily was waiting for her, hands in her pockets, Mrs Maddox knew exactly what she had decided.

It had been nearly ten years since she had last seen Emily. If Emily hadn't reintroduced herself, she would never have recognized her. But Emily remembered Mrs Maddox as well as if she'd seen her ten days ago.

While waiting for Mrs Maddox to unlock the door, Emily felt the same flutter of expectation that she'd always felt upon entering this shop. Mrs Maddox looked the same as ever, and had been one of those fierce shopkeepers permanently on the lookout for sticky faces and dirty fingers. She had several times made clear her disapproval of the amount Emily's mother spent on her. Now Emily saw a tired, lined woman in her early sixties, wearing the same brave red lipstick and still with an air of steely purpose about her, but no longer someone to be afraid of.

After Mrs Maddox had shown her around, they stood outside on the step in the cold bright sun and talked. There seemed little point in Emily disguising her enthusiasm. Mrs Maddox seemed to know from the start that she was keen, but, even so, she agreed that Emily could take a little more time to decide how she wanted to proceed, to go over her finances again with real figures rather than guesses, and to be sure she knew what she was doing. *But it's a very fair price so don't think I'll wait for ever.*

The rent was £8,000 per year, which was a little less than Emily had expected, and Mrs Maddox was prepared to take it in arrears, at least for the first six months, in order to help Emily get herself up and running. Any repairs or maintenance work would be the responsibility of Mrs Maddox, who would indeed be continuing to live above the shop. Any cosmetic refurbishment would be Emily's responsibility. Not, Mrs Maddox insisted, that Emily would be wanting to do any of that. The lighting worked perfectly well – Mrs Maddox had flicked a switch to prove it. Most of the shelves were good and solid – she had leaned her bulk upon one of them to demonstrate – and she would take care of the few that needed securing. Emily decided this wasn't the best moment to say that new lighting and shelving would be her first priorities.

She walked away from Humble Street overwhelmed with the need to talk to someone about it all. But it wasn't Sam she called but Arthur.

She didn't call Sam until she was back in London that night. She thanked him for tipping her off about the shops and told him how much she had liked Jack and Jill, how excited she was, how determined she was to make it work, how pleased she was that she would have him living nearby.

But while Emily enthused, Sam was thinking, *She came here and didn't she come to see me*, and as he took it in something shifted inside him, letting go. Emily hadn't come to see him. She hadn't noticed him at sixteen and she wasn't interested in him now and he realized then that she never would be.

And Sam was surprised at how easy he found it to put her aside in his mind. He was too confident and too happy to doggedly hold a torch for someone who was so completely blind to him. He still thought Emily was extraordinary. He still adored her quirkiness and vulnerability and was uplifted by her and transported by her loveliness. If he saw her again, no doubt he'd still fancy her rotten. But without any encouragement, without any sign from her that she had even noticed him, even when they were alone together, he told himself there was no point in thinking about her. He imagined that it would take only a couple of days before he would be able to put Emily out of his mind completely.

But then, before that couple of days came and went he had a call from Holly. Embarrassed at first, uncertain whether he'd think her invitation was a bit presumptuous, seeing as she didn't know him very well, she explained they had a space on their skiing holiday and asked whether he'd like to join them over Easter. And when she told him exactly who else would be there, he saw that he was being given one more chance to get it right. That it would be crunch time. Him or Oliver.

13

They were leaving for Magine on the Thursday before Easter and returning the Tuesday after.

Snow reports warned that it was warm enough to sunbathe and that mountain flowers were appearing on the lower slopes, but Magine was linked by a high-speed cable car to the massive Trois Vallées, with its glacier and year-round skiing so Holly could tell the others that the skiing was on, whatever the weather.

Caitlin wouldn't have minded if there was no snow at all. She could ski well enough but it had never been high on her list of favourite activities. She went to Magine because she loved Holly's chalet and because the men were gorgeous, and the warmer the weather the better. On really hot days she sunbathed at the mountain cafés in her bikini.

Like Emily, she'd been invited by Holly twice before, but either by accident or design, Caitlin wasn't sure which it was, she'd never crossed over with Emily before.

At six thirty on the Thursday evening, Emily, Holly and Caitlin were standing in Departures at Heathrow Airport, waiting for Leon and Sam to join them, and for Oliver to return to them. Oliver had arrived five minutes earlier, parked his bags and instantly disappeared again.

'Passport-tickets-money, passport-tickets-money,' Emily muttered to herself over and over again, until, with a sigh, Holly snatched her ticket from her with a red-leather-gloved hand.

'You, me . . .' She showed Emily the fan of tickets in her hand and Emily nodded. 'Sam, Leon, Caitlin and Oliver.' Emily nodded again. 'Watch,' Holly told her, 'they're all going in here –' she tucked them into a matching red leather handbag – 'where they will be safe.' She dropped her voice. 'Now, do you want me to take your passport?'

Emily shook her head. 'And don't let Caitlin hear you say that or I'll be crucified. She thinks you watch over me too closely, you know.'

Then Leon appeared through the revolving doors wearing a large green tweed coat and fur hat with floppy earmuffs. He caught sight of Holly, Emily and Caitlin and beamed his way towards them.

Caitlin stared at him pitilessly. Happy toad, off on his holidays, with his puffed-out chest and his dapper clothes. All that was missing was a silver-topped cane and a cravat – but perhaps he would get lucky in the airside branch of Aquascutum. She thanked God that Oliver had disappeared, wasn't watching Leon's arrival and laughing at her.

'Isn't this fun, fun, fun?' Leon said, clutching her to him and kissing her exuberantly. Seeing the look in Caitlin's eye he then held her away. 'And you, my dearest, are you happy to see me too?'

Caitlin laughed, despite herself, took his fat cheeks in her slim hands, and kissed him hard on the lips, leaving him with a look of stunned delight. 'Yes, I am. Very happy to see you.'

Keeping one arm around Caitlin, Leon kissed Emily and Holly.

'Are the others here?' he asked.

'All but Sam,' said Emily. 'And we've managed to lose Oliver.'

'Look after my bags for me and I'll go and find him,' said Caitlin. 'Come on, Holly, come with me,' she added throwing Holly a look that said don't argue about it. 'And look out for Sam, too. He'll be here any minute,' she called back to Emily over her shoulder.

The two of them walked off together through the terminal, Caitlin in a soft black leather jacket and jeans, Holly in a flowing green fur-lined cape. 'What is it?' Holly asked, turning to her.

Caitlin took her arm. 'I wanted to say that I've got a good feeling about this holiday. I think it's going to be fun.' She paused. 'And I wanted to say make sure that you put Oliver and Emily next door to each other . . . And I also wanted to say – ' she stopped, bit her lip, then looked at Holly and gave her a rather uncertain smile – 'am I mad or is Leon quite cute? In his own cuddly Kermit-y kind of way.'

'If you're going to stick with him you're going to have to stop being so horrible about him.'

'Really? Do I have to?'

Holly nodded. 'Yes, because he's sweet. I really think he is. And *very* good for you, so much better than the guys you usually end up with.'

And then, just as Caitlin was about to reply, they both caught sight of Oliver at the same time. He was some distance away but clearly on his way back to them, with one hand pushing a heavily laden trolley and a girl swinging from the other. When he caught sight of Holly and Caitlin he waved, looking very pleased with himself.

The girl was wearing a dark green denim jacket and in Caitlin's opinion was way too thin and way too pretty, with bouncy, shoulder-length hair and very long legs in her long straight jeans. At first it seemed that she was coming towards them reluctantly, but Caitlin quickly realized, watching the way she was laughing and only half-heartedly protesting, that she was putting it on and was really loving every second of being pulled along by him. 'Look at him,' Caitlin murmured to Holly. 'Look at how he's talking to her. No wonder everyone falls in love with him.'

As they drew nearer, Oliver leant close to the girl to point out Caitlin and Holly and Caitlin watched her look vacantly around and then catch her eye.

In the circumstances Caitlin was not about to pussyfoot around with a polite smile back. She gave the girl a put-him-down-or-you-die look and watched her pull up in surprise, then whisper something to Oliver.

'No, darling. That was Medusa,' Oliver replied, pulling the trolley to an unsteady halt beside Caitlin. 'This is Caitlin with her friend Holly.'

Then he introduced her to them both. 'This is Meribel. She's on our flight to Geneva.'

'Aren't you in the wrong place?' said Caitlin with a polite smile. 'Aren't you much closer to Lyon?'

215

Meribel gave a weary laugh. 'And I haven't heard that one before,' she said.

Behind Holly and Caitlin, Oliver caught sight of Leon and Emily coming over to join them and then his smile of relief broadened still further when he saw Sam appearing behind Emily, a hold-all over one shoulder. 'Sam! Great to see you,' he called out. 'Everyone, this is Meribel.'

Holly moved to welcome Sam. Caitlin kept her eyes fixed on Meribel.

'Oliver and I know each other through my sister,' Meribel explained to her, seemingly immune to the daggers in her eyes. Then she nudged Oliver playfully in the ribs. 'My sister who knows him rather better than I do.'

Oliver turned to the others. 'Meribel's on her own and I was saying that she should check in with us, so we can all sit together on the plane.'

Meribel fumbled in a fringed green suede shoulder bag and pulled out her ticket.

'And I was saying I wasn't even sure I was on the same flight.'

What, Caitlin raged, the *hell* did Oliver think he was *doing*?

'Good idea,' said Sam, standing very close beside Emily. 'Let's hope you are.'

'Shall I look at that ticket,' Caitlin suggested to Meribel, practically snatching it out of her hand. 'What's your flight number?' she demanded. 'What's your departure time?' She scanned the ticket quickly. 'Oh, what a shame, that's not going to work at all, you're leaving much later than we are.'

'Absolutely no problem,' Meribel said with an acid look at Caitlin. 'I've got some shopping to do. You guys go and check in without me.'

'Thanks,' Caitlin snapped. She knew she was being obnoxious, but Meribel was just poisonous and the sort of disastrous diversion they did not need. She turned to Oliver and forced a smile. 'If you hadn't disappeared, we'd have gone through already. You'll have no time to buy me that scent you promised me.'

'She's lying,' Oliver told Meribel. 'And Caitlin,' he added, 'Sam only arrived two minutes ago. I was watching out for him.'

'I'm a nervous passenger,' Caitlin joked, happy now that the threat had been disarmed.

'Then go, before you get your knickers into even more of a twist,' Meribel told her with a little laugh. 'Good to see you, Oliver.'

He kissed her goodbye. 'And you must say hi to Val for me.'

Holly glanced across at Caitlin, and Emily who'd heard him too, bit her lip and grinned at the two of them.

'Which "Val" would her sister be, then?' Caitlin asked Oliver, matching strides through passport control and on into the departure lounge. 'Val d'Isère? Val Thorens? They don't have quite the same ring as Meribel, do they?'

Listening to her, as she strode along in front of them,

Sam at her side, Emily smiled at Caitlin's words. Ahead of her Leon and Holly were already sliding their bags through the security checks and she slipped her handbag off her shoulder ready to do the same.

'And exactly when did you get to know Val so well?' she heard Caitlin ask then. 'I thought Nessa had been the only woman in your life for the past five years.'

'I can't help what you thought,' said Oliver.

'What?' Caitlin exclaimed. 'That is *news*. Are you saying you weren't faithful to Nessa?'

'More or less. One or two tiny lapses of concentration. Meribel's sister was one of them.'

'I don't believe it.' Caitlin laughed. 'So much for Mr Squeaky Clean!'

He sounded defensive. 'Speak for yourself. Don't tell me you've never done that.'

'I haven't! I've never two-timed anybody.'

If it was hard for Caitlin to take in, for Emily it was incomprehensible. Her first reaction was to feel as stunned and dismayed as if he'd been unfaithful to her, not to Nessa. Oliver did not do such things. Not Oliver. He was her champion, honourable and loyal. She wanted to turn around to him and force him to stop walking, make him stand still, look her in the eye and tell her it was all a big joke, that he was saying it to wind up Caitlin. Of course he wouldn't have been unfaithful to Nessa.

'Did Nessa find out?' Caitlin asked.

'She did about the second one. Not about Meribel's sister.'

'Oliver, I'm so surprised.'

'It happens. Nessa and I had been on the rocks a while.'

He shrugged. 'I wouldn't have done it otherwise. Change the subject, you're making me feel guilty.'

'So who was she? Who was the second girl?'

'Just a girl. No one you know. Stop talking about it, it was no big deal. I want to know why you were being so horrible to Meribel. Why did I feel I was being called to heel?'

'Because that's exactly what I was doing,' Caitlin told him. 'I wanted to remind who you'd come on holiday with because you looked as if you might have been about to forget. If you meet up with other people, make arrangements to see them instead of us – people like Meribel – Holly will think you're using her place like a hotel.' Caitlin knew she was taking Holly's name in vain, that Holly wouldn't ever think such a thing.

'Don't be ridiculous,' Oliver replied, then added so quietly that Sam and Emily had no chance of hearing him, 'I think it's because you know as well as I do that you and Leon are not going to last the holiday.'

Caitlin glared back at him. 'We're getting on better than ever.'

'Of course you are. But you were jealous of Meribel.'

'No I was not,' Caitlin whispered furiously. She looked away, watching Emily striding along ahead of them. *I wasn't jealous for myself!* Caitlin nearly said it aloud. *I was jealous on behalf of Emily. Not that you deserve her any more.*

They all made their way through the various security checks to their departure gate, whereupon Caitlin immediately dragged Leon away from the others and off towards the shops, hoping she might persuade him to spend some money on her.

Following her lead, Holly then cornered Sam, sat him down and started to tell him all about the chalet, how her uncle Richard Foy had bought it in 1960, before there were even any chairlifts in Magine. She drew out the story, explaining how he'd had to walk up the mountain with his skis on his back and had managed just one run down in a day.

And Emily and Oliver looked around and found themselves left alone.

'How about a drink?' Oliver suggested. 'Caitlin's rushed us through here so damn fast we've at least an hour to kill. Let's celebrate the start of the holiday.'

'The bar?' Emily suggested.

'Or shall we buy a bottle of champagne in duty-free and go and find some corner to drink it in?'

'Let's go to the bar.'

'You're right. We could end up missing the plane, couldn't we?'

Could they? Emily wasn't sure what he meant, but knew she wouldn't mind at all if it meant being left behind with Oliver.

In what she still thought of as duty-free, Caitlin peered around the shelves of cut-price cigarettes. They're alone, he's smiling at her, she's smiling at him, they're walking off together, he's taken her hand and she's moving closer, Caitlin noted with satisfaction.

Oliver held onto Emily's hand. For a few moments she was acutely conscious of it, hot and clammy in his, and then she made herself relax. After the non-event that was supper at Caitlin's, she was determined not to let this holiday become an endless agony over Oliver. She didn't know quite what she did expect of the holiday – there had, of course, been dreamy images of falling into his arms – but what she most wanted was to be relaxed around him again, certainly not to let him see the adoring, dumbstruck schoolgirl she felt she'd become. It seemed so unfair that all the confidence which had stood her in good stead for so long should vanish whenever she laid eyes on Oliver. It hadn't been this way when Nessa was on the scene. In the past Emily had had no problem talking to Oliver. Back then, she'd have been the one to throw an arm around his shoulders and suggest they went to the bar. But the moment she'd caught sight of him pushing his way through the doors into the terminal, a battered brown leather jacket slung over a shoulder, looking around for them – for her – then seeing her and giving her the most devastating smile in the world, she had collapsed inside in a heap of hopeless lust and confused love, and hadn't been able to pull herself together again afterwards. She hadn't liked what Oliver had admitted to Caitlin, had heard the warning that perhaps he wasn't all she thought he was, but it wasn't nearly enough to spoil the fact that she was alone with him now and that stretching ahead were four more days full of him.

During supper at Caitlin's, Emily had managed to talk to Oliver alone just once, an innocuous catching-up sort of conversation where he had told her about the split with Nessa and she had told him about leaving the Carrie

Piper Agency. She'd admitted that she'd done it only a week before, and he'd laughed and said exactly what she'd imagined he'd say. So you lied to Sam! And you promised, you *promised* me you were going to leave a year ago.

Now propped up in the bar against a little round table, with a vodka and tonic doing a good job of fortifying her, she was determined to move the conversation on. To be braver and bolder. But at first the conversation again stuck stubbornly to the mundane. She told him about Saltwater and her plans for moving to Cornwall. Even as she heard herself singing the praises of St Brides, she did wonder why she was telling him all this. What exactly she was hoping to achieve by emphasizing her desire to move a good three hundred miles away from London, from him. When she told him it was Sam who had found her a shop, his eyebrows shot up in surprise.

'Sam has found you a shop?' he repeated, for the first time sounding genuinely interested in what she was saying. 'Why did he do that?'

'But I might not go. I might stay in London,' she backtracked again. 'I'm not sure where I'm going or what I'm going to do.'

Oliver leaned in a little closer and stared into her eyes. Instantly Emily felt as if it was just the two of them alone together, as if the whole noisy airport had disappeared.

'How many times have you been back to Cornwall in the last two months?'

'I went to see a couple of properties up for rent. But I

222

only stayed one night.' Now he was making her feel defensive and she didn't know why.

'See Sam while you were there?'

'No. Why do you ask me that?'

'Anything you want to tell me?'

'What do you mean?'

'I wondered if my old friend might have been moving in on you.'

She shook her head emphatically. 'Of course not.' How could he have got it so wrong?

'Trevissey is wonderful, isn't it?' Oliver moved seamlessly on and Emily was left wondering if she'd imagined it, the flare of interest in his face. 'When I was there a couple of years ago I had a long conversation with Sam's father. He was picking my brains about the best way to get Sam home. He said that Sam was a genius and that it was a complete waste him being anywhere other than Trevissey, where he belonged. Don't you think that's sweet? That his dad said that about him?'

Emily nodded.

'As well as understanding all the technical stuff, apparently Sam has this incredible sense of colour. The gardens he's designed at Trevissey – ages ago, years before he went back permanently – are famous. People come from all over the country to see them. I read a piece about him in the paper saying how he clashes and mixes up his colours in this absolutely brilliant and original way.'

'I wish I'd seen Trevissey in the summer,' Emily said. 'But the way Sam described it, I almost did. It was as if it was real.'

'Make sure you do go back. You'll be blown away by what he's done ... OK, act normal,' he said, smiling broadly and looking over Emily's shoulder. 'Here he comes.'

Emily leapt back from Oliver, though she'd hardly been standing very close to him. What was worse, she could feel a giant blush burn her cheeks as soon as she caught Sam's eye.

'We were just talking about you,' Oliver told him as Sam threaded his way through the tables and joined them.

'Oh yes?'

'I was telling Emily about my last time at Trevissey.' Oliver turned back to Emily. 'What I hadn't got to was the bit about nearly breaking my back digging his rose beds for eight hours.' As he was speaking he was moving away from the table. 'Let me get you a drink, Sam,' he offered. 'What do you want?'

'A beer?' Sam suggested. 'Whatever you're having, thank you.' He took Oliver's place at the little round table. 'He did ask for it,' he told Emily.

'For what?'

'He did offer to dig up the rose beds. And of course he had to show us he could dig them up faster, harder, deeper than anybody else had ever done before.'

Emily laughed. 'That can't be so! Not Oliver.'

She had been a little concerned about how things would be between herself and Sam, whether there'd be awkward teenage embarrassment hanging over them despite the fact that nothing had happened that time in the kitchen at Trevissey, but she obviously wasn't a problem for Sam at all and she was relieved, even as a little part of her was the tiniest bit regretful too.

Emily thought how typical of Holly it was to invite someone whom she hardly knew skiing. As long as she had liked meeting them – and Holly had met Sam twice: once years ago and once at Oliver's welcome-home party – then she trusted that she would enjoy seeing them again. And for as long as Emily had known her, Holly had never been wrong. Her suppers, parties and holidays were always sprinkled with interesting new people as well as old friends. And so she hadn't been surprised to hear that Sam was coming skiing too.

'OK?' he asked.

'Sorry,' she laughed, shaking her head. 'I was in another world.'

'I'm sorry I interrupted you?' He raised his eyebrows at her. 'Was I in it too?'

'Bugger off, Sam!' But she was smiling back at him as she said it.

Another pause.

'Will you come shopping with me?' he asked. 'When I've drunk that beer Oliver's kindly fetching for me? I need to buy a present for my . . .'

She looked over to Oliver. He was paying the barman, and almost under the intensity of her gaze he turned and then waved at her. She waved back, unable to tear her eyes away.

'Emily . . .'

She forced herself to look back to Sam. 'Yes?'

Ever since the evening in the Pelican his words about

Oliver had been quietly repeating themselves in her head. And now she could see from his face he wanted to say them here again.

'Sam,' she cried. 'Don't tell me!'

He flinched. 'Present for my sister,' he said.

'There's nothing between Oliver and me. I wish there was, but he's not interested.'

He looked even more shocked. 'Oh, he will be. Give him a day or two. He's just slow to react. Once he realizes what's going on he'll be all over you.'

'And what's that supposed to mean?' she asked. 'What are you saying?'

'I'm saying I know Oliver. And I know that Oliver likes a challenge.'

'I thought you were his great friend. You shouldn't talk about him like that.'

'Oliver and I were great friends a long time ago. Not so much now.'

'Stop,' Emily hissed. 'He's coming back.'

And to her dismay Sam chose that moment to take her hand. 'Don't be cross. I promise, Emily, that I will shut up from now on. I will back off. What you choose to do is up to you.'

She slid her hand out of Sam's just as Oliver arrived back at the table, a vodka and tonic for Emily in one hand, a couple of bottles of beer in the other, and Emily caught his eye and knew that she hadn't done it quite fast enough.

'Beer for you.' Oliver dropped one down on the table in front of Sam, then chinked his bottle against Sam's. 'Cheers,' he said.

From then on Oliver seemed to freeze Emily out of the conversation, bombarding Sam with questions and anecdotes and jokes about their past together that deliberately excluded her, and even though Sam tried to steer Emily back in, she never lasted more than a couple of sentences. It was as if she was being punished. Eventually she gave up, knocked back her vodka and picked up her bag off the floor.

'I'm off. If you want me to help you choose that present for your sister, come and find me over there,' she told Sam, nodding towards the shops.

'No, stay with me, Sam,' she heard Oliver say as she moved away. 'We'll catch her up later.'

Emily headed first to WH Smith and bought Chris Manby's new novel, *Seven Sunny Days*, and then on into what used to be duty-free, where she wandered the aisles. In one of the mirrors, she caught sight of her pale washed-out face and she sloped over to the make-up section to sort herself out, brushing her cheeks with a bronzing powder before surreptitiously picking up a mascara and applying a coat, still thinking about what had happened in the bar. Why had Oliver suddenly become so unfriendly? He'd been like a big sulky kid. But what was it that was bothering him? Could he really have been jealous of her and Sam? What was he thinking?

'I don't know how you do that without a mirror,' Sam said behind her, making her jump.

'Ow!' she cried, wiping her eye, and what had been a tiny splodge streaked across her cheek.

'Isn't it great, what make-up can do?'

She rubbed at her face. 'Has it gone?'

'Not quite.' He came up close and gently rubbed her cheek with his thumb. 'Now it has. I'm sorry about that. And don't let Oliver upset you. He can be a moody bastard sometimes.'

'He doesn't fancy you, does he?' Emily asked. 'Perhaps that's what it was about?'

'No!' Sam shook his head. 'Definitely not. This has happened before. It's you he's bothered about, not me.'

'How do you know?'

Sam shook his head. 'Let's not talk about Oliver any more. Not now.'

'I agree,' Emily said, stepping back from him. 'We'll talk about Magine. You're going to love it, you know.'

'Hello, you two.' As Emily spoke, Caitlin's head popped up from the other side of the display cabinet.

'Oh, hi!' said Emily.

'What happened to Oliver?'

Sam couldn't miss the irritated disapproval in her voice. 'He's having a drink with Holly at the bar,' he said.

'But weren't you two having a drink together?' she asked Emily, ignoring Sam's explanation. 'Holly said she was going to buy some sunglasses. I thought she'd be here.'

'No,' said Sam. 'She's definitely at the bar.'

'Dammit,' said Caitlin, looking across to where Holly and Oliver were standing drinking together.

And then, belatedly, Sam understood everything. He saw what Caitlin was trying to orchestrate, the lengths she was going to in order to help things along between Emily and Oliver. He presumed Holly was in on it too, and even Leon perhaps. And what an irony it was that he, of all Oliver's friends, should have been invited along as a spectator.

On the plane, Emily slipped into her seat and watched Holly manoeuvre herself and a large hold-all down the aisle towards her, but when Holly reached Emily she smiled and then moved purposefully on, and Emily turned to see her take the seat two rows back, next to Sam.

So if Holly was sitting there, Emily thought, and Caitlin was going to sit beside Leon – she craned her neck to get a better look and saw Caitlin and Leon behind her, already sitting down across from Holly and Sam – then it had to be the man making his way down the aisle who was going to sit beside her.

Oliver swung his bag and his jacket up into the overhead locker, then slid around and into the space next to hers. When he turned to face her he was so close that she could breathe him in, feel the warmth of his body now pressed against hers.

'I was hoping you were going to be Caitlin or Holly,' she told him.

'I was hoping you were going to be Nicole Kidman.'

'Fair enough.' She grinned.

'At least you weren't wishing I was Sam.'

'Don't start on that again.' She looked away from him then, out of the window, seeing the great stiff wing of the plane there just in front of her, and a momentary burst of panic immediately overwhelmed the pleasure of sitting beside Oliver.

'I'm glad it's you and I'm very disappointed that you're not glad it's me. What do Caitlin and Holly do that I don't?' he asked the back of her head.

She looked at him. 'Sometimes they let me hold their hands while we're taking off. They let me bite them, if I get really scared.'

'Bite your own hand.'

'That's what I thought you'd say.'

He dropped his hand in her lap. 'There you are,' he said, obviously enjoying the way the conversation was going. 'How hard would you bite? Show me.'

They hadn't even taken off and instantly possibilities were fizzing between them. Emily had only a few seconds in which to make her choice: to go with it or to run away.

'Oliver!' She broke the moment, stumbling on his name, not knowing what else to say. She looked down at his hand in hers, at his stubby tanned fingers and short pink nails, and knew that the last thing she could do right then was pick up his hand and bite him.

Instead she lifted the hand off her lap and gave it back to him.

'So you've spared me?'

Then the engine noise increased and he saw her face drop in fear.

'Come here.' Instantly he put an arm around her and pulled her close. 'You *are* scared, aren't you?' She nodded. 'Poor baby. But you weren't nervous in the airport?'

'In the airport we were on safe, solid ground.' She sat back in her seat. Even Oliver's arm around her couldn't distract her now.

The plane started moving, taxiing out towards the runway.

'Go on, bite my fingers if you want to. Do whatever makes you feel better,' he offered.

She shook her head. 'I'll be OK. Talk to me about something. Distract me.'

'Sure.' He thought for a moment. 'So, which is the worst moment? Is it now? Or is it worse when we actually leave the ground?'

'Maybe you might choose a subject other than flying?'

'Oh, right, of course.'

Bing-bong went the intercom and the lights flickered off, then on, then off again. Emily watched the flaps lifting and dropping on her wing and she presumed final tests were being carried out, and that the wings were doing as they should. 'And nothing about how it's far more danger-ous to cross the road, or about how I'm more likely to win the lottery than be in an air crash,' she told him.

'If I was going to distract you, I'd be much more effective than that.'

The lights came on again and she closed her eyes and folded her hands in her lap.

He paused. 'I could say, Emily King, that in eight years, I've never stopped thinking about you.'

'Oh, God!' Against the tight restraining safety belt, Emily turned as far away from him as she could.

'Nice reaction! Thank you. Exactly what I was hoping for.'

'But, Oliver ...' she said looking back at him. She wanted to say she couldn't believe he'd said it, and said it so soon. That in eight years, she'd thought only about him, too.

'And stop smiling like that,' he told her. 'You're not allowed to smile. I'm being serious.'

'It's not a smile. My face has set like this. It's the shock.'

'Emily, don't joke.' He dropped his voice. 'I'm telling you, I adore you, every inch of you. I always have done. Ever since I met you and your rather enchanting pink bikini, three weeks before your seventeenth birthday. But I know you won't believe me. I know that you've forgotten about that time and that now you don't see me as anything other than a friend ...' He waited but she still said nothing. 'This is probably the last thing you want to hear, but I had to tell you.' He was sounding anxious now, pleading almost. 'Since I've been back, it's been driving me crazy not telling you. And now, having you beside me here, I've got no choice. I have to tell you how I feel. I didn't mean to, not straight away. I'm sorry.'

'Oliver, I can't believe it.' It came out as a whisper.

'No, let me speak,' he insisted. 'This is the first opportunity I've had to talk to you properly since I came home, so you have to listen. When I saw you at Caitlin's – I knew that you were going to be there – I thought I'd leave with at least a date to see you again, but it didn't happen. How could it not happen? We were in a one-bedroom flat and yet we never seemed to be in the same room at the same time long enough for me to say more than two words to you.'

'Oliver!' She was elated. She couldn't believe it. She turned to tell him so again, opened her mouth to say the words and saw clouds through the window opposite. And she realized that they'd taken off without her even noticing.

'Or I could say there's this book you might read called *Fear of Flying*,' he said more loudly, the gentleness and tenderness leaving his voice, 'which isn't actually about flying. We could talk about that. Have you read it? Do you know what it's about?'

'You bastard!' She turned back from the window and looked at him desperately. 'Don't think for one second that I believed any of that.'

'But, sweetheart, it worked! It worked! You weren't scared at all. You didn't even notice when we took off.'

'Oliver! You are horrible.' But her heartbeat was steadying again after its awful free-falling in shock and the only thing she was really thinking was *Thank God I didn't tell him how I feel.*

'Why am I?'

'Because you sounded so sincere. You went into so much detail. Remind me never to believe anything you say about anything ever again.'

'But are you OK? Now that we've taken off? You're not scared any more. You seem really pissed off now, so I presume that means you can't be scared at the same time?'

'I'm pissed off because you shouldn't joke about something like that.'

'Who said I was joking?'

Not again!

'I wasn't. You make me melt inside. It's the truth but you'll never believe me, will you?'

'Not now I won't.'

Teasing each other had been so much a part of their friendship in the past. She should have been ready for him – she would have been if everything else hadn't changed and got in the way. A year ago she'd never have been caught out so easily.

But even as the old familiarity returned, Emily was aware that something had shifted between them. Even joked about, Emily and Oliver *together* had been mentioned aloud and had therefore become a possibility, and there was a new awareness between them as a result. Twice she looked up from her book to find him watching her, and, looking down at his forearm and broad flat wrist – a Breitling now in place of the Swatch watch she remembered – and at her own narrow arm beside his, she thought how good they looked together, his arm and hers.

And she could tell that he was as aware as she was of his bare arm touching hers as they both read, or poured their drinks, or simply sat in silence. She leafed through the in-flight magazine, but didn't really read it at all. Arthur's voice was in her head, telling her that she was not to run away from this, that she had to stop worrying about what happened next. Let the future take whichever direction it chose. And listening to him again, she realized that it was panic that was making her feel this way, not a sudden distrust of Oliver. Enjoy the movement, she told herself. Have fun.

As they gathered around the carousel and waited for their baggage to reappear, Holly took Caitlin's arm and led her away from the others, ostensibly on a hunt to find a couple of trolleys. As soon as they were out of earshot of the others, Holly blurted out her confession to Caitlin. She'd had a rather difficult conversation with Sam.

'You didn't tell him!' Caitlin hissed. 'Not that we want to set Emily up with Oliver.'

'Yes, I did,' Holly admitted, shamefaced. 'And I told him why, too. But it wouldn't have made any difference if I hadn't. He'd already guessed everything anyway. I'd never have said anything to him but he was the one that brought the whole thing up.'

'And, let me guess – he thought it was a really good idea,' Caitlin said bitterly.

'Sadly, no.'

They found a line of trolleys and Holly felt in her pockets, found two euros and got one for each of them.

'Does he know she's never slept with anybody?' Caitlin asked.

'He does now,' Holly admitted.

'And I suppose he was really surprised?'

Holly shrugged. 'He was, a little, because it's unusual after all, but he seemed to cheer up after that, he said she must have had to withstand other Olivers before now, and what made me think this Oliver was going to be any different?'

'And you explained what made this Oliver different?'

'I did.'

'And what did Sam think about that?'

'He wondered how close she'd have to get before she realized she was wrong.'

'Glad he understands the problem.' They started to push the trolley back towards the others.

'Don't let's go back yet,' Caitlin stopped her. 'Wait with me here. We can see when the cases come through.'

'Walk back very slowly,' Holly suggested, 'or Emily will notice us talking and wonder what's up.'

'And what's up is that Sam obviously fancies Emily himself,' Caitlin said. 'Which is quite funny, in the circumstances.' She turned to Holly. 'What a good choice *he* was to bring on holiday.'

'I know, I know. Rachel did warn us—'

'That Emily liked him, *possibly* liked him. Not that he was besotted with her.'

'Maybe he's not.'

'But would it surprise you if he was?' Caitlin asked. 'Look at her.'

Fifty feet away, Emily was standing alone in the baggage-reclaim area. She had put on a pale blue wool coat and she stood tall and beautiful with her thick, wavy honey-golden hair tumbling down her back.

'If Sam's in love with her, he can't realize how hopeless it is,' Caitlin went on as they walked slowly back to join her. 'He didn't have much chance before Oliver appeared on the scene and he certainly doesn't have a hope now. The only chance for Sam is for Emily to get Oliver out of her system. Perhaps we should ask him to help us.'

'Which is sort of what I suggested to Sam.'

'You didn't! How did that go down?'

'Not brilliantly. He knows that Emily is infatuated with Oliver. But did not like the idea of us setting her up.'

'He wouldn't want Oliver to have first shot?'

'I suppose,' said Holly, 'and although of course we want things to work out for Oliver, I have to say I think it would be sweet if she ended up with Sam.'

'What else did Sam say on the flight, Holly?' Caitlin asked suspiciously. 'What's he done to you?'

'He asked how Emily would react if she knew what we were doing.'

'Perhaps a little badly?'

'Sam said that we shouldn't do something that we know she'd hate.'

'She'd go ballistic because she hates anyone controlling her. Who doesn't? But one day she'll be grateful to us. And, come to that, what *have* we done?' Caitlin stopped the trolley, pulling it to a sudden standstill. She didn't want to reach the others before they'd finished the conversation. 'Think about it. I've invited her around to supper and we've organized a skiing trip for her. Where's the big conspiracy? We're not talking *Dangerous Liaisons*. This happens all the time. It's what friends are for. You're getting distracted by her virginity again. And so is Sam.'

'Move,' Holly hissed, pushing the trolley forward again. 'She's watching us.'

Ahead of them, they could see that the carousel had started to turn. Caitlin caught Emily's eye and waved.

'We should talk about this again,' Holly said.

'I don't think so. What's there to say? What's done is done. Whatever happens next is not going to be because of us. It'll be down to Emily and Oliver. And Sam.'

In spite of the snail's pace, Caitlin and Holly had almost reached Emily.

'Sam said it was about the worst time to be doing this,' Holly added urgently. 'That now he's without Nessa, Oliver is determined to have some mindless fun.'

'He had some *fun* when he was with Nessa too.' Caitlin turned back to Holly. 'He told me about it on the way to the plane.'

'So what are we doing?' Holly asked, dismayed. 'Have we got him all wrong?'

'No, Holly!' Caitlin whispered, pulling a conspiratorial Holly-drives-me-mad face at Emily as she spoke. 'The point is that Emily needs to get him out of her system. If they end up having a one-night stand, so what?'

'But it would be so awful.'

'Perhaps it would be fun.'

14

As Holly had explained to Sam at Heathrow, Magine was a perfect hideaway, which was why he hadn't heard of it. A large village rather than a town and certainly not big enough to attract the tour operators, it had some lovely shops, just two hotels, one pizza house, one very good restaurant and less than a dozen commercially run chalets.

From the moment the six of them got onto the train it was clear that they need not worry about the snow. It was arriving with them, falling fast during their entire journey, so that when they arrived at their station, in a little town called Valorias, an hour and a half later, it was already deep. The taxis waiting to pick them up and take them on up the mountains to Magine had their snow chains on.

It was a further half-hour's drive up to the village. By the time they arrived, the snow had finally stopped falling but lay thick and even on the roofs of the buildings, and the few cars parked beside their chalet, had become soft vague bumps under a heavy white duvet of snow.

It was past midnight and Magine had shut down and gone to sleep, leaving a silence in the little village square.

Emily, who had been there twice before, looked around, at the little floodlit church in the corner, at the familiar pathways and shops and chalets. There was Holly's chalet, snow piled up against its grey stone walls, pale pink shutters all closed for the night. It had once been a barn and stood to one side of the village square, two minutes' walk from the cable car, one minute from the boulangerie. She took a deep breath of the clean, cold air and was hit by a childish rush of exuberance that made her grab hold of Sam, who was standing beside her and dance around him in her long blue coat.

'It's fantastic! It's so beautiful here,' Oliver agreed, catching her mood and spreading his arms to the sky, his breath rising up in a plume into the night sky. And watching him, Emily felt overwhelmingly happy, not just because he was there with her, but because they were all there with her. She realized she couldn't imagine having come with better friends. There was no tension between her and Sam, and even Caitlin was continuing to thaw faster than Magine in late April.

The chalet was warm and softly lit, homely rather than showy, with one huge main room with low beams and walls painted a washed-out china blue, rugs on the old stone floor and a couple of armchairs and two deep sofas pushed around a fireplace, the fire dying down in the hearth. Off this main room was a little kitchen. The fridge was already well stocked with food. Lying on the table was a note from Delphine, Richard Foy's housekeeper, to say that she would be coming in the morning with croissants for breakfast.

A narrow twisting staircase in the corner of the main sitting area took them all upstairs to two double and two single bedrooms and a couple of bathrooms. Holly divided them up, putting Caitlin and Leon in one double room and herself and Emily in the other, Sam and Oliver each getting a single room to themselves. Oliver's next door to hers and Emily's.

Perfect, Caitlin thought, walking into the bedroom she would share with Leon.

She dropped her bags on the floor, went over to the window and stood in the darkness looking out at the little square imagining the days ahead. She pictured the others leaving to ski while she'd take her time to get up, then perhaps she'd have a little wander around the town, then, later in the morning, she would take the cable car to meet them for lunch.

She heard Leon come into the bedroom behind her, put down his bag on the bed and take off his coat. Then he came over to join her at the window, and she felt his arms slide around her waist and pull her back against him. She'd known he would come to find her. They'd got too close on the plane for him not to take the first opportunity to get her alone.

She closed her eyes as she felt his arms tighten around her. He bent his head and slowly kissed the back of her neck, so lightly that she could hardly tell when one kiss ended and another began. She turned in his arms, her mouth reaching for his, and felt his hands slide under her sweater and she shivered as his fingers stroked her back. She touched his stomach and heard him groan.

The problem with Leon, Caitlin thought, as he pushed her back upon the huge double bed, undid first the buckle of her belt, then the button of her jeans, then pulled them down her legs in one fast, determined movement . . . The problem with Leon was that however critical of him she was to her friends, Caitlin found him irresistibly sexy. Get close to him and all those things she told everyone she couldn't stand, like his hairy body and his luminous white skin, she suddenly couldn't get enough of.

He was kissing her stomach, his rough chin grazing her skin, turning her insides to syrup. She reached down for him, pulling him up on top of her so that she could kiss him properly, and then she pulled the huge goose-down duvet over them both.

The next morning Caitlin woke up hungry, with a dry, foul-tasting mouth and her contact lenses stuck to her eyeballs.

She rolled her eyes to get the lenses moving again, then glanced across to Leon's side of the bed and saw that she was alone. She looked at her watch and saw it was just past ten. She got out of bed and cautiously opened her shutters, just wide enough to let a dazzling arrow of sunlight pierce the gloom of the bedroom. Seeing how glorious it was outside, she pushed them open all the way and looked out at a perfect blue-sky day.

Down in the square below her window people were walking about. Holidaymakers, dressed in brightly coloured ski clothes, carrying their skis and boards on their backs and making their way in twos and threes towards the cable car. She could hear the distinctive squeak of their ski boots against the fresh snow. A girl was pulling along a child and a bag of groceries on a plastic sledge, and some shopkeepers were sweeping snow away from their shop fronts, while others were shovelling paths across the village square.

The crisply perfect scene, all the fresh snow, the blue sky, the golden sun, the fact that it was the first morning of their holiday, that she had woken feeling full of love, all this combined to tell Caitlin that her dislike of skiing had to be put aside, that today she had to join the others.

And so, in a sudden panic that she was already too late to stop them leaving without her, she pulled on a T-shirt and a pair of jeans and ran out of the bedroom.

In the kitchen, she found Emily, Sam and Oliver dressed but clearly in no hurry to leave. She stopped in the doorway and smiled at the scene.

Emily was standing between her two men, eating a piece of toast, leaning against the kitchen cupboards in black lycra ski trousers and a heavy Equadorian sweater, standing on one ski-booted leg, while the other leg dangled in a bright pink ski sock. On her right was Oliver, looking gorgeous in dark red O'Neill trousers, sunglasses already in position holding back his hair, and concentrating hard on the task of making her a cup of coffee. As Caitlin watched him, he carefully poured in the milk, peered into the mug, then poured a little more, added half a spoonful of sugar, thought no one was looking and tasted the drink with the spoon, stirred once, twice, three times, then carefully handed it over to Emily.

Meanwhile, on Emily's left, was Sam. Dressed like

Emily in a thick sweater, he had on a pair of dark grey trousers and a moth-eaten bandanna, with a pair of sunglasses hanging around his neck. He had his head down and was busily adjusting Emily's other ski boot.

As Oliver handed over the coffee, Sam declared that the boot was ready. He undid the clips, knelt down on the floor and gently pushed it onto Emily's foot.

'Good on you, Prince Charming,' said Caitlin from the doorway.

Emily looked up. 'Good morning,' she said. She put down her coffee and stamped her boots on the floor. 'Thank you, Sam. That's so much better.'

'If I'm quick, will you all wait for me?' Caitlin asked. 'Please?'

'Take your time,' Emily told her. With Holly sitting in a towel upstairs, blow-drying her hair, there was no rush. She pulled out a breakfast chair for Caitlin and put another croissant in the oven to warm.

While Caitlin waited for her breakfast, she and Emily looked at a map and talked about where they might ski. Of the six of them Emily was definitely the least experienced, and she was determined that the others shouldn't be held back because of her. But Caitlin was just as determined to make sure that Emily and Oliver spent a good proportion of the day together. If Emily had a few crashes, there'd be all the more opportunities for Oliver to prove he was the perfect mountain hero by helping her back on her skis.

With sincere promises to look after her, Caitlin succeeded in persuading Emily that they should spend the first morning together. Oliver and Leon could snowboard another day and then Caitlin would retire from skiing altogether, but this morning they would all catch the Mont Julien cable car and then several chairlifts to reach the best snow on the upper slopes. They would spend the rest of the morning skiing back down to the Mont Julien café, which was to be found just beside the cable car. Most of the skiing would be very easy and Caitlin assured Emily that when they came to the two more difficult runs, both very short, her friends would help, even if it meant carrying her down. Emily was persuaded.

While Holly dressed, Caitlin browsed through her cupboards, eventually selecting a pair of ski boots that she recognized as ones she'd borrowed previously and then a familiar pair of skis, too. She pulled on a boot, trod down on a ski to test the bindings and found that they fitted OK – well enough to last the morning.

By the time she'd chosen herself an old pair of trousers and a jacket, Holly had abandoned her to join the others waiting in the square outside.

Caitlin emerged, ten minutes later.

'I can't believe what I'm seeing,' Holly told her, handing her a ski pass.

'It's me, isn't it, baby?' Leon crunched over to her in a pair of purple snow boots and gave Caitlin a warm kiss on the lips. 'Admit it.'

Caitlin predictably grimaced, then relented and kissed him back.

*

Caitlin hardly skied any more but she could remember which parts were fun and which were to be avoided. While she was happy to carry her own poles, it was Leon who found himself with her skis to throw over his shoulder and carry to the cable car with his own.

The cable car might have looked state-of-the-art, but their journey was still more reminiscent of the London Underground at rush hour. Nose-to-armpit, the six of them were pressed tightly among seventy or so other skiers and snowboarders for an uncomfortable fifteen minutes swinging up the mountain before they were disgorged at the summit.

Caitlin was the first to jump into her skis. She pointed out the Mont Julien café where they would end up at lunchtime and then she set off in a wide, gentle curve towards the first of the chairlifts. Watching Emily struggle to make a simple turn to join her, she hoped again that Oliver would take advantage of the chance to pick up the pieces.

Caitlin led them, turning all the time to see how the others were doing, skiing with effortless style and leaving deep regular waves in her wake. She was followed by Leon, Holly, Sam and Emily and then finally, bringing up the rear doing his duty and keeping a close watchful eye on Emily, Oliver.

The snow was deep but powder-fine and the further they went the more Caitlin forgot the others and concentrated on the wonderful skiing. Then, just as she was remembering to slow down and check on everybody again, she heard someone coming up behind her and turned to see that it was Oliver, obviously unable to bear any longer the slow pace at the back. Caitlin watched as he streaked past her, head down, leaning into his turns, kicking up great clouds of snow. Finally he reached the brow of a hill, brought up his knees, took off and disappeared over the edge and out of sight. *What a prat*, she thought furiously. Absolutely typical that he'd had to show off.

Emily didn't at all mind being left at the back. On her previous two holidays here she had survived skiing rather than relished it, but this morning she was loving every minute of it, especially since Oliver had disappeared, leaving her to relax and ski as badly as she usually did. The cold air whipped at her cheeks and, as she rounded the first bend and confidently moved her skis closer together, she cried out with exhilaration. It was a perfect, perfect morning.

With Oliver gone it was Holly who became Emily's minder, occasionally looking over her shoulder to check her progress and to ask if she was OK, and each time Emily managed to waggle a ski pole at her to show her that she was fine. Two more minutes and she saw Caitlin, Leon and Sam all waiting on the brow of the next slope.

Emily skidded to a halt just in front of Sam. 'What happened to Oliver?' she asked them all.

'Oliver is such a show-off,' Caitlin told her and she took Emily by the shoulder and pointed way down the slope to a tiny waving figure, waiting far below them. 'He had to make it clear how good he was. He'll relax now and be lovely.'

Immediately, before Emily had time to recover her breath, they were off again, this time obviously judging that it was OK to speed up a little, and Emily braced herself for the fall that she knew would come as a result. Just watching the others forever zig-zagging just ahead of her was enough to make her lose control.

After the first three falls, she got up happily enough, gamely dragging together her skis, taking her time, finding her poles, knocking the snow off her boots and setting off again, but gradually it became more difficult to recover the confidence that she had started out with and she began to think longingly of the café by the cable car.

Seeing them in a line waiting for her at the bottom of the run she knew that she was holding them up and that they'd enjoy themselves more if they could ski faster. *She'd* enjoy herself more if she could be left to ski more slowly. When she eventually reached the others, who had by now joined Oliver, she suggested to Holly that they should go ahead without her, arguing that in the time it would take her to ski the final run to the café, they could have got to the bottom, caught the chairlifts up once more and skied back down again to meet her.

It was agreed. One by one, Oliver, Sam, Holly, Caitlin and Leon skied over the brow of the hill and disappeared, leaving her alone. And because she knew that she could now relax completely, her skiing went to pieces.

Within seconds of setting off she was completely out of control, coming to a halt only by colliding with an old man and knocking him flying. She knew that he could have used some help getting up but Emily struggled to get over to him and in the end he waved her away. Just a few seconds later she fell again, losing a ski and sending a bright stab of pain through her left knee.

She got up carefully, tempted to take her skis off and walk the rest of the way to the cable car. But she didn't give up, found her poles and set off again, gingerly testing her knee with her weight and finding that it was bearable, just.

Now the fun had absolutely and completely gone. She'd thought she'd be fine alone, but the truth was that she would have loved to have someone else with her. As she made her way, heart in mouth, towards the last big run before the café – the slippery slope as she'd labelled it on a previous holiday – she kept hoping that she'd turn a corner and see them all waiting for her after all.

She began it knowing she was doing it all wrong. The certainty that she was going to fall again meant that she couldn't stop herself leaning backwards instead of forwards, though she knew she was committing the cardinal sin, and, of course, she was soon out of control again. Picking up speed, she found herself leaning further and further back until she was almost horizontal to her skis and hurtling faster than she'd ever skied before, frequently taking off as she streaked down the mountainside, able to do nothing more than cry out to anyone reckless enough to be in her way.

And then, with superhuman effort, she managed to turn both skis away from the downward slope so that she began to traverse across the mountain instead, still at extremely high speed, but at least going across the slope rather than straight down it.

She knew she had flashed past flags marking the edges of the piste but had no option but to keep going. The snow was getting deeper now, and every so often one ski would suddenly slow down without the other, forcing her to do the splits, but she somehow managed not to fall. Not until she slid into a thigh-high drift and came to a complete and sudden halt, toppling forwards head first into the snow.

At least she'd stopped. She had her head deep in the snow but she'd stopped. She tried to get up but her legs were twisted beneath her, still attached to both skis, and she fell sideways instead, buried up to her waist, half laughing, half crying, thankful that there was nobody to see her.

But there was. Following her tracks, determinedly poling himself along through the deep snow, came Sam.

When she saw him she fell back into the snow again and closed her eyes, thinking, *Why does it always have to be Sam?* But, of course, it was never going to be Oliver.

'I told them you'd need some help on this run but they said you'd be fine,' Sam said. 'So I said I'd come and find you and prove myself right.' He sat down beside her, letting her get back her breath. 'I've just won myself lunch.'

'No, *I've* just won you lunch.'

'Absolutely.'

He got down on his knees and dug into the snow,

scrabbling like a determined dog, deeper and deeper, until he managed to release her legs enough for her to be able to wriggle them out. Then he stood up and held out a gloved hand, pulled her to her feet and helped her snap her boots out of her bindings.

'Do you want to ski to the café or shall we walk?'

'I don't know,' she moaned, looking back the way she'd come. The rest of the slope now looked like a precipice. 'Can you help me?' She knew that she sounded pathetic, but she was so tired now and couldn't face another fall.

She followed him on foot, tramping along behind him, back through the deep tracks that her skis had made in the snow, back to the piste, and then he held her steady while she clipped herself back onto her skis.

'I'm fine,' she said for her own benefit more than Sam's, and they set off together once more, Sam skiing very slowly just in front of her, telling her exactly what to do, reminding her to lean forward on her skis, just a little, to keep her shoulders facing downhill.

Then a snowboarder whistled past Emily's ear, spraying a great cloud of snow all over her, and thwacked straight into Sam, sending him tumbling down the slope, and Emily immediately lost her balance and fell too, and again her knee twisted beneath her and once again she lost a ski.

She looked around for Sam and saw him about thirty feet below her. Picking up her lost ski, she stumbled slowly towards him.

She reached Sam and looked down at him, waiting for her, spreadeagled on the snow. Seeing her stony face, he started to laugh and reached up for her hand. 'And I'm meant to be helping you,' he said.

She took his hand and was assailed by dizziness, overcome with the desire to fall to the ground beside him. 'You must remember to keep your upper body still,' she joked weakly, 'and to flex your thighs.' His hand was still in hers. 'You were all over the place just then.'

'Do you think we'll make it to the café?'

She looked down towards it, not so far away, and nodded.

'How about I hang on to you and if we go down again, we go down together?'

'Very reassuring,' she smiled.

He stood behind her and wrapped his arms tightly around her waist, and they set off, Sam snowploughing outside her skis, checking her speed all the way down, his strength stopping them from running out of control. In this way, folded between his thighs and cocooned within his arms, she glided safely down to the café.

Once there, Emily thankfully jumped away from him – she had been much too close, she thought. Uncomfortably close. He took her skis and his and rammed them into the snow, then hooked both sets of poles around their tips.

They queued for two hot chocolates, which came in tall glasses, topped with Chantilly and shavings of chocolate, took them out into the sunshine, found a table facing the slopes and positioned their chairs so that they could sit side by side. There they sat, in companionable silence, watching the other skiers making their way down the slopes either to the café, or on to Magine.

How could it be, Emily thought as she watched Sam, that she could wait eight years for somebody, could finally reach a point where she could have a real shot at him, and then find herself interested in somebody else? After eight long years, yes, it was still Oliver uppermost in her mind, still the same old story, that if he called out her name she'd come running, but she couldn't deny any longer that she liked being with Sam. Sam who now seemed to have nothing on his mind at all beyond sitting beside her in the sun, getting a tan and enjoying the spectacular wipe-outs as people came too fast over the brow of the hill, and failed to stop in time for the café.

What had she hoped for? That Sam's feelings for her would last indefinitely without any encouragement from her? Until that moment she hadn't even properly admitted to herself that they had ever been there. Subconsciously, of course, she'd known they had, she'd been aware of them even in Ruffles Department Store, but she'd ignored them, pushed them aside even as she'd felt flattered by them, because there was no place for them in her life. And if now those feelings had gone, if the fact that he was sitting beside her now, so still, so at ease, without any urge to look at her, making little attempt to talk, happy simply to watch the slopes and wait for his friends to arrive, if that meant that he had changed, Emily missed the old Sam very much.

Through her impenetrable sunglasses, she stared at him, sitting handsome and relaxed beside her, his long legs stretched out in front of her in his battered, grey ski trousers, his small neat nose just starting to turn pink from the sun, a tiny smear of chocolate on his chin and his thick brown hair sticking up in vertical tufts, and told herself that as long as she still wanted Oliver, she had no right to miss Sam.

15

One by one, Emily watched the others ski up to the café, and pull up short at the sight of her and Sam sitting side by side in the sun. *You're too late*, she felt like politely informing them. *Not any more. He used to like me but he's stopped thinking like that now.*

They stayed at the café for lunch and when they rose to go Emily announced – firmly – that she'd had enough and was taking the cable car back down to the village. What she hadn't expected was Oliver overruling her, telling her that she wasn't going home, that she was spending an hour with him, having a lesson.

Anyone else but Oliver – *anyone* else – and the lure of the cable car would have been too strong. But he was offering to take her far away from the others, somewhere, he said, where they could concentrate. When Emily asked where exactly, he got out a map and showed her how it was possible to do as she wanted – go back down in the cable car to Magine – then walk through the village to the other slopes on the other side, the nursery slopes.

'The nursery slopes?' Emily spluttered.

'Not *to* the nursery slopes,' Oliver told her, '*beyond* them.' High above them, where, according to the map, there was a bubble lift. 'And above that – ' he pointed – 'all these wonderful, easy runs.' He showed her, tracing them down the mountainside with his finger. 'Perfect for you to get your confidence back.'

And so, while Caitlin, Sam, Leon and Holly left for more difficult slopes, Oliver took her away.

All too soon it became clear that while Emily was thinking romantic rendezvous, Oliver was thinking energy-sapping workout. She'd had a few lessons during her first skiing trip but knew she'd fallen into bad habits – Sam had spotted them too and had done his best to correct them before her legs turned into jelly and she could do nothing but fall over.

'Get your bum in ... Tuck your elbows in, weight forward, weight forward, look ahead, look ahead,' Oliver hollered at her as she skied past him again and again, and it was clear that he was getting more out of the afternoon than she was. After an hour, when she was finally getting the hang of parallel turns, of keeping her weight forward and her upper body still, she said she could ski no longer and Oliver was finally persuaded to take pity on her.

'You were like a man possessed,' she teased him, as she walked with wobbly legs towards a café for a quick drink before they made their way back to the bubble lift that Oliver had agreed they could travel in rather than ski all the way back to the village. 'You were terrifying. It was like you'd forgotten who I was, forgotten that you knew me at all.'

'I loved it. I loved telling you what to do. And it worked too. You improved so much.' He put his arm around her and said confidently, 'I could teach you so much more.'

Emily was sure he had said it innocently, that he had only skiing in mind, but once he'd spoken, the other connotation was the one left hanging in the air between the two of them.

Oliver responded to the long silence by laughing, enjoying himself as ever, and he squeezed her shoulders. 'I think you'd have a lot of fun.'

They sat opposite each other at a small square table, in the last of the afternoon light, glasses of brandy in front of them. It was getting colder now and Emily could feel stiffness spreading across her shoulders and a dull ache in her knee. She was weighing up the undoubted pleasure of looking at Oliver against the thought of getting back to the chalet and lying in a deep hot bath.

He took one of her hands in both of his and started to rub it gently. 'Are you cold?'

She looked down at her hand in surprise, then back at him, and he stopped rubbing and held it still.

'Why do I think you like Sam?' he asked her then.

She gawped at him. *Take your time to reply. Don't say the first thing that comes into your head.*

'I don't know.'

'Perhaps it was seeing him holding your hand, like this?'

She shook her head. 'Not like this.'

'Or perhaps it was seeing the two of you sitting side by side at the café just now, sitting so close.'

And it could have been you, she thought irritably but didn't say it. If you're jealous, if you're worried about Sam, why wasn't it you sitting beside me then?

'Do you find him attractive?' Oliver asked.

'I suppose I do.'

'I thought so.'

'Oliver. Nothing's about to happen between me and Sam. I don't want Sam.'

He was meant to ask her what she did want, and then she would have told him, but he didn't.

'Good,' Oliver said instead. 'Don't you think he's such an old woman?'

'I thought he was your friend!'

'A long time ago.'

'Sam said the same thing.'

'Yeah, he would. Oh, bollocks,' he said, dropping her hand. 'We're not such good friends any more.'

'Why not? Since when?'

'Since we fell out over a girl Sam was keen on. Years ago. He's not forgiven me.'

'Was it me?' Emily whispered.

'No! It was not you!' He shouted with laughter, making her jump. 'God, no. I'd forgotten that Sam liked you then. No wonder he's really pissed off with me now.' He sighed. 'Oh, Emily, stop looking at me like that, like you want to spit me out.'

'But you can sound so hard.'

Oliver drained the last of his brandy. 'I'm not hard. But I do have this urge to shove Sam away from you. I don't like him getting too close.' He abruptly stood up. 'And we must go or we'll miss the lift,' he finished. 'And they'll have used up all the hot water in the chalet.'

'Oliver, are you OK?'

'I'm fine,' he said impatiently. 'I just don't like to think of you and Sam. Do you mind me saying that?'

She shook her head. Mind? Did she mind? All she minded was that he was getting up and walking off just as he was starting to talk, but then what he was saying was true. If they didn't go, they *would* miss the lift and the thought that she might have to ski down to the village, in pitch darkness, overrode her wish to keep him talking.

They made it to the bubble lift with only a minute to spare. All the way down, alone in the little car, swinging gently in the darkness above the mountainside and then as they walked back through the quiet streets to the chalet, Oliver with her skis on his shoulder and his hand in hers, she waited for him to say something more. But he didn't and Emily, happy to have his hand in hers, didn't push him. Because it was clear that something was happening between them at last.

Back at the chalet, there was a brief lull in the early evening when Oliver, Sam and Leon were all asleep upstairs and Emily, Caitlin and Holly sat downstairs, already dressed for the evening, sprawled across the sofas in front of the fire eating crisps, reading yesterday's newspapers and drinking wine. Emboldened by two glasses on an empty stomach and by a new confidence that she could talk freely to Emily, that she no longer had to worry that Emily would flounce off in a huff, Caitlin found she had the courage to try a gentle interrogation.

She started off innocuously enough, asking about Emily's ski lesson with Oliver.

'It was fun,' Emily told her. She finished her glass of wine and refilled hers and Caitlin's. 'I could have done without Oliver taking it quite so seriously, but it was still fun.'

'You were so late back,' said Caitlin, 'we were getting worried about you. We were wondering what you'd got up to.'

'Nothing,' Emily said immediately, and then realized that she wanted to tell them. 'But he said if there was anything I'd like him to teach me, to let him know.'

Sitting in a deep armchair, out of Emily's direct line of sight, Holly chipped in, 'Will you take him up on it? That's the big question! Are you ready to learn?'

'No! Not like that,' Emily told her, serious now.

Caitlin quickly sat up on the sofa. 'Emily,' she said, full of purpose, 'let's not pretend any more. We know how you feel about Oliver. Is he what you've been waiting for? If he turned to you now and made it clear that he really badly wanted you, said all the right things, would you think this is it? He's the one? Would you jump into bed with him?'

'No,' Emily said. 'If that was all I was waiting for I'd have been to bed with someone else by now, wouldn't I?'

'I thought Oliver might make you feel it was worth it.'

Emily shook her head. 'Holly understands,' she said, looking over to Holly's chair. 'That's why she's not asking me these questions. It'll take more than someone saying all the right things.'

'Why? Give me a reason.'

Emily smiled. 'Whatever I say, just remember that they're my reasons. Not that I think you should have done the same.'

'Tell me,' Caitlin said more eagerly. 'Can you give me six reasons. And do make me think I should have done the same! Make me think *If only I'd thought of it like that!*'

'No chance.' Emily laughed. 'My reasons wouldn't have worked for you.'

'But I really would like to know what they are – hear it from you, for once, rather than from everyone else,' Caitlin said. 'I've wanted to ask you for ages.'

'Aren't there loads of reasons?' Holly piped up again from her armchair.

'No! Tell me what they would be,' Caitlin challenged. 'And none of that *sex is sacred* rubbish.'

'I'm serious,' Holly insisted.

'I am too.'

'I think of how Rachel was after Felix,' Emily said, interrupting them. 'That's my first reason.'

Caitlin shrugged, remembering.

'She made me realize that if the physical intimacy isn't matched by emotional intimacy, it breaks your heart. Like it broke Rachel's. And I've seen it happen too many times to want it to happen to me. That's why I know I shouldn't sleep with Oliver. Not for a long time. Not until I am sure he isn't going to leave me.'

Caitlin nodded. 'That's true. But that was how Rachel chose to deal with it. I'm not like that, I could have walked away with a smile on my face and he'd never have known.'

'Good for you. I couldn't.'

'But you can solve that simply by being discriminating, you don't *have* to stay a virgin,' Caitlin argued.

'And I am discriminating. Very discriminating. I want to do it with someone I love, who loves me. That's all. Reason one.'

'Because ninety-nine per cent of your friends exaggerate. Reason two.' Into the silence Holly piped up again from behind the sofa, 'And reason three,' she went on, 'because most of the time it's a bit disappointing. Emily shouldn't risk losing it all for a button mushroom. My advice is at least look before you leap.'

'Really?' Emily said laughing. 'Is that true? Everyone's making out it's better than it is?'

'You won't know until you try,' said Caitlin.

'It's a reason,' Holly insisted.

'Three reasons,' Caitlin said. 'Three reasons for staying a virgin. Aren't there any more?'

'Other reasons I've told you about already,' Emily went on. 'I like the anticipation. I wonder what's wrong with waiting, why we think we have to have everything so fast.'

'Fast tans, fast food, fast sex,' Holly interrupted. 'I agree with you. And endless foreplay sounds like a marvellous idea.'

'And I suppose it means you don't have to sleep in the wet patch,' Caitlin joked. 'There's another reason.'

'No, seriously,' Emily interrupted, 'think about the guys you lost your virginity to. Can you remember it? Do you still care about them now?'

'I never cared enough about him,' Caitlin answered. 'That was the problem at the beginning.'

'But he was completely in love with you, wasn't he?' Holly said. 'I remember you telling me about him, how bad you felt.'

'What about you, Holly?' Emily asked her. 'Do you still think about the man you first slept with?'

'Not if I can help it.'

'But don't you think that's sad? Don't you wish it could have been something special?'

Holly pushed herself upright so that she could look at Emily properly. 'Not really,' she admitted. 'I understand exactly why you do, but it simply wasn't like that for me. I didn't ever see my virginity as something I wanted to look after. It doesn't mean that I sleep around, doesn't mean I don't agree with you that sex can lead to emotional entanglements that can make you fall apart. But I don't believe it has to be like that. I think it can, simply, be good fun. Not something to worry about for twenty-five years.'

'I can only lose it once,' Emily said stubbornly. 'I want to get it right.'

'Five reasons. You have five reasons to stay a virgin,'

Caitlin said to Emily. 'I don't think that's enough. Not when I can tell you so many more reasons why you shouldn't.'

'Just give me one.'

'Because you'd enjoy it. Because it's such good fun.'

'I'll find out. And I'll find out with the man I'm going to stay with. And that'll make it even better. That's my sixth reason. Because if it happens with the right man, it's surely as good as it gets?'

'But that's so boring!' Caitlin retorted. 'You can't want to do it with only one man. That's such a waste.' She looked at Emily curiously. 'Have you *ever* been to bed with someone?'

'Once,' said Emily. 'I was sixteen and we did nothing at all.'

'Not Oliver, was it?' Holly asked, only half joking.

'No, not Oliver,' Emily confirmed. 'Before I met Oliver. And it was lovely. I'd do it again, if it felt like the right thing to do and whoever it was understood what wasn't going to happen. But it's not come up again, as it were. It just hasn't happened to me.'

'Emily,' Caitlin said, leaning in to her, 'all those reasons . . . the truth is, I don't need to be told what you believe in and why it hasn't happened to you yet because I know you better now. And I had just the same choices as you did, I listened to the same arguments. I don't regret the route I took, but I do respect you for choosing a different one to the rest of us. I used to think that you were too good to be true, that it was all part of an act, but I don't any more.'

'What do I say to that?'

'And now, I'm thinking "please hold on" and I never thought I would.'

'Why?'

Caitlin looked down at the floor, thought about it for a moment. 'In about twenty seconds, I think I may regret saying this.' She looked up at Emily again, and across the room Holly held her breath. 'I certainly wasn't going to say anything tonight. But now I'm going to.' She took a deep breath, sensing Emily bracing herself for some kind of an assault. 'I don't think Oliver's your man. I don't think he's ever going to be the one.'

Out of the corner of her eye, Caitlin could see Holly looking at her steadily but Caitlin was far more interested in Emily's reaction and she could see straight away that she had struck a nerve.

'Why? What do you mean?'

'I know how much you like him,' Caitlin said gently, trying hard to keep her voice very steady and calm, 'and while I have huge respect for your reasons for not sleeping with anyone, I still think Oliver is the main reason why you've not even come close. Oliver is the reason why you've not been tempted, why it is that you've not found yourself in bed with another guy since you were sixteen years old. I think you've come out on this holiday wanting to put everything you believe in to the test, hoping that you might get together with Oliver, that you might discover he's the man you've been waiting for. I think you're vulnerable. I think you might make a mistake.' She paused. 'And I'm not even sure that I like him any more.'

As Caitlin finished, Emily glanced quickly over to the staircase, the fear that Oliver might somehow overhear what they were saying there on her face.

'It's OK,' Caitlin reassured her. 'He's in his room and I'm talking too quietly for any of them upstairs to be able to hear a word I'm saying.'

'Anyone listening would know you were talking rubbish,' Emily finally retaliated half-heartedly.

'Really?' Caitlin asked. 'Are you sure?'

The anger was fleeting. Now Emily rubbed a hand across her face, more muddled than angry. 'I don't know . . .'

'I think what I'm saying is true,' Caitlin told her. 'Until this holiday I thought he was the one for you too. But I don't any more. I only hope you've got close enough to him to realize that for yourself. But I'm scared that you haven't, that you're still going to get swept off your feet by him.'

'Why don't you like him any more?' Emily asked.

Caitlin bit her lip. 'This morning, after we left you to ski on your own, Oliver started messing around, setting out to wind us all up, especially Sam. It was obvious that he had something on his mind.'

'What was it?'

'You.'

'Me?' Emily cried, and in her voice Caitlin still heard the hope.

'Yes, but it's not what you think. You were on Oliver's mind because he had finally picked up on the fact that

Sam likes you. *Really* likes you. He does, and you know it,'
Caitlin went on quickly, sensing Emily was about to protest. 'You might not feel the same way but don't pretend
that you haven't noticed. We all know he does. As soon as
Sam walked into the airport it was obvious that you were
the only person he wanted to see there.' Caitlin dropped
her voice again. 'Sam adores you. And Oliver knows it.'

Caitlin caught sight of Holly frantically shaking her
head and ignored her. 'And realizing that has got Oliver's
juices flowing. It's made him want you for himself.'

'Is that what you think too, Holly?' Emily turned to
her. 'Do you think what Caitlin is saying is true?'

It was difficult to interpret Emily's feelings at this
point, hard to tell if she was terribly hurt or emerging
unscathed, whether she believed a word of what Caitlin
was saying or was dismissing it entirely.

'I think Oliver can be very competitive,' Holly told her
carefully, 'and I agree with Caitlin that he was very
bothered about Sam this morning. He kept challenging
Sam about you, needling him.' Emily shrugged. 'But I'm
wondering whether that's simply because he likes you and
he wants to make sure you're OK.'

'I don't think so,' Caitlin said emphatically. 'Oliver
wants to get one over Sam. That's what his interest in
Emily is all about. That's why he suddenly decided to take
Emily off for a lesson this afternoon, having paid her
barely any attention at all. He hadn't realized how much
Sam wants her.'

Emily remembered the look on Oliver's face when he

came up to her and Sam at the bar in the airport and how he had reacted to what he thought he was seeing then.

Caitlin went on again, 'I think Oliver gets turned on by other guys' women. He always has done. He sees it as a challenge, and he loves a challenge. He saw me kissing Leon in the kitchen and it turned him on. The next thing I knew, he was trying to get me to do the same to him.'

'At your party?' Emily looked at her. 'When? When I was washing up with Leon? I thought Leon went a bit strange.'

Caitlin nodded. 'But he's cooled off me now because he has you and Sam to think about. And you are far more important to him than I ever was. Think what you represent . . . Don't you see? And the thought of Sam getting to you first . . . That's a big problem for Oliver.'

Had Oliver done this to Sam before? Emily wondered, wishing that she could stop herself. Was that why Oliver had suddenly appeared with Sam on that empty beach in Cornwall, when she was sixteen years old?

But even as a part of her acknowledged the possibility of truth in what Caitlin was saying, she had to deny it straight away because she hoped so badly that it wasn't true. Over the years she'd known him, there had never been any sign of this. Then a sneaky little voice inside her head told her, *But over the years there'd never been a Sam on the scene, never anyone with whom Oliver had to compete.* Yet she had made such progress with Oliver that afternoon. She'd just begun to feel that something might happen, really happen, between the two of them. And she wanted it to. She badly did. Why did Caitlin have to say this now, when she had finally, finally begun to feel there was hope between them?

Emily could see the concern on Caitlin's face, and on Holly's too as she peered at them over the side of her armchair, and she knew that neither of them wanted to hurt her, that both of them were looking out for her.

'I'm not angry with you for saying what you said. I appreciate your concern. But I'll show you that you're wrong.'

Caitlin shrugged. 'I had to tell you. But if I'm wrong, I'll be very pleased. I suppose you'll do whatever you think is right. I won't be judging you.' She grinned. 'As if *I* could ever judge *you*.'

And then they heard a heavy thud, thud, thud down the stairs and a freshly pressed Leon appeared around the corner of the staircase, closely followed by Oliver.

Oliver threw one quick glance around the room and went straight over to Emily, bending down towards her on the sofa. 'OK?' he asked affectionately. 'Not too tired? Not too stiff after the battering I gave you this afternoon?'

She shook her head, looking up at him, and he dropped his head and kissed her cheek and Emily put an arm around him and held him still for a few seconds.

He's working on her, Caitlin thought indignantly. It couldn't be a coincidence that Oliver was behaving like this right now. He was staking his claim. He probably knew that Sam was about to come down the stairs behind him and was waiting for him to catch them like that.

But Sam didn't come down. Caitlin looked back at Emily, at her perfect profile, her just upturned nose and her clear, flawless skin, her slender arm holding tightly onto Oliver, and thought she understood why Emily now mattered so much to him. He had always liked beautiful girls – especially when his friends liked them too – and Emily wasn't just beautiful. She was a rare prize. And Caitlin hoped very much that the prize was not about to be claimed.

Sam had still not appeared half an hour later. When Leon and Oliver disappeared into the kitchen offering to cook supper, Holly volunteered to go upstairs and fetch him down. She came back down a minute later, stood on the bottom step of the staircase and beckoned to Emily and Caitlin to follow her up.

Only half understanding where they were going and why, Emily found herself getting up and following Caitlin quietly up the stairs. At the top Holly led them along a short corridor and stopped outside Sam's door, which she carefully and quietly opened, and all three of them stood in the doorway and looked inside.

It was dark, the only light thrown in through the open door and a panel of glass above it, and the room glowed with a soft, intimate light. Emily's first thought was what a sweet but very feminine little bedroom it was, with a low ceiling painted a deep red pink.

The walls were painted white and in the middle of the room there was a bed surrounded by floating gossamer-fine drapes, gathered together into a bunch, creating the effect of a romantic billowing tent. She wondered suspiciously whether Holly had been let loose in this room, knowing it was just to her taste, and then her attention was caught by the bed itself.

Lying on it, half hidden by a cerise satin eiderdown, lay Sam. He was asleep, blissfully unaware of them all looking in at him. A long arm stretched out across the bed, his sleeping face turned towards them.

Emily had never watched a man asleep before. Her eyes flicked warily from his face to the bunched knot of muscles in his shoulder and then to the delicate skin that curved into his armpit. With an unexpected jolt in her groin, she caught sight of his nipple, dark and flat against his smooth tawny skin, and she felt herself blush.

'Doesn't he look flushed?' Caitlin joked, breaking the spell. 'Best we take off all those nasty covers.'

'Doesn't he look divine, you mean?' whispered Holly. 'Are you sure you don't want him, Emily?'

'We should wake him up. He's got to come and have supper,' said Caitlin.

'Make a noise, then. Say hello,' Holly told her, 'Don't just stand there staring at him.'

'Or shall we jump on him?' Caitlin suggested. 'All three of us? Don't you think he'd enjoy that?'

'You can't,' Emily managed to say. 'You mustn't wake him!' And then she turned away from them, towards the stairs, calling out as she ran that she thought she would go and help Oliver and Leon in the kitchen.

16

The next day everything changed.

When they awoke, it was not to the clear skies of the day before. The temperature had dropped and the clouds were low and heavy with the promise of more snow.

When she opened her curtains and looked outside, Emily's first reaction was to get straight back into bed, deciding there and then that she would not be skiing that day. She had gone up into the mountains in low cloud once before and found it utterly terrifying. She had been able to see nothing, had had no sense at all of where she was or where she should put her feet or where her friends had gone, and she was absolutely certain that she did not want to go through that again.

When Emily finally did get up and make her way down to the kitchen, still in her pyjamas, she found that Leon and Caitlin were already kitted up and eating breakfast together. And, as far as they knew, were expecting Oliver, Holly and Sam to join them.

'You?' Emily protested to Caitlin. 'I thought you hated skiing. What are you doing going up when it's like this?'

Caitlin shrugged. 'I've surprised myself. I had such a good day yesterday, I thought I'd do it again. And,' she said, blowing Leon a kiss, 'I like being with him.'

'Sweet,' Emily said, thinking how things had changed.

Then Sam came in, barefoot and dressed in jeans and a T-shirt.

'Sleep well?' Caitlin asked him.

'I'm starving,' Sam told them. 'I've spent the whole night dreaming about steak and chips. I can't believe you didn't wake me up.'

'You were too sound asleep,' Caitlin told him. 'We decided we couldn't do it to you.'

Sam wandered over to the fridge, found nothing that he liked and started opening and shutting cupboards. 'Have you eaten all the breakfast too?'

'There wasn't much. Delphine hasn't been yet,' Holly told him from the doorway, also barefoot and obviously having just woken up. 'If you're that hungry, you'll have to go into the village and buy something.'

'Come with me, Emily?' Sam asked.

She nodded, not meeting his eye.

'Croissant? Pain au chocolat? What do you fancy? Whatever, I need to go soon. I need to go *now*.' He looked her up and down. 'And you're wearing pyjamas.'

'I'll get dressed.' Emily stood up. 'Wait for me.' She brushed past Holly. 'We could buy the supper while we're out,' she told her.

'And I need to go to the bank,' Sam called after her.

'Have some fun, why don't you?' Holly said sarcastically.

'Oh, we'll have fun,' Sam said. 'Coffee, bit of shopping, perhaps some ice skating on the rink in the village. Yes?' He called to Emily.

'Definitely,' she shouted from the stairs.

'And don't you worry about Oliver,' she heard Caitlin add. 'We'll leave him a note to tell him where we are skiing. He can come and catch us up.'

Emily and Sam crossed the market square and walked on into the heart of the village. Emily knew exactly where to take him. She led the way through the narrow cobbled streets, so dark under the heavy clouds that the street lamps had come on again, and Sam followed her unquestioningly until she stopped outside a café tucked away down a little street called Rue Mathilde.

Although a few diehards were eating their breakfast outside, it seemed much more appealing to stay inside the café, with its whitewashed walls and steamy windows and red-tiled floor, the bittersweet smell of chocolate hanging in the air. Each little table was lit by an individual lamp and had a checked red and white tablecloth.

Emily stood beside Sam at the counter and looked down at all the mouth-watering patisserie and she heard her stomach instantly grumble with hunger. Each currant seemed plumper and more shiny than any she'd ever seen before, all the pastry more deliciously puffed up. Everything was so liberally sprinkled with pistachio nuts, chocolate or almonds that she wanted to eat it all. In the end she did the same as Sam and ordered a wonderfully fluffy-looking pain au chocolat and a croissant, warm from the oven, and they sat down opposite each other, pulling off pieces and dunking them in large cups of milky coffee.

It was strange, Emily thought, how despite everything

that was left unspoken between them, in that café, cocooned together for the twenty or so minutes that they stayed inside, they were so close. Nothing was said, they didn't hold hands or hold glances, and yet there was an intimacy between them and a trust that meant Emily knew she mattered to Sam, and Sam knew that he mattered to her. It lasted until they left the café. Outside, in the cold air, it didn't feel so certain any more.

When they got to the bank Emily left Sam, saying that she would wait for him in the street. She would look in a few shop windows while he queued inside. She watched him walk into the bank, then unexpectedly turn back at the last second to look at her, and it seemed to her that he was doubting whether she would be there as she'd said she would.

She wandered a little way down the street, looking in the windows of the shops, passing a toy shop that had opened since she'd been there last and then stopping outside La Coccinelle, her favourite shop in Magine. She would have gone inside straight away but for Sam's glance, so instead she made do with window-shopping.

La Coccinelle sold jewellery, all designed by its unlikely owner, Monsieur Gérard. He was huge and hairy with big fat fingers and a thick black beard, and he made the most simple, stunning jewellery. Rings, necklaces, earrings, brooches and bracelets, always intricately pretty but bold and dramatic too. Usually made of silver, but sometimes gold or platinum, sometimes with precious stones but more often with crystals, glass beads, jade, topaz and turquoise, everything was unique, and yet all undeniably M. Gérard's. Every time she came to Magine, his was the first shop she wanted to go to.

At first she'd wondered how such a shop could thrive in such a very small, traditional, conservative place as Magine, thought that only a few had discovered him, but then she'd asked Holly and had found out how famous M. Gérard was, how people came to Magine from miles around simply to visit him, that there was no danger of him closing down for lack of business. Ever since Saltwater had first taken shape in her mind, she'd been wondering if there was any way to persuade him to let her sell his jewellery there.

While she was still looking in the window, Sam caught her up.

'Let me buy you something,' he said impulsively.

'Lovely of you, but no.' She shook her head. 'For once I'm thinking about Saltwater, not me. How cool it would be to persuade him to let me stock some of his pieces there.'

'Go inside,' he encouraged her. 'Go and see if it's a good moment to talk to him. I'll wait for you.'

'Oh, God.' She swallowed. If she did, she would be confirming the reality of Saltwater.

'You are going to need stock,' he reminded her, speaking as if Saltwater was already a definite. 'Finding things to sell is going to be the hardest part of all.'

She gave him a worried look and went inside.

When she came out ten minutes later, Sam knew immediately that it had gone well. She danced her way towards him, and then hugged him delightedly.

'That's brilliant! You're on your way now.'

'He didn't say yes,' she said, smiling up at him, still in the circle of his arms. 'But he did say maybe.'

He could have kissed her then, and he knew that she'd have responded, caught up in that lovely moment of excitement, but she pushed herself up on her toes and kissed him on his cheek instead, and then before he could move she'd let him go and set off down the street again.

They spent the rest of the morning ice skating, first edging their way around the dilapidated ice rink and then getting braver. At one moment Sam caught her hand and led her around and around the rink, faster and faster, daring her not to let go, until finally she couldn't take any more and spun away from him, making it to the rails more by luck than skill rather than crashing in a heap in the middle of the rink. And Emily was angry with herself for her inconsistency, for her inconstancy, because she knew that if it had been she and Oliver here, skating together, she'd be enjoying it too and she wouldn't be thinking about Sam.

When Emily and Sam got back to the chalet it was nearly lunchtime. They walked into the kitchen together to find Oliver sitting at the table, reading a newspaper, one hand knotted in his hair, pointedly not looking up at their entrance.

'Hi,' Sam said brightly, too brightly, and Oliver glowered at him rather than smiled. It was obvious that he had been waiting for them, and waiting resentfully.

Oliver and Sam might once have been good friends,

but they certainly weren't now. Sam tossed the paper bag of pastries onto the table in front of Oliver and took off his coat. 'Help yourself,' he said, but there was no warmth in the invitation and Oliver ignored the offer.

'Where have you been?' Oliver asked Emily. He was so cross and aggrieved that Emily wanted to laugh and yet she felt her heartstrings pull.

'Getting supper, going to the bank.' Nothing about the ice skating or the coffee. 'I'm sorry we left you all alone.'

'I've been waiting for you all morning,' he said.

'Why?' Sam asked. 'Why didn't you go and find the others. They'd left a note for you. You knew where they'd be.'

'Because I was going to take Emily out for another lesson,' Oliver told Sam.

'I don't think so,' Sam said, looking out of the window.

'There's nothing wrong with the weather. If anything, I think it's brightening up.' Oliver turned to Emily. 'You are coming with me, Emily, aren't you?'

'But –' Emily looked outside, thinking if anything the weather was worse than before – 'I'm not sure I can ski well enough to go out in this.'

'Don't ask her to,' Sam interfered again. 'It isn't right.'

'Once we get high enough, we'll be above the cloud,' Oliver said, keeping his voice light, as if it was only the weather that was at issue.

'Bullshit, Oliver, of course you won't,' said Sam.

'It's all right, it's all right,' Emily intervened, hating them arguing over her. 'If you want me to come, I'll come,' she told Oliver. 'For an hour, no longer. Not when it's like this. Wait while I get changed.'

Sam looked at her and shook his head. 'Don't go.'

'Why not?' She smiled, trying to make light of it.

'Just don't go.'

I want to go. I need to resolve this. I want to know.

'No need to worry, Sam,' Oliver said as Emily moved to the door. 'I will look after her.'

'Do you mind if I come too?' she heard Sam ask him as she walked up the stairs. She stopped to listen.

'Yes, I do, mate, sorry to say. I'm going to give Emily another lesson and you'd be in the way. How about we all go out tomorrow?'

'But I'd like to come.'

'Look, Sam,' she heard Oliver say impatiently, 'you're not invited. You had her all morning, it's my turn now.'

Which was how Emily found herself alone on a chairlift with Oliver at two o'clock in the afternoon, swinging up a mountain when every other skier seemed intent on getting down.

The silence, deepened by the deep muffling cloud, was overwhelming. At first they both tried to make conversation but it didn't last, and for most of the ride up they sat listening only to the creak and occasional rumble of the chairlift.

What was she doing swinging up a mountain with Oliver? She didn't know. Was she happy to be there? She didn't know. Yes, yes, she was, of course she was. It was what she'd been wanting for so long. Beside her, he shifted slightly on his chair and then slid a familiar arm around her and she fell in against his warm body, reassured a little.

At the top, when they raised the bar and launched themselves away, Oliver immediately skied into the cloud and disappeared.

She was left all alone, once again, to think how mad she was to be doing this. How she had now set herself up for a neck-breaking fall simply because she was programmed to take advantage of every chance to be alone with Oliver. And she had vowed not to come out again, and she'd made that vow sitting in the snow in brilliant sunshine. What was she doing here in cloud so thick she couldn't see beyond the end of her ski pole? Trying to follow a man who seemed not to have thought of waiting for her, and who had now completely disappeared.

There was no choice now but to follow in Oliver's general direction and hope to pick up his tracks.

If Emily had been able to recognize where she was in the midst of this white-out, she would have realized Oliver had only skied forty feet away to where they had begun their lesson the day before. Finally she found him, his red ski jacket a beacon in the mist. She stopped beside him and told him that he'd damn well better look after her, that if he set off alone again she would never forgive him, and he apologized and after that stayed close.

In the end, Emily realized that as long as she followed Oliver and stuck to his tracks she was not going to ski over a precipice, and that softer snow meant slushier, slower snow that gave her time to regain her balance after each turn. With barely anyone else around, and silence but for the scrape and push of their own skis, or the occasional sound of their voices, Emily even began to enjoy herself again.

But she still didn't know why she was there. Oliver made little attempt actually to teach her anything and no further attempt to touch her and eventually, after half an hour or so, impatience started to build inside her again. Why had it been so important to go out together, if they weren't even going to talk? She was tired of trying to catch up with him, of feeling that he was always just out of reach.

'OK?' he asked her as she pulled up just above him.

'Just about.'

'Thanks for coming. I'm glad you did.'

She nodded.

He came side-stepping the few feet up the slope so that he was closer to her and she could look into his golden eyes, see the dent on the bridge of his nose where his sunglasses had been. He carefully edged his skis between hers so that he was standing very close.

'OK?' he asked again.

She shook her head miserably, then looked back at him and slowly he came towards her and she knew he was finally going to kiss her. He did, so gently that she hardly knew it had begun before he had moved away. *It's got to be more than that. Please after so long, let it be better than that.*

'Because you look miserable,' he said, sliding further away from her.

'I could do with a brandy.' She forced a smile.

And so they skied off again, Oliver leading the way to the mountain café they'd been to the day before. It was usually heaving with hundreds of skiers, but now there were only three other couples inside. Oliver bought two brandies and they chose a corner of the room well away from everybody else.

'You were great,' Oliver told her. 'You've done really well.'

'Thank you.' She shrugged. 'I had a good teacher.'

He took her hand across the little round table. 'I'm really glad you came out with me today. Sam was being a prat.'

She shook her head, looking down at her hand in his. 'He wasn't. He was worried I couldn't cope with the weather, that's all.'

'Sam wasn't worried about the weather,' Oliver told her. 'He was worried about me.'

'Why do you say that?'

He leaned forward across the table and kissed her again.

At first she didn't respond, then she felt his hand tighten on hers and tipped up her face to his, and let out an involuntary little sigh.

As if it was the signal he'd been waiting for, Oliver stood up and pulled her to her feet, knocking over his brandy glass so that it smashed on the floor. He wrapped his arms around her and pulled her hard against him, kissing her mouth, her cheeks, her ears, and she kissed him back, feeling light-headed, as if she wasn't really there, as if it wasn't really happening.

'So you *do* want me. Oh, yes,' Oliver murmured, his breath hot against her cheek. 'My sexy little fox. I think you want me.' He held her face in his hands. 'And I want you, Emily. I could take you back to my bed right now. I've been waiting for you for weeks. But I can wait some more, I've always wanted you,' he corrected himself hastily. He saw the look on her face. 'I can wait until you're ready. I won't rush you. I'll wait for as long as it takes.'

He kissed her again, his tongue driving inside her mouth, his teeth knocking against hers. But she couldn't give herself up to it. After all the waiting, all the longing, it still didn't feel real. She certainly didn't feel the electricity, the excitement that she'd expected. His kissing was clumsy rather than passionate, nothing like she remembered, and when he'd said she was his sexy little fox she'd had to fight not to push him away.

'Shall we go home?' Oliver asked, kissing the top of her head. His husky voice still suggested bed.

Go home to face the raised eyebrows and the smirks . . . and Sam.

It had to be done. 'Yes,' she nodded.

Unaware that anything might be wrong, Oliver dropped some euros on the table, took her hand and they left the café together.

When they reached the lift station and climbed the wooden steps to the top, it was to discover that the bubble had stopped running and wasn't expected to begin working again for at least half an hour.

'It's OK,' Oliver reassured her. 'Thirty minutes isn't long. I'm not even going to try to persuade you to ski down the last bit. We can wait.'

She looked at him standing beside her, his hand in hers and thought, *I just need more time to get used to him, that's all.* Perhaps it was bound to be a disappointment after so long.

'There is no way I *could* ski down the last bit,' she admitted. 'I'd rather stay here all night.'

They sat down on a wooden bench running the length of the station, Oliver with his arm clamped around her, neither of them talking but Oliver tapping his foot on the wooden floor, obviously more impatient to get back to the chalet than she was. Apart from the bubble operator, there was nobody else there.

When, thirty minutes later, the bubble still hadn't restarted, Oliver changed tack.

'Are you sure you don't want to ski down? We could be waiting here for hours.'

'What's the big hurry?'

He shrugged, looking at her, starting to smile. 'I want to tell everyone about you and me.'

'No!' she cried.

'What's wrong with that?'

'You don't want to tell *everyone*, you want to tell Sam. You don't care about the others but you want him to know.'

'Yes, I do. I want to put him straight.'

'You're awful,' she told him.

'No, I'm not.' He touched her cheek. 'I want the world – and Sam – to know that you're my girl.' He watched her reaction. 'And stop looking so happy about it.'

She made herself smile.

Ten minutes later, seeing that the snow was starting to come down harder and harder, she changed her mind. 'Show me the way home,' she said. 'I'll come with you if you promise to go slowly.'

'I've looked at the map and it should be really easy,' Oliver told her. 'Every run we have to do is green and we can trek through the trees just behind the chalet and ski right down to the front door. We'll be fine.'

But Oliver's impatience to get them home meant that despite his promise he skied faster than Emily could manage safely. The cloud was thick, and the snow was falling and it was very hard to see where she was going. All at once she was scared as well as miserable. What was she doing? she found herself thinking again and again, in between bellowing at Oliver to slow down. How could she have got herself into such a mess?

'We have to keep going,' Oliver called out to her for the fifth time now, looking as irritated with her as she was with him. 'It's only going to get more difficult. It will get dark and then how will we find our way back through the woods? We're going to be here all night if we don't get a move on.'

'I thought Magine was close. I thought you said it was a few easy runs and then the woods and then we'd be home,' she retorted.

'I did,' Oliver told her. 'Keep going.'

At long last they reached the woods. Again Oliver waited for Emily to catch him up and then led the way in, pushing his way past the branches of the pine trees and holding them so they didn't snap back in her face. The woods seemed pitch dark after the white world outside, but once they were used to the change of light, visibility was better than out on the mountainside. They made their way, half sliding, half tramping, moving slowly along a silent, spooky path, both of them concentrating too hard to talk.

'Go in front for a bit,' Oliver suggested after ten minutes. 'Take it at your pace.' He stopped and side-stepped off the path so that she could pass him and take up the lead.

She did so gratefully, keeping the twinkling lights of Magine as her bearing. Being in front was much easier and she began to go faster and faster, until it was Oliver calling out for her to slow down, but still she didn't stop. Not until she slid straight into a single strand of barbed wire that hooked her exactly at eye level and held her fast, bringing her to a sudden, horrible halt. She jerked her head backwards in reflex and felt her skin tear.

'I've cut my eye.' She said it so matter-of-factly that Oliver wasn't prepared for the thick red blood, creeping between her fingers and falling in fast, fat drops onto the snow.

He unclipped his boots and was swiftly at her side. 'Let me see. Take your hand away.'

'No.' She could taste the blood in her mouth, feel it running down her right cheek.

'It's barbed wire,' Oliver said incredulously. 'There's a strand of barbed wire between these trees. Who the fuck would leave wire here? What a fucking stupid thing to do.'

'Perhaps farmers graze sheep here in the summer, perhaps it's to stop them wandering off.' Her eye was cut and she was talking about local farming practices.

He stared at her hand held to her face. 'We have to keep going. You need a doctor, Emily.'

No! she wanted to bellow then. She hated that it was Oliver witnessing what was happening to her. She didn't want it to be him. She didn't want him looking at her face, have him be the one to tell her what he could see there. She wanted her mother. She wanted her mother there to look after her.

And then she thought that it wasn't her mother she wanted either. She wanted the one person who she knew could comfort her, who would be able to look after her and make her feel better. She wanted Sam. She desperately wanted Sam. She wanted to be with Sam. All she wanted was to get back to Magine and tell him so.

With that realization she could hardly bear to speak to Oliver. With her hand still stubbornly clamped over her eye, she became hell-bent on getting back to Magine as fast as she could.

Oliver followed her quietly. Perhaps sensing that he'd lost her, that it was over before it had even begun. As they walked into the empty village he caught her up and took her arm.

'Do you think this is my fault?'

'No, I don't.'

'Then stop, just for a second, Emily. Please.'

She stopped and turned, and looked at him, one hand still held to her face.

'I want to hug you. I want to make it better.'

She gave him a wobbly smile. 'And I want to get back to the chalet.'

He let his arms fall to his sides. 'It's Sam, isn't it?' he exploded. 'You want to get back to Sam.'

'What is this obsession with Sam?' She stared back at him, aware that this was a strange time to choose for a fight. 'This is not a bloody competition, Oliver. I am not a prize.'

'Why Sam?'

'It's nothing to do with Sam. If Sam wasn't there it still wouldn't be you,' she cried, as blood again seeped from beneath her hand.

Oliver saw it. 'I'm sorry, Emily,' he sighed. 'I can't believe I'm doing this, arguing when this has happened to you. I'm behaving so badly.'

'Oliver,' she said pleadingly. 'No, you're not. It's me not you.'

He shook his head. 'We'll talk about it another time. All we should be doing now is getting you home.'

At the chalet he moved in front of her to hammer on the front door while Emily waited, her boots still done up, suddenly too weak and shaky even to take them off.

But it was Holly and Caitlin and Leon who raced to the door in response to Oliver's call, not Sam.

Caitlin took one look at Emily, standing awkwardly in the darkness, one bloodstained mittened hand over her face, and took control. She padded out into the snow in her socks and took Emily's arm, helped her keep her balance while she bent down and undid Emily's boots. She led her inside, telling Holly to fetch a bowl of warm water and TCP and some cotton wool, pulled out a chair in the kitchen and pushed Emily gently into it, touching the hand still clamped over her face.

'Where's Sam?' Emily asked.

'Let me see,' Caitlin gently insisted.

Emily slowly removed her hand and looked up at her, immediately flinching at the cold raw air that took the place of her warm dark glove. She tentatively opened her poor, swollen, bloody right eye and found that she could still see.

Without flinching, without showing any sign that it was a nasty cut, Caitlin took a ball of cotton wool, smiled reassuringly at Emily, dipped it into the water and slowly and gently started to clear away the blood and, as she wiped, she told Emily what she could see.

The wire had cut Emily's lid vertically, through both her upper and her lower eyelashes. There was a tiny flap of skin on Emily's lower lid where the barb had torn. It was clear that Emily had closed her eyes at the moment of contact and her eyelids had done their job. Her lid was very swollen and she'd probably have a black eye in the morning, but otherwise it looked as if there was no serious harm done. Emily also had a cut across her nose which she hadn't noticed but, now that Caitlin mentioned it, she felt the pain there for the first time.

'Where's Sam?' Emily asked for the second time.

'He's gone,' Caitlin said. 'Having told Oliver *he* wasn't allowed to go off with other friends, we find that now Sam has done exactly that. Can you believe it?'

'Who's he with?'

'People he knows who came over from Valorias. He brought them over to the chalet for tea and they've driven him back to their resort. We were going to drive down and join them there tonight. But – ' Caitlin smiled – 'obviously we're not going to do that now. Not with you like this.'

'You can go. Of course you can. I'm fine.'

'I don't think so.'

'But someone has to go,' Emily cried, 'because someone has to bring Sam back.'

'I'll go,' Holly told her from the corner of the kitchen where she was making tea. 'It'll have to be me as I'm the only one insured to drive the jeep.'

Later it was agreed that Leon and Oliver would accompany Holly, and Caitlin would stay to keep Emily company.

A couple of hours later the shock hit Emily good and hard. She felt battered and shattered. She lay on the sofa in front of the fire with a glass of red wine and let Caitlin cook her some pasta for supper.

'Bad day for you, wasn't it?' Caitlin said as she brought the food through.

Emily nodded, on the verge of tears. Then she grinned

sadly instead. 'A very bad day. And I don't think Oliver would say it was much fun for him, either.'

'A bad day for Oliver won't do him any harm. Bit of rejection would be good for him.'

Emily knew that Caitlin understood exactly what she was saying. But she needed to talk and explain nevertheless, to run through the moment when it had all begun and the moment when it had all gone wrong.

'We all knew,' Caitlin confessed. 'We knew that this holiday was what you needed. That you had to spend time with him.'

Emily nodded. 'I did.'

'So we set you up.' Caitlin wasn't sure Emily understood what she was trying to say. 'We brought you here. We planned it all.'

'You did?'

Caitlin nodded. 'Do you mind?'

'Do I mind? I don't mind that you did that, no. All I mind about is Sam. I mind terribly about Sam.'

'What do you mean?' Caitlin asked gently.

'That I've wasted so much time over Oliver, I've probably ended up losing Sam.'

'You've done nothing wrong.'

'But I did, I did. I chose Oliver. Sam didn't want me to go out with him this afternoon. He asked me not to, and we both knew it was a kind of test. Oliver or Sam. And I went. I had to see. I couldn't trust my instincts.'

'Big deal! So what?' Caitlin laughed. 'He's a big boy. Sam will come around. Leave it to us. We can sort out Sam, just you watch.'

'No, don't,' Emily said tiredly. 'No more sorting out, please. It's the wrong time and anyway, it's up to me now. I'll talk to him tonight.'

But Sam, Holly, Oliver and Leon didn't make it back that night. While Caitlin and Emily talked, the snow came down fast, inches falling every hour, burying cars, roads, everything, and blocking off the road from Valorias to Magine.

The next morning it was still snowing, isolating Magine completely. Lower down in Valorias, the others could do nothing to help Emily and Caitlin and it was agreed, over a mobile phone call between Emily and Holly, that Leon, Oliver, Sam and Holly should go ahead and catch the train from Valorias and their flight back to London. Caitlin and Emily would have to stay put, pack for the others and wait for the snow to be cleared.

Then, on Tuesday morning, when they should all have been back in England, Emily and Caitlin woke to blinding sunshine and a brilliant blue sky. And with the sun came the snowploughs. They had left by lunchtime, managing to get seats on the afternoon flight from Geneva, and were back in London by the end of the day.

17

Six weeks after returning from Magine, Emily had moved to Cornwall. She took the lease on the shop in Humble Street two days after she arrived, after she had checked with Arthur that he wouldn't mind her moving into Dodger Point, just for as long as it took to find herself somewhere of her own to live. She had her eye on a cottage in St Brides itself, somewhere close enough to be able to walk to the shop, and close enough to Arthur's without camping on his doorstep. With Jennifer on the scene, and the two of them so obviously happy in each other's company, Emily did not want to get in their way for longer than she had to.

And thank God for Jennifer – Jennifer with her golden touch and amazing eye and her willingness to throw herself at a challenge. Since Emily had tentatively enlisted her help she was slowly, steadily transforming the little shop in Humble Street, leaving Emily to make the big decisions, but forever coming up with quirky wonderful touches that Emily would never have thought of, and that she knew were going to make all the difference.

She watched Jennifer now, painting a second coat on the walls, the rhythmic swish of her brush making the rough-cut diamond on her left hand twinkle in the light. Saltwater would open in two days' time.

Since Emily had come back to Cornwall, she had gone into overdrive to collect enough stock to open the shop in time for the start of the summer. Throughout it all, Jennifer had been at her side several times a week and they had become good friends. Opinionated and forceful when she was talking about something she knew about – and Jennifer knew about how Emily should tackle Saltwater – the reticence that Emily had encountered at the Pelican had evaporated, leaving only a disconcerting ability to go occasionally silent and a refreshing quirkiness that meant she was always fun to have around.

Jennifer had been sweetly untroubled by Emily's sudden arrival into Arthur's life, had had no problem at all with Emily moving into Dodger Point – she had known that it was a temporary measure, that once Emily had Saltwater up and running she would be looking for somewhere to live – and Emily was only embarrassed that she had taken a while to appreciate what Arthur had seen straight away. Two weeks after Emily moved into Dodger Point, Arthur and Jennifer announced their engagement.

Jennifer proved great to have around on a practical level, too. It was she who chose the stone-coloured paint for the walls, the exact shade of off-white for the stripped wooden floorboards, the deep red of the linen blinds in the window. And although Jennifer had left it to Emily to find most of the stock, she had such a good eye, and so many wonderful contacts, both in Cornwall and around the country, that Emily wondered what on earth she'd have done without her. Certainly, within a couple of weeks of taking on the lease Emily would have been on her knees in despair, because now that Saltwater had become a reality she understood how naive she'd been to think she could possibly have set up the shop without any help. It wasn't just an eye for colour and a knack for display that was needed, she realized belatedly, it was having the right contacts: knowing, or knowing of, designers and artists, handbag makers, candlestick makers, ceramicists, glass blowers, perfumiers to call on. It was knowing where the woollen mill was in Wales that sold the softest, prettiest blankets, how to track down a new scent that nobody else had discovered, which trade fairs to attend, and more besides. Jennifer knew about these things and Emily did not, and Emily remembered their bad start and shuddered at the thought of how she might have alienated her completely. It was in the back of Emily's mind to ask Jennifer to go into partnership with her, knowing that, in the longer term, she'd never be able to both maintain the stock levels and run the shop day to day. But that was something she was keeping to herself for now, at least until the opening day was behind her.

Together Jennifer and Arthur had come up with a list of local people she had to invite to the launch, and Emily again had to acknowledge how wrong she'd been, about both of them this time, not just about Jennifer. Why was it that she'd thought Arthur had few friends? Where had that patronizing preconception come from, that hardly any interesting people lived in Cornwall, that they only arrived in summer?

Among the names on Arthur's list was Sam's. She hadn't seen him since she'd returned to England. Having flown back into Heathrow, she'd left Caitlin at the underground and got back to her flat to find a message from him waiting for her, expressing concern about her eye, and she'd at once called him back and told him that she was OK.

She had put the phone down, knowing that it was up to her now and understanding why Sam was not about to make another hasty move in her direction. But instead of running out of the door to catch the first available train to Cornwall, she knew that she needed to sit tight for a while, wait for the right moment and not make a move towards him until her head had cleared from the fiasco of Oliver, until she knew it was the right time.

Once she'd moved to Cornwall, it would have been easy to drive over to Trevissey to see him but she hadn't and Sam hadn't come to see her either. Instead she'd spent the weeks driving all over the country finding her stock. She also knew that she hadn't seen Sam because they were both biding their time. There was a calmness there when she thought about him, because she knew that he was waiting for her to come to him, And as the weeks passed by, and spring came and with it the opening of Saltwater drew closer, Emily knew that the time to see him again was drawing closer too.

She hadn't spoken to Oliver since her return. She was surprised at how little she thought of him, finding that the memories of him faded as swiftly as the bruising to her eye, aware that she hadn't known him at all, relieved that she could let him slip from her life without a backward glance, that neither of them had ever said or done anything to make that slipping away more difficult.

Instead she felt a readiness to begin, an enthusiasm for the future in Cornwall that she had never felt in London. She was finally in the frame of mind that Arthur had told her she should strive for, full of confidence to go with what she wanted, whenever she found it.

Saltwater would open on her birthday. Holly, Caitlin and Leon, and Rachel were all coming down to the opening, which they hoped would turn into a spontaneous party for her afterwards. Only Jo-Jo, still filming in Italy, was unable to make it. Her friends hoped, of course, that it might be the occasion on which Emily and Sam got together, but there were no plans or schemes to help things along, none of the desperation in the air that there'd been throughout the discussions about Oliver.

On the day of the opening, 25 May, Emily was in Saltwater at seven in the morning, adding the final touches to the shop. The second coat of paint had dried overnight and a glass cabinet that had arrived the evening before could finally be put into place. Emily spent the first hour washing it and then filling it. The top shelf with scent bottles, very modern with gobstopper glass tops in pale blues and greens, and the bottom shelves with jewellery. Nothing yet from La Coccinelle – there had been no time for M. Gérard to make her pieces – but instead a range of items from other jewellers, some who had provided just five or six, others who had been able to supply a good deal more. The pièce de résistance was a series of necklaces from a jeweller in Ludlow in Shropshire, tracked down, of course, by Jennifer.

Emily worked hard, filling up and arranging the shop, leaving it only to buy a bacon sandwich halfway through the morning, enjoying being alone with her radio, the sunlight streaming in through her windows. Throughout the morning she had deliveries of more stock, glasses for the champagne – she'd pushed the boat out and ordered some, deciding the extravagance was necessary. And she had hired a local catering company to serve it and also to supply plates of canapés.

At around noon a bouquet arrived from Arthur and Jennifer, and then another from Rachel, Holly, Jo-Jo and Caitlin. And then, a short while later, the doorbell rang again and she looked up and saw Sam outside.

She stood up, feeling her heart start to pound, and went to let him in. The key was stiff in the lock and she struggled with it, all the time looking at him through the glass door, standing there. And all she could think was that here he was at last, her Sam, her sweet, lovely Sam and she wondered how she could have stayed away from him for so long.

'You've picked Chelsea Flower Show week for your opening. Can you imagine what my father said when I told him I was going to a party instead?'

'Oh, no!' She started to laugh. 'I'm so sorry. You shouldn't have missed it. I'd have understood.'

'He understood too, when I told him whose party it was.'

Sam handed her three perfect roses, pale blue tissue

paper wrapped around their stems, the flowers pale pink at the edges, getting slightly darker towards the centre, each a perfect cup filled with gorgeous, gently scented petals. He came closer and stroked one with a fingertip, then bent his head to smell them.

'They remind me of you,' he said.

'Thank you, Sam. They're beautiful.' And they were – the most beautiful roses she had ever seen.

'And now I have to go,' Sam said apologetically. 'I wanted to give you these now, before I saw you again tonight, but I really can't stay.'

'I'd like to come back with you, you know how much I want to see Trevissey again, now that it's all coming alive. I've been waiting for the summer.' She laughed nerously and there was suddenly a formality in her voice.

'So that's what you've been waiting for,' he teased. 'Well, the sun is out. It's hot. The roses will be opening as we speak. Come whenever you want to.'

'Tomorrow?'

He nodded, then looked around the shop. 'And this looks fantastic. I can't believe it's the same place. You'll have customers beating down the door.'

'Sam,' she said, not knowing quite what to say, but acutely aware that it was up to her this time. 'I've missed you. I've been thinking about you, all the time I've been here.' And then she added in a flustered rush, 'I'm so pleased to see you again.'

He looked back at her, warmth, love, suddenly there in his eyes. He took two steps towards her.

'And I've missed you too. More than you could ever

imagine. But now, dearest Emily, I have to go. I really have to go. And I'll see you properly tonight,' he said, leaving her giddy with longing for him. And then, before she could stop him, he had gone, saying only that he'd be back for the party.

At Dodger Point later that afternoon she sat for a while in the kitchen in feverish excitement. Arthur, listening to her, knew exactly what it was about, knowing it wasn't her party she was anticipating, not the party that was stopping her from eating or keeping her talking and talking and talking.

Then, finally, when Jennifer arrived and Arthur packed Emily off to change, she lay on her bed in her little room at the back of the house, letting her mind still. Then she got up again, stripped off her clothes and stood naked, looking at the marble whiteness of her body in the mirror, turning to look at her bottom, at the line of her thighs, at the way the whiteness gradually changed to a golden brown around her shoulders and down her arms and she wondered what Sam might make of her, whether he would like what he saw, what it would be like to make love with him. Not just how it would feel to let go, at last, but physically, what it would feel like, whether it would hurt, whether it was possible that it might be wonderful first time around. She knew it rarely was, remembered Caitlin's and Holly's warnings, and yet, if it was with Sam, whatever happened, surely it couldn't be a disappointment?

She pulled open the door of the small single wardrobe and pulled out the dress she was going to wear that she'd found in Notting Hill with Holly, just before she left

London for the last time. A sea green halter-neck dress, the top half fitting close, made from thick stretchy silk which floated out around her legs.

Emily stood at the edge of the crowd at her party, holding a glass of warm champagne, searching through the faces for Sam. She had kept an eye out for him since the beginning, and an hour later he still hadn't arrived. All around her the noise of her party swooped and dived. The doors and windows had long since been thrown open and people spilled out onto the usually quiet street, the lights and noise on that glimmering evening attracting the attention of the few passers-by.

It was going well, if noise and numbers proved anything. Having sat out the first half-hour with Arthur and Jennifer and the girls from London, wondering if anybody was going to show up, suddenly Emily found the room was full and now still more people were arriving. She presumed they would last as long as the drink did.

At seven Arthur took it upon himself to propose a toast to the success of Saltwater. Then Emily stood up and thanked them all, thanked Arthur and Jennifer most of all and all the while scanned the room for Sam. Then, just as she was finishing speaking, she saw him standing in the corner of the room. When she caught his eye he smiled at her, lighting her up so that the grumbling headache she hadn't even been aware of instantly lifted, the panic subsided, and she was transformed from looking decidedly half-hearted about the whole evening to glowing, beautiful, mesmerizing.

When she had finished thanking everybody for coming, Sam moved across the room to her side and told her she was brilliant, kissed her hard and hugged her tightly so that she could feel his heart beating fast against hers with all the promise of what was to come.

Emily glided through the rest of the party. On a high, knowing he was waiting for her, savouring the anticipation, as she circulated and did a perfect job of looking after her guests.

And then, almost abruptly, the party was over, the tail-enders straggling out of the door, talking about restaurants and catching last orders, and Emily was left with just the girls and Arthur and Jennifer, and Sam.

'So,' said Caitlin, draining her glass of champagne, 'who's clearing up?'

'Not me,' said Emily. 'The caterers.'

'That's all I need to know. It's not down to us. So we can go and find something to eat?'

'Good idea,' Emily said, even though she couldn't imagine eating, going along with it even though she was thinking, *no. No, I do not want to do that. Not at all.*

One by one they filed out of the shop. Emily locked up and they set off down the street.

'I've called the Pelican,' Arthur told her. 'We've got a table at ten thirty.'

'Great.' Emily smiled. 'Lovely idea.'

But she and Sam never made it to the Pelican. The others ambled slowly through the streets, and it wasn't until they reached Arthur's and Holly's cars that they realized Emily and Sam weren't with them.

18

In the car Sam and Emily didn't speak, but he kept hold of her hand all the way to Trevissey.

Outside the house Sam stopped the engine and Emily opened the door of the car and stepped out, waiting for Sam to come around and join her, and then together they walked through the archway cut into the wall and into the gardens. Feeling the grass beneath her feet, she stopped, bent down and slipped off her sandals. The grass was spongy and cool between her toes.

Silently Sam slipped his jacket off his shoulders, passed it to her and she pulled it around herself gratefully. Emily could tell that there was a purpose to Sam's stride. He was heading somewhere specific. In the moonlight they passed the huge greenhouses but he led her past them, then cut around the side of the house until finally he stopped and turned to her, and she knew that whatever he was bringing her to see was here.

She looked around but could see nothing different. They were standing beside the old pear tree where Sam had lifted her up and she'd found the platform high in the branches.

'What is it?' she asked, curious.

'Damn it for not being daylight,' he replied, 'but still I had to show you tonight. It wouldn't be the same if you saw it tomorrow. You have to see it tonight, on your birthday, on the night of your party for Saltwater.'

'But what is it?'

He took her hand and led her over to the pear tree, put his hands around her waist and once again lifted her up. This time she found there was an old rope looped around the trunk of the tree and she used it to pull herself up and onto the platform.

She stood in her dress and her bare feet and Sam's jacket, looking out across the grounds, to where one garden ended and another began, and still she could not see what it was he wanted to show her.

Then Sam pulled himself up behind her and slipped his arms around her waist. It felt so indescribably perfect that she found she had no voice to ask him again.

He crossed his arms around her. 'Do you see those arches dividing this garden from the next?' he asked. 'Do you see those seven arches?' She nodded. 'There's a rose growing up each of them. It's the same rose that I brought you this afternoon, only none of those is flowering yet. Not quite yet.'

She nodded again. She could see where he meant now. In the light of the moon she could just make out the shoots twisting and spiralling, and, high up on one arch, a single rose was starting to flower.

'That rose is very special,' Sam told her. 'It's one of the three roses that we're launching at Chelsea this year.'

'It's beautiful.'

'And the reason Dad was so cross about your party being tonight wasn't because he wanted me at Chelsea. It was when I explained that *you* couldn't be there that he was really put out.'

'Why?'

'Because I've taken a leap of faith.'

She leaned back against him, still not sure what he was going to say, yet knowing it was about her.

'It's your rose, Emily,' he told her. 'It's called Emily, after you. And usually, if a rose is being named after someone, and the someone hasn't died, then they turn up at the flower show to celebrate. But then, to be fair, usually the recipient of such an honour knows about it in advance. And I didn't tell you,' he went on. 'I thought it would be nicest if you found out today, on your birthday, on the night of your party. I gave the roses to you this afternoon but I managed not to tell you their name because I wanted you to see them here, now, with me. It's why I had to leave so fast.' He grinned at her. 'I knew if I stayed another second I'd tell you everything that I wanted to save for tonight.'

She turned in his arms. 'Oh, Sam, how can you have done that for me? I think that's the most lovely thing that's ever happened to me.'

And before Sam could stop her, she'd leapt straight out of the pear tree, landing in a heap on the grass below.

'Emily, you are stark raving mad,' Sam called, immediately jumping down after her, relieved to see her getting to her feet, laughing at his concern.

'I knew it was a soft landing,' she told him before she set off again. 'I guessed I'd survive. I want to see Emily close up.'

At the arches he reached up and pulled the single flower down so that she could look at it.

'How beautiful it is,' she said, reaching forward and burying her nose in its soft folds.

'Read the catalogue entry before you thank me too much,' he said with a grin. 'You might change your mind.'

'Thank you, thank you, thank you,' she said, hugging him tightly to her.

He hugged her back, then bent and kissed her gently.

She looked up at him, watching his eyes. 'What do I do now, Sam?' she asked. 'If a girl gets a rose named after her, I don't know but I think there must be some kind of payback due, don't you?'

'Kiss me,' he told her and she stretched up and did what he said.

'And then what do we do?'

'And then you put your arm around the back of my neck, like this,' he murmured against her face, lifting her arm, and she wound it around his neck and clung on to him. 'And then I kiss you again.' She stretched her other arm around his neck. 'And I kiss you again and again and again,' Sam said, 'and I never stop, I just keep kissing you for ever.'

They stood in the moonlit gardens, Emily in bare feet, Sam in his shirt, grass stains on his knees, kissing each other until kissing was no longer enough. Then Emily took his hand and led him underneath the arch of Emily roses to the little summer house.

When they got there, it was Emily rather than Sam

who jumped up the step and tried the handle of the door. It opened, and it seemed natural and inevitable that she should lead him inside. Stacked up along one wall were deckchairs and sun loungers and along the other were the cushions for them. Without waiting for Sam to say or do anything, Emily walked over, picked up an armful of cushions and chucked them on the floor, then sat down and looked up at him. 'Come here,' she said, reaching out for him.

He sat down beside her and she could tell that he was unsure about this moment.

'It's all because of the rose,' she joked. 'Look what happens when you give a girl a rose.'

'Emily, Emily, Emily,' he groaned, burying his face in her neck.

'Yes, Sam,' she said, holding him close, 'I know you're concerned about doing the right thing. And you *are* doing the right thing. We are doing so much the right thing. This is what I've been waiting for. This is how it should be. You don't have to worry, because I know it is. I know what I want to do, and that's to be with you. You're everything I've been waiting for, everything I ever wanted to find.'

He touched his hand to her face and then kissed her again, tenderly, softly, and she could feel herself opening out for him, long slow ripples of lust flowing through her. She slipped her hands under his shirt, feeling his ribs rising and falling, then moved down to the flatness of his belly.

'Don't talk,' she told him. 'You don't need to tell me anything. You don't need to tell me that you love me, you certainly don't need to tell me that you'll marry me. You don't even need to tell me you'll respect me in the morning.'

He said nothing, just reached for the tie at the back of her neck with infinitely gentle hands. He moved his fingers slowly down her back, then around to the soft flesh of her stomach and to the curve of her hips. She pulled her dress over her head and then grabbed him to her, finding she wanted to push against him, be passionate and rough, not gentle or sweet any more.

Later, Sam got up and she heard him rummaging in the corner of the summer house and then felt the delicious warmth of blankets being carefully draped over her, and then, with his arms around her, she fell asleep.

As dawn broke across the gardens she woke up again and beside her, almost to the second, Sam woke up too, saw her there beside him and smiled a smile of such sweet happiness that she felt her eyes burn with tears.

'I can't promise any croissants for breakfast,' he said, kissing her. 'But I can run to the house and get some toast and coffee.'

She snuggled deep under the blankets, keeping her arms around him. She wondered if she was different. If what had happened had changed her. But she knew that it hadn't at all. It wasn't who she was that had changed, it was how she led her life. Because from now on her life had Sam in it. She wasn't alone.

'Everyone told me it's not so good the first time,' she said.

'And what do you think?'

She turned in his arms and kissed him. 'I think that I need something to compare it with.'

Epilogue

Emily King (Heritage rose) – 'Unique Blanche' ×
Hybrid tea 'Monique'
× 'Constance Spry'

There are some roses that one is rather doubtful
about introducing to the garden and at first Emily
seems such a rose. Truly beautiful, its colour com-
bines a mixture of pale pinks and gold. Emily is
capable of considerable climbing feats, especially
into trees but has a tendency to ramble in the
opposite direction to where you were hoping,
especially when exposed to the cold. Hates the
snow, which can affect the bloom, but in its favou-
red habitat richly rewarding, a flawless, perfect rose
with a wonderful heady scent. Climber 5'5".

Acknowledgements

Special thanks to Jill Bevan, Charles Davies, Michelle Scorah, Petra Reitmayerova, Louise Cripps and Louise Voss, Chris Manby, Alex Roads and Miranda Fricker, and to my Barnes and Unicorn friends for all their advice and enthusiasm and to everyone else who came up with great reasons for staying a virgin (but didn't act on them). Also to Caroline Gardner, particularly for pointing me in the direction of the Cockpit Studios and for having a shop as gorgeous as Fig, and to David Austin for showing me around his wonderful nurseries in Albrighton and for taking the trouble to explain the intricacies of cross-breeding roses to me. His excellent books, especially *Old Roses and English Roses* (Antique Collectors' Club), were also very helpful. As was John Armstrong's book *Conditions of Love* (Allen Lane) and *Been There, Haven't Done That – A Virgin's Memoir* by Tara McCarthy (Time Warner International). Huge thanks to everyone at Pan, who once again have made publishing a book such fun, especially to Imogen Tayler and Lucy Henson. Thanks again to Jo Frank for her great editorial eye and such wise words. And lastly thanks to my family, especially Tom and Jack, and, of course, most of all to Ant.

Six Reasons to Stay a Virgin is one of several new novels that include the name Nessa O'Neill following a charity bid at an auction in support of War Child.

calling on lily

For Ant

and in memory of my father,

Graham Hartley Davies

My true friends have always given me that supreme proof of devotion: a spontaneous aversion for the man I loved.

Colette

1

You don't often see a good-looking man in Welshpool. To see four at once, on a rainy Friday in February, with no girls in tow, was too good to be true. Kirsty stopped abruptly and caught Lily's arm.

'Look at them, on the other side of the street.'

Lily screwed up her eyes, wondering what she was referring to, and saw four men, slowly making their way towards them. They were walking three abreast and one behind, dominating the pavement, forcing everyone else to divide, muttering, around them.

Before Lily could get a proper look, Kirsty grabbed her arm and hustled her off the High Street and into a tiny cobbled passageway. Hidden, they stopped beside a deserted clothes shop.

'They're crossing the road,' Kirsty said, edging out to get a better look. 'Keep still and look at the clothes. Any minute now, they're going to walk right past.'

Smiling at the speed with which Kirsty had moved into action, Lily watched her whip out a lipstick from under her coat and slide it quickly across her mouth, then consider herself in the glass reflection. She slapped both her cheeks and wiped her cold nose with her hand.

'You're such a tart,' Lily told her.

'No I'm not!' Kirsty grinned. 'But you have to admit

it's sod's law. If you go out with no make-up on and looking like a dog, gorgeous men *will* walk up the street towards you.'

Kirsty had wild black curls, sparkling blue eyes and pale, flawless skin. Under a thin summer coat, she poured out of a low-cut top that was tucked into jeans so tight she'd been practically vacuum-packed into them. The last thing anyone was going to notice was the lipstick.

Out on the main street the men were getting closer.

'Josh,' one said loudly, the voice now so clear that he had to be almost beside them. 'Do you *seriously* want to look around the castle? It's raining and it's miles away. Or did you say that to get rid of Hal?'

Lily took a sneaky look. The guy who was talking was tall and well built, with cropped brown hair and soft dark eyes.

'No, Hal's safely at home,' Josh replied, looking at his watch. 'Come on, lard-arse, you could do with the exercise. It's only four o'clock. We'll be back by five.'

Kirsty considered them carefully, trying to decide whom she'd say yes to first. Either of the first two, she decided. And the third's not bad either. Lily could have the fourth one. Like his friends, he was probably in his late twenties or early thirties, but while they were growing older gorgeously, he had traffic-light orange hair that was fast receding at the forehead, plump pale cheeks and beady eyes. He was wearing a rugby shirt tucked into his jeans, with the collar up against the wind, and was hanging back from the others, hunched over a kebab and dripping a trail of grease and juice and bits of meat on to the pavement. And if that's from the Taste of the Orient kebab van, she told him silently, you're not long for this earth anyway.

At the front, Josh was wearing a dark coat buttoned high up to his chin and a navy stretchy hat pulled down to his eyes. Kirsty had never seen someone wear a woolly hat and look so good in it, certainly no one older than ten. But beneath the hat were lovely eyes and lofty cheekbones, and the short coat revealed a pair of long, long legs.

'Hey, we could chuck Hal in one of the castle dungeons,' said the one with the kebab. He wiped his chin with his hand, and started to laugh. 'Save us the hassle of looking after him.'

'Oh, ha,' said Josh in a bored voice. 'No. Llanygoed will suit us just fine. The cottage is perfect.'

Lily wondered who Hal was and what was going to happen in Llanygoed. For a second, she thought, quite calmly, that they might be planning a murder. She concentrated hard on the voices, trying to hear everything that they said.

'Don't tell me you lot are bottling out?' Josh challenged them all, stopping suddenly, his words causing Lily's heart to beat even faster in sudden panic. 'It's much too late for that.'

He stared at them, waiting for an answer, but nobody spoke.

'Does anyone have any better ideas?'

The other three stood awkwardly on the pavement.

'Come on, guys,' Josh said impatiently, turning against a sudden gust of wind and rain. 'We've been through this a million times.'

Still the others didn't speak.

'We can't wait here for ever,' Lily whispered from the passageway, her teeth chattering. 'I'm freezing.'

Kirsty shrugged. 'As long as we need to. I'm not moving.'

'And I can't stand these terrible clothes any longer!' Lily hissed back. 'People might think I like them!'

'Don't be such a snob! And don't you dare move. They'll notice you and then they'll shut up. Something is definitely going on.'

Lily rolled her eyes and looked back at the window, noticing that the mustard-coloured dress, which she had come to think of as a permanent feature of Welshpool, had been joined by a pair of matching mustard earrings.

'No, Josh, I'm not happy about this,' someone said. 'I never have been. It can't be the only answer.'

On the street Josh paused and pulled out a packet of cigarettes. His head bent low as he struck a match, long fingers cupping it against the wind and rain, before flicking it out into the road.

'You're not the sharpest knife in the drawer,' he said, looking up at the guy with a grin, 'but can't even you see we have no choice? We've been waiting for Hal to change his mind for months! And we can't wait any longer because the wedding's in the morning.' He stopped for a second, challenging them all. 'We've got him down here, against all the odds and now, what else do we do? You lot

4

haven't produced one single good idea. And in the long run he'll be grateful,' Josh insisted. 'We're saving him from a fate worse than death. Amber's such a bitch she'd win best of breed.'

'But it's his *wedding*!' the other guy replied. 'Think of all the people, the cake, the presents – the matching bathrobes that I chose with such loving care – the vicar, the honeymoon . . .'

'Think of his vows.' Josh was adamant. 'And how he'd never give up on them. He'd be reciting his own prison sentence. As his best man and ushers it's our duty to look after him.' He paused. 'So we'll stop the wedding, stop him marrying Amber.'

Absolutely, thought Kirsty, who hated people getting married.

'But they can't!' Lily cried, and for a moment Kirsty thought she might be about to confront them.

'Shut *up*! Keep *still*,' she begged, grabbing Lily's arm.

'They can't do that!'

Somehow the four men didn't notice them and slowly moved off again. Lily and Kirsty immediately walked out into the street and tucked in behind them.

'We'll have dinner at the Little Goose at about eight.' It was the one called Josh speaking again. 'Then we'll drive back to Llany-welshy-whatever, get him trashed and put him to bed.'

Kirsty bristled at his words.

'He'll probably sleep beyond midday,' Josh went on. 'And by then it'll be too late.'

'How are we going to keep him here? Won't he go

5

back to Oxford as soon as he wakes up?' It was the dark-haired one talking again.

'Oh no, Charlie,' Josh said, sounding surprised that he hadn't understood. 'If he tries to leave, you're going to stop him. Rich, Alex,' he said, nodding at the other two, making sure they were listening to him. 'It's up to the three of you to make sure nothing goes wrong. When he wakes up tomorrow you mustn't let him leave. I'll have gone to Oxford, to see the bride, break the news that he won't be showing up.' He shrugged. 'She'll get over it,' he said confidently. 'Give her a week or two and she'll have got her claws into some other poor sod.'

'It's all we can do,' said the kebab eater. 'As Josh says, she's a hound.' He moved swiftly up the street, beginning to leave the others behind. 'Forget the castle, we're not here for the sightseeing,' he shouted back to them. 'And we said we'd get some beers. Hal will start to miss us if we're not back soon.'

Kirsty and Lily watched them until all four disappeared into the off-licence.

'Can you believe that?' Kirsty looked at Lily with glee. 'And they're all alone!'

'Can't see things changing for the guy with the kebab. Even with you around.'

Kirsty blew her a kiss.

'And you heard what they said,' Lily went on. 'They're in the middle of a kidnapping, they're not going to have time to get to know you!'

'They don't need time to get to know *us*,' said Kirsty. 'It's just important that they know *we're* here – we're an important local attraction. Pleeease! How often is it we get an opportunity like this?'

'You know,' Lily said, looking puzzled. 'I've always given people such a hard time for calling you Thirsty Kirsty. Why is that?'

'Don't ask what they call you!' Kirsty put her arm around Lily's shoulders. 'Come on,' she cajoled, 'all you have to do is come with me to the Little Goose. We know when they'll be there.'

Lily nodded slowly. She wanted to talk to Kirsty about what they'd heard, wanted to ask her if it could possibly be for real, but Kirsty was too bound up in plotting and scheming and working out how she might engineer a meeting and was almost oblivious to what they'd actually said.

'Home,' Kirsty said. 'We need time to get ready. Let's go back to your sister's.'

*

It was a steep, wet climb. On either side of the wide street were solid, sodden black and white buildings, their ancient gutters pouring arcs of rainwater out on to the pavement. Shouldering space between them, giving the street a lovely higgledy-piggledy look, were tiny cottages and an occasional Georgian townhouse. And all along, branching off at regular intervals, were narrow alleyways with names like Bear Passage, where the lichen and moss grew rampant between the slippery wet cobblestones.

Sometimes these alleys would open on to an utterly unexpected courtyard and it was in one of these that Lily and Kirsty had spent most of Lily's first summer in Welshpool, sitting outside in the shady dappled sunlight, idly eating lunch. They'd met a week after Lily's arrival, sharing the last outdoor table, one hot July day.

It hadn't been entirely spontaneous. Kirsty, preparing for a solitary lunchtime with *OK!*, had looked up to see Lily walking hesitantly down the cobbled pathway towards her. Kirsty had been captivated, not just because she knew everyone in Welshpool and Lily was obviously a stranger, but because Lily looked amazing. A wisp of black lace held back her short blonde hair, and she wore a loosely crocheted black cardigan over a violet bra top, cut-off black jeans and flat leather sandals. She had golden brown legs and dark purple nail-varnish. The kind of girl who Kirsty wished would stay on, would move in down the street, and liven up her beloved, boring town.

Of course she was probably only in Welshpool for a few hours, how many people stayed longer? But even so, as the girl moved indoors to choose her lunch Kirsty made a swift decision and dived in behind her. By the time they'd finished queuing for the soup, they'd begun to talk.

Later, sitting languidly in the sun, their empty bowls pushed to one side, Lily explained that her decision to come had been made on the spur of the moment. That she'd got a sister in Welshpool, called Grace Somerville who'd bought a house about six months ago, and that she was going to spend some time with her. Kirsty had flinched. Of course she knew exactly who Lily meant. Everyone knew Grace, or knew of her. She was their local Miss Haversham, living out a life of miserable isolation in

8

a lovely house in a quiet back street a little way out of the town.

Kirsty had nodded non-committally, waiting to see if Lily was going to say more. But Lily had fallen silent, transported back to the flat in Manchester where she was staying at the time, listening again to her sister weeping brokenly down the telephone, protesting in the same gasping breaths that she was absolutely fine. She had known with sisterly intuition that she should get to Grace as soon as she possibly could.

Lily had shaken the image from her mind, and looking up she'd smiled at Kirsty and had started to describe what it was like being met at Shrewsbury station and driven through the early evening sunlight, into what felt like the middle of absolutely nowhere, where not even Macdonald's had penetrated. Kirsty laughed, but Lily had meant what she said. As the hills had become higher and more beautifully desolate and the villages had fallen away, she had grown silent, looking out of the car window wide-eyed. She had noticed signposts to Welsh Harp Hollow and the Long Mountain and had felt an unexpected glow of anticipation.

'Where are you from?' Kirsty had asked.

'I've been at art college in London,' said Lily, squinting at Kirsty in the sunlight. 'I've just finished a post-grad in three-dimensional design.'

Kirsty was momentarily silenced.

'Call it pottery!' Lily reassured her, laughing and showing even pearly white teeth. 'But I grew up near Chester. We used to come here camping. I don't remember it but I think that's why Grace has come back.' Lily fished a pair of sunglasses out of her back pocket and settled them on her small nose.

'And how long might you stay?'

'Dunno, it depends on Grace. But I'd imagine about a month. She wants me to help her paint her house.'

Kirsty nodded slowly.

'And what about you?' Lily asked. 'Have you always lived around here?'

'Sure,' said Kirsty. '"*Does neb byth yn ymadael!*"' She grinned at Lily. 'Nobody ever leaves. The furthest I got was when I was sent to boarding-school about thirty miles away. But I love it. I always have. I couldn't be anywhere else.'

Lily laughed. 'Well, while I'm here, I've got to see you again. Please! You can imagine, I know *nobody*. And Grace can't face a trip to the video shop let alone a night in the pub.'

Six months later Kirsty was feeling confident that Lily would stay put, if not with her sister, then somewhere else near Welshpool, and if not for ever, at least for a few months more. Although the freezing winter winds had put paid to the alfresco lunchtimes and the rain had fallen almost incessantly since Christmas, Lily had stopped talking about when she would move on.

Now it was so dark that the alleyways had become a little menacing, the bright lights of the nearby shops emphasizing how spooky and silent they were. Lily and Kirsty hurried past them, then moved off the High Street and began to head out of the town.

Lily was deeply relieved that her sister had chosen that weekend to go to see their parents and wouldn't therefore walk in to find Kirsty in her house. Grace couldn't even stand to be in the same room as Kirsty, and hated Lily spending so much time in her company – time spent away from her – missing the point that Kirsty provided vital light relief. What others saw in Kirsty – why others felt better for being with her – completely passed Grace by. She could make Lily laugh at nothing, but her loud voice and relentless good humour made Grace itch to slap her. Even more, it was Kirsty's avaricious accumulation of all the most personal, most embarrassing gossip that really drove Grace crazy, knowing that Kirsty would have an absolute feast on all the disastrous details surrounding her own love life.

'She's like a dirty great bluebottle who finds the shit and then just loves spreading it everywhere,' Grace had said bitterly. 'And don't you ever tell her what happened to me.'

*

When Lily had offered to come to stay with Grace she'd had little idea of what she was letting herself in for. She and Grace had had a bust up a year earlier, but it had never occurred to Lily that she might not be able to regain the easy friendship that had always previously been there between them. But she had arrived to find the new Grace was someone she hardly recognized. Alternately weeping or bitingly aggressive, she was negative about everything and everyone, particularly Lily, and still refused to forgive her for her part in what had happened the year before. If Lily had presumed that her arrival would smooth things along, pick up the pace of Grace's recovery, she was wrong. The weeks passed but Grace's black moods did not. Still Lily had hung on, patient and gentle, tirelessly listening, encouraging Grace to talk, night after night, hoping that, in time, she'd come to terms with what had happened to her.

Six months later, Lily was close to admitting she'd failed and, if anything, that Grace was in even worse shape than when she'd arrived. When she announced to Lily that she was going away for the weekend, a miracle in itself, Lily felt a leap of delight at the thought of a whole weekend without her. Now with the stag party in town she was even more relieved that Grace was safely off the scene.

She played the boys' conversation over again in her mind. It was unbelievable that after all that she and Grace had been through, she of all people would overhear such a conversation. To Lily it was amazing that these men could have so much confidence that they were doing the right thing, and were prepared to hurt so many people. She hadn't been able to do it for Grace.

A year ago Grace had had a fiancé. He was someone Lily had disliked at first sight and only loathed more the longer she knew him. At first Lily had been hardly able to do more than voice a doubt, but when they became engaged she'd resolved to try to tell her sister how she felt. It had sent an immediate icy wind whipping between them. Grace had been livid that her little sister had questioned her judgement about anything, let alone her choice of husband. In tears, she'd spat out, an inch from Lily's face, that it was only because Lily was jealous, because she couldn't get close to anyone herself, that she hated Jeremy. Lily had swayed in shock, totally taken aback by Grace's anger. She remembered staring at Grace in disbelief, telling her that she was wrong and that it was only because she loved her that she had decided she must say what she felt.

'And what *was* that exactly? Tell me again!' Grace had demanded.

'That I don't think he loves you. Enough,' Lily had replied quietly, not adding that in her opinion, he was about as good a catch as a bucket of crabs. And he'd probably given her them already.

*

Stop thinking about it! Lily told herself now. She grabbed Kirsty's arm and marched her up the steep hill, putting her sister firmly out of her mind.

'In! In! I'll go all frizzy,' Kirsty cried when Lily eventually unlocked the front door of Grace's house, pushing past her and making her way towards the kitchen. Lily followed, letting her keys and coat drop to the floor. She stood still for a moment, ignoring Kirsty's chatter, and lightly touched the walls. The hall smelled of Green Smoke paint even though it had been dry for a few days. It still surprised her every time she walked in and for a moment she felt almost nostalgic for the anaglypta wall paper and the old pizza-effect carpet Grace and she had ripped up with such relish. But the new colour emphasized the uncluttered simplicity of the house and highlighted the beautiful vaulted ceiling and curving central staircase. It had taken a long time to persuade Grace that style didn't always mean that your clothes were black and your house white, but the effort had definitely been worth it.

'All that work. Bet you wish this place was yours,' Kirsty said.

Lily followed her, thinking that it was true, her footsteps loud on the floorboards, newly stripped and sanded by her. She walked over to the windows, which opened out on to a large garden, and drew shut the heavy curtains. Behind her, Kirsty headed straight for the freezer and took out ice and a frosted bottle of vodka, orange juice already at her side.

With a glass in each hand, Kirsty pushed open the sitting-room door with her foot. She handed one glass to Lily and lowered herself on to the sofa.

'So, who would you pull, then?' Kirsty asked, forcing off her trainers and curling her feet underneath her. 'I liked that one called Josh. Bloody gorgeous. I bet they're all loaded.'

Lily put down her glass. 'I just can't believe we heard them say all those things,' she said. 'And sorry, Kirsty, sorry, but I didn't *like* them. Whoever Hal is, he's picked a bunch of bastards for his friends.'

'You're so predictable.'

Lily laughed. 'I don't care what you think, you old slapper.'

Kirsty shrugged, enjoying herself. 'So what? I keep the

locals happy.' She looked at Lily with a light in her eye. 'You, on the other hand, have no fun at all.'

'Oh, leave it out,' Lily said. 'If I don't choose to shag for Britain that's up to me.'

Kirsty let it rest. She wasn't going to risk irritating Lily tonight. Not when she might refuse to go to the pub. She lay back on the soft, dark brown moleskin sofa, stroking the arm with her hand and wondering if moleskin had once meant real moles.

Kirsty couldn't have admitted it, even to herself, but from the moment they'd first met she had found Lily completely captivating. She stared endlessly at Lily's thick straight eyebrows and olive-green eyes, listened intently to her soft laugh and continually analysed her clothes. How or why Lily did even the most trivial things was of vital importance to her. She followed Lily's example and fitted hair-clips of butterflies and flowers into her own dark curls, sorted expertly through the same piles of gorgeous tops and jackets in the vintage clothes shop, and drove miles in search of the same pair of sunglasses that Lily had worn on that first day they'd met.

To Kirsty, Lily was cool, part of an urban, sleeker world. She wanted to know everything about her: if she coloured her hair, if she took drugs, if she liked sushi and where she lost her virginity, whether she thought ankle boots had had their day, how often she saw her parents, whether she could cook. But they talked about more serious things too, about the collapse of the farming industry and the devastation wreaked by foot and mouth, and urban sprawl, and Kirsty was relieved to discover that the terrible rural crises that one after another were destroying so much of her own family's livelihood hadn't entirely passed Lily by.

Lily was welcome relief. They had been born into similar enough backgrounds, and although Lily had been through art college while Kirsty had gone straight to work from school, Kirsty knew straight away that she had found a kindred spirit. She was happy to sit for hours at the weekends, watching Lily at work on her pottery in the old brick workshop in Grace's garden, warmed by the portable kiln, and enthusiastically reading all Lily's old art college textbooks.

'So what are you going to wear?' she asked now. 'Grey trousers?'

Lily swallowed back irritation at Kirsty's perfect knowledge of her wardrobe and nodded.

'I think I'll make a bit more of an effort,' Kirsty wondered aloud. 'Do you mind if I borrow something?' She looked at her watch. 'It's nearly six now and they're getting there at half seven. Let's get to the bar at about ten past and have a few drinks before they arrive.'

*

After Kirsty had gone Lily went upstairs and flopped on to her bed. Kirsty had been almost humming with excitement. But then, Lily acknowledged, how often did such a potent combination of sex, scandal and gorgeous men land on your doorstep?

The way Kirsty went after men reminded Lily of a fish gliding powerfully across the ocean bed, picking up everything in her path, but spitting most of it out again almost straight away. Lily couldn't remember a time Kirsty had gone out with a bloke for longer than a week.

She didn't doubt that Kirsty would get in with the stag party. It was inconceivable that she would leave the Little Goose without having checked them all over. What they were planning to do wouldn't bother her in the slightest. But it did bother Lily, terribly. Could these guys really be contemplating such a thing? In the low, expectant tone of the conversation on the High Street, Lily had sensed their excitement. They had talked with a mistaken romanticism, as if they were plucking their man from the scene of danger, swooping heroically at the final hour, to hold him in a secret hideout until the crisis had past. They'd been serious, she thought. They were going to do it.

She got up and walked across to the window, drawing shut the blue velvet curtains. Whoever Hal was, however unstable, however lacking in self-preservation, self-awareness, however grateful they might think he'd be; how could they take the chance that they were wrong? If they liked him, even just a little, how could they allow themselves to get so carried away? How could they take it so far?

Lily stood between her curtains and looked out at the deserted, lamplit street, pressing her fingertips against the cold panes of glass and watching the rain streak the window like tears. And what about his bride? It was bad enough that they were doing this to Hal. But what about her? How would she feel, Lily wondered? What might she do?

Grace had been sent four times around the village in her wedding car before it was finally established that her fiancé was not going to turn up at the church. She had still not got over it. Lily could not let it happen to someone else.

2

Alex's grandmother, Peggy Topham, had been delighted for her cottage to be used by her only grandson and his young friends while she went to visit her sister in Cheltenham. In her keep fit class she'd talked about it so much that the group had come to a chattering untidy halt in the middle of a routine and the instructor had petulantly switched off her music and had folded her arms, taking several of them back to their schooldays.

Her cottage was on the edge of a wood, tiny and pretty, with a black cat and three small bedrooms, the sort of place Little Red Riding Hood's grandmother might have lived in. Alex and the others took great care of it, careful not to break the delicate chairs, tread in the plate of cat food or block the antiquated loo. They didn't notice how a couple of pictures had bounced off the walls with the force of the slamming doors, or how the stacked-up beer-cans were threatening to overwhelm the kitchen.

Upstairs old copies of *The Field* were piled high on each of the small, carved bedside tables. In her own bedroom, Alex's grandmother had trustingly left her high, bouncy bed covered in a white lace bedspread, the pillows plump and laundered.

Josh walked along a narrow upstairs corridor his hair wet, a towel wrapped around his waist, his bare feet leaving large wet footprints on the old oak floorboards, and hammered on Hal's bedroom door.

'Go on in. I'm just dropping the kids off at the pool,' came a voice from the bathroom next door.

'Hal! You're an animal.'

Hal laughed over the sound of the flush and appeared in the doorway. 'What do you want?' he asked, bending his head and following Josh into his bedroom.

Hal was tall, easily the tallest of the five of them. He had huge hands and size thirteen feet and a thick thatch of caramel hair that looked as though it had been cut with a Flymo. He loped rather than walked and the tiny cottage bedroom seemed much too small for him. When Josh didn't answer he came round in front of him.

'What's wrong?' He asked, then a shaft of hurt crossed his open, smiling face. 'Don't *do* this to me. I keep telling you. My wedding is not a point for discussion.'

Josh closed the door with a click. 'What do you mean?'

'I mean it's happening. All organized. Dress fitted, guests arrived, speeches written, cake decorated, flowers arranged. There's no going back.'

'But you wish there was?'

'I didn't say that,' Hal said calmly.

There was a long silence. 'Even if I told you I'd slept with her?' Josh said, desperately. He sat down slowly, unable to meet Hal's eye, and picked at the bedspread.

'Yes, you bastard. Even if you told me that,' Hal said eventually. 'I already know.'

'Amber has *told* you?' Momentarily Josh was thrown

off track. 'She cheated on you, Hal!' he said indignantly, quickly back on course. 'You shouldn't be marrying her. What's to stop her doing it again?'

'Nothing. Apart from the fact that we love each other.' Hal stood resolutely in front of him. 'And we didn't when you two got it together. I reckon I can live with it.'

He moved over to the tiny leaded window, undoing the locks and letting in the clean night air, and Josh saw that once again he was getting nowhere.

'How could you still ask me to be your best man?'

'It's hard to explain. Perhaps because I'd probably have slept with her if I'd been in your place. I was like you then. I hated you when she first told me but I forgive you for it now.'

Hal went silent for a moment, looking out into the dark, watching the swing of headlights travel along a distant lane. 'I always knew you'd freak when you realized Amber and I were serious, and I suppose you thought it was a fun way of making sure she forgot about me? You're so bloody heartless, Josh.'

He turned back from the window, bent under the bed and unearthed a pair of black socks. He sniffed at them and then sat down next to Josh to pull them on. 'You should never get married. Remind me to drag you from the altar if you ever get near.'

*

The silence between them was broken by the noise of taps being turned on next door. 'You finished in the bathroom?' Charlie yelled, thumping on Hal's door.

'Yeah. Go ahead.' Hal called back.

'I'm sorry,' said Josh. 'And it didn't happen like that.'

'I know it didn't,' Hal said. 'Amber told me you were so crap in bed that she'd never do it with you again in a million years.' He laughed. 'Hard to believe. And I really do forgive you, Josh. I can forgive anybody anything tonight. You're still my best mate as well as my best man. And, anyway, if we fall out now, I haven't got time to find another one.'

Josh didn't smile. Hal's dignity filled him with self-disgust. 'I'll leave you to it,' he said getting up. 'The others are coming down, we'll open a bottle in about ten minutes. I'll see you then.'

'I'll be there. And . . .' Hal hesitated. 'Forget it, Josh. I have. Please. I don't care about the past.'

Josh couldn't get back to his room fast enough. How impressive Hal had been. How unruffled, unfazed, how certain he'd been about what he was doing. For a brief, terrible moment Josh had to seriously doubt what he was planning. But then he shoved the thought resolutely away. *I am right*, he told himself, *I know I'm right*. He slammed shut the flimsy bedroom door in frustration and the pink rosebud walls shook with the force. He wished he'd been able to talk to Hal properly at some stage, at any stage, before they'd come this far. But the fact that he'd slept with Amber himself had always stopped him dead in his tracks. Hal would never have believed that Josh didn't have some ulterior motive and would only have despised him for bringing her up. And what could he have said? Don't you see that she doesn't love you? Don't you hate it when she rips you to shreds in front of all your friends? Don't you realize that the only two things she finds truly attractive about you are the drop of blue blood and the pile of cash? He couldn't bring himself to say the words even though they were true.

Hal was so impulsively romantic, so happy to see the best in everyone, so quick to fall in love. If he'd only left it a few months longer before proposing, Josh was sure that Amber would have slipped up so badly that even Hal would have seen her for what she was. But he hadn't waited, and so now Josh was going to have to take drastic action. He unwrapped his towel and walked naked into the tiny *en suite* bathroom, feeling overwhelmed by all the doubts and regrets and wishing there was a powerful, painful shower in there to blast them all away.

*

By seven o'clock the main bar of the Little Goose was filling up fast. It was positioned half-way up Vincent Street in a beautiful sixteenth-century timber-framed building with a flagstone floor, head-crackingly low doorways and bulging whitewashed walls. The sort of place, far off the beaten track, that was still unused to tourists.

When Simon Campion, the landlord, had bought the Little Goose and moved in six months earlier, he had been uncomfortably aware of the uncanny similarities between his new acquisition and the Slaughtered Lamb in *An American Werewolf in London*. Sitting in an unobtrusive corner on a weekday evening, trying to decide whether or not to make an offer, he had half expected the locals to surround him and carry him out. A man at the bar wouldn't meet his eye and growled if he came too close, and the landlady's wildly sprouting body hair suggested that she had unwisely left the safety of the pub on the night of a full moon.

In his first six months, Simon had tried hard to change things. He had added five bedrooms, and had bought the next door building, knocked a way through and begun his restaurant. In theory, the Little Goose could now appeal to everyone. The pub went on much as it always had done, with weekly darts matches and a quiz night, and was used by the same old regulars as always as their nightly watering hole. But through a low unobtrusive archway, the restaurant served such enticing, imaginative food that people were being attracted from far and wide. Once they'd established that Simon was all right, the locals were delighted. It was wonderful to have such a place on their doorstep, and they were proud that Welshpool was now being talked of in the same breath as neighbouring gastro-ville, Ludlow.

Tonight there was an old black collie lying like a shag-pile rug on the floor of the pub and a couple of weather-beaten old men standing at the bar in baggy tweed trousers and braces. A game of darts was being watched by most of the room. Good-natured insults loaded with innuendo were being lobbed back and forth between some spotty teenage boys and a table of seven or eight girls.

When Kirsty and Lily walked in they were beamed at by the old men, whistled at half-heartedly by the boys, and given a brief, hostile once-over by the girls. The old dog stretched, stood up and walked over to Kirsty, nosing enthusiastically at her crotch.

'Get your face out of it, Laddie, you can get lost up there,' called out a sharp-faced girl with thin hair held viciously in place by several combs.

The whole room roared with laughter. Kirsty walked over to the girl and put both hands around her neck, pretending to strangle her.

'Join us?' the girl offered.

There'd always been a little friction between them, Kirsty's posh boarding-school preventing her from ever being wholly accepted by this girl and her friends. As a teenager, it had bothered her terribly. Now it had long ceased to matter. But she was grateful for the little peace-offering and at any other time would have pulled up a chair, but just then the door banged open and a gust of freezing air blew into the room.

'I know this place looks like shit but the food's surprisingly good.' The hooray twang sounded even louder in the suddenly silent bar.

Kirsty shifted nervously, knowing just who they were without looking over.

'Shut *up*, Alex, you tactless git.'

So you're Alex, Lily thought, watching ginger kebab man survey the room, his eyes darting quickly from side to side as he looked around for his friends. Standing next to him, a good foot taller, was Josh.

'Hello, gorgeous,' Kirsty murmured in Lily's ear, seeing where Lily was looking, and staring at Josh too. 'You can bend me over a bar-stool any day.'

Almost as if he'd heard, Josh looked across the room and took them both in with a casual glance. Then he let his eyes slide carefully back to Lily. She looked back at him with calm disinterest.

Seeing that the others hadn't yet come in behind him, Josh steered Alex across to the bar. The barman had his back firmly turned away from them and was drying a pint glass with a towel. Josh stood awkwardly, shifting from foot to foot. Next to him the two old men stood quietly drinking their beer, savouring the awkwardness, their eyes alight with enjoyment. Josh was reluctant to call out as it would get everybody else's attention as well as the barman's, but Alex had no such qualms.

'Excuse me, old chap,' he began loudly, 'could we have a couple of beers over here?'

The barman turned.

'We'll have two pints of your local brew. The Shropshire Lad,' Josh said, trying to be conciliatory.

'Two pints, what! I *say*. Oh jolly, jolly good. What a simply smashing idea!' said someone at Alex's shoulder, exaggerating their voices perfectly. Alex turned to him in surprise. The man was about their age and had a face pitted with acne and pale, aggressive eyes.

'You've got straw in your hair,' Alex told him in an amused drawl, not in the least intimidated. Instinctively the man went to touch his head and then stopped himself, furiously. Alex smiled at him with satisfaction, picked up his beer and moved away, threading through the tables, Josh following close behind.

'Still want to score?' Lily asked Kirsty, watching the

exchange but unable to hear what was being said. 'Don't tell me you fancy *Alex?* Look at those jodhpur boots. He probably wears spurs in bed.'

'And keeps a riding whip under his pillow,' Kirsty agreed.

They took the boys' places at the bar, slid on to a pair of stools and ordered a couple of glasses of wine. Lily was quiet, imagining catching the groom alone as he came out of the gents'. 'You don't know me but there's something I must tell you,' she'd begin. Then in another blast of icy night air the other two ushers arrived with the groom himself. Lily and Kirsty looked at him, fascinated to see who all the fuss was about.

The three searched the room until they caught sight of Alex and Josh sitting at the back, then went over to join them. Lily and Kirsty watched Josh leap up to greet them.

'I'll get you a drink,' they heard him say.

'That's unusually generous of you,' Hal grinned, sitting down and rubbing his cold hands together.

'He's got his eye on a chick,' Alex whispered. 'Who happens to be sitting at the bar.'

'Don't you ever rest?' Hal said, looking at Josh.

There was an uncomfortable pause.

Josh said quietly, 'It's your stag night. I think I'm allowed to buy you a beer.'

He got up and left them.

'Alex has booked a table in the restaurant,' Charlie said brightly, pointing at a doorway.

'And? What then?' Hal asked, having visions of lap-dancing Welsh girls in G-strings and stilettos.

'Then we're going back to Pen-y-bont.'

'Penny-a-bonk,' Alex drawled, deliberately mishearing Charlie's awkward pronunciation, 'sounds like my kind of place.'

The Little Goose quickly filled up until all the tables around the bar were crowded with people. Then, just as the boys were starting to talk about moving on, the barman rang a brass bell and announced that that week's quiz was about to begin. Every table was to make up a team. Little blue biros and sheets of paper were hastily handed around and immediately there was a buoyant hush to the room. There were to be twenty questions, the barman explained. A read-through of the answers and then twenty more.

'You're the local, did you know about this?' Josh asked Alex.

Alex shook his head. 'We'll cream them,' he said gleefully, grabbing the paper and pen. 'The peasants will revolt.'

Charlie, already in despair about the plans for Hal, stared at Alex and imagined stuffing the paper and pen into his small round mouth. He adored Hal, and Josh, but several times he had come close to punching Alex. He never wanted to see him or Richard, the third usher, ever again.

But forever in the back of Charlie's mind was the fact that the four of them were Hal's closest friends, and he would never hurt Hal by saying anything too offensive. Charlie knew that, in a simple enough way, the four of them represented all the extremes of Hal's own personality. Alex and Richard had known him through school and then had gone with him into the City. Like Hal they owned thousands of acres and loved dogs and the countryside, and with them, Charlie presumed, Hal could have boring conversations about set-aside and forestry grants. But, Charlie decided, it was with him and Josh that Hal had proper fun. In just a few years of knowing each other, they'd gone running with the bulls in Pamplona, clubbing at the Fridge, drinking in the Red bar and bungee-jumping in Battersea, flying for the weekend to Amsterdam, or Barcelona, and rock-climbing in Thailand. It was because of Charlie that Hal had finally dropped his Husky into a dustbin and because of Josh that he rode a V-Max motorbike to the job he was about to leave. It was with Alex and Richard that Hal had grown old before his time, but with Charlie and Josh that he'd grown young again.

Chill, Charlie told himself now. He took a mouthful of beer and tried to relax, but now he wished he were anywhere else, doing anything else. He loathed Welsh-pool, loathed the rain, and felt an icy ball of panic rolling around inside him every time he remembered what they were planning to do to Hal.

'Catch!' said Josh, throwing him a cigarette, well aware that Charlie was on the edge, not sure what to do about it.

'Are you ready?' shouted the barman, questions in hand.

'Yes!' everybody roared back, shifting in their seats with anticipation.

'Hang on!' It was the scrofulous youth from the bar,

speaking out from the back of the room. 'I've got a question. Why do posh gits make good ventriloquists?'

The room went quiet.

'Because they always talk out of their arses!'

Then he exploded into laughter.

'And why have toffs got long, thin willies?' a girl shrieked out when the noise had died down a little. She waited for a brief second, looking at the five of them, and then answered with surprising force, 'Because they're tight-fisted *wankers*!'

'And why do all the sheep around here need chastity belts?' shouted Alex angrily, standing up before anyone could stop him.

'Oh shut up!' Josh said in exasperation, pulling him down again, and watched his face glow as bright as his hair.

When Josh plucked up sufficient courage to look around the room again, he saw several people staring in anger and one table of youths that looked as if they'd relish a fight. He gingerly turned sideways and noticed a voluptuous, pretty girl splayed on a bar-stool smiling at him. He grinned back at her, relieved that here was one person, at least, who didn't want him to drop down dead.

'Come on, guys. Let's not hang around here. I'm starving,' he said, laughing in relief and knocking back his drink, eager to get away.

*

'What are they doing?' Kirsty hissed to Lily at the bar. 'They're not staying for the quiz. And once they're eating we've lost them.'

'Undo some buttons and pretend to be a kiss-o-gram,' Lily suggested. 'It's perfect casting.'

'Thanks. But what do we *really* do?' Kirsty said, exasperated that Lily wasn't taking the problem seriously enough. 'We'll have to have dinner too.'

'No way,' said Lily. 'I'm a potter, not a merchant banker.'

'It's all right, I know Simon *very* well,' Kirsty raised her eyebrows suggestively. 'He owes me a lot more than a couple of dinners.'

'Get thee to a nunnery!'

'I'm going to go and ask him.' Kirsty knocked back her wine, jumped off her stool and disappeared out of the room.

Lily waited, listening to the quiz questions with half an ear, and watched the boys with interest as they got up and threaded their way through the tables towards her, noticing even in those few moments how much they all deferred to Josh. He had his back to her, but then he turned, still talking and joking over his shoulder to the others. And looking at him properly for the first time, Lily found herself entranced too, caught up in his wonderful eyes and quick smile and by the golden energy that emanated effortlessly from him. As he walked towards her, he pulled off a thick chocolate coloured jersey, taking half a T-shirt away with it, and gave Lily a quick glimpse

31

of a brown stomach that would have done anybody proud. He caught her watching him and grinned back at her, and unable to stop herself, she smiled back.

All five then slowly filed past her as they made their way to the restaurant. He'll be a complete bastard, she told herself. There was no mistaking that sleepy, sexy, arrogant look in his eye. It didn't surprise her at all that someone who looked like him would concoct such an outrageous plan and think he could get away with it. As she thought about it, Lily was flooded with absolute determination not to let him succeed. If he hadn't exuded such nonchalance, such confidence in his own supremacy, had not been quite so good-looking, quite so able to fool around with the others despite everything he had in mind for later, she might not have felt it quite so strongly.

Would it be enough if she simply caught Hal alone and told him what she and Kirsty had overheard? She doubted it. And even if Hal believed her and confronted the others, there was no guarantee that they wouldn't try to spirit him away immediately. The best thing would be for her and Kirsty to let the evening go ahead as planned but to find out somehow where they were staying in Llanygoed. They could wait until the morning and then pick Hal up and take him back to Grace's. Whatever they had to do later on, what was most important now was that she and Kirsty shadow the group for the rest of the evening. Not something she'd have any problem convincing Kirsty about, Lily reckoned.

Out of the corner of her eye Lily could see her already hurrying back, pushing hard against the wall of people now at the bar.

'We're on,' she said in excitement. 'He's put us right next to their table. Let's go.'

Lily was wearing bootleg dark grey velvet trousers and a silvery blue top edged with downy feathers that she'd found in a vintage clothes shop in Chester. It was nineteen-forties and very skimpy. Her blonde hair was held back by a slide, accentuating her large, clear eyes. As she walked into the restaurant with Kirsty everybody watched her.

'My God, it's Gwynnie,' whispered Charlie.

'She's stunning,' Hal agreed.

Josh considered her. Would she seem quite so lovely if he had caught her eye on the escalator in Harvey Nichols or brushed against her in some club, he wondered? Would she stand out against all the models and actresses who moved through the revolving doors of his offices every morning? Or was it the unexpectedness of finding her here that had knocked him for six? As fast as he asked himself the questions he knew the answers. Lily would stand out anywhere. She was too small to be a model and she didn't have the sleek, expensive look of the girls he knew in London, but she looked even better for that. He wished he was seeing her in different circumstances, some time when he could have engineered an opportunity to get to know her. Tonight he had to concentrate on Hal, and he knew he shouldn't do anything that might jeopardize his plans. She would have to remain forever in his mind as the one who got away.

3

Kirsty and Lily sat down at a neighbouring table. Lily chose a bottle of Pinot Grigio and lit a cigarette off the candle. The wine coursed through Kirsty, who had barely eaten all day, and she looked at Lily, her eyes glittering. She leaned forward, putting the candle to one side.

'Sod the blokes. I'm really pleased to be here with you. This will be one great dinner!'

'I haven't been to a restaurant since I left London,' Lily said.

'So you've never eaten here with Grace?'

'God, no. I can never get her out of the house.'

'Bring her here some time. It would do her good.'

Lily nodded, knowing that she'd never persuade Grace. She arched her back, putting her sister out of her mind.

'So what's it with you and the chef?' she asked. 'And why don't I know about it?'

'I'll tell you in a minute. When I know he's not about to jump out of the kitchen and hear me.'

Lily nodded. 'Okay. Wait until we've ordered.'

'It's not that I've *not* told you anything. There's just nothing much to tell.'

'But enough to get a table and a free meal out of him.'

Kirsty smiled up at the waiter arriving at their table to take their order. 'I'll tell you later,' she told Lily.

When they had both chosen from the menu and the waiter had left them alone again, Kirsty turned back to Lily.

'Let's talk about you for a change. Have you decided how long you're going to stay?'

She poured more wine into Lily's glass and held her breath, hoping that Lily was going to say she would stay on indefinitely. She knew that Welshpool had gradually begun to rise in Lily's estimation, that the isolation, initially so overwhelming, now seemed protective and benevolent, that the clean cold air and the bustling friendliness of the town had become something Lily loved too. But she also knew that Lily had had jobs lined up in London and that she had to be thinking about what she was going to do in the long term. Working and earning and getting on with her life.

'I don't know,' Lily said, knocking back the wine. 'I could imagine staying for ever, but I can't – I'm in Grace's house, and if I stay much longer she'll drive me crazy.'

Kirsty pulled a face. 'Go! Leave her now! If it was me I wouldn't have lasted a week.'

'I've promised myself that if it gets too bad I'll look for a cottage. If I worked a bit harder I could sell enough stuff to pay the rent.'

When their starters were laid down in front of them, Lily's scallops were dwarfed by Kirsty's plate of roast pumpkin risotto, a Little Goose speciality. Kirsty gazed at her plate in wonder, acknowledging that this was why she was size fourteen and Lily was only a ten, but not caring at all.

As Lily ate she looked around the dining-room with interest, careful not to catch the eye of any of the men at the table. The room was colourwashed a deep pinky red which looked wonderful against the exposed beams in the ceilings and walls, warm and comforting against the cold of the night. Tables and chairs were tucked into alcoves and corners, and twelve more people ate at a Jacobean oak table in the middle of the room. And all around them was the loud drone of satisfied eating and drinking.

They sat in mellow silence for a few minutes more, working through their food and happy to let the atmosphere wash over them, then Lily dramatically put down her knife and fork.

'Kirsty, I'm not going to let them get away with it. I want to stop them,' she said.

Kirsty looked at her doubtfully.

'Don't get involved,' she said. 'You don't know the circumstances.'

'Something like this happened to Grace.'

Kirsty tensed. No one in the town knew what precisely had happened to Grace. There were some facts and of course everybody had speculated, but only in a concerned kind of way. Seeing her out on the High Street, head down, avoiding eye-contact, most people who encountered her were filled with pity.

Kirsty was no longer one of those people. Perfectly sympathetic before she had met Lily, she now found Grace irritating beyond belief and was forever teetering on the brink of telling her so, holding back only out of respect for Lily. She disliked the way Grace wafted around the house in her dressing-gown, pale and tearstained, while Lily bent double dragging dustbin sacks out to the back gate, and how, as far as Kirsty could see, she had taken advantage of Lily's arrival to absolve herself from the responsibility of every single aspect of running her house.

Lily had some idea of what Kirsty thought but she didn't care, confident that if only Kirsty knew all that Grace had been through she would understand how fragile she was, and how Lily had to give her all the help in the world. Until tonight, Lily had never felt like telling Kirsty what had happened but now, suddenly, as they sat together, the words poured out of her.

'Jeremy was never good marriage material,' she concluded with a sigh. 'The last we heard of him, he was swimming with dolphins off the coast of Ireland.'

Kirsty put her hand over her mouth but she couldn't stop herself laughing. Lily grinned tolerantly.

'So, don't you admire these guys for sticking their necks out?' Kirsty demanded, serious again. 'Isn't that just what you should have done for Grace? Surely you're contradicting yourself! You should have done the same for Grace and saved her all that agony. She'd have thanked you for locking her up for six months if it would have saved her from the wedding day!'

'Oh, I don't know, I don't know!' Lily groaned. 'And I couldn't have done anything about it. There wouldn't have been any point.' She shrugged. 'Perhaps in the very, very early days I might have said something without sending her off her rocker, but I didn't. And then she was in love. I tried to say something then and nearly lost my

37

life. So, after that I kept quiet. Anyway, she knew I wasn't bowled over by Jeremy.'

'What about your parents? Did they try to say something to her too?'

'It's not that they don't care,' Lily said slowly. 'I know that they care.' She looked hard at her plate. 'But they don't want to hear about it, or think about it. They like things to be happy . . .' she paused. 'Anything difficult, no thank you.' She looked up at Lily. 'They haven't been to see Grace once. They gave her some money towards her house, but they'd never come down and stay with her.'

'I'm sorry,' Kirsty said.

'So it was always up to me. And so I decided to tell her what I thought of Jeremy. And how miserable I thought she'd be if she married him.' Lily winced. 'I was being mild, but it was like I'd lit a rocket.'

She drank some more wine. 'The point I'm getting to is that in the end Grace weighed up everyone's reactions, whatever they were, and made her own decision. And that's what was important. In the end she was free to do that. It was up to her, not me. Who am I to say what makes her happy?'

Kirsty didn't look convinced.

'And the same goes for this lot. Who are they to say how this guy *Hal* lives his life? It's not up to them.'

'But sometimes your friends know you best of all,' Kirsty replied. 'Better than you know yourself. And they can see the disaster you're walking into when you can't. Sometimes a friend will put you straight.'

'No,' Lily said. 'It may be the best thing for Hal. He might be walking into a disaster. But it makes no difference.'

'Surely you're not being much of a friend if all you say is what people want to hear.'

Lily nodded. 'But there's a time and a place, and there's some things you talk about and some things you leave alone. And then there's the point beyond which you've gone too far.'

To Kirsty's dismay Lily's eyes promptly filled up with tears.

'I bet Amber's absolutely lovely. All this will be because those stupid men don't want to lose one of their mates.'

'Okay,' Kirsty said, touching her hand. 'I'm in there with you. You're right. We can't let it happen.' She thought for a moment. 'You know we'll have to drive him to Oxford tomorrow? It's the only way we can be sure that he'll make it on time. Can you get away?'

'But your car's in the garage,' Lily despaired.

Kirsty thought for a second. 'Grace has left hers here, though.'

'There is no way I can involve Grace in this.'

'You don't have to,' Kirsty said, chasing the last grains of rice around her plate. Just borrow it, you're always doing it. We'll be back by teatime.'

Lily knew that Kirsty was right. Grace probably wouldn't ever know the car had gone.

There was a man coming to their table, Lily saw in surprise when she looked up again. He was moving purposefully, wearing a long, expertly tied white apron, and he had Kirsty in his eye. And for once, Kirsty had done well, Lily thought, promptly swallowing the last of her food.

He stopped beside Kirsty and crouched down beside her.

'So why didn't you call?' he asked quietly, ignoring Lily for the moment.

'Don't be boring,' Kirsty said, not looking at him.

There was a nasty silence. It wasn't the first time Lily had witnessed someone being given the brush-off by Kirsty. Lily wondered how much charm she had wielded just a few minutes earlier in order to get them a table, and felt embarrassed at Kirsty's abruptness now. When on the pull, Kirsty was a lethal combination of out-and-out flirtatiousness and down-to-earth good humour and men fell for it over and over again, but when she was no longer interested she showed a brutal detachment that took people completely by surprise.

'The scallops were great!' Lily muttered into the heavy silence, tapping her plate with her fork, but Simon was being bombarded with get-lost vibes from Kirsty and didn't hear her.

'We need time for a proper conversation, Kirsty,' he said, standing up again, 'and we're going to have one.'

Kirsty finally looked up at him.

'Not now!' He caught Lily's eye and smiled. 'I don't want to ruin everybody's dinner. But soon. Okay?'

'I'll call you.'

'Make sure you do,' said Simon, 'and enjoy your meal.' He nodded to Lily and left.

'What was all that about?' asked Lily the second he was out of earshot.

'Nothing much. Honestly, he's not worth the effort.'

'Oh yes he is. Tell me what's going on.'

'You haven't seen him without any clothes on,' Kirsty smiled grimly. 'Best to keep away.'

'You're not serious? Have you seen him with no clothes on?'

Kirsty sighed and didn't reply.

'Hey, I've known you for six months, I see you practically every day and yet I know nothing about this at all. When did it start?'

'About five days before it finished. Not long ago. But it was nothing. A couple of dinners. I didn't tell you because there was nothing to tell.'

Lily looked steadily back at her. 'Are you sure? And if it's all finished, why do I think he doesn't know that yet?'

Kirsty shrugged.

'Okay.' Lily said. 'So we're not going to talk about it.'

She gave Kirsty a long look. In the months since Lily had known her this had happened once or twice before, but as none of the previous guys were anything to write home about it had been a blessing that they'd been binned so swiftly. But this man, Simon, was completely, wonderfully different. Even in the few seconds that Lily had had to take him in, she'd known that Kirsty would be mad to let him go.

'So!' Lily said, changing the subject and nodding in the direction of the boys. 'What are we going to do about them? We'll need to know where they're keeping Hal for a start. Llanygoed's such a tiny place. It shouldn't be hard.' Lily paused, watching them. 'And you know, the more we see of them, the less I like what I see.'

'I agree. I'm sure the ginger one is a gerbil. And the little dark-haired one gives me the creeps. But,' Kirsty looked them over again, 'I'd say the other three have definite potential.'

'So you're including the groom?'

'*Hal*,' said Kirsty, rolling his name on her tongue. 'Maybe. Depends on what happens to him tomorrow. But either of the other two.'

'They're all yours.'

Kirsty grinned. 'So, how are we going to infiltrate? Lose a contact lens?'

'But we don't wear them.'

'So we'll never find it.'

'Okay then,' Lily said, convinced. 'Do it!'

Straight away Kirsty said, 'Fuck!' loudly and clutched her right eye.

'Oh, Kirsty! Have you lost your contact lens?' said Lily. The boys immediately stopped their conversation, scraped back their chairs and all stood up.

'Keep still,' said Charlie, immediately coming over. 'I can see it on the floor.' He moved over to their table, bent down on hands and knees, and studied the floor close to Lily's ankles.

'While you're down there . . .' said Alex.

'No, bugger, it's just some dust.' Charlie gazed longingly up at Lily. 'Hi,' he said. 'I'm Charlie.'

Josh moved swiftly over to intercept.

'You'd better stay away,' he told Charlie firmly, knowing that Charlie had seen nothing remotely resembling a contact lens, and pushed him gently back towards a chair. 'He's as blind as a bat,' he told Lily, shoving Charlie down. 'So he'll only squash it.' Then he held out his hand. 'I'm Josh,' he said.

Next to them Hal started patting the tablecloth in gentle patterns.

'I don't think we're ever going to find it,' he told Kirsty.

'Is it hard or soft?' said Alex, coming to join him.

'Disposable,' said Kirsty.

Alex belched in response and then sat down again and poured himself a glass of wine.

'Better take the other one out,' suggested Charlie. 'Isn't it much worse with only one in?'

Behind them the waiter was hovering with his main course.

'Come and have a glass of champagne with us after dinner to celebrate my stag night?' Hal offered and the others immediately all backed him up.

'Stag night? Congratulations! We'd love to,' said Kirsty. 'Wouldn't we?' she nodded at Lily.

So far, so good, thought Lily. 'Thanks. That would be great,' she said.

'The groom's sweet,' said Kirsty as they waited for their main course. 'I was wondering what he'd be like.'

'Anyone in this room that you don't fancy?' asked Lily.

'You know something?' Kirsty mused, ignoring the question and pouring more wine into her glass. 'One thing

I will never, ever have is a hen night. I can't think of anything worse. No men, all your girlfriends snapping at each other.' She sighed dramatically. 'I *know* none of mine would get on.'

Lily laughed. 'One glass and she's off. And I'm not so difficult to get on with. Don't your friends get on with me?'

'What do you think?' Kirsty said, then she laughed. 'No, they do. Of course they do. But I can think of nothing worse than pissed women with blown-up condoms on their heads throwing up in the loos of some cheap Italian restaurant.'

'No, Kirsty! Think Harvester Inn at the very least.'

Kirsty laughed. 'And you must have some grim friends.'

Lily glanced over to Hal. 'Just like he does.'

They both went quiet, watching them all around him, eating and laughing, passing things for him to try, having a good time.

When their own main course arrived Lily stared at it suspiciously. Having witnessed the fall-out between Kirsty and Simon, and because their meal was for free, she wondered whether it might have arrived raw or doused in pepper, but she had underestimated Simon. When her plate was put in front of her, Lily vowed that it was the most beautiful meal she'd ever seen. Seven wedges of pink Welsh lamb, roasted with anchovies, garlic and rosemary, had been built up into an intricate, layered castle and was sitting above a round of perfect mashed potato. Lily took a mouthful of lamb, so tender it could have been eaten with a spoon.

'Heaven,' she exclaimed with pleasure. 'I wasn't sure about the anchovies but they're not fishy at all.'

'It's the best thing I've ever had here apart from Simon,' Kirsty agreed.

'You can't say that!' Lily told her. 'Not when you're not going to tell me what's going on.'

*

Later, the boys called Lily and Kirsty over to join them and they all squashed up on the two oak settles running down either side of their table and drank a couple of bottles of champagne.

Squashed between Josh and Charlie, Lily saw straight away that Josh was determinedly keeping Hal's glass full. And yet still Hal seemed unaffected, talking coherently about how he'd been left a celebratory bottle of whisky on the doorstep of the cottage by a neighbour. Lily looked at his huge gentle hands and the soft hair falling into his big blue eyes. You're so lovely, she thought. I hope you marry her, and that she deserves you.

She was also aware of Josh's hard thigh pressing against hers. I'm part of the game, she thought. Part of tonight's entertainment. He knows he's gorgeous and he knows he can pull just about anyone, and so tonight he'll try it on with me. For once, Lily found it amusing, her decision to ride to Hal's rescue making her invincible, one step ahead of anything he could do or say.

Opposite her, she could hear Kirsty getting on surprisingly well with Alex.

'Did you have to speak so loud in the bar? You're such a big mouth,' she heard Kirsty tell him.

'Cheers,' Alex replied. 'You have a big mouth yourself. A big, red, beautiful mouth and I want to kiss it.' He refilled Kirsty's glass and opened an engraved cigarette case.

Kirsty looked back at him, for once completely silenced.

'When can we arrange it?' Alex said. He selected a cigarette and clapped shut the box. 'Give me your telephone number.'

'No chance.'

Josh turned to Lily, smiling. 'He won't give up easily, not now.'

'I think she can handle it,' Lily replied, noticing threads of gold in his green eyes.

'It's time he met someone who could keep him in order. She was perfect from the moment she first opened her big mouth.' Josh paused. 'Has she got a boyfriend?'

Lily nodded. 'So, how long have you known Hal?' she asked awkwardly, wanting him to stop staring at her.

'Not long. A couple of years,' he answered, abandoning his decision to leave her alone.

'And what's the bride like?'

'Perfect, they were made for each other.'

He lies so effortlessly, she thought.

'What about you?' he said, softly. 'Anyone made for you yet?'

For a moment Lily paused. I'm drunk and he's good-looking, she warned herself. But in the morning I'll be sober.

'No, not yet.'

He's about to betray his best friend. I don't like him at all. But his smile was as infectious as a yawn and she couldn't stop herself smiling back.

Then, breaking the moment, Charlie tentatively stretched across her and caught Josh's sleeve.

'I need to talk to you,' Charlie told Josh, nodding towards the gents'.

Damn, thought Josh, wondering what was up. 'Don't go away,' he said to Lily.

He tried to stand, then realizing that he had no room, climbed up high on to the bench beside her. Lily immediately felt the hairs rising on the back of her neck even though he didn't touch her. Josh stood for a second to get his balance and then hopped gently to the floor and followed Charlie out of the room.

*

'Sorry,' said Charlie once the door of the gents' was closed. 'Was that bad timing?'

'Don't worry about it. What's up?' Josh asked, sensing trouble.

'I'm sorry,' said Charlie. 'But what I have to say won't come as any surprise. I'm not doing it. I wanted you to know now.'

Josh tested his weight against a basin and then gingerly leaned back. 'It's okay,' he said, well prepared for the conversation. 'I knew you'd feel like this.'

'It's a mad idea. And in any case,' Charlie went on as if Josh hadn't spoken, 'Hal will just go and get married next weekend instead.'

'No, he won't.'

'What?'

'That's the whole point!' said Josh.

'Why? What do you mean?'

'I know that Hal's going through with this only because he's too much of a gentleman not to. He told me so tonight.'

Charlie looked stunned. 'What did he say?'

'That it was too late to do anything else – you know, the guests, the cake, his parents, her parents.'

'My God,' said Charlie.

'But what if we take the decision for him?' Josh looked intently at Charlie. 'Make it easy for him. Don't give him the option of getting there tomorrow. He's not going to go and marry Amber next weekend! He'll be so bloody relieved.'

Charlie still looked unconvinced. 'Are you guessing or did he definitely say he didn't want to go ahead?'

In his own mind Josh was doing the right thing. He took a deep breath and chose his words with care.

'He said that he couldn't back out because it was all organized and because he couldn't hurt Amber that much. But that he wished he could.'

'He *said* that? He said that he wished he could *back out*? Those actual words?'

'Yes.'

'Shit.'

Charlie shook his head, but he was believing it. Because it all fell into place. The weeks Charlie had spent waiting for Hal to change his mind, his own certainty that this engagement was wrong, all convincing him that what Josh was saying now was the truth.

'So we do it for him,' Charlie repeated. 'Do the others know about this?'

'They don't need to. They're on for it anyway. It's only you who's bottling out.'

Charlie walked over to the basin and stared at himself in the mirror.

'Okay, I'll do it,' he told himself. 'You've convinced me. Bloody hell, we'd better be right. What a mess. What a terrible mess. Can you imagine how horrendous it's going to be tomorrow?'

'Awful,' agreed Josh. 'And I'm the one to tell everybody.' He paused for a few seconds. 'What should I do? Tell Amber, or wait till the service is about to begin and tell the whole congregation?'

'You can't do that to her.'

'But if I tell her too early she might still manage to find Hal and persuade him to come back.'

'Not with us there to stop him.'

'That's why you three have got to stay on in the cottage. If we pour enough down Hal he won't wake up till midday. Plenty of time for me to get to Oxford, to Amber's house, and persuade her that Hal's changed his mind. If I manage to convince her she'll start cancelling everything straight away.'

'But if he changes his mind, decides he wants to go through with it all, I really don't think I can stop him,' Charlie warned.

'Charlie! You'll have to. He's very fond of her, he'll feel

absolutely terrible about it. Of course he'll *say* that he wants to go. You'd do the same thing. But you mustn't take any notice. He mustn't marry her! You have to agree not to let him out of the house!'

Charlie looked at him uneasily, but he repeated Josh's words to keep him quiet. 'I won't let him out of the house.'

Josh relaxed a little. 'We're doing the right thing,' he said, putting an arm around his shoulders.

They made their way back to the table and sat down again, but Lily was talking to Hal now and Josh had no opportunity to work himself back into the conversation.

'Hal,' he said eventually, plunging in. 'We should be off. We'll be stripping you,' he joked, 'but don't let it concern you.'

'Is that all of us?' said Alex, immediately unlacing his brogues.

He's so public school, thought Kirsty.

So this is it, thought Lily. We've got this far. Now we must wait until the morning. She got up quickly and moved towards Kirsty, who was still talking to Alex.

'I'm coming, hang on a minute,' Kirsty said, wanting Lily to leave her alone. 'I'll see you outside.'

'Sure, I'll get our coats.'

She stood on the pavement outside and looked up at the sky, then jumped as she felt someone take her arm.

'Good bye, golden girl,' said a velvety voice in her ear. It was Josh. His kiss was as light as a feather, soft on her cheek. 'Finding you was a revelation,' he whispered. 'I didn't know people like you lived here. I wish I'd more time.'

More time for what exactly? Lily thought, looking up into his pussycat eyes. She rested her hands gently on his shoulders.

''Bye,' she said, and leaned forward and kissed him slowly and softly on the mouth. He started, and she watched his eyes as surprise turned instantly into lust, but before he could regain the initiative and grab her again, she moved out of reach.

Seemingly unaware of what Lily had just done, Hal carefully took her hands.

'Next time I'm in Welshpool . . .' he said seriously and then laughed at the look of doubt on her face. 'Honestly! I mean it. I'm coming back – sober. It's a wonderful place and I've seen hardly anything at all.'

'She lives on Green Lane. Over the hill and round the bend,' said Kirsty, joining them.

The rain clouds had disappeared, leaving the night clear and cold, with a deep, black sky and silver stars. The tarmac glittered wet in the dim street-lamps. There was no one else in sight and a wonderful sense of end-of-the-evening quiet.

'We're off,' said Hal, walking unsteadily down the middle of the road with his shoes in his hand.

'Look after him,' said Lily earnestly to Charlie.

She left Charlie and ran after Hal down the road, catching his arm. 'Good luck for tomorrow,' she said, looking up at him.

'I'll need it,' he replied. It was dark, and his eyes were so far above her that she couldn't make out the expression on his face. Then before she could say any more, Charlie joined them and clumsily tried to turn Hal back towards the group.

'How are you getting there?' Kirsty asked Alex.

'I'm driving. And no, I'm not too pissed.' Alex pointed his alarm key at a dark green Golf GTi parked a few cars away. 'Come on, guys, or we'll be here all night!'

He stood holding back the front seat while Charlie, Richard and Hal squashed into the back.

Lily and Kirsty waited until they had driven out of sight.

'So what do you think you were doing?' Kirsty said grinning.

'What the hell. It was good for him – to know he hadn't got me all neatly worked out.'

'Good for you too. I'll bet you're still weak at the knees. And it *is* that cottage on the side of the lane. Off the Builth Road. It's called Pen-y-bont.'

'How do you know all that?' Lily asked, still thinking that up close Josh had been completely irresistible.

'Alex told me. It's no secret, after all.'

'You don't fancy him, do you?'

Kirsty smiled and shook her head. '*Me?* Fancy Alex? Of course not! It was just a bit of fun.'

'Our rescue can wait until the morning, can't it?' Lily said as they walked home. 'I'm so tired.'

Kirsty nodded. 'As long as we get there early enough.

The wedding's at three thirty. Hal should be in Oxford by two at the latest.'

'What if the others wake up and stop us leaving with him?'

'We'll cross that bridge when we come to it. I hardly think they'll fight us for him.'

'Poor Hal,' Lily shook her head.

When the time came for them to go their separate ways, Lily stopped, feeling closer to Kirsty than ever before. 'Stay the night? Grace is away. You can have her room.'

Kirsty nodded and slid her arm through Lily's and they set off down the road, matching strides.

*

The Golf bounced at high speed down a tiny rutted track and came to a rocking halt outside the grey stone cottage.

'Welcome home,' said Alex. He felt in his coat for the key, then shoved against the door and turned the lock.

Hal felt particularly sick. The fresh air outside the Little Goose had momentarily cleared his head but Alex's rally-style driving had done him no favours. He sank to the floor, head in his hands.

'Oh, God. What have you done to me?' he moaned.

Won't be long now, thought Charlie, looking down at him as Alex heaved him up and helped him into an armchair.

'Music, camera, action!' Hal commanded unsteadily from his chair. 'Where are the girls?'

'On their way,' said Josh, appearing in the doorway with a case of beer.

But the beer was barely touched. After all they'd drunk at dinner, and with the plan for the next day cutting a heavy swathe through the party, it was only twenty minutes before Josh and Charlie put their arms around Hal and half carried him into Alex's grandmother's bedroom.

'Like getting into a boat, she keeps moving,' Hal slurred, face down on the bedspread, trying to lift his legs up on to the bed one at a time and ending up half kneeling on the floor.

'I'll get you some water,' offered Josh, going into the next-door bathroom. He found a tooth mug and rinsed out a manky brown sludge from the bottom, deciding as he did so that this would be the only glass he'd allow Hal to drink. He needed all possible advantages, and the worse the hangover, the better.

When Hal and the others had gone to bed, Josh went back downstairs. He sat in the dark, silent sitting-room deep in thought, alternately knocking back sweet sherry from a tumbler and blowing immaculate smoke rings towards the dying embers of the fire. He didn't go to bed and, as the dawn light finally broke across the hills, he quietly opened the back door of the cottage and slipped outside.

4

At five to seven Lily left her bedroom. She'd set her alarm for half past six and had been fully awake the moment it began to ring. Feeling surprisingly clear-headed and energetic, she'd dressed in navy jeans and trainers.

'No, no, much too early,' protested Kirsty drowsily as Lily flung open the door to her bedroom.

'Get up,' ordered Lily. 'The more time we have the better.'

'Make me a cup of coffee,' Kirsty moaned, face down in her pillow, feeling terrible.

Over breakfast, Lily suggested they go by bicycle.

Kirsty's headache gathered force with the thought. 'A *bicycle*!' she repeated in disbelief. 'You are *so* Famous Five!'

Lily stood up, taking their plates over to the sink. 'Don't be pathetic. And anyway, I liked the Famous Five. Dick and Julian were lovely boys.'

'You're sad.'

Kirsty looked a bit more perky after her coffee and Lily judged it the right moment to try again. 'A car could wake them up. It's so quiet there,' she pleaded. 'It's only a couple of miles. It'll do your head good.'

'No! No! No!' shouted Kirsty, her hands over her ears. 'The hills are the size of Everest and it's frigging February!'

'You're such a slob. It's a lovely sunny day. Come on,' Lily begged.

'Listen,' Kirsty paused. 'I am *not* a going-on-a-bike kind of girl! *And* I've just woken up.'

Lily looked at her, knowing when she was beaten. 'Okay, I'll go on my own.'

'See what's going on, how many of them are still there. Try to talk to Hal, then come back and get me and the car.'

'And you make sure you don't do a thing,' Lily told her. 'Not a thing. Actually I know what you're going to do. You'll go straight back to bed.'

Lily left the house by a back door and walked through the long wet grass to the shed that housed her bike and her pottery.

She wheeled the bike away from the house and set off.

As she cycled slowly up the first, hideously steep hill she had to squint against the pale early morning sun. A little while later she stopped for a moment to get her breath and leant against her bike, looking through a gateway at the awesome landscape spread out before her. As always, the vast, panoramic beauty of the scenery took her by surprise. Head down, cycling up a sunken lane, it was easy to forget where she was. Now Lily looked out for a minute across the endless undulating hills and valleys mapped out in the early sunshine for hundreds of miles around her. It was utterly still, utterly silent: no people, no cars, not even the sound of the wind in the trees or the chirp of a bird broke the spell.

She knew that a couple of bends later she would come

to the tiny rutted track that belonged to Pen-y-Bont. Taking a deep juddering breath she set off once more, suddenly feeling overwhelmed with nerves. Her hands, slippery with sweat, slid around the handlebars and, as she cycled towards the track, one foot suddenly kicked itself off its pedal and she nearly came off with it. She freewheeled for a moment and grabbed hold of her back brake, which immediately began a noisy, resentful groan of complaint.

She took some deep calming breaths, trying to steady her nerves and her stomach, and with one eye on the potholes she made her way towards the cottage.

It was as if the house itself was fast asleep. Upstairs, curtains were drawn across the two tiny latticed windows, like eyelids, and the front door was still ajar, like a mouth fallen half open. The Golf was parked outside.

Lily looked at her watch. It was just past eight. She left her bicycle on the grass and slipped silently in.

Much of the kitchen was in deep shadow. She could make out several empty cans of beer and a jar of tomato chutney surrounded by ash and crumbs on an old pine table. The room was filled with the pungent, morning-after combination of wine and cigarette smoke. She walked through an open doorway and found herself in a sitting-room with a large brick fireplace, the ashes still glowing a bright, pale pink. She opened another door and there, lying on a sagging velvet sofa under a brown wool blanket, was Charlie, fast asleep.

Lily quietly shut the door again, tiptoed away and turned towards the stairs. She climbed slowly, trying desperately to outguess the creaky floorboards but choosing the wrong place to put her foot on almost every stair. At the top were two small doors, one to the left, one to the right. She tried the left one, having to half bend her head to get through, and there was Hal.

He was tucked tightly into heavy, white cotton sheets so that only his sleeping face was showing. He was so pale and still that for a moment Lily went cold, but then he made a tiny sound in his throat and she sighed with relief. If I wake you up now, while the others are asleep, I can get you out of the house without them even knowing I was here, she thought. She crept towards him.

'Wake up, wake up,' she said softly. 'Hal!' Hal did not stir.

Have they given him pills? she wondered. If so, they *could* have killed him. She reached into the bed and touched his bare shoulder and again whispered his name, but there was still no response. Lily hesitated for a second, worrying that if she shook him awake he would shout and bring the others in. She crouched down and stroked him gently on the soft skin of his cheekbone, looking down at his sleeping face. Finally Hal stirred and a strong arm wrapped around Lily and drew her close, pulling her on to the bed beside him. For a few seconds she lay stiffly, her eyes wide open, her nose pressed uncomfortably deep into his armpit.

'Hello, sweet pea,' he murmured gently, into her hair.

Lily shot upright. He thinks I'm Amber!

'It's Lily,' she whispered. 'Be quiet!'

'I thought I was dreaming.'

'I had to wake you! You've got to get up. They're going to make you miss your wedding.'

'What?' Hal smiled, opening his large sleepy eyes but making no attempt to sit up.

'I'm really sorry,' she said. 'They don't want you to marry Amber. They've been planning this for ages. They want to keep you here. You've got to come with me now, before they wake up. Before they can stop us.'

Lily was just about to throw back his sheets when a voice from the doorway said calmly, 'I wouldn't do that.'

Lily screamed. It was Charlie, dishevelled and heavy with sleep. He rubbed his eyes. 'I wouldn't do that,' he repeated, 'because he's stark, bollock naked.'

Hal sat up in the bed.

'Did you hear what I said?' Lily asked Hal urgently, and then she turned to Charlie. 'Tell him!' she commanded. 'Tell Hal your plans for today.'

Charlie stayed silent.

'Is it true, Charlie?' asked Hal suddenly completely awake. 'Can you really hate Amber that much?'

'Lily, if you don't mind,' said Charlie, turning to her.

'No. Let her stay. I can obviously trust her more than I can you.'

'You say that,' Charlie said quietly, walking further into the room. 'But I'm trying to stop you making the biggest mistake of your life.'

'How can you say something so corny,' Hal yelled at him, 'about something so important to me?'

'I want to help,' Charlie remained calm. 'I'm not going to stop you going to your wedding. If it's what you really want. But I'm giving you a final chance to get out.'

'But why?' shouted Hal. 'Why would I want to do that?'

'Because deep down you *know* this is wrong.' He stopped, waiting for Hal's response, but Hal didn't speak. 'I'm not going to start cataloguing Amber's faults. That wouldn't do any good, but you have to believe we wouldn't go this far if it wasn't something we were sure about ... God knows, we've tried everything else.' Charlie fell silent.

'You're wrong,' said Hal. 'You've been wrong from the very beginning. Although why I should need to convince you I still don't know. And I'll never, ever forgive you for this.'

It was as if all the fight, all the uncertainty, suddenly went out of Charlie. He looked back at Hal, nodded meekly and moved towards the door, then turned back again at the last moment. 'I'm sorry,' he said, from the doorway.

Lily followed him downstairs, where Charlie sat down at the kitchen table and put his head in his hands.

'Coffee?' she suggested and he slowly got up again, rummaging in a cupboard above the sink.

'What were you doing up there?' he asked. 'What do *you* know about all this?'

'Not a lot. Enough to decide I wanted to stop you.'

'Interfering woman.' He smiled weakly. 'God, it's a mess.'

'It's not too late. It can all go ahead.'

'What a mess! What a mess! What a fucking mess!' Charlie banged his hand heavily against the wall. 'Of course Josh was wrong. I *knew* he was.'

He looked back at Lily, full of despair. 'How have I let this happen?'

'But it's not too late.'

Charlie ignored her. 'It doesn't surprise me that Hal won't change his mind now, he's a good bloke and he's not going to leave Amber in the lurch. That's why we all thought we should make the decision for him. And Josh is so unimaginably persuasive. You end up believing anything. Anything he wants you to believe.'

He banged two china cups, as thin as eggshells, into their saucers and brought them over to the kitchen table. 'Sorry about these,' he added, pouring in the coffee. 'We can't find any mugs.'

'Tell me what's wrong with her, why you thought it was worth all this? You wouldn't have got involved in all this with no reason.'

Charlie sat down.

'Oh, there's reason,' he said. 'But that's not why we did it.'

Lily looked taken aback. 'But I thought . . .'

'What we wanted to do was give Hal his first real opportunity to think about it. When he's with Amber, it's impossible for him to see straight.'

'And now you're surprised that, thinking straight, Hal has no intention of changing his mind?'

Charlie didn't answer.

'Tell me what she's like,' Lily said instead.

'She's mesmerizing.' He looked at Lily. 'Amazing. I met her with Josh. Hal was still in Japan. Josh and I went to this drinks party in Clerkenwell.'

In his mind Charlie saw Amber walking into the party out of the night. He and Josh had been propping up the banisters, keeping an eye on the new arrivals, when Amber had walked in. Cold and beautiful, with long brown hair as smooth as chocolate.

'When I first met her I thought she was fan-bloody-tastic. When she and Hal got together I would have swapped places with him any time. We all would have done, in theory.' He paused. 'Then Josh put the theory into practice. He had no idea that Hal was that serious about her. None of us realized. And then, just two months ago, they announced they were getting married.' He looked at Lily and shook his head. 'He's completely mad. And God knows why she wants to marry Hal. At least Josh was tough enough to handle her.'

'So when did she and Josh get together?'

Charlie sighed theatrically. 'After the party she got brought in on a production Josh was working on. He's an agent, film and television, and she's into the make-up or something. Then Hal left his job in Japan and came home, Josh had a big party to welcome him back and invited Amber. And she and Hal got together. Josh had lined her up and he wasn't going to let Hal get in his way.'

'And neither was she,' said Lily. 'So why would she want to get married?'

'Well, she probably liked the idea of the dress and the

lifestyle too. She'll have her reasons. Amber always has her own best interests at heart. I'm sure she's worked out that marriage will be good for her.'

Lily felt her enthusiasm for rushing Hal to the church draining away.

'On her part it is not exactly a question of lifelong commitment,' Charlie went on. 'But it would have been for Hal. And he's a good catch. He's classy and eligible.' Charlie nodded to her. 'And he's going to inherit a fortune.'

Lily sat glumly staring at her coffee, feeling depressed. Still believing that Hal had the right to make his own mistakes, but wishing that this didn't have to be such a bad one.

'He'd better hurry up if he wants to arrive on time,' she said, looking suddenly at her watch. 'Who's driving?'

Charlie stirred in some sugar and fished a packet of aspirin out of his jeans. He popped out a row and threw them back with a mouthful of coffee. 'He thinks Alex is going to drive him,' he said, wincing at the taste, 'but he's not. He's never going to agree to drive Hal. Ever. He loathes Amber. He'll hold to the plan whatever Hal tells him.'

'Does anyone else have a car?'

'No.'

'What about Josh?'

'Josh took the other one back to Oxford at five this morning.'

'He did what? And what was he doing, leaving for Oxford so early?'

'Er . . . Well, I think Josh left to talk to Amber.' Charlie shifted in his chair and suddenly wouldn't meet Lily's eyes.

'So by now Josh's been in Oxford for about an hour. And what do you think he might have been saying to Amber, Charlie? While you've been sitting here with me?' She looked at him, thinking he'd been doing it knowingly, deliberately. 'You bastard!' she exclaimed, standing up. 'I thought you were on Hal's side now!'

'Fuck it! I don't know!' Charlie shouted, angry in his confusion. 'What's being on Hal's side? I don't know *what's* right.' He stood up again and walked outside.

'Yes, Josh left first thing this morning to see Amber. Yes, I should have told you sooner. Or even better, told Hal. What will Josh have said to Amber? I don't know!'

'You sat here drinking coffee because you're scared of Josh,' Lily called after him. 'You bloody coward!'

She left him, took the stairs two at a time and charged back into Hal's room. He was sitting on the end of the bed in a white shirt, staring out of the window.

'Which tie do you think?' he asked her, picking a handful off the bed and letting them drop back through his fingers.

'You should call Amber. Now,' Lily said, trying to sound calm. 'Right now. Let her know it's all okay and that you're on your way, with me. Josh left early this morning and he might have tried to convince her that you've done a runner or something.'

'I'll kill him!' Hal dived into his overnight bag and pulled out a phone. Lily left him to it and ran back down the stairs and straight into Charlie, who was waiting for her at the bottom.

'Lily!'

'I'm taking Hal to Oxford,' she told him, pushing him away from her. 'I'm going home to get the car and I'll be back in about twenty minutes.' She stared into Charlie's face, thinking that without Josh to steer him Charlie couldn't come up with anything else.

Then she left them, freewheeling down the lanes, forcing herself to keep pedalling hard up the hills. As she stopped outside her sister's house and got off her bicycle, Kirsty came out of the front door in a stretchy tight pink suit and a large straw hat.

'I know it's February but this is my favourite,' she said. 'And Hal will want us there. We're saving the day.'

'Fine, Kirsty,' said Lily, 'just get in the car.'

'But what about you? You can't go in trousers. You've got no make-up on and you're covered in sweat.'

Kirsty looked Lily up and down. It would be the understated look, but Lily was so striking that no one would guess her outfit wasn't deliberate, and she could do her make-up in the car. Kirsty walked around to the boot, opened it and laid down her pink jacket, then went to climb into the back, leaving the front seat for Hal.

A few minutes later they arrived back at Pen-y-bont. Hal was standing outside the cottage waiting for them, dressed in his morning suit. He looked immaculate and very handsome, his spiky hair flattened wetly down. Kirsty let out a dreamy sigh. 'He looks so young,' she said. 'Like he's waiting to be taken to boarding-school.'

Lily agreed. She could see Hal's blue eyes were dark with worry and his mouth was set in a grim line. Standing next to him, Charlie and Alex were rolling a spliff.

Kirsty was secretly loving the drama of it all and beamed when she saw Alex. She immediately jumped out of the car.

'Get in, because we're off,' ordered Hal.

Lily joined them. 'You okay now?' she asked Hal, gently, ignoring the other two.

'I need to get to Amber,' Hal told her desperately. 'I got through once on her parents' phone and some arse told me it was unlucky to speak to the bride before I saw her in the church. Now there's no answer there at all. And I've tried her mobile and it's switched off. I can call other people from your car. Just get me moving.' He jumped into the car without looking at Charlie or Alex.

'You could come too,' said Kirsty brightly to Alex as she climbed back into the car.

'No fucking way,' snapped Hal.

Lily put her foot down, driving faster through the country lanes than she had ever done in her life before. As they rocketed through the centre of Welshpool, she caught glimpses of startled familiar faces staring after her. All my efforts to mingle with the locals and I'm confirming their worst suspicions, she thought. That I couldn't fit in, that I'm getting out at top speed, and I don't care if I kill half of them on the way. At the Shrewsbury service station she filled up with petrol, drumming her fingers on the roof of the car, for once willing the petrol to suck up the money even faster. As she queued to pay she watched through the window as Hal tried again and again to get through to Amber. Then she raced back out, dumping a hastily gathered bag of Polos and drinks on to Kirsty's lap. Hal took a deep breath and stretched in his seat.

'Thanks, Lily, but you don't have to drive like a maniac the whole way.'

'Be cool. I'll get you there in one piece,' said Lily.

'Mineral water for you?' Kirsty asked her from the back seat as they sped towards the M54, hoping that Lily might have changed the habit of a lifetime and bought herself a sweet, fattening can of Tango. Lily hadn't: she stuck out an arm behind her and took it from her.

In the front seat Hal selected a tape. 'What can that bastard have done?' he muttered, more to himself than to anyone else.

I hate people who prefer the taste of water, Kirsty decided, stabbing a straw into her Ribena, then holding it away from her pink skirt.

She caught Hal's eye in the mirror and smiled and touched him gently on the shoulder.

'Want some?' she offered.

Hal shook his head. He looked out of the window, imagining how it would feel to be running for it, the wind with him, swooping over the fields and hedges in fantastic leaps. He forced himself to sit still.

'You two must be wondering what the hell is going on,' he said. 'Christ, I am!'

He was silent for a few moments then started again, forcefully. 'Whatever *anyone* has said to you,' he looked hard at Lily, 'Amber is a wonderful person. And I don't want to end up with some horsey Sloane who wishes Barbour did a range of underwear.'

Lily and Kirsty laughed.

'Sounds as if you have someone in mind,' said Kirsty.

Hal smiled at her, grimly, in the mirror. 'I do. She's called Lucy and she's my ex-girlfriend. My mother loves her.'

'Well, she's surely not the only alternative,' Lily said.

They hit heavy traffic and crawled towards the M6. Hal wondered who else he might call.

'Your parents?' Lily suggested. Hal grimaced.

'What would they say? They'd be relieved, like everyone else, it seems, if I missed this wedding. Not great for Amber, of course, they'd admit that. Wouldn't wish it on anyone. But they'd be bloody ecstatic when it came to me.'

'Why!'

'I don't know. It's not as if they don't want me to get married off to *someone*. Josh must have poisoned them against her.' Even Hal was aware he didn't sound very convincing.

'They'd help me out now. They're decent, lovely people,' he went on. 'But what could they do that I can't do? At this moment they'll be no nearer to her than I am. I'd prefer they didn't know.'

'Don't worry, it's not far now,' Lily reassured him, putting her foot down again.

Sitting in the back, Kirsty kept missing what was being said. She felt like a child again, swallowed up in the noise of the old car, watching her parents' heads nod and shake. She leaned forwards, squashing herself between the two front seats, butting in to the murmured conversation, determined not to be left out.

'So, Hal,' she shouted. 'What's everyone got against her?'

Hal took a deep breath. 'Different things,' he shouted after a pause. 'Richard and Alex are odd about women, full stop. And they don't like her taking me away from them.'

'I don't understand,' said Lily. 'Loads of other guys must have this happen to them. Gradually no one left to meet at the pub, or do things with at the weekend. One by one everyone getting married. But other guys don't resort to sabotaging their friends' weddings to stop it happening.'

'Look,' said Hal. 'Richard and Alex are much, much worse than the other guys! It's just taken me twenty years to realize it. Josh and Charlie always thought I was mad to have anything to do with them.' Hal shook his head. 'Josh and Charlie too,' he said sadly. 'They've set me up. They'll have had this planned for months.'

'They did it because they care about you,' said Kirsty from the back seat.

'I doubt it,' said Hal. 'This is all down to Josh.' His voice shook. 'Getting me down to that cottage. Missing my *wedding* day!'

'It'll be all right,' said Lily.

'So you'll never ever forgive them?' asked Kirsty.

'Fuck no,' said Hal. 'Bastards.' He looked down at his phone. 'God, I wish I could get through to her.'

'Could Josh have put her off, do you think? Done

something to stop her answering your calls?' Kirsty asked, tentatively.

'There is nothing that Josh could say that would persuade Amber not to be in that church, waiting for me. She loves me.'

When, eventually, they made it to the motorway it was almost empty of cars. It was just past eleven thirty. The sun broke through the clouds and Lily gingerly pushed the car towards a hundred.

They had gone less than a mile when, for the first time in her life, she saw a police car in her mirror and knew it was after her. She braked hard and watched the needle slip back down to ninety, eighty-five, eighty, but it was no good. The police car flashed its lights, gave a burst of its siren and indicated that she should pull over.

Lily watched the pair of policemen saunter over to her in her mirror. She gritted her teeth, knowing there was little point in protesting.

'Run out of runway?' one asked with a patronizing smile.

'I'm sorry,' Hal groaned to Lily. 'I'll make it up to you somehow.'

It took half an hour to be charged and so it was nearly twelve when they came off the motorway. They drove through Evesham and towards Broadway, Hal no longer needing the map, guiding them urgently on through one honey-stoned Cotswold village after another.

Any other time and we could stop for lunch, thought Kirsty, looking at all the tiny shops and the olde-worlde signs advertising cream teas. But it was not really a place she wanted to stop in: architecturally perfect and yet clipped and maintained to such a level that it felt as if the tourists blocking up all the roads, swarming on the perfect green, and flowing in and out of the gift shops, were the only people there.

How serious was that extra half hour delay? Hal wondered, telling himself that if she were waiting for him half an hour ago, she'd be waiting still. In his heart he felt that it couldn't matter. That with this much effort they *must* have succeeded.

They pulled off the main road on to a narrow unmarked lane and, at last, picked up speed again. Every time they turned a corner Lily wondered if this was it, if this time Hal would say *stop*, and they would see his church and know that they had made it. But instead he told her to turn again, and again, leaning up close to the windscreen, one hand on the dashboard in readiness to propel himself out of the car door the second he could. They turned again, into an even smaller lane. Ahead of them and to either side long grassy meadows stretched steeply away from them, the hedges yellow-green in the sunlight, new buds and leaves waiting to unfurl. And then Hal said, 'That's it.' He pointed through a veil of yew trees to a little church set back from the side of the lane.

'Amber's parents live about two minutes further down the lane.'

'There's something pinned to the gate,' said Kirsty ominously as they passed by.

Lily pulled over and parked, tucking the car as much into the side of the lane as she could. Hal got out with

Kirsty and they waited for Lily to climb through the passenger's side before they set off across the road, three abreast, supporting Hal on either side.

'It's Amber's writing,' said Hal, stunned.

They stopped at the gate and looked at the discreet white card, somehow knowing what the words would say. And yet, when Lily did read the words, slowly, one by one, her insides froze with icy shock. It was with regret that Mr and Mrs Aisling announced that the marriage of their daughter Amber to Mr Henry Summer was postponed. Tea was available at Mill House and they were requested not to leave presents.

Hal studied the note long and hard. He finally turned to Kirsty and Lily and raised his fingers to his lips.

'I'd better find out what's happened,' he said. 'Thanks, you've been great.' He took a deep breath and turned away from them.

They let him go, watching in silence as he made his way down a little path away from the church, out of an ornate wrought-iron gate, and then into the lane ahead. They stood, side by side, as his tall, solitary figure loped away from them in the sunlight, until finally he disappeared from view.

5

'We can't go to the reception! It would be like gate-crashing a funeral.'

'Well, if Hal doesn't like it he can tell us. How else are we ever going to know what happens?' Kirsty looked beseechingly at Lily. '*Please.* We can't just turn around and go home. Not now. Don't you want to find Josh? Tell him what you think of him? Don't you want to know what he said to Amber? Don't you want to know if Hal has managed to sort things out?' She paused for a second, racking her brains for something more persuasive. 'Get a quick look at her? See what all the fuss is about?'

'*She's* not likely to be there. She's hardly going to feel like hosting a reception.'

Kirsty reconsidered. 'Well, depends if Hal's found her. They may have sorted it out.'

Lily hesitated. 'I don't think so,' she said doubtfully.

Kirsty lifted her feet off the dashboard and slipped them back into her shoes. 'I am not going home,' she said determinedly. 'So go back without me.' She tried the handle of the car door. 'Unlock it!'

'Hang on a minute.'

'Look,' said Kirsty, 'I'm going to that reception. I don't want to let them all just disappear out of my life. Not yet. It's the best fun I've had for years.'

Lily put her head in her hands.

'I'm only being honest,' Kirsty went on. 'Admit it. We don't *really* care about Amber, or Hal! We don't even know them. It's just a bit of fun. So, stop being so antsy and come and have a cup of tea and a piece of cake. Or go home, alone.'

Lily looked at her. 'Oh sod it. Let's go!' she said eventually and Kirsty heaved a sigh of relief.

It was over half an hour since Hal had left them. For a long while they'd simply sat in the car and watched fascinated as a steady procession of guests had walked past them, clutching hats and bags and presents, on their way to the church. They'd watched as, one after another, people had read the note pinned to the church gate. Unable to hear what they were saying, all the same Lily and Kirsty could make out exactly what they were thinking. Some people seemed horrified, holding hands to their mouths in shock, making big eyes at each other, others couldn't seem to have cared less, and one gaggle of pretty girls had stuffed their fists in their mouths, failing to suppress a great, unanimous gale of laughter.

Kirsty and Lily cruised slowly down the lane, rounded a bend and saw a sign ahead of them with an arrow and 'Wedding Cars' pointing towards a field. There was matting laid down in the entrance and about twenty cars parked just inside. There, ahead of them, was a huge, cream marquee, fluttering and pulling at its ropes, and nestled discreetly behind it, a lovely Cotswold farmhouse. At the sight, Lily felt a familiar thrill of anticipation that turned swiftly into a lurch of sickness. Seeing it all wonderfully spread out, waiting for a reception that was never going to take place, brought a huge lump to her throat. She glanced across to see if Kirsty had felt it too, but Kirsty had almost climbed inside her make-up bag and was oblivious to Lily or anything else.

As they tentatively got out of the car, the sun disappeared behind a cloud and an unsettled breeze whipped at their clothes and hair. Kirsty felt the goosebumps rise on her arms. She grabbed her hat with one hand and Lily with the other.

'You're right. I don't look smart enough,' Lily panicked as they tripped across the field.

'No, you don't. But don't worry about it, masses of people don't dress up for weddings. No one will notice. The important thing is not to tell anyone who we are. We'll find out what's happened, have a quick nose around, and then we're out of here.'

'What if –'

'*No one* will notice us,' Kirsty interrupted. 'It'll be packed full of people – there's nothing this lot like more than a good scandal. They'll all be gossiping away, enjoying themselves. No one will take a blind bit of notice of us.'

'You're right.'

'So don't worry.'

'And what if Josh's there?' Lily said, half dreading it, half relishing the opportunity of telling him what she thought.

'He won't be,' said Kirsty. 'This is the bride's patch. He won't want to hang around.'

They walked in beneath a double arch of entwining pink roses and cream ribbons, and through a short tunnel. Lily just had time to register that it was surprisingly quiet when she found herself in a big, brightly lit, silk-lined marquee, half filled with ornate tables and chairs. Suspended high up on the central poles was an avenue of huge, flamboyant flower arrangements.

Lily took them in at a glance, her attention elsewhere. At the other end of the marquee, sitting in a lone, defiant cluster, were thirty or forty people. Around them hovered a huge army of super-attentive waitresses serving tea and, in the corner of the room, a string quartet was gamely serenading everyone with a complicated piece of Bach. Apart from them, the marquee was completely empty.

As Lily and Kirsty walked in, conversation died immediately away. There was a brief second where it might have been possible to turn on a heel without catching anybody's eye, but the moment passed and neither Lily nor Kirsty did anything.

Lily had never felt such an outsider. She forced herself forwards and walked towards the curious tea party, the music accompanying her footsteps, feeling like she was floating, her feet silent on the hessian floor. At the last minute she lost her nerve, changed direction and veered off towards the tea tables, but a girl rose from her place to bar the way.

The girl was stunning, with porcelain skin and hair that tumbled down her back in long red ringlets.

'Bride or groom?' she asked with an open, friendly smile.

'Bride,' said Lily quickly.

'Groom,' said Kirsty at the same time.

The girl stared at Kirsty long and hard. 'What the fuck are you doing here?'

Lily was aware of the other guests, faces expectant, tea-cups frozen in mid-air.

'Nice to meet you too,' Kirsty snapped back. 'For God's sake! He hasn't murdered anyone.'

Lily jumped in. 'We're friends of Hal's,' she said quietly. 'And we wanted to see if he was okay. We don't want to upset you.'

'Come on Mel, darling. Come and sit down. Stop giving everyone the third degree,' came a rather careworn voice from among the smattering of guests. A heavy, gentle-looking man of about sixty heaved himself off a gilt chair and came across to put a protective arm around the girl's shoulders.

'I'm Jonathan Aisling and this is my *other* daughter, Mel.' He offered his hand and smiled wearily at Lily and Kirsty. 'Need we say more?'

A group of guests, hanging on to every word, all gently shook their heads in sympathy.

'You can imagine that we think unspeakable things about Hal. But that's no reason to lynch you two. Come and have a cup of tea.'

'We're so sorry about all of this,' Lily said to Mel's father.

'He's a bastard. A total, utter bastard,' said Mel passionately. 'You can tell him so when you see him. From me.'

Looking at her, Lily realized that Mel was probably only about sixteen. Her chin, wobbling now with tears, was full and very young and the eyelashes that swept half-way down her cheek were those of a child.

She gently lifted her father's arm off her shoulders. I wonder if Amber looks anything like you, Lily thought, watching the lovely face break into a smile as she wiped her eyes and pushed her father back to his guests, reassuring him that she was okay.

'Can I come and talk to you two for a second?' She asked them more quietly. She glanced around at the other guests. 'You're the only friends of Hal's to come,' she paused. '*Not* surprising.'

'Of course,' said Lily and Kirsty in unison.

'Here, have some,' Mel said, moving them over to where tea was being poured.

Behind her the quartet had moved on to the beautiful, sad adagio from the Bach double.

'Aren't they awful,' whispered Mel. 'I told Dad to shut them up, tell them to go home, but apparently it's Mum's idea. She thinks it'll make people forget what's going on.'

Lily nodded. 'Like on the *Titanic*.'

They took their cups and a plate of tiny sandwiches and sat down at an empty table.

'Sorry about what I said. I'm all over the place.' Mel shrugged bitterly. 'It's all so terrible. You know, I'm more upset about this than Amber! She didn't even cry.'

'Is she here?' Kirsty asked, looking around the marquee.

Mel shook her head. 'Erm, no actually,' she said sarcastically. 'After she spoke to Josh this morning all she wanted to do was get away. She took about an hour to rearrange her flights and then she was gone.' Mel looked at her watch. 'She'll be leaving Heathrow about now.'

'Oh my God!' said Kirsty admiringly.

'She's gone on her honeymoon. My sister's pretty cool.'

'She didn't give Hal much chance to explain. How *could* she leave? Didn't she want to speak to him?' said Lily indignantly.

'Was there something he wanted to say?' Mel shot back. 'I thought he had Josh to do all that for him.'

Lily rocked back in her chair. She was certain that she and Kirsty should not get more embroiled than they already were, that what had happened and was still happening was so precariously balanced that she and Kirsty must not interfere any more. The wrong explanation now, to Amber's kid sister, could screw up everything, ruin what slim chance Hal had of ever sorting things out. If, indeed, he still wanted to. She hoped that Kirsty felt the same way and wondered whether she could count on her to keep her mouth shut.

'Hal was set up by Josh,' Kirsty told Mel, dramatically, right on cue, and Lily's heart sank. 'He didn't mean *any* of this to happen.'

'Don't give me that!' exclaimed Mel furiously.

'Leave it out, Kirsty!' Lily insisted, exasperated. 'It's nothing to do with you, or me, or even Mel. It's to do with him and Amber.'

'But Amber's gone, and Hal's not here. Someone has to tell them all what really happened.'

'No! Everybody has had too much to say already. Let Hal sort it out now.'

'There's nothing to sort out. Amber's gone, and Hal is never going to get her back,' said Mel. 'He was here about half an hour ago. When he realized that she'd gone he went crazy, shouting at my dad that it was him who'd been left at the altar, not Amber. Luckily none of this lot were around,' Mel waved her hand towards the other guests. 'There's nothing he can do now, it's too late. Amber's never going to forgive him for putting her through this.'

'Even if he didn't mean to?' asked Kirsty.

'Wait,' Lily told her, cutting in. 'We only met Hal last night. We don't really know him at all. Yes, he seemed determined to get married but the truth is we just don't know. I think the best we can do is accept that Hal is the one to sort it out, that if they're meant to be together then ultimately, this won't put them off.'

'But what could Josh have said?' Kirsty insisted. 'What could be so convincing that she buggered off without even giving Hal a chance to explain? If Josh's spun some clever lie, by the time Amber gets back from her holiday she'll have had two more weeks to think about it. She'll probably be even more certain she doesn't want to marry him. And Hal can't do a thing. Not unless he flies out to join her.'

'Well, I hope he doesn't do that, because I think Josh's gone with her,' said Mel, quietly dropping an unexpected bombshell.

Lily went cold.

'Just after I'd said goodbye to Amber, I realized he'd vanished too,' she went on. 'All this morning, I kept asking her how she was going to get to the airport, but she always changed the subject and wouldn't answer. And then after she left, I got it.' Mel paused, suddenly forlorn. 'Josh must have driven Amber himself.'

She looked at them despondently. 'There was a bag of his over there in the corner, and then it was gone. He went to the airport with her and I bet he's gone on the honeymoon too. God I hate her!'

'Surely that should be *him*?' said Kirsty.

'I wish I could but I can't hate Josh,' Mel replied sadly.

He wouldn't do it, Lily told herself, acknowledging at the same time that everything she knew about Josh so far suggested that he would. The Josh she'd met the night before would positively relish the idea of eloping with someone else's fiancée. Perhaps, she mused, this was all one big set-up. Carefully worked out so that Josh could get Amber back for himself?

'So you two didn't even know them before yesterday?' Mel said. 'Nothing *you* can tell me then, is there?' Understanding suddenly dawned on her face. 'I bet you weren't even invited to the wedding!'

'Nope,' Lily replied, smiling back at her. 'We met Hal in Welshpool last night. Do you mind?'

A small black and white terrier trotted importantly past with a large pink ribbon tied around his neck. Mel scooped him up into her arms and buried her face in his neck.

'Of course not.' She laughed, balancing the little dog

on her lap. 'My sister hadn't known him much longer and she was planning on marrying him.' She paused. 'And where's *Welsh Pool*?' she said. 'Sounds awful, like the kind of place you get taken to on a biology field trip.'

'It's in mid-Wales, on the border with Shropshire.' Kirsty smiled icily. It was okay for her to knock Welshpool but not anyone else.

Mel set the terrier back on his feet and fed him a sandwich. 'I should get back to my friends.' She scraped back her chair and was just rising to her feet when she noticed that her father was doing the same thing. He chinked a saucer against his tea-cup and looked pointedly across at her and she sat down again.

Jonathan Aisling looked steadily around the marquee.

'When I heard the news, I would go so far as to say that I became concerned for my daughter's sanity,' he announced, staring down at his shoes. All around, people stilled, stricken faces looking up at him. 'Yes,' he added solemnly, 'it really was *that* bad.' He paused for effect and then allowed a smile to twitch the corners of his mouth. 'I'm talking about the day she told me she was marrying Hal!'

The audience laughed appreciatively in a burst of relief.

'I'm not going to say it's better she found out now – I doubt that Amber will ever have a worse day in her life. And I wish I could make it different for her,' his voice wobbled. 'But I can't.' He stopped again and cleared his throat. 'I'd like to thank you all for coming, for supporting us here today, and I'd like to propose a toast.' He paused again, and looked around the room. 'She's not here because she decided not to waste the honeymoon. So, in her absence, to our dearest, darling elder daughter, Amber.'

The guests started cheering and clapping and hammering the table in appreciation and Jonathan Aisling's face broke into a grin. At his smile, the cheering got even louder and for a while he forgot his speech and gave himself up to them. But eventually the wisecracks and whistling died down again and he raised his glass.

'Amber,' he repeated. 'May you survive this. And when you are ready, have a wildly irresponsible, fantastically indulgent, utterly enjoyable time, *without him*!'

'Hear, hear! To Amber!' shouted people in unison and everybody stood up as one and raised their glasses.

Lily could feel the huge wave of support for the Aisling family, and she thought that if Hal happened to walk in at that moment, the wedding guests would fall upon him like a pack of hounds.

'Finally . . .' Jonathan Aisling hardly had to raise his voice for the guests to fall silent once more. 'There's some tea – if you haven't eaten it all – and then you can push off home and leave us alone!'

Everybody laughed at his abruptness. Mel shook her head, smiling proudly.

'He's always like this,' she said.

Jonathan Aisling's speech opened the floodgates. He had released them from embarrassment and had given them the go-ahead to let rip. Suddenly there were shrieks of laughter, and a mad, animated chatter where before there'd been a decorous, deferential hush. The quartet rapidly switched to a noisy jig and a few people even began to dance, one couple immediately executing a series of complicated rock and roll moves.

'There's *always* someone who does that!' Kirsty commented to Lily. 'Why?'

They watched as the man ostentatiously twisted the girl into what looked like a painful half-nelson.

Lily laughed. 'They're sad people who have no friends,' she said, grimacing as a little girl wandered into the couple's path and was nearly sent flying.

Next to them a rugged, attractive man with greying hair and a too-red face started talking in a very loud voice to a couple of pretty middle-aged women.

'I once gave Hal two pieces of advice,' he said, watching Lily and Kirsty with half an eye, 'and he didn't listen to either of them.' The man paused, picking out his words carefully. 'I said to Hal, one, never dance in public.' The two women smiled, unsure whether this was a reference to the rock-and-rollers. 'And two,' he went on, 'just because you enjoy a good gallop, don't necessarily buy the horse.' He looked at the women with glee. They laughed politely. 'Bloody idiot didn't take my advice and now look at the mess he's in.'

'Really!' one of the women exclaimed, delicately nibbling at a profiterole and seeming to misunderstand him completely. 'How many horses have you bought then?'

'None! But, Kitty, that was a *metaphor*!' He said despairingly.

'The truth is, Kitty,' the other woman explained to her

slowly, shooting a piercing look at the man as she did so, 'Jimmy here can't talk, he's been married four times! And as for horses, he falls for anything that comes between his knees.'

Jimmy raised his eyebrows.

'It's why I adore *you* so,' he said to her. Then added, silkily, 'Although, don't you only come for a title?' He caught her hand.

'Bastard,' she hissed.

'But I adore you,' he repeated, kissing her palm.

'I'm sorry, you've lost me completely,' the dim woman complained.

The man let the woman's hand go.

'Now *she's* rather fetching!' he told them both, loudly, gesturing to Lily. All three looked her over appraisingly.

'If you want to get away, get away now,' Mel advised. 'Jimmy's okay, can even be quite funny, but he's a complete lech. You'll need a Stain Devil to get rid of him.'

Lily had had enough. Jimmy was hurriedly working out the cork of a bottle of Bollinger, so she turned her back on him and grabbed Kirsty's arm.

'I'll let you go. Thanks for listening. Sorry if I was rude,' said Mel quickly. 'Keep in touch,' she called over her shoulder, moving back to her friends.

Walking close together, Kirsty and Lily strode the length of the marquee without looking back. As soon as they were through the entrance they ran, laughing and relieved, back to the car. They flung themselves in and slammed shut the doors.

'Wow!' said Kirsty.

'Let's get out of here,' said Lily starting the engine, suddenly overcome with a violent tremble.

'I'm starving,' said Kirsty. 'Wish I'd got some more of those sandwiches.'

'We'll stop on the M40. Eggs, chips, sausage.'

'And baked beans, bacon, mushrooms and a large Diet Coke.'

6

A week later, Kirsty and Lily knew no more than when they'd left Amber's wedding reception. While Lily was ready to put it all behind her, Kirsty was eaten up with an inquisitiveness that got worse day by day. One answer would have been to ask the Little Goose for a booking number or address and to write to Hal, but that might have meant a conversation with Simon, whom she wanted to avoid at all costs. And so, eventually, she too resigned herself to not finding out any more, guessing there was no likelihood of the boys ever getting in touch with her.

That eventful Friday had been Kirsty's afternoon off. She worked a four-and-a-half-day week and, as usual, had chosen to spend her Friday afternoon with Lily, wandering along the High Street in the rain. They'd meet at the entrance to the covered market before making their way across town to the Courtyard for lunch. Kirsty never wanted to go further afield, not even to Shrewsbury or Oswestry. She made the effort to moan regularly about Welshpool, but actually wanted to be nowhere else.

Her parents tried persistently to nudge her out of the house, comparing her with her younger brother, Dan, who had travelled since he was eighteen, catching up with his family for only a few weeks each year. But Kirsty had no interest in doing the same. Relaxed and confident on her own turf, Kirsty thrived. Away from home for more than a couple of weeks and she always grew desperate to return.

Kirsty worked in a creeper-clad warehouse nestled against the hills on the outskirts of Montgomery, a few miles from Welshpool. She was the general manager of an agricultural suppliers partly owned by her father. Nearly everybody she knew had thought she was mad to take the job. Her schoolfriends had been aghast, arguing that if she had to work in a shop, why couldn't it be somewhere like the florist's, or even the underwear shop on the High Street, where she could have got them discounted Wonderbras? Instead of which, she'd be selling things like chicken coops and cattle prods. Kirsty had retorted that she'd rather help a gorgeous young farmer into a new pair of wellingtons than a fat old bag into a size eighteen corset.

From her first day, Kirsty adored it, as she had known she would. Five years on, she still took pleasure in every sale. She had improved her knowledge of farming to the extent that she could advise with authority, and thrived on all the close relationships she had built up with her customers. They loved her back. Old men who'd never confided in their families or friends in their whole lives would find themselves chatting to Kirsty, taking her into their confidence. She was so good at listening, so disarmingly straightforward, that many people pulled up in the forecourt simply to see her. In the course of her five years, there'd been more and more they'd needed to say.

Even before foot and mouth, the farmers who provided

her with almost every penny of her income had been pushed ever closer towards extinction. Kirsty had become used to hearing tales of desperation, a farmer who had given up his sheep to the RSPCA, another who had shot his calves because there was no point taking them to market. It had been an extreme and yet ever-worsening situation, and Kirsty had veered from despair and anger to disbelief that so little was being done to help, knowing that by the time public attention had caught up with the situation too many farmers would have fallen permanently by the wayside.

And then came foot and mouth. First one young heifer, tender on her feet, and suddenly whole herds of animals condemned to slaughter all around her. Farms closed down, villages empty. The smell of disinfectant heavy on the air. The crack of the gun, the strain and despair etched into faces everywhere.

For a few months public attention had held, but all too soon it was easier to think that because the barricades had come down and the footpaths reopened life in the countryside had returned to normal. In a way it was true – but what had been desperate and relentless before was, too often, impossible now, and for some it had been one crisis too many, tipping some men over the edge, to give up tragically and permanently.

On a practical level Kirsty tried everything she could think of to prevent the warehouse from going under. Gradually she had widened the range of goods on sale, introducing, alongside the sheep dip and baler twine, some pony nuts, tiny plastic bags of hamster food, lawn seed and puncture repair kits for wheelbarrows and bicycles. And as a result she widened her customer base, bringing in the hill-walkers and holiday makers when they started to return, the weekenders and people from the town.

And then one day she'd been stock-taking in the back when the bell had rung and Simon Campion had walked in. Just as she'd always predicted, he was tall, dark and handsome, and was looking for a pair of wellingtons.

'We might not have any your size,' she'd said, doubtfully, staring at a huge pair of Caterpillar boots, surprised to be almost lost for words.

'Hey, my feet aren't *so* big!' he'd laughed, picking a random pair off the shelf. 'These'll do.'

'Try them on?' Kirsty had suggested.

He bent down and unlaced a boot, resting his arm on the wall to keep his balance. He was wearing jeans and a heavy navy ribbed jumper that had tiny wisps of hay clinging to the front. He was rugged and dishevelled, full of energy and vitality. She'd loved the way he'd looked up at her, smiling easily, brown eyes warm. Straightforward, uncomplicated, liking what he saw and not bothering to pretend otherwise.

'I'll have them,' he'd said, pulling out a grubby chequebook from a trouser pocket and stomping back into his shoes, not stopping to retie the laces.

She had taken his cheque, waved away the card and rung it through the till while he looked over her shoulder, studying the flea powders and cat collars displayed behind her.

'What a great place,' he'd said, looking around. 'You've got everything under the sun.' He'd paused, thinking. 'What was it I wanted?' He'd scratched his black hair, searching for inspiration. 'A rabbit hutch! A really big one,' he remembered. 'With a wheel.'

'Rabbits don't have *wheels*,' Kirsty had said dismissively, leading the way to the back of the shop, praying that he wasn't buying it for himself.

'I know I shouldn't ask you out straight away,' he'd said from behind her, making her knees go suddenly weak. She'd managed to carry on walking. 'But I don't want a rabbit hutch.' She'd stopped then and turned around. 'If you say yes, you'll be saving me from coming back hundreds of times to buy all sorts of things I don't need.' He'd looked at the shelves stacked high around him. 'Like wild bird seed and curry combs.'

'But I like the customers who do that,' she'd said.

'Oh damn, of course you do!' he'd laughed. 'Go on, say yes.'

'Go out when?'

'Tomorrow night? I'll cook you supper.'

When Simon had moved to Welshpool the town had been awash with the news, curious as to who this handsome man was, single-handedly taking on crumbling, beautiful Pond House, where he planned to live, and the Little Goose, where he planned to work. Quickly, they'd realized that his cooking was far better than the usual goujons of plaice and melon drenched in port, and that the Little Goose would be flying upmarket. At roughly the same time *World of Interiors* photographers were spotted taking pictures not only of Pond House but of the whole town. Simon was putting Welshpool on the map in more ways than one.

His very public love life provided more rich pickings for the local gossip vultures. Since he'd moved in, there'd been a stream of what the bridge club liked to categorize as 'Twit' girls, all obviously completely unsuitable, showing off their Fendi baguette handbags in the local Co-op, or trying to pay for half-a-dozen free-range eggs with a black American Express card. Confidently, the bridge club ladies had told each other that it was only a matter of time before he met either Lily or Kirsty. It had taken four months.

'Okay. I'll see you tomorrow,' Kirsty had smiled. 'Shall I come to the pub?'

'No, come to Pond House. You know where it is?'

Kirsty had nodded.

'Good!' he'd said calmly. 'And thanks for the wellingtons.' It was only after he'd climbed into an old black Porsche and disappeared in a puff of smoke and dust that she'd realized he'd left them behind.

*

Oh, Simon, Simon, Simon. Kirsty paced in time to the words, her head down, her feet keeping to the squares of the pavement because that would mean she would see him again. I did love your cooking . . . and you, she half thought, before she forced the idea out of her head. She was on her way to meet Lily for a quick shop and was very late. She looked at her watch, swore and broke into a half jog.

At first she'd been confident that she could slip out of the relationship with Simon as simply as she'd got into it but he hadn't given up easily. When the stag party had appeared the week before, it had seemed as if they were heaven-sent, providing her with enough fun to drive Simon out of her head. But it hadn't worked at all.

She didn't want to talk to Lily about it because Lily would never understand and yet, at the same time, she desperately wanted to tell her everything. It had never happened to Kirsty before, this churning panic every time she thought about a man. When she'd arrived at Pond House for dinner, that first time, she'd felt confident, completely on top of the situation, proud of how she looked, at ease with the thought of the evening alone with him. But seconds after he'd opened the front door she'd been engulfed by nerves. It was to do with the way he'd stared at her, and how she'd looked beyond him into a huge dark hall lit only by a log fire. It was a warm, flickering, hypnotizing, flame-lit world and she had suddenly felt as if she were entering the lion's den.

The look on Lily's face, when Simon had come up to them in the Little Goose, had told her better than words ever could that Lily was not going to understand and that her decision to hide her fling with Simon from Lily had been a wise one. Far from being on Kirsty's side, she'd been very impressed with Simon. It was as if she hadn't expected Kirsty to pull it off with someone so cool and so much older. Now, Kirsty knew Lily would be impatient, pushing her to make a go of it with him, not remotely understanding why Kirsty wanted to detach herself before things had really begun.

Rounding the corner, Kirsty saw her propping up one of the pillars at the front of the market-place. As Kirsty approached, Lily smiled and raised a hand in greeting.

It was February the 13th. All around them people were marching in and out of the newsagents and Woolworths, armed with cellophaned red roses, satin padded cards and pink envelopes.

'I'm not even going to think about Valentine's Day,' Kirsty announced later, standing alongside Lily in the card shop, reading poems over Lily's shoulder. 'Roses are red, violets are blue, sugar is sweet, but I'll suck you,' she recited. 'Jesus! Give me Purple Ronnie any day.'

'Sshhhh!' Lily cried, pink with embarrassment, wishing Kirsty didn't have to speak in quite such a loud voice. She shoved the card back into its rack.

'What are we doing here anyway? I'm not sending any.'

'Nor me,' said Kirsty decisively, biting her lip.

Lily took her arm. 'Really? Nothing for Simon? When *are* you going to tell me about him?'

'I don't know. There's nothing more to say. Tell me something about your love life for a change.'

'You know there's nothing to tell.'

'Ah, but surely there was *once*. Wasn't there?'

'Wrong time, wrong place,' Lily said ambiguously, smiling brightly, closing the subject.

'I'll get it out of you some time,' Kirsty said seriously. 'You owe it to me. And then I might tell you about Simon. I'd stay out for a drink,' she added, 'but Dan's come home and I said I'd be back to see him. I'm sorry.'

'That's fine, I'll go home. Cook the dragon some soup.'

'Send her a big kiss.'

'Oh, right,' said Lily.

'I'll call you, we could get together some time over the weekend.' Kirsty turned and walked away, then looked back. 'And if you get any cards, I don't want to know.'

Lily slowly made her way home. She saw that lights were on in the kitchen and guessed that her sister was already there. The hall was in darkness and Lily turned on the overhead light, calling out as she did so. There was no reply.

She went through the house, switching on all the lights, quietly calling her sister's name, until eventually she found Grace in the television room, curled up on the sofa in the dark with a packet of Wotsits, children's television flickering cartoon colours around the room.

'Why didn't you answer? You must have heard me.'

Grace stared at her. 'Drop it,' she said, aggressively. 'You've only just walked in.'

She stood up and brushed crumbs off her jumper, scattering them on to the floor, then scrunched up the crisp packet and threw it into a bin before pushing past Lily and making her way upstairs.

For God's sake, Lily thought to herself, breathing out a shaky sigh, taking in the collection of cups half filled with tea and the crusts of a sandwich lying on the floor. She turned off the television and switched off the light, anger rising like bile inside her.

Needing to get out of the house, she left everything as it was and went back outside, to the small, numbingly cold outhouse built at the back. Her teeth chattered as she opened the padlock on the door and she told herself she was being ridiculous, imagining herself freezing at her wheel, becoming a lifesize piece of ice-art. Once inside, she switched on an overhead light and an electric radiator, retrieved some wet clay and slapped it on to the table in front of her. Still in her coat, she sat down and looked at it, then picked it up again, forcing her stiff hands to begin work.

Boxes and crates of half-finished vases and cups took up almost every foot of space. Huge bowls and fruit plates balanced precariously on top of each other, alongside outsize dishes and milk jugs. In the back were a small portable kiln and several makeshift shelves filled with finished work – bold, colourful designs, flowers, fish and fowl in jewel bright colours. This was the beginning of Lily's studio.

Fingers sticky with clay, she pushed back stray strands of blonde hair, tucking them behind her ears. Every time she bent her head another section came loose and fell forward, and soon there was enough clay on her cheeks to give herself a face pack. She knew she wasn't going to make anything good but still she carried on, stabbing at the piece of clay with a cold finger. She felt like moulding a face of Grace and sticking nails into it but worried that her anger was so strong she might actually make the magic work.

Finally, Lily admitted to herself that it was time to move out. That she couldn't stand staying with Grace any longer. If in all the time she'd stayed she felt she'd helped Grace at all, she wouldn't have been so sure it was time to go. Now all she wondered was what had taken her so long.

How she'd afford to move to anywhere else she couldn't imagine. Once upon a time, as she'd put the finishing touches to her plans for London, there had been a commission from the Registry, a big department store in Chelsea, which was looking for a young designer. She'd complacently turned it down, figuring that moving to Welshpool and looking after Grace was going to take up most of her time, not realizing how unlikely it was that she'd ever be offered anything as good again. Now she kicked herself, only too well aware that she'd sold far too little in the last six months and that her savings were gone.

The Registry offer had come in months ago. When she declined they'd said that she was to get in touch if anything changed. And now everything had changed. It would be a long shot but she'd follow up the invitation in the morning, she decided. And if they said no after all, she'd get off her backside and try somewhere else.

Gradually she brightened up, wondering if perhaps this was the time to move away from Welshpool, to Manchester or even back to London. And yet she didn't feel at all sure about going, not just because she'd miss Kirsty but because she was enjoying herself and she wanted at least one whole summer before she moved on. Somehow she'd get the money together and rent a cottage with a studio, she decided, and Kirsty could move in too.

After an hour she cleaned up, locked the studio door and made her way around the side of the house, letting herself in through the back door into the warm silent kitchen.

She went up to Grace's room, knocked, and then, when Grace didn't respond, opened the door. Grace was lying on the bed reading a magazine.

'Hi,' Grace said, without looking up. 'What's going on?'

'I was thinking how it was time I moved out.' Lily spoke the words before her brain was in gear but Grace didn't flinch.

'About time,' she said coldly, turning a page.

Lily came and sat on the bed next to her and saw that Grace's eyes were filling with tears.

'Don't cry.'

'Please don't go,' Grace whispered. She put down the magazine and looked up at Lily.

Lily moved further up on to the bed, hoping that this was the breakthrough between the two of them. 'If I went it would only be up the street. I'd still see you every day. But admit it, Grace,' she smiled gently, 'I've been driving you insane. I certainly don't make things any better.'

'You ought to have seen me before you arrived.'

'I heard you, on the telephone every night, remember? But this is your house, and you've always said you're better living alone. I get under your feet. Up your nose.'

'Will you please stop telling me what I want. What's best for me. I'm telling you, I don't want you to go. I need you here.'

'No, you don't. I make things worse,' said Lily, ignoring the edge that had crept into Grace's voice. 'I've been here six months and look at us. We're at each other's throats all the time. I can't remember us ever being like this before.'

Lily reached out to touch Grace's skinny thigh, hoping that she might nudge Grace to acknowledge how they once were, but immediately Grace flinched out of reach. 'Grace,' Lily said gently, 'I'm not talking about next week or even next month. But I think I might start looking for somewhere. Somewhere close by.'

'You're serious, then?'

'Yes.'

Grace's mouth hardened and Lily braced herself. The new Grace would move seamlessly on to the attack.

'You go, Lily,' she agreed. 'You're right, I *am* better alone.' She paused and looked at her with cold eyes. 'Mother-so-Superior, with your do-goody crap.'

'What?'

'You heard me.'

Lily bit her lip, holding on. 'What's going on?' she said, still trying to sound gentle. 'How have we got to this?'

'Don't you know?' Grace sat up abruptly. 'You arrive here – uninvited, if I remember rightly – ' She spoke fast, her voice rising steadily, 'Telling everyone who'd listen that I couldn't cope on my own, that you were *so worried* about me.' She paused. 'You stay for six months. Which messes me up completely. And now, you tell me you're moving on again.' Angry tears started to trickle down her face. 'How can you say that!' she suddenly sobbed.

'Grace, please!'

'You never cared about me. You weren't worried when Jeremy ditched me. You were delighted! It was what you'd expected – what you'd told everybody else to expect too.'

Lily had had enough. Of the past six months of letting Grace get away with saying what ever she wanted, of fetching and carrying, listening and supporting, and never retaliating.

'It's not true,' she yelled back, making Grace start in surprise. 'Everything you think is all twisted up.' Lily stared at her. 'And it's been miserable living here with you.'

Grace was still and silent.

'And I'm bored of being miserable,' Lily told her. 'I'm bored of you. It's never even occurred to you, has it? That I might decide to go. In all this time you've never once thought about anyone apart from yourself.'

Lily stared at Grace without seeing her, not noticing how slack and grey her face had become. 'I'm sorry you had a hard time, but I left my friends, gave up my flat, lost a job, all to be with you because I was sorry. And no, since you mention it, I wasn't delighted to do that. It was a lot to give up.'

'Are you leaving now?' Grace asked quietly, in a flat dead voice.

In answer Lily stood up and went over to the door, turned away from Grace without saying any more, and then lifted her hand in goodbye. She walked away, down the stairs, her heart thumping. For a moment she stood silently in the dark hall, then went to the telephone.

'Come over,' Kirsty told her as soon as she heard Lily's voice.

After the phone call, Lily went back upstairs and packed a bag and then she left the house.

It was a black night with no stars visible and the cold night air was like a slap against her cheek. Wheeling her bike out into the lane, she was overcome by everything she'd said, horrified that she could have gone so far. But, she reminded herself, for how many months had Grace been saying far worse? She thought of all the times she'd ignored the insults, turned the other cheek, and her blood boiled again. It had all gone on long enough, and whatever the consequences, Grace had had to hear it.

Street lights hadn't yet come to Green Lane and, as Lily cycled blindly into her third pothole, her bag swinging precariously around her back, she wished she had a light. She began to notice every shadow, and then every clatter in the wind became something menacing. Cycling faster, she felt a cold tightening of fear and imagined her hackles rising like a dog's. She pushed on, holding the bag still with one arm, and kept going until she was out of the side streets, when she could freewheel through the centre of town and then out again, finally tackling the last steep climb towards Little Venus Farm. As she dropped her bike and made her way around the house to the back door, Kirsty opened it and reached out to pull her in before kissing her on her icy cheek.

Later, they sat by the fire.

'Give it time,' Kirsty advised. 'I'm sorry, Lily, it must have been horrible.' She made a face. 'I don't know how you lasted so long.' She paused, savouring the pleasure of finally speaking her mind. 'She was a total nightmare!'

Lily shook her head, not liking to hear it. 'Not always. She used to be great.'

'So,' said Kirsty, changing tack. 'If she used to be great, then deep down, she'll feel awful about you. Some time, when she's cooled off, she'll know what you said is true.'

Lily nodded.

'She'll realize. You'll get her back. She must have some Lily genes in her somewhere! Jeremy can't have taken away her entire personality.'

'He turned her into a nervous wreck. Before him, she was . . .' Lily sighed and looked up at the ceiling. 'Oh, I know you find it hard to believe but she was great . . . *I* was the one who moaned about everything and she'd cheer *me* up.'

'Then give her time.'

Lily nodded, knowing that Kirsty was right. 'Before she met Jeremy, she never had any problems,' she went on. 'She was really *sorted*. Apart from men. She always had useless taste in men. But it never used to bother her.'

'Well, finally there's something Grace and I have in common!'

Lily shook her head. 'You don't have useless taste. You just don't give anyone a chance.'

'I know,' Kirsty smiled. 'I dump everyone too fast. You sound like my mother. But I'm holding out for the right guy. What's the point in wasting time with the ones you know are wrong. I need the tingle factor.'

Lily shook her head. 'Don't give me that! Simon Campion made you tingle! Even in the restaurant, when you were supposedly giving him the push.'

'No, he didn't. It never felt right. And when it doesn't feel right, get out of there.'

'It doesn't always feel right straight away.'

'Rubbish. Think of Josh!'

Lily laughed. 'How has this conversation turned back to me? Okay. *Yes!* Straight away, I thought Josh was . . .' She paused. 'Nice.'

'Lily, this is fantastic! What an admission! And now you're not to change the subject. We are going to talk about him some more.'

'Get away from me! You're striking when I'm at my most vulnerable. I don't need this interrogation right now. How can you do this to me?' Lily laughed.

'Beats talking about your sister. And, for God's sake! What's wrong with you? You're telling me you fancied Josh, that's all. It's not as if we're talking about your serious drug addiction. Or your sexually transmitted diseases.'

'Oh, them,' Lily grinned. 'Anyway, I didn't like him.'

'Of course you didn't. That's how it's bound to start,' Kirsty said dreamily, 'but then somehow, some day, some place, you'll realize that you got him wrong. And fighting, fighting against it all the time, you'll fall in love, get married, and live happily ever after.'

'You should write blurbs for Mills and Boon,' said Lily. 'And isn't our hero currently on holiday with his best friend's ex-fiancée?'

'I forgot about that.' Kirsty screwed up her nose then immediately returned to the pursuit. 'Tell me again. How, *exactly*, did you feel? Was it straight away? You said you didn't fancy him at all when we saw them in the street?'

'It was when we were in the pub,' Lily said. 'I had to wind my legs around the bar stool!'

'To stop yourself doing what?' Kirsty asked, laughing.

'Jumping on him.'

'And then?'

'I don't know. I suppose I imagined him taking over.'

'In the bar or somewhere more private?'

'Enough!' Lily stopped short the conversation just as Kirsty was getting into her stride. 'We'll never see them again. And now, knowing what he did to Hal, I'd never ever dream of seeing him again.'

'Of course you wouldn't,' said Kirsty.

7

At dawn Grace stood motionless in the middle of her bedroom. She'd been making herself wait for seven o'clock but at some point her body had swung itself out of bed and she'd found herself standing there before she knew it had happened.

She sat down in the middle of the floor, then shuffled over to the wall and lay back against the radiator, feeling its heat uncomfortably through her T-shirt but lacking the will to move away. She stared sadly at her feet, picked at a toenail, then lightly ran her hand the wrong way up her calf, taking perverse pleasure in the fact that her stubbled legs looked as unattractive as she felt. Then, for a long time, she simply sat there, arms around her legs, resting her chin on her knees, unable to summon up the energy to think coherently.

When she couldn't bear the burning in her back any longer she stiffly stood up again, feeling as if even the radiator was conspiring against her. She wandered aimlessly around the room. She touched her hairbrush and lifted a pair of jeans off a chair, folded them carefully and packed them slowly away, all the time putting off the moment when she'd confront the fact that she was alone again.

She sat at her dressing-table and applied a layer of

mascara. As she caught her eye in the mirror her mind's eye saw Lily back on her doorstep, finger on the bell. She imagined opening the front door with a great, happy smile, the wonderful flood of relief as she led her back into the house. She imagined all the things they would do together, how she would beg Lily's forgiveness, and talk to her as she had used to and as she had wanted to for so long. They would be inseparable from that moment on, Kirsty cast aside.

It was what she'd wanted from the moment Lily had moved in – a chance to talk about the terrible falling apart over Jeremy, to try to explain why she had been so angry and so unforgiving. She imagined that what had happened between her and Lily must have been played out in one way or another between sisters over and over, across time.

It had been thoughts of Lily, even more than Jeremy, that had eaten away at her in the weeks following her doomed wedding day. Much as she hated herself for falling for such a shallow, worthless, unreliable bastard as Jeremy, she could satisfyingly heap all the blame upon his head, whereas with Lily, kind-hearted, generous-spirited Lily, that hadn't been possible. At the time, she'd been deeply insulted that Lily, her little sister, had had the nerve to challenge her, and completely defeated when she'd been proven right. In the longer term Lily had forced Grace to see things about herself that she wished weren't true, things that made her feel ashamed. It had led to a defensive, corrosive anger that had eventually forced Grace to move away.

Once in Welshpool, Grace had slid further and further

away from the person she used to be. Alone every day, the insecurities born from being dumped at the altar grew and mutated until they dominated her entirely. The only thing that provided her with any energy was her anger. Somewhere, deep down, Grace still knew this was all wrong, that Lily had done the only thing she could, and Grace knew too that she'd never be happy until she freed herself from this bitterness. But until Lily announced that she was moving in, Grace had had nothing to aim for. With Lily there with her, she'd desperately hoped she could break the spell and begin again.

But it hadn't worked out. It was as if her mouth and her mind had belonged to two separate people. She'd sometimes taken *herself* aback with the things she'd found to say to Lily but still, as she'd watched Lily's eyes flicker at a particularly well-placed barb, she had felt a poisonous surge of elation. Why she should want to do this, when deep down she was unbearably grateful that Lily had come to her rescue, she really didn't know. But being bitter and twisted had become addictive, and Lily didn't help matters by being so relentlessly nice. Night after night, Grace would replay in her mind what she'd said and be eaten up with self-loathing and shame, but she never changed, and the further she left her old self behind, the more complicated and difficult the return journey became.

Grace left her bedroom, walked down the hall and paused for a moment outside Lily's door. Much as she wanted to open it, she knew that it would make her feel even worse. So she moved on, into the bathroom, where she could turn on taps and end the awful silence that was beginning to consume her.

As she bent over to drop in the plug, she was acutely, painfully aware of what she'd lost. It was like an electric shock sending a great jolt through her body. She sat down on the edge of the bath. *Lily*, she whispered aloud, startling herself with the sound.

I'm so sorry. She was aware of her loudly thumping heart and she clutched the sides of the bath. Moments from the past, a jumble from across the years, now fell over themselves in their haste to get her attention. I've turned into someone else, someone none of you know, she realized.

Grace remembered driving Lily towards Welshpool on her first evening. At one point she had leaned in towards Lily, smiling conspiratorially, about to tell her some story. As she had done so, she had caught a look of unconcealed relief on Lily's face, as if, unexpectedly, Lily had been told it was all going to be all right after all, and in a fraction of a second Grace's mood had changed. She remembered the swift surge of fury at Lily's complacency and how she had wanted to wipe away her confident smile and cut her down, how much she wanted to retain the upper hand. She remembered what she had said, and Lily's stunned look and the brief surge of power, and hated herself for being such a bitch.

Of course I appreciated what you were doing for me! Sitting there in the car beside me, leaving behind God knows what to be with me. But knowing that only made me feel even worse, even more guilty. And it's been driving me insane.

Grace stood up again in agitation, no longer able to sit still. She moved to the basin and started vigorously brushing her teeth.

And I'm sorry for everything that I said last night, Grace told Lily. She spat into the basin, then allowed herself a brief, grim smile because, actually, Lily owed *her* an apology for the last night. It had been a case of the mouse that roared and Grace had still not quite got over the shock.

You try having a little sister who's such a flaming all-round perfect person, she told Lily, suddenly wanting to defend herself. Who's so organized, and unruffled and so bloody smug. She finished brushing and moved back to the bath, testing the water with her hand. A little sister who makes you feel insignificant and useless. I don't think you would have coped with it any better than me.

And then, she thought sadly, *you* fall in love with someone, and get engaged, and see how it feels when it dawns on you that no one envies you after all. That actually they all pity you for being with such an arsehole. But stand your ground even so, hold firm, have the courage of your convictions, just so that you can find out, as the church bells are ringing, that even he doesn't want you. You'd have gone crazy too.

I'm sorry that I tried to marry someone so useless. I'm sorry that I couldn't see what I was doing. Grace thought back to the image of her father, grey-faced, walking back to the wedding car with the news. And I'm sorry Jeremy didn't want me and that I put you all through so much . . .

After months of trying to talk, this torrent of unspoken words was so loud and clear that she felt Lily had to be hearing them, had to be understanding and forgiving her. But even if she wasn't listening, Grace realized that just thinking the words through had been detoxifying, that she felt a little calmer, a little less desperate.

She wondered if she was glimpsing a new start, one that she still wasn't quite ready to embrace but that was there, just ahead, waiting for whenever she could make a move towards it. It would take one brave casting off of the black robes of her mourning, of the anger and bitterness and isolation that she had wrapped herself in for so long. And with that casting off, perhaps she'd find the confidence to believe in herself again. She picked up an ancient bottle of Badedas and squirted a long green stream into the bathwater.

And then the doorbell rang. She listened carefully, wondering how long it would be before whoever it was gave up. Then it rang again in three short bursts and one long one and suddenly, in a swoop of joy, she knew it was Lily, Lily giving her another chance, Lily arriving like a reward, just as she had turned the corner on her own. She wiped under her eyes and raced out of the bathroom, overwhelmed with gratitude.

'Lily! Lily! I'm coming,' she shouted as the bell rang again. She flew to the front door, her heart thumping. 'Am I pleased to hear you!'

She drew back the bolts, grinning with delight as she swung it open, to be confronted by a swaying, rustling, colossal bouquet of lilies pushed unceremoniously into her face. Around the side of the flowers peeped a bright-eyed gnome of a delivery man.

'Expecting them, were you?' he beamed. 'Aren't they gorgeous? Just sign here and they're all yours. I'm sorry I'm so early, but we've got a lot to deliver today.'

She took his pen.

'So then,' he said, smiling kindly, angling his head to read the little white card attached to the cellophane. 'Would you be the Lily herself? Or are you Kirsty?'

Grace looked up and smiled a grey, ghoulish smile.

'Oops!' said the little man, shocked by the awful emptiness in her eyes.

'I'll see that they get them. Thank you,' she said quietly, taking the flowers off him and stepping back into the house.

She closed the door, feeling as if she could shatter into tiny pieces at any moment. She walked straight to the kitchen, where she laid the flowers carefully on a table and wrenched the lid off the swing-bin. She pulled out the half-filled rubbish sack and opened it as wide as it could go, ensuring that she could stuff the entire bouquet into the sack without the sight of a single flower poking its head through the top. Then she tied the yellow strings tightly together and dumped the sack outside her back door.

Blood roared in her ears. She recognized the same deep

stab of hurt that had assailed her once before, when she had sat alone in her bedroom, looking down at her delicate cream silk shoes.

She leaned her cheek against the cool painted door-frame of the kitchen and wondered if she was about to throw up. So this is what happened when she let down her guard. When she allowed herself to think that just maybe she was turning the corner and that maybe she could hope for a break, a little help along the way. It hadn't been Lily at the door, and disappointing as that was, she could cope with that. But then, for a brief moment, she'd thought the flowers had been for her. A double whammy of rejection. This was an omen, a warning of how strong she had to be. Proof of how foolish she was to hope that fate might have been kind to her now.

She pushed herself upright and left the room. As she reached the stairs she was confronted by water, stealthily sliding down each newly stripped and sanded and polished step towards her. And everywhere there were bubbles made by the Badedas. Some were breaking free from the rest and were hanging gently in the air, catching the light like Christmas baubles, while others, glistening and twinkling, had piled high on top of each other like a huge frothy cake and were being majestically carried towards her down the stairs.

Gritting her teeth, refusing to give up and collapse on the stairs in a heap, she walked through the water. She splashed to the bathroom and found the water slopping and pouring over the sides of her bath. She plunged in her arm and pulled out the plug, then turned off the taps so hard it was unlikely she would ever get them to turn on again. Then she left the room, thinking she should get dressed before she tackled the mopping up.

She opened her wardrobe doors, searching for something to wear, and stared blankly at the tangled knots of dirty black jumpers and thick black tights that seemed to fill every shelf. Suddenly a gut-wrenching wave of hopelessness caught hold of her and threw her back on to her bed.

Tears ran down her face and into her mouth, sliding into her hair and collecting in pools in her earholes. She got back into bed, pulling the duvet high around her face, and eventually, she fell asleep.

*

'He is so safe you could have a picnic under his tummy.' Kirsty waited for a reaction but Lily wasn't listening, all her attention on the big brown mouth that was nudging persistently around Kirsty's pockets. 'He used to be a polo pony so he got called Chukka,' Kirsty continued. 'Rather witty, don't you think?' she added sarcastically. She offered the horse a carrot and he took it immediately, swallowing silently without even a crunch. 'Here, give him one,' Kirsty urged, handing Lily another carrot.

The bone-crushing hooves took a step closer as the horse immediately moved in on Lily. She held her ground and timidly stuck out a hand, flat, as she had always been instructed, and before she knew it her fingers had been delicately avoided and the carrot was gone. The horse stood tall above her, crunching happily, a trail of saliva swinging out of its mouth. Laughing, Lily ducked out of range, but the horse suddenly sneezed and bits of carrot and froth sprayed straight into her face. 'Disgusting!' she spat, picking bits off her tongue.

'Riding him is like sitting in an armchair,' Kirsty went on. 'Wouldn't you like to try?' She looked at Lily persuasively. 'Go on! It'd be a laugh – we need to do something wild and crazy today . . . And, let's face it, there's not a lot of choice.'

'What do you mean?' Lily said, suspiciously, latching on to the *wild* and *crazy*.

'We need something to take your mind off Miss Home Alone.'

'I didn't know you liked horses.' Lily made it sound like she was accusing her.

'Like them, yes. Like *riding* them, not much. Unless it's a special occasion.'

'Why? Is there something wrong with them?'

Kirsty shook her head and smiled. 'Lily, don't fuss! It's just I hate breaking my nails and smelling of manure. Poor things,' she went on sadly, aware she'd lost ground, 'they're so sweet, and they spend their lives looking over the fence, just waiting for someone to take them out.'

'Oh,' Lily sympathized, heartstrings successfully pulled.

'And there really is no one else. They're both in their nineties – in horse years – and so they're a bit too slow for most people.'

Lily shrugged.

Taking her response as a definite yes, Kirsty had them tacked up almost before Lily realized what she was doing.

'Here, give me your foot,' Kirsty demanded, leading Chukka over. She stood beside the horse and linked her fingers to take Lily's weight and toss her up into the saddle.

Lily knew she had no choice.

'I thought polo ponies were meant to be small,' she said, as Kirsty gave her such a powerful leg up that she nearly flew straight over the horse's back.

The next thing Lily knew, she was charging backwards at high speed, the horse's hooves slipping dramatically on the cobbled stableyard. She glanced across to Kirsty in wide-eyed terror, and let out a little scream, but Kirsty took one look at Chukka and immediately started to run, heading for the large open gate that led out of the yard. Chukka meanwhile, still managing to canter backwards, took one stride too many and backed solidly into a wall, whereupon he leapt forward again as if someone had stuffed a firecracker up his backside.

Desperately hanging on, Lily watched the scene around her unfolding in slow motion. Ahead of her, Kirsty was still running, her head thrown back, arms and legs pumping, occasionally casting desperate glances over her shoulder, valiantly trying to get to the gate before Chukka. But beneath her Chukka rose to the challenge and determinedly extended his stride. As Kirsty reached the gate and sent it swinging shut, Chukka reached it too. As his escape route closed in front of him he seemed almost to hold in his breath, managing to squeeze himself and Lily through with barely six inches to spare.

Puddles of ice cracked and split under the pressure of

his galloping hooves, sending pistol cracks echoing out across the empty fields. With Lily still aboard, he left the track behind and moved on towards a large grass field, spread white with frost and boxed in by high black hedges.

This horse is having the time of his life, Lily thought furiously. And probably at the expense of mine. Her hat was tipped low over her eyes, her empty stirrups clanked against her ankles and she felt as if her teeth were being shaken out of her head.

'Slow down you bastard horse, slow down,' she yelled at Chukka, thinking how this was the stuff of too many bad films, wishing all the same that a rugged hero on a black stallion was waiting in the wings to materialize at a gallop beside her. Instead, all she could hear was Kirsty shouting her name over and over again.

Lily looked down at the ground, hard and stony and blurring with the gathering speed and took in the two stirrups, swinging beneath her. Without much hope she thought she might as well try to stuff her feet into them and, before she knew it, it had worked. Straight away the canter felt very different and she cautiously looked up again, realizing with surprise that she could now stay on quite easily. The relief flooded through her, filling her with euphoria, and instead of pulling on the reins she forgot herself and leaned forwards into Chukka's mane, pushing back her hat and encouraging him on. Giving herself up to the ice-cold air, the warm sun on her face and the wonderful, flying freedom of the gallop.

From the sound of drumming hooves behind her she

knew that Kirsty was now managing to give chase. She sat as still as she could in the saddle, not wanting to unwittingly send some signal that would cause the horse suddenly to change direction, or turn on a sixpence, like she'd heard polo ponies could.

'Stop!' Kirsty gasped desperately, the wind whipping away the sound of her words. 'He'll jump the hedge. Stop! Pull up. Pull on the reins!'

Lily felt herself wobble alarmingly. The horse, aware that Kirsty was creeping up alongside, put his ears back aggressively and then barged suddenly sideways, nearly losing Lily and forcing Kirsty to back off.

And ahead of her, on the brow of the hill, loomed the hedge, wide and huge and unyielding.

I can do this, Lily thought confidently, gathering herself up for the leap.

The horse barely checked his pace. He met it cleanly and Lily was shot high up into the air. For one exhilarating moment she knew what it felt like to fly.

By the time Kirsty's head popped up on the other side of the hedge Lily had managed to sit up. At the sight of her, still in one piece but covered in mud, with Chukka standing guiltily by her side, Kirsty's face broke into a huge smile of relief.

'Chukka, you fucker!' she admonished the horse.

Chukka hung his head, still blowing hard.

Before Lily could speak she had disappeared again, making her way down the other side of the hedge to reappear in an opening just a little further down. Lily hadn't known it was there. She heard Kirsty click her tongue at her tired horse, encouraging him to trot over to Lily. When he drew alongside, Kirsty leant over and took a strong hold of the nearest rein, but there was no likelihood Chukka was about to take off again. Both horses stood, still recovering, sending huge white plumes of breath into the frosty air.

'I didn't ask him to jump that fuck-normous hedge,' Lily said despondently, carefully standing up. 'I thought I would stay on.'

'You were brilliant.' Kirsty winced on her behalf. 'Totally brilliant. You stayed on for ages,' she paused for a second. 'Forgive me?' she asked pleadingly. 'I am so sorry he did that! It was as if he'd taken speed!'

Lily laughed.

'You know,' Kirsty went on and nodded earnestly at Lily as she spoke, 'I think it was at least as awful for me. At the beginning, it was quite funny, the sight of you bouncing out through the gateway. But suddenly, you were going so fast! And then, when I knew you were going to jump the hedge . . .' Kirsty shuddered. 'It was *horrible!*'

Kirsty leant across to Chukka and slapped his neck. The horse's ears flickered forwards. 'Useless animal. I thought I could trust you!'

'And we weren't meant to be going that way,' Kirsty told Lily as they eventually rode back into the stableyard. 'I suppose I'll understand if you say you've had enough . . . But we could carry on. There are no more fields, just lanes. And I *promise,* I promise that they're so knackered now they won't go faster than a walk.'

'Oh, I really believe you! About as much as I believe that this horse is ninety years old.'

They wandered slowly out of the yard again, down into the drive beside Little Venus Farm, Kirsty's home. Then they followed a long snaking lane that took them low across the hills.

Side by side the two horses ambled contentedly down the middle of the lane, their eyes half shut, their heads drooping, flicking back the occasional ear at the conversation that ebbed and flowed above them. It was hard to imagine Chukka had any other speed. Soothed by the gentle, swaying rhythm of the walk, it wasn't long before Lily and Kirsty were lulled into silence.

The pale winter sunlight splintered through the bare hedgerows, and the dark tarmac of the lanes, still dusted softly with early morning frost, caught the sun and sparkled. Behind them, dark imprints of the horses' hooves stood out sharply against the white of the road, marking their passing by. From her new-found height Lily could look out over the hedges and across the quiet fields. Kirsty was right, she thought. There probably was no better way to empty her mind.

As soon as she'd thought it, Grace was there, filling it again. But this time, perhaps for the first time ever, Lily felt no accompanying twist of pain. It was as if Grace's power, which had grown so strong as to overshadow Lily's entire life, had finally been stemmed. Her ivy-like ability to smother and reshape had been taken away. This time Lily could disregard Grace and not crucify herself in the process.

She had acknowledged more than once how strange it was that such an intense relationship had sprung up between them, aware that theirs was the kind of relationship one might have associated with couples rather than siblings. How it had become so all-consuming she didn't know, recognizing only that it was born out of tensions that had been there since the very beginning, that all Jeremy had done was expose vulnerabilities between them that had always been there.

Grace was seven years older and had bossed and mothered Lily from the moment she had been born, a relationship that could not survive comfortably into adulthood. As Lily had grown up, Grace had always fought off any threat to her dominant position, had seemed more and more insecure every time Lily showed signs of going her own way, especially when it seemed she was choosing a better route than Grace.

'Why don't you go back and get your things,' Kirsty chipped in, intuitively, 'and make sure she's all right.'

'You really think so?'

'No,' Kirsty laughed. 'But if you go back you'll put your mind at rest and find it easier to move on *for good*. And then, we're going to find a house together. It's high time I left home, and this is the ideal opportunity.'

'Yes, please!' Lily exclaimed, making Chukka suddenly start in fright.

'Then we'll do it. Let's start looking this afternoon.'

*

When they re-entered the stableyard, Kirsty's mother came walking out of her kitchen to catch them. She was tall and pretty, in Armani jeans and a heavy cream jersey, and she looked as though she meant business. She held up a bit of paper to Kirsty and raised her eyebrows.

'Simon Campion called,' she announced in a low, hopeful voice, allowing a suitably momentous silence to follow her words.

Kirsty lifted her feet from the stirrups and cast a quick look across to Lily.

Lily shrugged. 'Chukka here says Simon's a good bloke, and you should call him back.'

'Chukka's had his balls chopped off, so he doesn't know anything about it . . . Oh God! This is not what I wanted to hear,' Kirsty moaned. She swung her leg over the front of the saddle and slid off her horse.

'Kirsty. You *are* going to call him back?' her mother said worriedly.

Kirsty ignored her and led the horse towards its stable.

What is the matter with you, Kirsty thought. You haven't even met him. You know nothing about him.

'He sounded *terribly* nice.'

'I'm sure the wolf sounded terribly nice when he knocked on the door of the three little pigs. He probably sounded just like Hugh Grant,' Kirsty said sharply, disappearing into the dark stable. 'What's wrong with you?' she shouted from inside. 'Why are you so desperate to get rid of me?'

Kirsty's mother looked at Lily helplessly.

Kirsty appeared again, a saddle over her arm. 'Well, don't be surprised if this little pig gets served up for dinner,' she said, stalking towards the house. 'Roasted by the great chef. With a little balsamic vinegar and a sweet apple sauce.'

8

The wind changed, blowing in from the east, and the wide blue sky was hidden once more by racing black clouds. With nothing better to do, Grace spent most of her days watching the rain slide down the windowpanes as the wind blew wildly down the chimneys. Her only diversion was to go out walking, which she did most afternoons. She wore black wellingtons and wrapped herself up in a huge orange rubber coat that she'd bought a long time ago, when she'd been keen on someone who'd wanted to take her sailing. The relationship had lasted only a few days but the coat had stubbornly stuck around for a good ten years and showed no signs of getting lost. Grace expected it to outlive her. She knew it only added to her already rather eccentric image but she didn't care.

Day by day, she began to map out the hills and valleys around her, putting together a dark web of steep lanes, overgrown footpaths and muddy bridleways, and slowly she began to feel better. Each day she ventured further, walking fast and silently up the dauntingly steep hills, sometimes plunging down again into low-lying cloud that prevented her from seeing more than a few feet ahead of her. She thought she should have a dog to keep an eye on her and give the walks a purpose.

Occasionally she would meet other walkers but she

never stopped to talk. It had been so long since she'd had a passing-the-time-of-day kind of conversation with anyone that, now she found she quite wanted to again, she couldn't think of what to say.

She knew she was being self-indulgent, acknowledged that without a little money of her own and the indefinite loan from her parents she could never have chosen to hole up for so long. And yet, without money, she'd have been forced back to people and the clutter and pressure of a job, and that might have made a difference. As it was, she reminded herself most days that she was wasting her life but still the admission was an idle one, not something she felt ready to do anything about.

Since the awful morning with the flowers, she had treated herself like an out-patient, battered and bruised, who needed pampering and fussing over. With no one to indulge her, she became her own nurse, filling a hot water bottle each night, putting fresh sheets on her bed every other day and keeping well stocked up with chocolate and magazines. And yet, even as she did this, she was aware that the days of playing the invalid were drawing to a close. She couldn't ignore the fact that since Lily had gone, she had finally felt stronger, and that a new restless energy was now trickling through her, sending her prowling around the house, making the long walks addictive. Miserable as she still was, the tight-lipped anger against the world had finally begun to lessen its hold. That morning had marked the moment when the torrent of panic and tension that had coursed through her for so long finally burst its banks and began to drain away.

In theory she wanted to see Lily before too many more weeks went by, but in practice she still felt a strong need to keep to herself. It was as if her recovery was still so new and fragile that it could break apart again if she got the slightest buffeting, even one harsh word, and so, apart from a brief call to her parents to check where Lily had gone and to make sure that she was all right, she continued to let the days pass by.

She could afford just a few more months before she would have to find a new job. Before the fiasco that was Jeremy, Grace had taught maths at a large school for girls in London and it was only because of him that she'd given it up. After their wedding, they had been going to live in Scotland and she had saved enough to give herself a few months to settle in before she found another school, somewhere in Edinburgh. Now she began to keep an eye out for jobs in the local papers and, at the same time, renewed her subscription to the *Times Educational Supplement*. She knew there was only a slim chance she'd actually follow up anything but at least she could feel she was starting out again.

She also pored over the small ads, fascinated by the things people wanted to sell, overcome by insane urges to buy a knitting-machine or a Belling cooker or even a catering pack of luxury disposable glasses in the unlikely event that she ever had a party.

Then, one Friday morning as she lay in bed drinking tea and reading the papers, an ad caught her eye that she couldn't resist. The address was a farmhouse about a mile and a half from Green Lane and there were five puppies for sale. I have to have one, she thought with instant conviction, absolutely certain that this was what she needed to turn her life around. Before she could doubt what she was doing, she made a quick telephone call to let the owner know she was on her way, hurriedly got dressed and within fifteen minutes had left the house.

As Grace neared the farmhouse, what she was planning finally caught up with her. She stopped the car in the middle of the lane and sat for a moment. She heard her mother's voice telling her it was ridiculous. That she had absolutely no idea what she was letting herself in for.

But, even as she forced herself to think sensibly, all she was aware of was that she wanted one now, that she couldn't wait. That it was *because* dogs were for life that she wanted one, that she'd noticed it was the boyfriends who were just for Christmas. Her life hadn't turned out quite as rosily as she'd imagined it would. She shouldn't be living in a dark wet lane in mid-Wales all on her own. She should be in bright, noisy Edinburgh, blissfully happy. She wanted a dog more than anything in the world. She would buy a dog that she would grow to love, and yet would never have met if everything had happened as it should. She started the car again, imagining him sitting beside her on the front seat.

The address led her to an old black and white farmhouse that looked as if it had sunk two feet into the mud spread all around it. She stopped the car and watched a few hens clucking and pecking in the verges of the lane beside the house, while others charged hopefully through the mud towards her. She pulled on the handbrake and got out. There was a thin line of smoke curling out of a wobbly chimney and she noticed that the roof was missing over half its ancient slate tiles.

She picked her way gingerly towards the house, avoiding rolls of uncoiled barbed wire, tractor tyres and sodden bales of rotting straw, and knocked gently on a front door that looked as if it would fall off its hinges if she pushed it. At her knock it opened immediately and a white-haired old woman poked her head around the door at Grace.

'I've come about the puppies. I called you about ten minutes ago.'

The woman stared at her for a few moments. 'I know who you are,' she said irritably. 'You'd better come in.' She put a hand to her head as if to wiggle it back into place and re-establish an unreliable current, then she turned and disappeared back inside.

Grace followed her uneasily, quickly sliding off her wellingtons, reminding herself as the front door slammed that no one knew where she was, suddenly picturing herself still there six months later, chained up and being fed Pedigree Chum.

They made their way along corridors tiled in cracked and curling linoleum, the walls getting narrower and narrower the further they went, the ceiling so low that spiders' webs hung down and brushed against Grace's forehead. Finally, they halted outside a heavy oak door.

Looking at her properly for the first time, Grace saw that the woman would once have been rather beautiful. She was tall and imperious with clear light blue eyes, a straight nose and a haughty aristocratic arch to her eyebrows. As she looked appraisingly back at Grace, she slowly wound a long loose strand of white hair back into a green jade hairclip.

'Emily Hodge,' she said, offering Grace a half-hearted smile. 'I can't stand letting them go. It's not you.'

'It must be hard,' Grace said smiling back at her.

'I've been breeding dogs on and off for fifty years,' she said with pride, 'and so I've done this many a time.' She spoke in clipped cut-glass tones. 'But it doesn't get any easier.' She stuffed her fists into her jacket pockets and thrust forward her hips. 'Know anything about looking after them?'

'No, not a lot,' Grace admitted.

'Then when you've chosen him, or her, you get straight down to Kirsty Williams's in Montgomery. Tell her I sent you. If you're quick you'll catch her before she goes for lunch. You know where I mean?'

Grace nodded briefly and looked away. The woman put her hand on the door's handle.

'She's a wonderful, wonderful girl. And she'll sell you everything you need to buy, and tell you everything you need to know.'

Oh, what a pleasure that would be. Grace smiled grimly and nodded. 'Thanks for the tip,' she said.

'Right then, let's go and have a look at them.' Emily Hodge threw her bony frame against the heavy door, which opened stiffly.

To Grace it was abundantly clear that she was living on the breadline. Her suit was worn and shiny with age, her skin had that thin translucence that spoke of lack of nourishment, her house was freezing cold and falling down all around her, her chickens were starving. One glance through the door told Grace where what little money she had was surely going. The room was warm and bright and newly painted, with a big wooden bed for the bitch. While Emily Hodge didn't look as if she'd had a proper meal for weeks, the puppies were fat and shiny with good health and bursting with energy.

Grace dropped to her knees and opened her arms to them. Within seconds they were climbing all over her, licking and jumping, worrying her trouser legs, chewing and nipping at her fingers with their piranha sharp teeth.

Grace knew very little about dogs. Some were black, some were chocolate and others were black and white and they were all tiny and incredibly sweet and that was about all she knew. After a few minutes playing with them, she picked one black and white one out and held him up in front of her, wondering how she was ever going to choose one. He responded with a tiny high-pitched bark at her, and a desperate wriggling in her hands as he struggled to get closer to her. She brought him in against her chest and he reached up to her face, managing to get in several quick licks to her nose and mouth before she held him away again.

'We're going to have to have some rules,' Grace told him. She smiled over at Emily Hodge. 'But I think it's got to be this one.'

With the puppy loose in her car, looking out of the window and whining continuously, and falling off the seat whenever she went around a corner, Grace left the farm-house with repeated reminders to visit Kirsty ringing in her ears.

She felt both elated and terribly nervous. It was so long since she'd had anything new to think about, to look *at*, let alone look *after*, that, once home again, as she watched the puppy scamper clumsily around the kitchen, then lie down to whine at the space under her kitchen door, she found herself suddenly wanting to rush away, finding his loneliness and misery at being taken away from his brothers and sisters too much to take.

And, overwhelmingly, Grace wanted to see Lily again. Lily was so capable. Lily would know how to look after the puppy, would love the puppy. And it would bring them together, happy again too.

She sat beside the puppy in her kitchen for what felt like hours, both of them pushed up against the Aga, drawing comfort from its warmth. She touched his long satiny ears and told him that it was going to be okay, living with her. That she was going to look after him, that he didn't really want to run away from her and go all the way back to Emily Hodge's because he was going to have a lovely life. As she rhythmically stroked his coat, and watched as he fell asleep, she thought he was the loveliest thing that had happened to her for ages, and that she'd even stomach a trip to Kirsty's warehouse if that was what he needed her to do.

She would go to Kirsty as Emily Hodge had suggested and see which way the wind blew. Perhaps she might even venture a question or two about Lily. For all their differences, Grace trusted that Kirsty was a good friend to Lily and wouldn't deliberately scupper a genuine attempt by Grace to make things up. If Lily would allow a thaw, Kirsty would have to let her know. But, for the first time, she knew that she couldn't count on Lily wanting peace between them, that their last argument had been so terrible that it could well take months to patch it up again.

Lily had made it clear that Grace had run out of chances, had used up her nine lives, and Grace had no way of knowing for sure unless she talked to Kirsty.

She stood up, careful not to wake the puppy, found him an old blanket and made him a temporary bed in her scullery. She shut him in there, took her car keys off the kitchen table and left the house.

*

She had to sit outside the Warehouse in her car, steeling her nerves. She unclipped her seat belt and studied the building ahead. She felt as nervous as if she were about to storm it. It was just one storey, she noticed, but big and impressive, built of old red brick and probably once part of the farm next door. It had high wide doors positioned at each end, tall enough to allow horses and carts, and later tractors and trailers, to drive straight in. She could see through the corner of one of the doors into the cavernous space within. It would make a stunning house, she thought.

At the far end a couple of men were unloading sacks of grain from the back of a lorry, a forklift truck moving neatly back and forth between them. Grace watched them for a moment, taking in their sweat-streaked faces and their dusty clothes, bemused that Kirsty would choose to work in such a place, but thinking, nastily, that everyone found their level sooner or later. Finally, she told herself to move. She switched off the radio and looked at herself in the mirror. In the glove compartment there was a stick of lipstick that had seen better days and she found it and put some on. Then she slammed shut the car door and strode confidently across the forecourt, presuming that the shop itself would be empty and that she'd have Kirsty all to herself.

She was wrong. Just inside the door, a man was half turned towards her, casually studying a row of bottles of Organic Tick Treatment for sheep. As she entered the shop he looked up at her and grinned. Completely unexpectedly, she felt herself flush with sudden warmth and a raw awareness that she had forgotten she could feel. Behind her the door shut with a clunk.

He was gorgeous. Gorgeous enough to make her want to throw herself at him and beg him to carry her away. Wow! she thought, in a moment of stunning clarity. You would make me so, so much better. Lift me up in those strong arms and never let me go.

Seconds passed and she found she couldn't take her eyes off his face, but, having smiled so irresistibly, he then dropped his gaze back to his bottle and didn't notice the effect he was having on her.

Kirsty had noticed. 'Can I help you?' she said, coming over from the other side of the shop. *Bitch*, she wanted to add, seeing the love-stricken look on Grace's face. 'What are you doing here?'

'Perhaps you can,' Grace replied, coming back to reality with a bump and trying hard to sound normal. But she couldn't bear the distraction of Kirsty straight away and so she left her and wandered off, looking half-heartedly around the shop. She touched things lightly with the tips of her fingers, trying to concentrate on what she was looking at but unable to stop herself staring back again at the man.

She loved the way his dark hair curled gently on to the back of his collar as he bent forward slightly to read the label, the brightness of his warm brown eyes and the shape of his long fingers as they held the bottle. But it wasn't as if there were just one or two things that stood out about him. It was an overall impression – a strong sense of promise. Promise that time spent with him would be full of fun and wonderful, and that if you were the one he fell in love with, you could never do better.

Grace sighed. 'I've just bought a puppy,' she announced eventually, turning back to Kirsty. 'Tell me what I need.'

'A muzzle,' Kirsty said.

Grace saw the man suppress a grin. She flushed with embarrassment and stared at Kirsty with complete, open dislike. How could she have thought she would ever, *ever* broach the subject of Lily with her? She'd rather drink the bottle of tick treatment. One day, she was going to make sure that Lily saw this girl for what she really was.

'A puppy!' Kirsty repeated more gently, a pasted-on smile on her face, trying not to be too harsh. 'So, how are the carpets?'

Grace glared back at her.

Don't do that to your face, Kirsty thought. It really does you no favours.

'What sort is he?' Kirsty went on, continuing the attempt at conversation, the smile staying in place. 'Or is he a she? Is it very sweet?'

If it hadn't been for the man, Grace would have already marched out of the shop. But because of him she wanted to stay, had to stay. And if that meant she had to talk to Kirsty she was prepared to endure it.

She gritted her teeth. 'It's a he. And yes, thank you, very sweet.'

Rather than continue the conversation, she stalked away again, over to a selection of dog beds and dragged a large wicker basket from out beneath a shelf. It was lined with a deep blue and white gingham quilt, soft and inviting.

With her arms folded, Kirsty watched Grace from across the room.

How come I'm so useless that I don't know what breed my dog is, Grace wondered? I never thought to ask and Emily Hodge must have thought I knew.

'What's your puppy's name?'

'Hodge.'

Kirsty's attention was caught. 'Is that who you got him from?' she asked, coming over immediately. 'Emily Hodge?'

'Yes. I was there this morning,' Grace told her, taken aback by her sudden interest.

'And Mrs Hodge sold him to you?' Kirsty persisted.

'Yes,' Grace told her impatiently. 'Why shouldn't she have done?' Despite everything between them, Grace wanted to know more. 'Why are you asking me that? Why shouldn't she sell me the puppy?'

'No reason,' Kirsty told her. 'Don't worry. It's good news.'

'But why?' Grace insisted.

'Because,' Kirsty said, 'the fact that she's started to sell her puppies again . . .' Grace saw with amazement that her eyes were full of tears. 'I didn't know. It's important. It means that she's carrying on.'

'Carrying on what?' Grace shook her head. 'I don't understand.'

'Her son died eighteen months ago,' Kirsty told her shortly.

'Oh God, that's terrible!' Grace thought back to the dignified, determined strength of frail Mrs Hodge. 'How did he die?'

'On the farm.'

Grace could tell that Kirsty did not want to say any more to her. She was looking at her in a way that made Grace cringe. As if she was thinking, what do you really care? What do you know about tragedy, sitting there in your lovely house, distraught because your boyfriend left you? Grace didn't like that look. She turned away, back to the dog beds, hurt and defensive and angry that Kirsty could make her feel that way.

'You don't want a wicker one,' Kirsty called after her dismissively, walking away from her. 'That's for older dogs. He'll chew it to bits.'

Grace looked glumly again at the dog bed and realized that Kirsty was right. She supposed she should get something plastic or wooden. She bent down and tried to put it back where she had found it, but got it solidly wedged between two shelves. Trying hard to drive it back in, she eventually got to the point where however she angled her tugs it wouldn't move at all. Let the witch sort it out, she told herself angrily, still unable to stop herself wrestling on.

'Don't expect her to help, she never does,' said a deep voice from high above her. 'I wonder if she could be sent somewhere to be genetically modified?'

Grace looked up. The man stood over Grace as he spoke but he was smiling and looking at Kirsty, not at her. She stood up and stepped out of his way, blowing her fringe off her hot flushed face. Then he crouched down at her feet and carefully studied the bed.

In a wild, fairytale moment Grace imagined him looking up at her, gently taking hold of her hands and pulling her down beside him, tumbling them both backwards into the gingham quilting. Instead, he quickly pulled the bed free and then slid it smoothly back into place.

'Thanks,' she said shyly, wishing she could think of something more interesting to say.

'Pleasure,' he replied, standing up again.

But the fact is, there wasn't a line that would have worked any better, she realized. The way that his eyes immediately slid away from hers told her plainly, painfully, that she was not holding his attention at all.

In the old days, I would have had a good shot at him,

Grace thought sadly, as he wandered back to Kirsty at the other end of the shop. But clearly not any more. Somewhere along the way she had lost whatever it was that made men like him sit up. So when he'd come over to help her there had been friendliness in his face and nothing more. It was a shock. All her adult life she had floated in the soft warm water of admiration, effortlessly attracting any man she liked. But this was like standing under a bitterly cold shower. She wondered where he lived and if she'd ever see him again. The thought that he could simply be driving through her life, on his way to somewhere else, dropping in for just a few minutes in the course of her eighty or so allotted years, was unbearable.

'For God's sake, can't you pick up some of this stuff? Does everything have to be on the floor?' Grace snapped at Kirsty, making her way back towards her. She pointed to some cases of Puppy Chum and a few bags of Winalot stacked up around the till. 'I want some of this. But do I dare pull a bag out? It looks as if the whole lot would come down!'

Kirsty bit back something far more insulting. She didn't want to descend into some sort of cat-fight, she just wanted Grace out of her shop as swiftly as possible. She glared back at her, grimly hoisted a bag of biscuits up into her arms, added a tray of puppy food and, balancing awkwardly, went to the till and started totting up. From behind her, Grace quickly picked out a collar and lead, a water bowl, a food bowl and a book on puppy care. When Grace had paid, Kirsty wasted no time in holding the door open for her.

Grace walked over to her car, followed at a distance by Kirsty carrying the dog bed. Neither of them offered to break the silence. Walking around to the boot Kirsty chucked the bed down on the ground beside her and turned away.

'I'm sorry about all that,' Grace blurted out, surprising herself as much as Kirsty. 'I really am.'

Kirsty turned back towards her. 'What did you say!' Kirsty was wide-eyed, staring at her, surprised. 'I don't think I heard right!' She grinned at Grace.

Grace tried but couldn't quite follow through. For all her good intentions, she couldn't say anything more. Didn't want to put away all the protective thorns and spikes that had marked out their boundaries for so long.

'I do care about Mrs Hodge. And her son,' she said instead. 'I thought she was wonderful.'

'Yes, she is,' Kirsty agreed. 'It wasn't an accident,' she added abruptly. 'He killed himself in the barn. He couldn't make the farm work any more.'

'Oh no!' She'd known it had got bad enough to make such awful things happen, but being confronted with the reality of it was completely, unbearably different. 'The farm where I was this morning?'

Kirsty nodded. 'He'd taken it over when his father died. He was their only child. After he died Mrs Hodge moved back in. She said it was a matter of honour.' Kirsty sighed. 'But of course she couldn't do anything with it. The farm's finished.'

Grace was terribly touched. Not just by what Kirsty was telling her, but by Kirsty herself, by all the intensity in her voice that she'd never had the chance to hear before.

'She likes you,' Grace told Kirsty hesitantly, not sure if she was going to get her head bitten off. 'I could tell straight away. Whatever you're doing for her,' she smiled, 'I think it must be helping her a little.'

Kirsty shrugged. 'Thanks. But in the end, she's lost her son. What can anyone do? Nothing that will bring him back to her. But if she's got the puppies, I think it's a good sign.'

Grace nodded.

'I'll see you around,' Kirsty told her and she turned and walked back to her shop.

When she had finished loading the car, Grace opened the driver's door and got in, then sat for a moment watching the key tremble in her hand, not yet able to drive away. She breathed deeply, forcing her nerves to steady, taken aback by the reaction that Kirsty had provoked in her, surprising herself by how much she cared about what Kirsty thought of her. She'd always known that Kirsty thought very little, and she'd always told herself that it didn't matter. But of course it hadn't been true and she'd resented Kirsty for taking Lily away from her, and resented Lily for appealing to Kirsty, for winning Kirsty's respect in a way that she knew she couldn't.

First poor Mrs Hodge, then Kirsty herself, two emotional encounters that made her desperate for the quiet safety of her house. She rubbed at her face. But she would go back soon and visit Mrs Hodge, she decided. Maybe take her a present and show her how well she was looking after her puppy. It couldn't hurt and she might just like the company.

She started the car. And then there'd been that man. Who could he be? Kirsty's little warehouse wasn't exactly a motorway service station. Not the kind of place one would pop into on the way to somewhere else. He had to live, or at least be staying, nearby.

She drove home, knowing she was going to get another chance with him. Perhaps not straight away but some time when she was more prepared, when she could focus on him properly. He might not have noticed her today but one day he would. And in the meantime she'd better shape up, buy some make-up and fake tan. Get a hair cut and some highlights and spend the last of her savings on some new clothes.

Because my heart is set on you, she sang out, suddenly inspired. She took a corner much too fast and a huge hedge loomed in her windscreen, forcing her to brake hard and concentrate on her driving. Stop fantasizing, she told herself sharply, concentrate on Hodge! And for a while after that she did. But long before she reached home her mind was elsewhere again. She had morphed back into the butterfly she'd always been before. Honed from long sessions at the gym, wearing new clothes, with her hair shining in the sunlight, she saw herself walking, bright and beautiful, towards him.

*

One down, one to go, Kirsty thought, turning back to Simon.

'I've been waiting,' he said, 'for rather a long time. The service here is terrible.'

Kirsty didn't smile, even though her heart had been hammering in her chest from the moment he'd first walked through the door. She busied herself with tidying up after Grace, wishing she didn't have to do this now.

'Did your mother say that I called? Again.' He paused, waiting for a response. 'God, I must be desperate.' There was amusement in his voice.

Still Kirsty did not reply.

'I've missed you.' He followed her about the shop, trying to get her to look at him.

'Lie down for a moment and I'm sure the feeling will pass,' Kirsty snapped. She turned around, wanting the whole thing over and done with as quickly as possible.

'Is that an offer?' Then his smile disappeared as he saw that she was serious. 'Looking at your face, I somehow don't think so.'

Kirsty pursed her lips. 'Just give up,' she said sadly.

Simon came closer. 'Why do you say that?' He frowned. 'I don't understand.' He lifted a curl of her hair and wound it gently around his finger, then tucked it slowly behind her ear.

Nor do I, she thought. Not really. Bracing herself, she stared back at him silently, her face impassive, hands by her sides.

'You and your friend managed to eat all my food and drink all my wine . . . so it can't have been my cooking,' he mused.

'It isn't that,' she murmured, her ear burning at the

touch of his fingertip, momentarily torn between pushing him away and falling into his arms. Pushing him away won.

'No, it isn't,' Simon agreed, sounding sad. 'So it has to be me. Yes?'

It was as if, now that he had looked into her eyes, he had seen with shock that she was serious.

'I don't want to see you any more.'

He shook his head. Kirsty turned away because she couldn't bear the look on his face.

'Well,' he said, eventually. 'Rest assured. The message is received, loud and clear. That doesn't mean I understand a word of it. But if you want me to go, I'll go. I'm not the sort to hang around.'

He walked away, wishing she would respond, even to look at him, then stopped and looked back at her again. 'This is it, you know? No more chances. I won't be back for more.'

'I'm sorry, Simon,' Kirsty said miserably, keeping her eyes down. 'But I mean it. I can't. I don't want to get involved.'

Yet even as she was saying it, she was feeling none of the usual sense of relief. Instead she felt stupid and cowardly and couldn't bear what she was doing. But she didn't say anything, and then it was too late.

When, a moment later, she did look up, Kirsty saw that Simon was picking up his wallet and keys, which he'd left on a table by the till. And she saw straight away that everything had changed. He was a stranger again, not hostile, not aggressive, but suddenly unfamiliar and completely impenetrable. He looked at her and she saw with a nasty shock that there was now no reaction at all in his eyes. Either that or he's a bloody good actor, she thought. It was as if he had successfully withdrawn from her everything she had ever touched, taken back any part of him she had ever laid claim to. And she found she felt no relief at all, just sickness at what she'd done.

As he walked towards the door, she saw him afresh; the springing black hair no longer hers to slide her fingers through, the broad shoulders that were now turning away from her, no longer hers to wrap her arms around. His mouth that had once closed, smiling, over hers, now as unapproachable as a stranger's in the street.

She wanted to tell him that she was sorry, that she hadn't meant what she'd said, that she'd panicked because he was so serious about her so soon and that was all, but she couldn't do it. She watched through the window as he got into his car, thinking of all the things they would never do again and all the things they had never done. And with a sharp twist of pain she wondered how quickly he would fall into bed with someone else. She imagined his bed, rumpled white sheets half covering an unknown female form.

Out beside his car he looked at her once more through the window and raised a hand in goodbye, then drove away.

All Hal could remember was the name of the road. He had hoped that perhaps he could stand outside all the houses on Green Lane, one by one, and that her house would give off a different aura so that he could divine which one it was. But instead he'd walked up and down the little lane several times, sizing up too many possibilities, and had had no helpful jolt of recognition. And there was nobody about to ask. He'd expected it would be quiet, but not so deserted that in three-quarters of an hour of loitering he'd seen no one at all. Now there was nothing for it but to start knocking on all the doors. And if that didn't work he'd find his way to the Little Goose and see if anyone recognized her name.

He had tried a couple of houses without luck when he saw a car turn the corner into Green Lane and drive towards him. He stared at it gratefully, waiting as it swished through the puddles and came to a halt about fifty yards away. Then a fair-haired girl got quickly out and walked around to her boot. Hal watched as the girl stood with her hands on her hips, staring down into her car, then roughly began tugging at whatever it was she had inside. He watched her struggle for a few seconds, trying to decide what it could be, and then he strode towards her, wanting to help.

He'd known almost immediately that the girl wasn't Lily, but as he got closer he decided that she had to be Lily's sister. They were the same height and they shared the same colour hair and there was something about the way she swung her head at the sound of his footsteps. But whereas he guessed Lily would have then sauntered towards him with a grin, this girl looked quickly down again, as if she hoped he might change his mind and disappear before he reached her.

'Can I help?' he offered with a smile.

'Be my guest,' she replied from the depths of the boot, wondering what it was about herself and dog beds and tall, thirty-something men.

'I thought you were someone else. Actually someone I'm trying to find,' he said, stepping around her and tugging it out.

She shrugged and forced herself to look up at him. 'Tell me who and I might be able to help.'

'She's called Lily,' he paused. 'And she looks like you. Do you have a sister?'

'Yup,' the girl said, moving to the back seat and bringing out a tray of tins of Puppy Chum, answering as if she didn't really care either way. 'And she's called Lily. But you should have called first. She doesn't live here any more. You need to get back in your car, drive down the hill, through the town and out the other side. She's staying at Little Venus Farm. Ask someone when you get closer and they'll tell you which one it is.'

Relief shone for a moment in his face. But still he hesitated. He could do as she suggested, leave it at that, jump back into his car and have nothing more to do with her, but something held him back for a second longer. He wanted to know if this girl was always so awkward, why she spoke of Lily so sharply, why Lily no longer lived there?

Hal took the bed in one hand. 'Lead on,' he said. 'I'll help you get everything inside.'

Grace led the way to her front door. It had rained all night and she stretched over several large puddles on her way. Not wanting footprints on her pristine wooden floors, she hoped Hal would notice them and do the same. She turned the lock and pushed her way in and she could hear him following her down the hall.

What she wanted to do was go straight to Hodge, but she didn't want this man to see Hodge too. If she opened the scullery door, she'd be giving him an excuse to hang around and she absolutely didn't want him to. And yet, without opening the door, how was she to know if Hodge was all right? If he'd survived all that time away from her? She stopped in the doorway to the kitchen and listened but could hear nothing.

'So tell me who you are and where you come from,' she snapped at Hal, sounding like a bad-tempered Cilla Black. She added more softly, 'And why you're looking for Lily.'

Hal didn't answer and her words hung on in the air.

'Perhaps I should have asked you that before I told you where she was?' she encouraged.

'Yeah, you should have done,' Hal agreed. 'And probably before you let me in. But don't worry about it.'

He followed her into the kitchen and placed the dog bed gently on the floor. He didn't know how to answer her, how far to go. He thought about why he'd come, the hope he had that somehow, by bringing Lily back into his cocked-up life, she would make it all better. He looked around the room thinking how outrageous it would be if he started to cry.

'My name's Hal,' he started, 'and I need Lily's help.' He went over to a window. 'I'm calling on her, in an hour of need.'

Grace was shocked at the hopelessness in his voice. This was not what she'd expected, not at all what she wanted to hear. She'd been so certain he would be just another pushy guy who fancied his chances with Lily. Someone momentarily entertaining who could then be sent on his way. Instead, here he was, in her kitchen, a man she'd never met, needy and sad and obviously gearing up to bare his soul to her. She wished she hadn't let him in. She wanted to be with Hodge, not him, wanted to preserve what remained of her fragile good humour, which she could feel was already fast slipping away.

But Hal was oblivious.

'She's the only one who can make things better,' he said, still staring out of the window. 'Lily is the only one she might listen to. Because everyone else is tarred with the same brush.' He turned away from the window and looked at her. 'But you don't want to hear about all this, do you?' he realized, belatedly. 'Why should you?' He frowned and rubbed at his forehead. 'I'm sorry. It's driving me crazy. And so I find myself talking about it to complete strangers.'

He moved away from the window, making for the kitchen door.

'What brush is everyone tarred with then?' Grace asked, stepping around him and beginning to put away her shopping, thinking that as he'd got the message, she could afford to be rather more sympathetic. 'What did you do?'

'What I did, and what my fiancée, Amber, thinks I did are very different things.'

'Oh, I see. And Lily could put her straight,' Grace finished the sentence for him. 'Well, go on. You have to go and ask her. I'm sure she'll want to help.'

'You think she will?'

'Of course she will.' She waited for him to move on.

Hal nodded. 'Down the hill, through the town and out the other side,' he recited back to her. 'Thanks.'

She stood up to follow him out, relieved that it had been so easy.

'So what does Amber *think* you did?' she asked impulsively, thinking it was definitely safe because Hal was now moving purposefully through the door.

Hal looked back at her bitterly. 'Ruined our wedding day.'

'Oh!' Grace still had no sense of what was coming, thinking he was probably about to describe a lost ring, or a drunken brawl in the middle of a speech.

'How?' she asked.

Hal stopped in the doorway.

'Oh, you know how it goes,' he said dryly. 'We were going to meet at the end of the aisle . . .' He paused. 'But we didn't.'

Grace caught her breath.

Immersed in his words as he was, Hal was aware that she'd reacted rather strangely, as if she'd been hit in the stomach by a well-struck rugby ball. He went on, actually revelling in the power of his words, almost as if it had all happened to someone else.

'We didn't get married.'

'What went wrong?' Grace croaked out. 'Come back and tell me.'

'My best man went wrong.' Hal came back eagerly and sat down at the kitchen table opposite Grace. Weeks on, he still had the compulsion to talk about it at every opportunity. 'On the morning of our wedding,' he swallowed hard, still completely unable to accept what Josh had done, 'he – my best man – drove up to see Amber, my fiancée, in Oxford. And he told her that I wouldn't be showing up.'

Grace stared back at him, as still as a statue.

'And she believed him. Well, you would, wouldn't you? Would you suspect the best man of lying about that? Of course you wouldn't. So by the time I showed up it was too late. There was nothing I could do. My wedding had been cancelled, postponed to be precise, most of our guests sent home, and my bride had gone on our honeymoon without me.' Hal smiled grimly. 'Superb story, isn't it! Until it happens to you.'

He looked at her, waiting for her reaction, confident

that she would be suitably outraged and disbelieving, but Grace didn't speak. He leant forward, wondering if she was all right, and the silence went on. For a moment it seemed as if she was fighting back tears. He sat quietly, touched that he'd had such a powerful effect.

'I don't believe it!' Grace said eventually not looking at him. She took a deep breath and Hal heard a strange break in her voice. 'I just don't believe it.'

Hal nodded solemnly in agreement.

Grace lifted her head and stared at him solemnly, and then unexpectedly she started to laugh.

Hal looked at her in amazement.

'I'm sorry!' she cried, the look of surprise on his face just making it worse. She covered her mouth with her hand and bit hard on her lip. 'I can't help it!' She could feel the muscles gathering around her mouth, trembling with the awful effort of keeping straight. 'I'm really sorry,' she said, her voice breaking again. 'You must think I'm a terrible person to laugh at you.'

She took a couple of breaths, telling herself that she couldn't do this to him. But then she caught sight of his sweet baffled face and had to turn away.

Hal smiled awkwardly, thinking she was mad.

Grace shook her head and tried again. 'I know you must think I'm mad,' she finally managed to get out, in a normal voice. 'Really, I'm laughing at myself, not at you.' She closed her eyes for a second. 'It's the coincidence. You and me. You sitting here and telling me that.' She shook her head. 'It wasn't funny at all. It must have been so awful for you.' She went on, her voice steadier, managing to look at him properly with no further threat of laughter. 'This time, you picked the wrong person to tell.' She paused. 'Oh,' she said wiping her eyes. 'I'm crying now!'

'If you cry now, I will have to walk out of the door.'

Grace smiled. 'I got dumped at the altar too.'

Hal's eyes widened. 'No,' he replied firmly. '*I* did not get dumped at the altar. And neither did Amber.'

Grace considered him for a moment, weighing up his words and the force with which he'd said them. Then she got up, walked over to the sink and filled up the kettle. Yes, you were dumped in a way, she thought. Because if she'd really loved you, she would have waited for you. She wouldn't have let this happen.

Wanting to diffuse the tension, Grace decided it was now the right time to open the door to her scullery, thinking that Hodge would bound out and buy her a little time, but he was at the other end of the room, lying fast asleep against the radiator, his eyes tightly shut, spotted tummy turned up to the ceiling, one fat paw giving an occasional paddle at the air.

She shut the door on him again and turned back to Hal. How to explain what she meant? How to explain how she could have laughed at what he'd just told her? She had laughed with relief. It was as if this strange meeting had been orchestrated for her benefit, set up to give her the final go-ahead to pick up the pieces of her life. It was proof that she wasn't crazy to think about the man in the warehouse, that it was okay to stop worrying.

That if she once turned her back and dropped her guard, her past wouldn't immediately spring on to her back and drag her down again.

'I owe you a proper explanation,' she said.

*

They were still talking two hours later. Grace offered him lunch and when he agreed, looking at his watch and deciding that Lily could wait just a little while longer, she made them fat omelettes with a tomato salad and French bread, flipping the omelettes over immaculately so that the melted cheese oozed out from underneath them.

When she'd eaten every last tiny speck of omelette it was all Grace could do to stop herself picking up her plate and licking it clean. But she restrained herself and sat, mopping up the last of the tomato juice with her bread, and listening to Hal, unable to ignore – in the midst of all his misery – how light-hearted she felt.

She felt so charged up she found it hard to concentrate on what Hal was saying. All she wanted to do in those moments that required a reply was shout that he should give up on Amber and get on with his life, that he should start again, just as everyone had always said to her. But *she* had never listened and she knew he wasn't going to either. She of all people knew it was far too soon for him to hear the truth. So she forced herself to shut up and let him talk on.

'Lily is my best hope,' he told her again. 'Because she saw what happened. She did all she could to help work it out for me.'

'She would,' Grace agreed.

'Eventually, of course, I will persuade Amber to listen to me, and then I can explain and we can pick up the pieces and get on with our life together. I don't doubt that. But first of all she needs to hear it from someone else. And that someone else is Lily.'

'Wouldn't Amber even read a letter from you? Give you just one chance?' Grace asked. *If she wanted you back she would.* She knew that if Jeremy had tried to make contact with her she'd have given him every opportunity, any time. Even yesterday she'd probably still have listened.

'Think what she's been through,' Hal defended Amber. 'Think how that arsehole must have made her feel. I'm not a bit surprised she doesn't want to have anything to do with me. But with Lily talking to her . . .' Hal sighed. 'If Lily talked to her, told her what really happened . . .' He was looking somewhat unsure. 'I know I'm asking a lot. And Lily doesn't owe me a thing. God knows she did enough at the time, taking me all the way to Oxford, zipping down the motorway in that little car. Getting caught by the police . . .'

'Oh, she did, did she?'

'She was wonderful,' Hal repeated. 'She was so furious with Josh, my best man. It was like she was going to do anything to stop him. She was on a mission.' He looked at her quizzically. 'Perhaps now I can understand where all that came from.'

Grace shook her head. 'It wasn't because of me. Lily's always jumped straight in. If she cares about something she always wants to get involved.' She looked at him, seriously doubting how much even Lily could do to help him now.

Hal drained his cup of coffee and stood up. 'Well, I suppose I should get on with asking her.'

Grace stood up with him.

'It was good to meet you,' she said, walking with him towards the door. 'I know you still feel awful, but you've done a great job cheering me up!' They moved out of the kitchen. 'So. There's some comfort for you.' She smiled at him.

By the door he pulled her close to him and gave her a hug. 'I hope you don't mind me doing that,' he said.

Grace shook her head, taken aback by how lovely it felt.

'And you'll be fine, you know that, don't you?' he said. 'Better than fine. You're going to do brilliantly.' He paused, looking down at her. 'Seriously, I'm pleased that I made you laugh about him. Even if you did completely freak me out in the process.' He let her go. 'Mad woman,' he said. 'No wonder he ran a mile.'

'Watch it, you! You've only just met me. I don't think you know me well enough to say things like that.'

'I'm sorry!' Hal grimaced. 'You're quite right.'

'I hope it works out for you too, Hal,' Grace said seriously. 'And if it doesn't . . .'

'Don't say it,' Hal said firmly, cutting her off. 'I'm going. Off to find your sister.'

She waited while he put on his coat.

'That's nice,' she said, touching it, now wanting to prolong the conversation, not wanting him to go.

'Isn't it?' he agreed, doing up the buttons. 'Amber gave it to me last Christmas.' He looked at her. 'I could pass on a message to Lily? From you.'

Grace shook her head.

Hal let it rest. 'Then wish me luck!'

'Good luck,' she said.

It was raining now in light little bursts that barely broke through the sun, and the wind was gusting, blowing his tawny hair into damp little peaks. He'd got half-way to his car when he turned back to her suddenly.

'How about coming with me?' he called.

Grace's heart leaped. 'What?' she shouted back, hearing him perfectly well.

'Come with me. Now! Take the plunge. While I'm here to break up the fight.' He put out his hand encouragingly.

Grace hesitated. She looked at him, so big and reassuring, and thought how much easier it would all be with him standing there beside her. But still she hesitated.

'No,' she called. 'There's stuff I need to sort out. I'm not ready to see her yet.'

Hal shook his head. 'Not true.'

He waited in the rain, sure she would come.

She looked at him, agonized for a moment more, then ran out towards him, jumping over puddles as the door slammed shut behind her.

10

Hal stopped beside a navy blue TVR and opened the passenger door.

'So this is what she saw in you,' Grace joked as he guided her into the soft leather seat.

'Yes, if all my friends are to be believed.'

Hal got in and the engine started with a throaty growl.

'By the way,' he said, following signs for the town centre, 'put me straight. If you and Lily fell out about three weeks ago and she moved out, and you haven't spoken to her since . . . I presume it was you who enjoyed my hugely expensive bouquet of flowers?'

Grace looked across at Hal and shook her head. 'You don't want to know.'

They drove down the hill, through the town and out the other side. Concentrating on the narrow twisting roads, Hal could not take in much of the landscape around them, but as they began another steep climb he allowed himself an occasional glance between the hedges. When he'd mentioned to Lily that he wanted to come back here, he'd meant it, and it was because he'd got a few tantalizing glimpses of the places he was now being led through.

Just as they neared Little Venus Farm they had to pull over and stop for a passing tractor, and for a few seconds Hal could gaze around him. The southern counties were

overrun with cars, carpeted with concrete, but here there
was little sign that the landscape had changed in the last
thousand years. Hal could see just one or two houses
below him and, to the west, what looked like a small
village, but overwhelmingly his impression was of the
thick woods, deep valleys and rich green hills, stretching
away further than he could see, rippling out across the
horizon, powerful and reassuring. With bright sunlight
beaming through the bruised black clouds, heightening
the purple of the ploughed earth and the dazzling green
of the rain-drenched grass, it was a magical sight.

'Sometimes I hate it,' Grace admitted.

'I can't believe it!'

'No, I do! You look at it and think it's all so idyllic,
but you're going back to London tomorrow. You have no
idea how peace and quiet can crack you up. How empty
it makes you feel.'

Hal glanced across at her.

'Give me a great big traffic jam any day.'

'I didn't realize. I'm sorry.'

'Don't be. I can get away when I want to. I've got
money and a car and a family to go to. But there are some
people who don't ever get away.' She was thinking of Mrs
Hodge. 'Peace and quiet's not what they need.'

'No. Of course it's not.'

She smiled at him, wanting to lighten the atmosphere.

'And it rains so much. That's why everything's green,
even in August. It's our own form of water torture.'

They drove on, following the lane until they neared
Little Venus Farm. 'What am I going to do if she's not

there?' Hal asked as they pulled to a halt. 'Do you think she'll be there? What does she do with herself all day?'

And what am I going to do if she doesn't want to see me, Grace wondered.

'I don't know,' she shrugged. 'When she lived with me, she potted, or whatever she calls it. She was in her shed for most of the day. But here, I don't know.'

From a window, Lily watched them get out of the car. She saw Grace staring up at the house, looking nervous, biting her lip and Hal by her side in a chocolate sheepskin coat.

Lily didn't know what to do. Her brain whirred and clicked, putting together the information faster than she could consciously think it through. Hal on her doorstep. Hal and Grace side by side. How close? Look at the way she leans into him. How had it happened? How had it happened? At the awful thought that Grace was involved with Hal, Lily's heart plummeted. Stay away from her, she wanted to yell at him. You're a disaster zone. Don't do this to her! She can't take it! Grace, stay away from him!

She very nearly shouted it from the window. She saw Grace pause as they made their way to the front door and touch Hal's hand, and then she couldn't wait any longer and threw herself down the stairs just as the bell rang.

Having asked Grace to come with him, Hal knew that by doing so he'd almost certainly done away with any opportunity to talk to Lily immediately. Even before Lily opened the door, he had already decided that he would stay only to fix up a time to meet her later, knowing that she would not be able to concentrate on him with her estranged sister standing over his shoulder.

He knew he would find it desperately hard not to start talking to her straight away. For the four hours of the car journey from London he'd thought about nothing else – which nuggets of information he could give Lily to help her convince Amber of his love, the heartfelt words he would ask Lily to say on his behalf.

It had come to him suddenly that morning, as he had sat at his desk at work, that Lily was his best and perhaps his only chance. He had stared blankly at the meaningless words on his screen, and then suddenly there was Lily. Far removed from everything, untainted by all that had happened. As his idea had begun to form he had been filled with an exultation which immediately transformed itself into a blind panic that if he didn't get to her straight away, circumstances might change and she would some-how be prevented from helping him. He had paced his office for a few moments, letting his run of thoughts assemble themselves, and then he had left the office, stalking down the long corridors until he was outside and running the short distance to his car.

And now here he was outside her house, knocking on the door, anticipating the moment when it would finally open. And now it *was* opening and she was there, standing in front of him. Seeing her, so lovely and reassuring, it was all he could do not to push his way in front of Grace and grab hold of her, but he forced himself to hang back for just a few moments more.

Lily looked from him to Grace and back to him again.

'You!' She laughed in wonder, leaning into him for a kiss and taking hold of his arm, ignoring Grace for just a moment longer.

Hal grinned. 'Yes, me.'

'And you!' she said to Grace, forgiveness already twitching her cheeks into a smile. 'What are you doing here?'

She turned back to Hal again, asking the silent question.

'No,' he answered, shaking his head. 'I couldn't sort it out. I haven't managed to see her. Not yet.'

Lily's face crumpled in sympathy. 'Oh God, Hal. I so hoped it would be all right.'

She'd forgotten what he was like. How sincere and straightforward he was. Seeing him now, the notion that he might have got together with Grace was ridiculous.

'But you can't have come all the way from London just to tell me that it didn't work out?' Lily asked. 'Have you?'

'Don't make it so hard!' Grace butted in. 'He has come all the way from London to see you. He needs you—' she paused and said emphatically, 'you *have* to find a way to persuade Amber to give him another chance.'

Lily turned back to her, finding it hard to take in what she was hearing.

Grace stared back. 'I know. I know. You must think all this is really weird.'

But it wasn't what Grace was saying, it was who she'd become, that Lily could hardly believe. She could hear enthusiasm and confidence in Grace's voice, see a new sparkle in her eyes, and the fact that she showed any concern at all for someone else marked a radical improvement on past form.

'What is going on here?' she demanded indignantly. 'I turn my back for just a second, and the next thing I know, my agoraphobic sister is walking up the drive, practically hand in hand with someone I would say she should steer clear of at all costs.'

Grace laughed delightedly. 'I knew this would freak you out. It was why I couldn't resist coming too.' She turned to Hal. 'But Hal's lovely! Why do you say that about him?'

'Yes, bloody hell,' Hal agreed, 'what have I done?'

Lily said, 'No! I'm sorry. It's not what you've done, it's just . . . you're in the middle of a crisis, and I don't think Grace needs that right now!'

'Because I'm terribly delicate. Is that right, Lily? And being involved in a crisis might just send me jumping over the precipice?' Grace laughed but there was a defiant edge to her voice. 'Seriously, you don't need to worry. And I've only just met Hal. Literally, just today, because he turned up at home, looking for you. And he and I talked a bit.' Grace paused. 'Then we had some lunch and then the only thing left to do was to come and find you!'

'Fine. Absolutely fine,' said Lily, feeling rather ticked off, still catching up with the new Grace.

And the new Hal, too. Changed almost as dramatically, but in his case definitely for the worse. Trying to be bright and happy and falling in with the banter, he couldn't quite cover up his desperation. In the weeks since she'd seen him, it didn't look as if he'd thought to wash his hair, and his eyes were red and tired, his skin looked grey, and he looked very thin under his heavy sheepskin coat.

There was too much going on here, Lily thought looking from one to the other, not knowing who to start with. There was so much Lily and Hal needed to talk about and so much to say to Grace. But she and Grace could catch up any time. It had to be Hal she took care of first.

She started decisively. 'We can't talk here,' she told them both. 'Kirsty's parents are inside and Kirsty will soon be back.' She stopped and considered what to do. 'Hal, I'm on for it. I'm with you, whatever you want me to do. Of course I am. I'll do anything. And Kirsty too,' Lily went on. 'I'm sure she will help too, if you need her.'

'Maybe, although I have the feeling it's you Amber will listen to.'

Lily raised her eyebrows. 'Oh! I wondered what it was, exactly, that you were going to ask me to do.'

Hal nodded. 'Please,' he said, his voice full of intensity.

'Yes,' Lily said again, firmly. 'Of course I will. But we need to talk about it properly, discuss what I should say. How I get her to meet me. When and where.' She paused. 'How long are you here for?'

'I've got the day off tomorrow so I'm staying the night in the Little Goose. How about meeting me there? I'll buy you some supper. Bring Kirsty with you.'

'But not me,' said Grace. 'Definitely not me.'

'No,' said Lily, grinning at her, 'you are not invited.'

Lily turned back to Hal. 'There's one other thing,' she said, more seriously, 'something I just have to know.' She found herself holding her breath. 'The fact that you're here, the fact that there's hope for you and Amber. It must mean that Josh didn't go with Amber on her honeymoon?'

Ever since Amber's sister had told them that Josh had left with Amber, Lily had suspected that the true cause of the wedding-day fiasco was that Amber and Josh had never been able to give each other up. That it had been carefully set up by the two of them. A desperate last-minute plan to ditch Hal. By holding Hal in Wales, Josh had saved Amber from an excruciating confrontation on her wedding day. He had given her the chance to run away rather than face the music and admit to Hal and everybody else that she couldn't go through with her marriage. Whatever she and Josh would have to contend with when they finally did come home, it would, at least, be done in private.

But Hal was aghast at the question. 'What? Of course not!' he said, bristling and defensive. 'Why ask me that? He and Amber were finished ages ago. Of course he didn't go on the fucking honeymoon!'

'I'm sorry. It was just something Mel said at the reception.'

'You went to the reception? You met Mel? What else don't I know?'

Lily flinched. 'So what?' she said defensively. 'It's not that terrible! We only wanted to make sure you were okay.'

Hal winced at the look on her face. 'I'm sorry,' he said. 'I'm so wound up. And I was taken aback at the thought of you in there with all of them.' He grimaced. 'So, what did sweet little Mel say to you?'

'Nothing much.' Lily was panicking that she was about to put her foot in it again, that maybe Hal was the only one still in the dark about Josh and Amber. 'Just that she thought Josh might have . . . might have taken Amber to the airport.'

'Mel thought he took her to the airport!' Hal looked stunned. 'No,' he said emphatically. He shook his head. 'No. He wouldn't do that to me. And anyway, I'd have known about it. He might have taken her to the airport but he didn't jump on the plane.'

'Then they're definitely not—' Lily stopped. Hal hadn't ever thought that they were.

So Lily still didn't know if Josh had taken that final step on to the aeroplane that would have put him completely, permanently out of bounds. Hal seemed sure he hadn't, but Hal had been wrong about Josh before. And yet, she agonized, wouldn't Hal have heard about something as important as this? It wasn't the sort of thing that could have been kept away from him. It had to be true, she decided, trying not to grin into Hal's face. Then, as fast as she acknowledged the thought, she stamped it out. Josh didn't interest her. Even if he hadn't taken Hal's place on the honeymoon with Amber he was still a deceitful, double-dealing, untrustworthy scumbag. Not the sort of guy she would ever waste her valuable time thinking about. She had her standards, and whatever he looked like, however he had made her feel, she would stick to them. And in any case, she reminded herself sharply, there was absolutely no likelihood of ever seeing him again. He lived hundreds of miles away in London and the only person they had in common was never going to speak to him again. But you know where he works, a little voice reminded her, because he'd told her in the Little Goose. He worked in South Kensington, just off the Fulham Road, and one day, perhaps, she might find herself there and bump into him again.

'You can rest assured that Amber and Josh are not living together on an island paradise,' Hal told her. 'Actually he turned up at my flat a few days ago.'

Lily leaped upon the information. So he *had* spoken to Josh again.

'But I'm not telling you about it now.' Hal turned back to Grace. 'Because I am going to check in at the Little Goose and leave you two in peace.' Seeing Lily's face, he grinned at her. 'You're just dying to know, aren't you? But you'll have to wait.'

As he walked to his car he called back to her, 'I will tell you about it tonight. And don't savage each other. Be nice!'

He opened the door and then looked at Grace. 'And I'll come and say goodbye to you tomorrow, before I go.'

As Hal's car took the first bend, Grace let out a deep sigh. Lily looked across at her and guessed that with Hal no longer there she wasn't feeling so strong, daunted by the possibility that they might now have to confront the awfulness of the night Lily left.

'Isn't it cold?' Lily said to break the silence. She jumped up and down. 'We should get into the house. Come and have a cup of tea?'

'I came without my coat. I'm completely freezing,'

Grace agreed, still staring vacantly down the road. Then she turned to Lily. 'I don't want to go inside. Do you mind? I can't face making polite conversation with Kirsty's mother. Can you lend me a jumper or a coat? Then maybe we could go for a walk.' But before Lily could answer, a look of sudden panic crossed Grace's face. 'Oh, I have to go home.'

'Why?'

'Because,' Grace said, 'I've left someone at home waiting for me.'

Lily's eyes widened.

Grace smiled. 'I love him and he loves me. And if I don't get back soon he will probably be up the stairs and tearing down my bedroom door with his teeth in frustration.'

Lily laughed. 'You've gone and bought a dog!'

Grace looked crushed. 'How did you guess?'

'But Grace, you're completely mad!' Lily told her without thinking. 'You'll never look after him! It's ridiculous. You have no idea what you're letting yourself in for.'

'What!' Grace spluttered. 'Was that you or my mother speaking just then?'

'I didn't mean it,' Lily cried hastily. 'Honestly!' She didn't want to remind Grace that only a few weeks ago she'd barely been able to get herself dressed.

'You mustn't speak to me like that,' Grace insisted. 'Or you'll spoil everything. I'm fine now. I'm perfectly capable of looking after a puppy.'

*

The further they walked, the more Grace and Lily relaxed. At first the conversation between them came in fits and starts, but gradually Grace began to talk. As it had been so long since Lily had seen her like this, she shut up and let her keep going, limiting her responses to the occasional 'hmmm' or nod, all that was necessary to let Grace know that she was listening.

When they reached the bottom of the hill, Grace finally paused for a moment to catch her breath. The strong wind and the effort of talking and walking at the same time had brightened her eyes and pinked her cheeks and the rain had washed her face clean of make-up.

'Do I sound better?' Grace asked unexpectedly. She breathed deeply and swallowed. 'You must be able to tell. I feel so much better. Not just because of the puppy, but meeting Hal today. It was strange.' She paused, struggling to find the right words. 'Like I'd come full circle.'

'It's closure,' Lily told her.

'Oh,' Grace said doubtfully. She paused for a moment and started to smile. 'I'm sorry,' she bit her lip, 'for that evening. And for calling you Mother Superior. And for saying all those terrible things. I didn't mean any of them. You've been everything to me. You're my rock. But even so I had to push you away and stand up on my own.'

Lily looked back at her. 'I'm sorry too.'

'Do you know?' Grace said brightly, changing the subject. 'Today, I met ...' She stopped again. It was on the tip of her tongue but she changed her mind at the last second, torn between wanting to talk about him, and superstitiously imagining that her chances would disappear if she spoke about it out loud. 'I suppose,' she said instead, 'that what I needed to realize was that everyone else wasn't leading such perfect lives either. I realized it, talking to Hal.'

Lily nodded. Looking at Grace, she felt old, with an overwhelming desire to protect her sister, to keep her safe and make sure that nothing could interfere or spoil it all.

'I want to say something,' Lily said quickly. 'We must hang on to how we are now. I don't think we should ever try to analyse why we fell out. I don't think we should talk about it at all. There's no need, is there? Neither of us really meant those things.'

Grace paused before replying. She saw the point and yet at the same time she hoped that one day they would be able to talk about the past again. Not just to go over why Lily left, and certainly not to dredge up old hurts, but because there were things she wanted to talk about. About her engagement. She had questions that still needed answers, impressions that maybe Lily hadn't always been honest about what had gone on, suspicions that important things had been swept under the carpet because, perhaps, it was felt that Grace couldn't deal with them. And the doubts and questions were still there between them, unresolved.

But it could wait. For the time being, she knew that Lily was right. That if they talked about it now this fragile *détente* would be shattered. They were not yet on firm enough ground to have a conversation rather than a row and she didn't want to lose Lily again so soon. So she shut up, and smiled back.

'I've missed you,' she admitted, turning towards Lily. 'I really have. And I don't want to talk about that night either. Apart from to say that I'm sorry. Again.' She screwed up her face. 'Tell me I wasn't as awful as I think I was.'

Lily opened her mouth to reassure her, but Grace went straight on. 'No. Don't! Please.' She winced. 'I was as awful as I think I was! Talk about something else. I want to hear about everything that's been going on while you've been away. Tell me how it's been, living with the lovely Kirsty.'

Lily laughed. She's amazing, she thought. Unbelievable. How can she be like this? And why, why if it's all so simple, couldn't she have been like this a few weeks ago, when I was still living with her? Those six months had been so grim that Lily, despite her best intentions, couldn't quite forget them. Not because she resented Grace any more, but because the psychological bruises Grace had given her had still not entirely faded. She had been left with a wariness that she couldn't drop to order, a new sense of self-preservation that told her not to let down her guard too soon, because, despite Grace's best intentions, it could all start up again. As it had done before.

I'm rushing everything, Lily decided. And it has to happen slowly. Let's see the puppy and make another date and leave it at that for now.

But running through Lily was a new awareness that it wouldn't be so easy to pick up where they had left off as and when they felt like it. That as much as she wanted to protect and nurture and preserve her sister's new state of happiness, a bombshell had arrived in the post that morning, forwarded on unwittingly by Grace. Something which meant it might no longer be possible to pop in and see Grace whenever she wanted.

Lily cursed the timing. The letter from the Registry was in response to an earlier one from her. Just after she had left Grace, Lily had enquired whether they were still interested in the possibility of her designing a range of kitchenware for them. They were. It seemed that by turning them down all those months ago, she had only fanned their interest. Now they were suggesting the possibility of a whole range of work that would keep her fully employed by them for at least the next three years. Crockery, tiles for the walls and for kitchen floors. It was an amazing opportunity, at once massively exciting and deeply terrifying. If she pulled it off it would bind her to them through what would probably be the most important stage of her career. She would emerge at the other end so well established and well connected that, she imagined, she could then turn in any direction she wanted and be sure of a certain level of success.

To design for the Registry would be a huge coup. Their products combined quality with cutting-edge designs that inspired worldwide devotion. Based on the Fulham Road, in an old art deco furniture warehouse, the Registry called itself a general store but it had a globetrotting faithful clientele that would think nothing of flying in for a Saturday afternoon browse around its five exquisite floors. It was the sort of place that Lily might have hoped to work in several years after having left college, at the peak of her career. That they had suggested she might go there straight away was the most flattering thing that had ever happened to her. The fact that she'd had to turn them down, the most galling. And yet some of her wasn't at all sure she wanted to rise to the challenge right now.

Having read their letter, she'd sat at the kitchen table, holding it in her suddenly sweaty hand, feeling like she was sitting not just at the other end of the country to them but on another planet. Much as she knew she should call them immediately and arrange a meeting, she couldn't bring herself to do it, panicking that she didn't want to give up the cosy undemanding world she had built for herself. She wondered whether her doubts were simply because she was extremely lazy and didn't like the idea of being tied down to work of any sort, or if she was right to doubt whether it was really for her. And there was Kirsty and the cottage they were just about to rent together. What would happen to it? Where she might work from hadn't been mentioned in the letter but, if they did give her the job, Lily wondered if they'd be content for her to live in Welshpool.

How badly did she want to stay? How much did she want to go? What if the two were mutually exclusive? She had been wondering and worrying throughout the day, and had got nowhere. Eventually she'd realized that without meeting them she simply couldn't know the answer to either question. So finally she had called them and had set up an interview, and then she'd sat at her window, drumming her fingers on the ledge, and had waited for Kirsty to come home. And then Hal and Grace had walked back into her life instead. At least now she'd be able to kill two birds with one stone, she comforted herself. Perhaps the Registry in the morning, Amber Aisling in the afternoon.

Walking with Grace, Lily decided not to tell her about the Registry. Whatever else came up between them, she knew this was one ingredient to leave out for now. And later, as she sat beside Grace and the puppy, she knew she'd definitely made the right decision. She didn't need to work out that she couldn't just slip her news casually into the middle of a conversation. It was going to change everything between them, all over again, and it could wait at least until she'd had the interview and found out if she'd really got the job.

*

When Kirsty arrived home she quietly shut the door of her car so as not to alert her mother that she was back and ran silently up the two steps to the front door. She trod lightly past the kitchen door, through the hall and up a flight of stairs to Lily's bedroom, and saw the closed door that told her that Lily wasn't in.

'Where are you, where are you? Where the fuck are you?' she hissed at the door before charging back down the stairs again and outside once more. This time she slammed the front door and then jumped back into her car, calling Lily's number with her mobile as she backed out of the drive. But Lily's phone was switched off and Kirsty didn't know where to find her.

She drove aimlessly along dark roads trying to decide

what to do, turning randomly left and right until she had no idea where she was. Finally, she turned into a little lane so narrow it was practically impassable. Brambles and nettles so tall and strong that they had grown out from each side to meet in the middle. They scratched and pulled at her car as she passed, slowly ripping a way between them. Her headlights picked out puddles so deep and huge she worried that the car wouldn't make it through them. When one threatened to block out her headlights she conceded defeat and pulled over into a boggy gateway. She turned off the engine, opened her window and lit a cigarette, inhaling deeply enough to make her lungs flinch in surprise at the sudden bombardment of smoke.

Thank God she'd got rid of him, she thought. She really couldn't bear clingy men. No more pressure, no more dopey, love-sick looks, no more horrible feelings of being trapped. She was free of him. He wouldn't call her mother ever again. And thank God the town would have to find some other source of excitement. Miserable sad people, eaten up with interest in her because there was nothing going on in their own boring lives. Urghh, she shuddered. That awful moment in the warehouse, when she'd felt as if she might die with the agony of watching him drive away, was only a reaction to the shock. She wasn't denying he was a nice guy, just not the one for her.

Where the fuck have you got to, Lily? she thought again, chain-smoking another cigarette. She urgently needed to tell Lily about what she'd done. As if by speaking about it out loud she could convince herself that she'd done the right thing. Having not wanted to talk to Lily about Simon at all in the past few weeks – because she'd known Lily would have encouraged her to hang on to him – she now felt safe telling her all that had happened. By chucking him, she'd earned the right to some emotional support. It had been a traumatic day, and Lily couldn't knock her when she was already down. If she could only find her.

She finished the cigarette and started the car again, turning around and driving back along the dark lane until, eventually, she recognized where she was and found her way home. It was only six thirty but as black as midnight.

This time she got out of the car and didn't hurry, walking to the front door and pausing on the way in to call hello to her parents.

'Lily's gone to her sister's,' her mother shouted from the kitchen. 'She told me to tell you she'd be back about six thirty.' There was a pause. 'So, about now.'

Kirsty raised her eyebrows at the news and stalked slowly on towards the stairs.

'And she also said to tell you that Hal has turned up. That he's taking you both out for supper to the Little Goose.'

Kirsty stopped on the first stair and bit hard into the soft skin of her thumb. No way, she panicked. There was no way she could face the Little Goose. She couldn't bear to see Simon again so soon.

She dragged herself up the stairs towards her bedroom, ignoring her mother's friendly call to join her in the kitchen. And then, as she opened her bedroom door, the second piece of news belatedly arrived at her brain and she found herself turning mechanically and making her way slowly back towards the kitchen and her mother. 'Did you say Hal?' she asked, standing in the doorway.

*

Ten minutes later, Lily poked her head around the door and waved hello.

'Lily,' Kirsty snapped, standing up immediately, 'I've been waiting so long. Where have you been?'

'To see a man about a dog. You know where I've been!' Lily smiled, not noticing Kirsty's pinched face. 'I asked your mum to tell you, so don't get stroppy and pretend you don't. And I guess you've also heard that Hal's here and that he wants to take us out tonight?'

'Yes. But I can't.' Kirsty ushered her out of the kitchen and into the hall. 'I can't go to the Little Goose tonight, not now.'

Lily looked at her and said nothing. Instead she led her upstairs and into her bedroom and sat her down on the bed.

'I just can't do it,' Kirsty said. 'It's too soon.' She closed her eyes and fell back on the pillows and groaned. 'Simon came around to the warehouse today. And I told him I didn't want to see him again.'

'So?' said Lily cautiously. 'You told him that ages ago. I didn't know you were still seeing him.'

'Well, I was.'

'You're so secretive! When? How many times? How many times since we had dinner at the Little Goose, the night we met Hal?' She looked at Kirsty, tilting her head sideways, her eyes questioning. 'And why didn't you tell me?'

Kirsty shrugged. 'He's turned up at work a few times. And we went out, maybe three or four more times. It was nothing serious. And I haven't seen him since you moved in here. Not until today.'

'Why didn't you tell me?' Lily asked again. Kirsty didn't answer. 'I know why,' Lily said. 'Because you didn't want me to interfere when you decided his time was up. That's right, isn't it? You knew we all liked him and you didn't want anyone to give you a hard time. And now, today, you've done the dirty deed and you want me to tell you what a brilliant thing it was to do. That it's all okay.' Kirsty, shocked, couldn't think of what to say. 'How do you feel about it?' Lily asked, an edge to her voice. 'Was it difficult? Easy? Was he upset?'

'I feel crap,' Kirsty burst out angrily, pushing herself up against the back of the bed. 'How do you think I feel!' She looked at Lily, still surprised that Lily was reacting like this. 'I didn't expect to but I do.' Then she heaved a sigh, hating her admission. 'No. That's not true. I'm okay. It was the only thing I could do and I'm glad it's all over. And Simon was fine about it too.'

Lily pulled a chair out from under a dressing-table and sat down. 'Had you slept with him?' she asked curiously.

Taken aback, Kirsty stood up abruptly and went to the other end of the room, over to a chair piled high with clean clothes. With her back to Lily she started matching socks and didn't answer for a few moments. 'It's got nothing to do with it,' she said eventually. 'And, anyway, none of your business.'

'Sorry.'

'But yes. Actually,' Kirsty said defiantly, now turning around, 'I did. Make something of it!'

'You're like one of those bugs, aren't you? A praying mantis. I think it's them that do that,' Lily said.

'God! Thanks a lot. What was that for? I haven't done anything wrong. I haven't hurt you! No, don't you smile at me like that now, you little cow!'

'I'm sorry,' Lily apologized. 'Okay, you don't actually kill the men off. But you know what I mean. Know that it's true. You should sort yourself out.'

'And what do you mean by that?' Kirsty replied, her voice trembling, not liking the patronizing tone. 'Lily, I've got a tidy knicker drawer but I haven't got a life. At least I do something. At least I'm alive!'

'Really,' Lily said, anger rising. 'Thanks so much. You should think why you need to attack anyone who makes you feel uncomfortable. Attack them, or in Simon's case, get rid of them.'

'Not true! I don't,' Kirsty exclaimed. She stopped pairing the socks and started putting them away in drawers, telling herself to calm down. She hadn't wanted to hurt Lily. It had burst out before she'd known what she was saying. She knew that much of what Lily was telling her was the truth.

'I do it,' Kirsty told Lily in a quiet voice, 'when they

make me feel claustrophobic and panicky and pressured into being someone I'm not. And Simon did all those things.'

'Oh, crap,' Lily scoffed. 'How can you say that? He adored you! And he was lovely to you.'

'I know he adored me,' Kirsty told her smartly. 'And that's what I didn't like. He didn't know me. He had me down for someone I wasn't, and it was impossible. And he was too old and serious and he'd read too many clever books and he had had too many high-powered girlfriends and I didn't like it.' Kirsty stopped at the disbelieving look on Lily's face. 'He's thirty-six, Lily. He's so much more grown-up than me. And we weren't suited in other ways too,' she said firmly. 'We didn't have similar interests. We weren't into the same things.'

'Like what?'

'Things like TV and shopping,' said Kirsty, now starting to smile too. 'Oh, stop looking at me like that! Stop doubting what I'm saying.' She threw a balled-up pair of socks at Lily's head. 'Listen to me and believe me,' she demanded. 'What I'm saying is that I'm much better off without him and you should trust me on that. Now stop asking me about him and tell me about Hal.'

'Thirty-six is so old, isn't it?' Lily said sarcastically. 'You're mad,' she told her, going over to the corner of the room to retrieve the socks and tossing them back to Kirsty. 'Mad to let him go. Why didn't you have some fun? Get to know him a bit better. You haven't given it a chance.'

'It's a shame he didn't meet you first. You'd have made a perfect couple.'

'Oh, Kirsty, shut up,' she said, coming to join her on the bed.

'Simon and I are over. And don't try to analyse me, Lily, because you're not very good at it.'

'I'm sure you're right,' Lily snapped back. 'But I can't say what you want me to say.' She sat back too quickly and banged her head against the wall. 'You don't really want it to end with him. You sounded convincing for a while but only because you're trying your best to convince yourself.' She paused and rubbed her head, and looked up at Kirsty. 'Ow!' Kirsty didn't respond. 'What is it with you? On the one hand, you're happy to pull men left, right and centre. And yet the minute someone like Simon comes on the scene you run a mile.'

'It's true.' Suddenly all the fight went out of Kirsty and she gave up. 'Actually, I feel totally shit about it. I don't know why, but I've never really cared about any boyfriend I've had. I used to look at my friends, desperately in love, and think, that looks nice. But always from a distance. I could never imagine feeling like that myself.'

'What are you afraid of?'

'I don't think it's that I'm afraid of anything. It's not as if I've had a traumatic experience or a bad childhood to blame it on. I just don't want it like everyone else does.'

'Well, looking at the arseholes I've seen you with, I don't blame you. But you have to admit Simon was different.'

Kirsty smiled sadly. 'I know. Why did I think I wanted *him* to go?'

'Poor Kirsty,' Lily said sympathetically.

'This morning, it was almost as if I was playing a game, trying out different phrases on him.' She shook her head. 'Why didn't I see how I'd feel now? I so want to tell him I didn't mean it. That I've come to my senses.'

'What shall we do with you?' Lily said smiling.

'Don't joke about it,' Kirsty said flatly. 'I miss him and I wish I hadn't done it.' She looked away and Lily saw a fat tear slide out from under her eyelashes. She had never seen Kirsty cry before. 'I didn't realize in time. But I knew it as soon as he drove away. And now he's gone.'

'Oh no,' Lily cried. 'Stop it! I can't bear it. It's not so bad. Don't be so sad! You have to get him back. That's what you've got to do. Tell him you've made a mistake.'

'It's not a question of telling him anything, doing anything differently. I think it's a question of how I get over him.' Another tear slid down Kirsty's face. 'Because he made it absolutely clear that I wasn't going to have another chance. Oh, what's the matter with me?' she demanded angrily, turning to Lily.

Lily sat in silence.

'The End,' Kirsty said abruptly, to finish the conversation. 'I don't want to talk about it any more. I definitely don't want to hear your plans for winning him back. And tonight,' she went on firmly, 'you are going to the Little Goose on your own. I'll wait up for you and you can come home and tell me everything that Hal said. I want to know everything that is going on.' She paused, wondering if Lily had forgiven her for the earlier outburst. 'Why exactly is he here?' she asked, curiously, turning the conversation away from Simon once and for all. 'I suppose she wouldn't have him back?'

Lily shook her head.

'How can I possibly not come and hear what he says? But I can't, I can't. Oh, God, the timing!'

'We could go somewhere else.'

'No, go there, without me. I wouldn't be good company tonight and, anyway, I think it's you Hal wants to talk to.'

'He'd like to see you. I know he would.'

Kirsty shook her head. 'No, not tonight.'

'If you're sure.' Lily got up. 'I'm sorry if I said all the wrong things just then. I think you should get him back. But I'm doing what you want. I'm not talking about it any more.'

Lily leaned down and touched Kirsty's shoulder. 'You'll be okay?'

Kirsty nodded and opened her bedroom door. 'For now. Have a good time. I'll see you in the morning.'

11

You can't help but see good-looking men on the Fulham Road. As Lily paused for a moment, tucking herself into a shop doorway, she saw another one striding towards her. He was in the middle of a conversation on his mobile and he was walking with his head bent, not looking where he was going. At his side a girl in a pink coat with long shiny brown hair and spindly legs encased in long shiny brown boots trotted to keep up with him. As the two of them swept past her, Lily's heart skipped a beat as she saw that the man was Josh.

Although she knew that she was near where he worked, and although a tiny bit of her had been longing to see him, when it really happened it was still such a surprise that she found herself holding her breath as he walked by. She watched the two of them stop just beyond her and saw him take his phone away from his ear and pull the girl to a halt. Smiling down at her, Josh planted a kiss upon the girl's upturned forehead and then another, more tenderly, on her cherry red lips. The girl leaned in to him, obviously hoping for more, but Josh laughed and put his hands on her shoulders, steering her slowly around until she was turned away from him, facing back the way they'd come. Then he gave her a gentle push and immediately went back to his mobile, walking away down one of the side streets without turning back. The girl stood as still as a statue for a few moments, watching him disappear, and then with a little secret smile of success she bounced into a jaunty walk, passing by Lily once more before making her way down Walton Street and out of sight.

Lily didn't expect the sight of Josh to have such an effect on her. Irrationally and overwhelmingly, she longed to be that girl.

She wandered down the road feeling let down and lonely. She was having an interview, *the* interview, with the Registry in less than half an hour. People would kill for such a chance. She slid the palms of her hands down her skirt. She couldn't let him spoil it, not Josh.

But he was so gorgeous. The memory of him didn't do him justice at all. Maybe it was the dark suit, cut so that it set off every beautiful line and angle of him. Or the tender, sexy smile that he'd given his knock-kneed girlfriend. And probably, she admitted, it was something to do with the fact that, this time, he had been completely oblivious to her.

She walked on, focusing on the dramatic art deco building that housed the Registry, just a few hundred yards away from her, forcing her mind to start to concentrate on what lay ahead. She would spend her last few minutes wandering through the store, slowly working her way up the floors towards her interview on the fifth, preparing herself by getting a sense of some of the things they had on sale.

She walked up a couple of shallow stone steps and in through two frosted-glass doors and found herself in a vast central atrium. She was in the heart of the store. She stood still for a moment, taking in the bustle and the buzz, the expectant purposeful looks on the faces of the shoppers as they made their way towards the escalators, or tap-tapped across the mosaic floor to the ground-floor departments. And dotted among them were others like her, standing still and allowing the atmosphere to wash over them.

Lily had been to the Registry before, many times, but this time she was seeing it with a different eye. As she stood in the middle of the atrium, she couldn't believe that she was here to become part of it, that her designs could possibly be good enough to be displayed in the huge lit-up alcoves she could see all around her. Josh faded from her mind as she began to concentrate on how to convince them that they were right to be after her.

She turned slowly, looking all around, and then tilted backwards to stare up at the pale blue and white stained-glass dome of a ceiling, glistening miles above her. She knew it was time to go. She took a slow trembling breath, told herself to be cool, that she could do it, and moved towards the escalators.

There were three of them to interview her. One man with hair dyed grey and long fingernails cracked a few terrible jokes at the beginning and then, when she didn't laugh, turned nasty, passing her pieces to identify from their stupendously expensive 'antique corridor' on the fourth floor. She thought about dropping one on his toe and asking, politely, what it had to do with her own work, but she wanted the job too much. His two colleagues were much nicer. She'd met them once before, when they'd come up to her stand at her end-of-year show and had embarrassed and flattered her with their noisy interest in her work. Today they gracefully sidelined their colleague, reiterating their own excitement ten times over, stressing how perfect Lily was for them, making it impossible for the other man to speak up and for her not to relax and blossom and tell them all about what she did and the sort of things she'd like to work on next.

Afterwards she stood outside, dazzled by the sunlight, feeling euphoric and released and slightly disorientated too. She looked down the street, suddenly feeling buffeted by all the sounds. She looked around, wanting to find somewhere quieter where she could think about it all. It had been so straightforward that already she was beginning to feel a little disconcerted, almost wishing that they'd given her a harder time, or held back a little on the enthusiasm so that she might have had more to work on. She heard a clock chime and realized that she had been inside with them for forty-five minutes. Long enough, then, for them to get a good sense of her, however relaxed it had been.

She started walking without thinking where she was going. She'd already killed an hour in the Fulham Road before the interview and there was nothing she hadn't seen before, but she set off again anyway. She was finding it hard to recall the details of the interview. She remembered that the nice two had explained that they would bring her up at their next directors' meeting and how the grey-haired man had illustrated the point by pretending to gag. She knew he'd caught her look of disdain and she wondered whether he'd try to sabotage her application. If he failed, and she did manage to get the job, any position made available to her would be for an initial six months. They'd explained that the successful applicant's brief would be to provide the Registry with several one-off pieces, whatever she liked, that they could display and sell on the fourth floor, and also to create a series of dummies, the idea being that these would, eventually, replace some of their current in-house designs. If okayed by the board, her dummies would then be sent on to one of the factories in Stoke-on-Trent to be mass-produced and sold under the Registry logo across the country. She would be providing the staple range for all their kitchenware. How amazing it would be, Lily thought with a surge of excitement. And it *could* be her. They had definitely liked her. All she had to hope for was that they didn't like everyone they saw as much.

Hal had promised her lunch that day but at the last minute he had had to stand her up, and now that she thought about it, she realized that the bubbling in her stomach wasn't only due to nerves. On the way to the tube she stopped at a deli and bought herself an enormous baguette. Then she turned up Pelham Street, keeping her eyes open for somewhere to stop, and eventually veering off course to sit down on a bench under a flowering cherry tree. The sun was warm on her face, and when she'd finished her baguette she sat on, happy to enjoy the sun, and put off the evil moment when she faced the sweat and stink of the underground. I love being back, she thought, closing her eyes and tipping back her head. And not just in safe, pretty Chelsea either, but in all of London. Not for the first time, she wondered if she should come back for good, give up Welshpool now that Grace didn't need her any more.

She got on the tube and as the train rattled towards Hammersmith some of her euphoria dissolved. By the time she got off again and headed towards the bridge she realized that she was tired. Not so much footloose as footsore. She walked over the bridge towards Barnes, and half-way across she stopped beside a green and gold-leaf lamp-post and leaned out over the river, looking down to the slick black water flowing fast beneath her. There was a group of seagulls just below her, bobbing amidst the driftwood and the plastic bottles, and further upstream a bony heron hunched down on a rock.

There'd been other questions she'd wanted to ask the Registry people, she remembered now. Did they care where she lived? How often would they want to see her? How much feedback would they give her? Would she be part of a team of designers or was she on her own? How quickly would they want her to start? Imagining actually starting work, she felt a great lurch of panic. She sniffed in the salty river smell and breathed out again, aware that she was on the cusp of a huge change, that everything she knew was turning around and reordering, settling down again in new formations. Looking out at the river, she felt as if she was leaning out on the edge of her life.

The water swirled hypnotically beneath her and the bridge shifted slightly under her feet. She jumped back in alarm, grabbing hold of the lamp-post, and the moment was broken. I don't want it, she suddenly panicked. This shouldn't be my first job. I haven't any experience. It's too much. I don't want this job.

She made herself let go of the lamp-post and looked around self-consciously, wondering if anyone had noticed her, or had worried that she'd been about to jump, but there was nobody else about.

She walked on, leaving the bridge behind, then turned right and set off up Lonsdale Road. She was borrowing the flat of an art-school friend who had left that morning for a long weekend with her boyfriend. It was on the ground floor of a big white stuccoed house, with high ceilings and lovely light rooms.

Josie, her friend, had crossed over with Lily for just one night, long enough to find her the spare key, to clear some hanging space in her wardrobe for the interview clothes, and to ensure that she got Lily wrecked the night before her interview. She could stay for as long as she wanted to, Josie had reassured her, it was all hers, apart from the slim chance of Beth, her little sister, turning up to sleep on the sofa on Friday night. But Beth had her own keys so Lily was not to worry about her.

It had been wonderful for Lily to see Josie again. Lily could tell her about the giant steps that Grace was finally taking, without needing to explain anything about the past. Josie had known Grace for years and had been one of the guests waiting with mounting dread for the denoue- ment in the church, as the rumours about Jeremy had escalated until they had zig-zagged and bounced around the pews like bolts of forked lightning.

And then, after a bit, the conversation had moved away from Grace and on to Lily, Josie demanding that Lily bring her up to date with her sex life. 'Non-existent, of course.' Josie refused to believe there was still no one that Lily fancied. To shut her up, Lily eventually told her about Josh, not that there was anything much to tell. She described the night when she had sat beside him in the Little Goose, and then having started to speak about him she, of course, had to explain why they'd met. And so she told Josie about the stag do, and how strange it was that she had become embroiled in another wedding-that-wasn't, albeit a different version.

Josh caught Josie's attention. Although she was, of course, interested in what he'd engineered for Hal, far more it was because he seemed to have got under Lily's skin. Josie had always found it disconcerting, the way Lily could slip along seemingly so unruffled, never falling in love, leaving each relationship completely unscathed, never knowing what it felt like to be hopelessly infatuated by someone. Hearing Lily unsuccessfully masking her interest in Josh, floundering around as everyone else did when she tried to sound nonchalant and unconcerned, even disapproving, Josie wanted to shout a great 'Yes!' in triumph.

'But you must see him again,' she insisted. 'You've got to find him while you're in London, hunt him down! I've never heard you talk like this about someone before.'

Lily looked at her incredulously and shook her head. 'Hunt down Josh! No way. That is *not* my style.'

'Oh, *Lily*!' Josie shouted, full of exasperation. 'You know, sometimes I could . . .'

'You could what?'

'I don't know,' Josie said, deflating again. 'Something bad.'

'Don't you do anything,' said Lily, taken aback. 'Don't you dare!'

'Don't worry. I won't. But don't you ever think you're missing out? You should live a little! Do the wrong thing for once.'

Lily laughed uncomfortably and brushed it away and started to tell her about other things.

While Lily talked, Josie had cooked her the one meal she knew how to do – grilled chicken and fried potatoes – and listened through the doorway. Afterwards she had lain on the sofa smoking, a glass of wine in one hand, letting Lily wash up.

She was impressed with Josh. Perhaps it was because Lily's description of him had unwittingly given him a heroic quality but, whatever the reason, she found herself intrigued by him. She liked him for doing something rather than just talking about what a disaster the girl was, for being prepared to take the flak. She'd never heard anything like it before. And she warned Lily against underestimating his resolve. What would he do if he knew Lily was about to play negotiator between Hal and Amber?

'He's gone this far already,' she said theatrically, think-

ing aloud and suddenly sitting bolt upright on the sofa.
'So how much further would he go a second time?' What
might he do when he realized that Lily was still determined to set Hal and Amber back on course? It might not
be a question of Lily hunting him down after all! Was Lily
safe?

She got off the sofa and appeared in the kitchen
doorway.

'Does anyone know where you're staying in London?
Is there a way he can find you if he wants to?'

Lily had whispered back that she was becoming para-
noid, and what had she had to smoke?

Josie had gone early the next morning and so Lily was
left to open the door later that same Thursday afternoon
to a blast of cold air and silence. It was like walking into a
completely different place. She unbuttoned her coat and
hung it at the bottom of the stairs, then walked through
into the sitting-room and over to a window that she'd left
a few inches open. Then she bounced down on the sofa.
As soon as she landed she was up again, moving over to
the wall to flick a switch on the central heating and then
into the kitchen to make a cup of tea.

She had one further ordeal to get through. In its way,
it was something she was as nervous about as her interview at the Registry – but she wasn't quite up to it yet.
She flicked on the television. *Pet Rescue* was about to
start. She would watch *Pet Rescue* and then she would do
it. Make the dreaded telephone call to Amber. Take the
plunge and see if there was any chance of persuading her
to meet up while Lily was in London. And once she'd

done that, she could start to think about other things, like the Registry and calling Kirsty and Grace, and seeing if there was any chance of an evening out with some friends.

She had Amber's number programmed into her mobile by Hal, ensuring that she couldn't lose it, and so, when the suitably sentimental theme tune started to play, she went through to Josie's kitchen and keyed it in, still with no idea of what she was going to say if it was picked up.

When somebody answered the phone she started in shock, but she managed to inquire, in her best caring, gentle tone, whether she could speak to Amber Aisling.

'Who is that?' a girl asked suspiciously.

'My name's Lily. But you . . . she,' Lily fumbled, 'you . . . she . . . you . . . won't know me.' Lily pulled herself together. 'I wanted to talk to her. Not for long. But I wanted to tell her something important.'

There was a long, suspicious pause. 'Okay, hang on and I'll see if she's free.'

Lily heard the receiver being put down and then a whisper, cut off by a hasty hand over the receiver.

Then the receiver was picked up again. 'This is Amber,' said the same voice. She now sounded clipped and rather confident. 'What did you want to tell me?'

Lily knew the next sentence was make or break but it had to be done.

'Well,' she said gently. 'Hal's asked me to get in touch.' She waited but the girl didn't respond. Lily went on. 'He asked me to call you because he knows you won't speak to him, and you don't trust any of his friends. And he can understand why. But I'm not a friend. I've only met him once before. So he thought you might listen to me.' She paused and swallowed, then proceeded again, still speaking as gently as she could, as if Amber's response was entirely dependent on how she said the words.

'I met him on the Friday night of his stag do. The night before what should have been his marriage to you.' She waited again, allowing Amber an opportunity to come back at her with something. To shout at her and tell her to get lost, perhaps, or even to break down and sob with relief that Hal had made contact. There was nothing.

'I'm calling because I think you should know the truth about what happened.' She hoped Amber was still there. 'And the truth is that Hal was terribly deceived by all his friends. So were you, I know,' she added hastily. 'And if only you hadn't left so fast,' Lily speeded up, thinking she'd said enough, 'none of this would have happened.' The last bit was hers but she thought it was worth pointing out. There was more long silence on the other end of the phone. 'He loves you, Amber. All this is crucifying him.'

At least she's let me say it, Lily thought, as she waited for a response. And now it can never be unsaid. Even if I get no further, I have passed on Hal's message.

'Lily,' the voice spoke very gravely. 'Thank you very much.'

Lily waited for more. 'Is that all?' she said, desperately not wanting her to hang up so soon.

There was another long pause and then the girl whispered, 'Don't let's make this worse.'

'But is there anything I can tell him?'

The voice spoke up again. 'I suppose you could tell

him that there's no point him doing this? That getting friends to make phone calls on his behalf is not going to help anything. That it's not, actually, going to make a blind bit of difference.'

'Don't you love him any more?' Lily asked sadly.

There was another long silence.

'Thanks so much for calling.' The girl now obviously felt it was time to go. 'I really don't want to talk about it.'

'Wait!' begged Lily.

'It's much better if we end this conversation now.'

'Why?'

'Because!'

'Tell me why, please.'

'Oh my God! Leave it alone!' She sighed in exasperation. 'What do you want me to say? That I've realized in the time we've been apart that he's not the one for me?'

Lily was taken aback at the way she trotted out the corny, awful phrase. 'Can't you do better than that?'

'Okay, how about I hope we can still be friends? What do you want me to say? You tell me!'

'I wouldn't know. I'm surprised you don't know. I'm surprised you don't know what to say to someone you were prepared to marry,' Lily said bitterly. 'Who you know still loves you and doesn't deserve to be treated like shit.'

There was silence on the other end of the telephone.

'What's wrong, Amber?' Lily asked.

'Oh, please!' The voice snapped back. 'Don't tell me you still think you're talking to Amber!'

Yes, Lily thought helplessly, I do. I did.

She could hear the girl breathing on the other end of the phone as she waited for Lily to respond but Lily couldn't think of anything to say. Then the voice spoke again, now mimicking Lily's words.

'*He loves you, Amber*,' she sighed theatrically. 'Oh, he's absolutely *crucified* without you.' She paused. 'Well, actually there *is* something you can tell Hal. From me. You can tell Hal that Amber was standing right beside me throughout this entire conversation. And that she suggests he gets on with his life now, and forgets about her. But you know what? She doesn't much care either way!'

'You shouldn't be enjoying this so much,' Lily told her bitterly. 'You're not in a soap opera.'

'Thanks for calling,' the girl said just before Lily hung up.

'Urgghhh!' Lily shouted in frustration. You bitch! If Amber was anything like her friend, thank God Josh got Hal out of the wedding. And fuck Hal for getting her involved like this. She hated them all. She lifted up her hands and saw that they were shaking with tension. Immediately she called Kirsty to let rip.

Kirsty, having initially thrown up her hands in horror as Lily recounted what had happened, was, in the end, philosophical. At least after a call like that they were left with no doubt that Hal was well rid of a monster. Even if it wasn't Amber herself on the phone, anyone with friends like that did not deserve Hal.

'This is good,' Kirsty told Lily confidently, 'because now you can come straight home.'

Kirsty didn't like Lily being in London. It made her

insecure. 'There's nothing else Hal can ask you to do and now you've done the interview you may as well come back. Oh my god! I can't believe I haven't asked you about it! How was it? Did they sign you up on the spot?'

Lily couldn't bring herself to contradict her or admit that being in London had been far better fun than she'd remembered and that the thought of coming back didn't fill her with quite as much glee as Kirsty would have hoped.

'So when *are* you coming back?' Kirsty demanded.

'Sunday. It's not long, Kirsty. And while I'm here I want to see a few friends. And Hal's taking me out for supper on Saturday night. He wanted me to have lunch with him today but he had to cancel me.'

'Which friends would those be then?' Kirsty asked.

Lily laughed. 'Oh, you don't know any of them,' she said, winding her up. 'But there's Linds and Charlie and Charlotte and Toe and Tracey and Martha and Hels. My proper friends. You know, the ones I wish lived in Welshpool.'

'Oh all *those* friends. I wouldn't bother calling them. They've been on the phone to me, actually, to say that they think you're really boring. Apparently you go on about Welshpool all the time and they're a bit sick of it.'

'Piss off!' Lily laughed.

'Lily,' Kirsty said, suddenly serious, 'remember the cottage we were going to get together? I've just seen the most perfect place. It's called Owl Cottage and it's in Montgomery, right in the town, and it's got a stream running through the bottom of the garden. And it's black and white and so pretty and about four hundred years old. It belonged to an artist. But he's just died, left his studio in the garden all ready for you. You will be coming back, won't you?'

How did she know there was any doubt? Lily wondered, touched that Kirsty was so in tune with her. The studio in the garden whetted her interest. And Montgomery was absolutely lovely. Why not at least have the summer there to decide where she was going to go next? She didn't want to be in London in the summer.

'We could have barbecues and parties in the garden.'

'With all our hundreds of friends,' said Lily drily.

Kirsty laughed. 'Well, invite some of yours down from London. Or we could always borrow Grace's!'

'What do you mean?'

'She's suddenly a different person. I see her everywhere I go.'

'I didn't realize there were so many places to go to. And how's Simon, by the way? Seen him anywhere?'

'Oh, no,' said Kirsty breezily. 'I'll tell you more when I see you. Talk about Grace, not me.'

'But has something else happened between you two? Have you sorted it out? Just tell me that?'

'Not with me, no. He's met someone else.'

'No!'

'Yes. Her car's parked in his drive.'

Simon couldn't have met someone else, Lily told herself, furious, not taken in by Kirsty's easy tone. Not so fast. He and Kirsty had barely been apart three weeks. What the fuck did he think he was doing? Kirsty and

Grace could do with poison tasters to check out their men, she thought, wondering how she might set up the service.

*

That night Lily had arranged to meet two of her former art college friends, Stella and Steph, who were living with a guy called Badger in a stark, trendy warehouse conversion in King's Cross. There'd been space for Lily too, and she'd still been considering whether to move in with them when she and Grace had had their fateful telephone conversation and she'd decided with some relief that she had to go to Welshpool instead.

What was it? she thought now, as Badger handed her a beer and showed her around. Had she changed so much since she'd last seen them, or had they? Or was it just that what little they'd had in common had been lost once the familiarity of day-to-day life in college was gone? Whatever it was, she felt now as if she hardly knew them.

'King's Cross,' Steph told her smugly, coming over to join her, 'has become the new Hoxton. Not,' she hastily reassured Lily, 'that Welshpool doesn't sound dead cool. Some of my best friends live in Wales.'

Lily thought Steph would find it much more dead than cool and thank God she was unlikely ever to make the two-hundred-mile journey to find out. But the warehouse was amazing and Lily had to admit it would have been fun to live there, if she could have got used to the complete lack of privacy. All the internal walls were suspended and had gaps of at least a foot at the top and bottom. Whatever happened in either the bathroom or the bedroom would be heard everywhere else.

A state-of-the-art internal lift took them up to the most spectacular roof terrace, and immediately she thought she could live with the floating walls if she could have this too. It was wonderful, and as she stood there sipping her beer and looking out across London she could understand why they felt they had arrived on the top of the world.

When Lily told them where she was being taken by Hal on Saturday night they laughed, taking it as an invitation to draw up a hit list of all the fabulously cool places that they frequented. Places like Aqua and Marley's and VoiceMail, they told her. Lily had nodded blankly. Then they would take her on to a couple of clubs.

They started off in the early evening in the West End, then moved deep into Soho, Steph, Stella and Badger moving her purposefully around the town as strategically as if she was the queen on a chessboard. By eleven, Lily was gliding down the streets in an intoxicated haze. She knew she'd never be able to remember where she'd been taken but, as she carefully selected another cocktail, a delicious pear daiquiri, in a slick bar somewhere in Wardour Street, she decided she didn't care. It simply felt wonderful to be out.

Later, she laid her hot cheek against the cool white-tiled walls of a loo somewhere deep in the bowels of Soho. They were brilliant people, she thought smiling. They were genuinely kind people who she could live with for ever. But she did miss Kirsty. It would have been fun to have had Kirsty with her now.

By half-past one they had moved across the Monopoly board of London, ending up in a club not far from where they had started out, full of dramatic deep shadows and candlelight, with vast high ceilings and glinting stone floors. As they queued to get in she could feel the beat of the music thumping through her, so loud her heart seemed to re-set to beat in time to the music.

For a while Lily danced and drank a little water, and then a huge wave of tiredness swept through her and she knew she had to go home. The others would stay until seven or eight and usually she'd have joined them, but all she wanted was her bed.

She motioned to her friends that she was going and they led her away from the dance floor, mouthing to her to keep in touch and smiling and kissing goodbye, then disappeared back into the heaving crowd. She left the club, grateful for the air and for the sight of a long line of taxis waiting to ferry her home.

She paid off the taxi driver and stumbled through the front door, the steady beat of music in her head already being drowned out by the insistent beat of a hangover, brewing before she'd even had the chance to sleep. Somehow she managed to pull off her tiny skirt and skimpy T-shirt, drop them on the floor, then drag on another T-shirt to sleep in and to make it to the bathroom. They'd drunk nothing like as much as her, she thought, looking at her haggard face, picturing them still dancing. She slung herself across Josie's bed, too out of it even to get under the duvet, and let the welcome clouds of sleep immediately gather her up and float her away.

A little later, she found she was still half awake. Through the daze she took in the fact that somewhere in the room a high, persistent peeping, like a half-hearted alarm clock, had stopped her from dropping off to sleep. She climbed out of bed and padded around the room in the shadowy grey light and traced the insistent peep to her mobile. She pulled it out of her bag and squinted at it suspiciously. What the hell? What did it want? She was sure she'd turned it off before she'd gone out. She looked more closely and saw that she was being warned that the batteries were low, and also that she had a text message.

If you are interested, she scrolled down, *in my side of the story*, she scrolled down again, *call me tomorrow*.

She pressed and pressed, not registering the message at all, and with relief she saw the lights go out. Then she threw the phone into her handbag, padded back to the bed and slid under the duvet, too sleepy to take the message in, or to think whom it might have been from.

12

Kirsty couldn't believe that Simon had met someone else so fast. The fact that it was someone with such a ridiculous name as Mimosa McAlpine would have made her laugh if she hadn't been so miserable, because he had so obviously fallen back into old habits. She would be a stunning size eight and as thick as a barn door. Obviously not someone who should get too fond of Pond House, but no doubt having some fun while she kept his interest.

Three weeks had gone by since she and Simon had split up. Whereas every break up in the old days had prompted a celebratory party with her friends, this time all she wanted to do was stay at home. Initially she tried to deny that it was Simon keeping her there and still made the odd effort to keep in touch with other friends, but without Lily around to distract her she quickly began to give in, finding herself thinking about Simon obsessively, all the time. Without Lily there to encourage her into action, there was no possibility at all of Kirsty making contact with him. She was too much of a coward to do it on her own. And now that Mimosa had arrived with the spring, it seemed to confirm that their relationship was truly over.

Her mother's constant refrain, *it's such a shame about Simon*, and the fact that it never occurred to her mother that this was any worse for Kirsty than it was for her, that she might be twisting the knife every time she mentioned his name, made it easier for Kirsty to decide once and for all that she was leaving home. She was too old to have to put up with it. When her mother proceeded to tell Kirsty all about Mimosa, Kirsty left the house and promptly joined the books of all the local estate agents, determined that if the Montgomery cottage fell through she would have alternatives already lined up.

Maybe I'm finally growing up, Kirsty thought miserably, when she realized she was recognizing most of the contestants on *University Challenge* as they returned to do battle in the later rounds. Maybe this despair was a necessary evil. Perhaps she had to go through all this heartache in order to ensure that she never lost another Simon, if she was lucky enough to meet someone half as good as him ever again.

Kirsty didn't want to come face to face with him but she was not averse to spying on him, particularly if there was a chance of a glimpse of Mimosa. She cruised several times past his house but never saw her. All she saw, every time, was her car. A scarlet, shiny, in-your-face Mercedes sports car, sitting there on the gravel, smug and proprietorial. Why didn't Mimosa ever drive her car, Kirsty wanted to know? Why didn't it ever, ever leave Simon's drive? Probably because Simon was keeping her housebound. Housebound and knickerless, she thought bitterly. She wanted to push the car out between the gates and down the hill that stretched away from Pond House, down to the conveniently placed Montgomery Canal lying at the bottom. Now she understood why the scorned lovers she read about in the *Daily Mail* so often focused on the cars, daubing them in pink paint, or better still, paint-stripper, or setting them on fire.

Having spoken to Lily in London, Kirsty found herself once again edging towards Pond House in her car. This time, for once, it was a valid journey. The conversation with Lily had finally stimulated some desire to see people, and she'd called up some friends and was on the way to meet them in a pub near Simon's village, for a drink.

It was seven thirty as she drove towards Simon's house, and very dark, much too dark to hope to see anything of interest, like Mimosa. But as she got close to the delicate wrought-iron gates, she saw that there were bright lights coming on in the drive and then the door of the house opened in front of her. This was it, she thought, this time she was going to see her.

Kirsty slowed and changed down into first gear. It was frustratingly hard to get a proper look, as there was a huge bank forcing a sharp right-angled turn just a few hundred yards ahead of her. At the most there was just four seconds' staring time.

The front door was open, spilling light out into the drive, and she watched fascinated, expecting some leggy, tarty human equivalent to the car to come stepping out into the darkness. But the girl who suddenly appeared was wearing jeans and wellingtons and a thick stripy jumper and, even over the noise of her engine, Kirsty could hear her laughing.

Kirsty just had time to take in a face shining in the lamplight and then the solid black bank came up hard and terrifyingly huge in her windscreen. She hit it at about ten miles an hour, with her mouth open in shock, and heard herself make a painful *oof* of protest as the steering-wheel shoved into her, knocking all the breath out of her chest, and then the engine died.

She slowly lifted her head. She could hear that she was groaning in desperate breaths as her shocked lungs struggled for air, and her ribs felt so painful that she wondered if one of them was broken. She sat for a moment, trying to stop herself making such an awful noise, willing herself to recover before Simon emerged to find out what had happened. But in the wing mirror she could see she was too late. Simon was already appearing through his gates, and then, when he saw her car, was breaking into a run. Lovely, lovely, darling Simon, Kirsty thought miserably, as he raced towards her, completely unattainable.

And behind him, more hesitantly, came the girl, chubby-faced and fluffy-haired, sweet-looking and appalled.

Oh please no, Kirsty thought despairingly, more affected by the sight of Mimosa than by the crash. It was worse, far worse than crashing the car, to realize that Mimosa was not the red-taloned, predatory bit of totty she'd conveniently presumed her to be.

Simon came around to her side of the door and opened it swiftly.

'What happened?' he asked, looking grey in the light of the car. 'Are you all right?'

'It's okay,' Kirsty groaned, feeling utterly humiliated. 'I'm fine.'

'You'll have to come inside.' He straightened up, glancing away from her back down the lane to where Mimosa was cautiously making her way towards them. He ran his hand through his black hair. Then he turned back to her. 'Looking at your car, we don't have much choice.'

'Surely I was going too slowly to do any damage?'

Kirsty stared up at him with miserable eyes. She bit her lip at his brusque words, feeling tears start to wet her cheeks. Yet even when he was being curt, Simon was still more capable and reassuring than anyone else she'd ever known. At that moment, in pain and shock, she would have died for the comfort of being wrapped up in his arms.

Mimosa arrived and leaned in over his shoulder.

'Don't cry,' she said, smiling. 'You'll be okay. Come in to the house and I'll give you a drink. I'm sure Simon can get the tractor to pull your car into our drive.'

Kirsty shook her head. 'I'll phone my dad. I've got my mobile.'

'That's ridiculous,' Simon snapped at her. 'You're outside my house.'

In the darkness Kirsty saw Mimosa shoot Simon a surprised, questioning look.

Any mental agility that Kirsty could usually rely on seemed to have departed her brain. She was sure there was a brilliant reason why she should wait, alone and vulnerable in the dark lane, for her dad to come and pick her up, but somehow nothing came to mind. Much as

Kirsty did not want to walk up 'our' drive into the Happy Families household that was now Pond House, she seemed to have no choice.

And it was much worse than she thought. Mimosa took her arm and helped her out of the car, leaving Simon to jog back to the house to find a rope and get the tractor. She led her through the front door, and there, just inside, in the flickering hall she knew so well, was an open bottle of champagne on the dark oak table and two glasses sitting on the flagstones beside the crackling fire.

No, no, this is what we did. You can't be doing it too. Not like this.

She looked around the hall, half expecting to see a pair of knickers dangling off the huge stone mantelpiece.

'I can't come in. I don't want to interrupt your evening,' she said woodenly.

'Oh, that doesn't matter.' Mimosa waved it away. 'We were staying in anyway. We were just going to fetch more logs when we heard you crashing your car.'

She took Kirsty over to the fire. 'Come on, warm yourself up,' she suggested. She drained one of the glasses of champagne, refilled it and handed it to Kirsty. 'Don't worry,' she smiled. 'I haven't got germs.'

Kirsty took it from her and gave her a sidelong glance. No, she thought. Mimosa wouldn't have germs. She was nothing like Kirsty had expected. Pretty but not knock-out, with heavily mascara'd eyelashes and determined blue eyes. She wasn't slim but she had athletic legs and big breasts. And if the firelight revealed the stripy jumper to be definitely more Laura Ashley than Kookai, that, sadly, was no reason to dislike her. Under different circumstances they might even have become good friends.

Outside Kirsty could hear Simon opening heavy doors, and then the tractor spluttered into life and chuff-chuffed past the window, out through the front gates and on towards her car.

'Come and sit down, you poor thing,' Mimosa told her with a beaming smile.

Kirsty did as she was told, thinking how much Mimosa seemed to be enjoying the situation. Not if you knew about me and your boyfriend, she thought wearily.

She sank into a deep tartan armchair and leaned forwards to warm her hands on the fire.

'And you mustn't worry about Simon. Now he knows you're all right, he'll be having fun. Doing the knight in shining armour bit.'

Not for me he won't be.

There was a pause.

'Do you know, that was how Simon and I met?' Mimosa told her enthusiastically. 'He was my knight in shining armour too.'

No doubt she wanted to sound bright and conversational but her words came out unnaturally loud, and after she'd said them she swallowed hard. It left Kirsty in no doubt that Mimosa did know about her and Simon. Knew exactly the score between them. More than that, it was as if she was telling Kirsty that she knew, wanting to show that she wasn't about to be intimidated by her.

You've got it wrong, Kirsty thought, if you're thinking

like that. I'm not about to challenge you for him. You're nothing to me.'

'I'd got a flat tyre in the Safeway car-park, and Simon offered to change it.'

'How romantic,' said Kirsty.

'Yes. It was actually!' Mimosa smiled determinedly at Kirsty. 'Come on, baby, change my tyre! He was perfect.'

As Mimosa talked, she started to relax, leaning back in her chair, and settling herself down to tell the story.

'It was dark and pissing down with rain, I'd found the jack and the spanners but I'd been working up the courage to get the wheel off for about half an hour! And then, suddenly, there he was! His car was parked right next to mine and he was on his way home. God, I was so grateful!' She heaved a happy sigh at the memory. 'And then the most amazing thing was, we went for a quick drink at the Little Goose and realized we knew each other already! We hadn't seen each other for years but we'd been at nearby schools and we'd been to all the same parties. I couldn't believe my luck! When I was fourteen I'd fancied the pants off him.' She drifted off, a fatuous smile now on her face. 'And then before I knew it, I was moving in here. Of course he tells everyone that it was only my car he was interested in!' She laughed.

'And was it?' Kirsty asked without thinking.

'No!' Mimosa looked surprised and then rather irritated. 'Of course not!'

She disappeared into the kitchen and then came back out again a few moments later with another glass of champagne and an enormous bowl of crisps. She sat down opposite Kirsty.

'That was very quick,' Kirsty ventured, 'you moving in.'

'I don't think so,' Mimosa told her swiftly. 'It felt right. And if I see something I want, I tend not to let it out of my sight.'

Ho hum, Kirsty thought. She supposed she should have thought the same.

She wondered what had led Mimosa to the Safeway car-park in Welshpool. Why had she come at all? Had she been passing through the town on her way to somewhere else, and had only decided to stay because of Simon, or was she always going to stay on? But she couldn't bring herself to encourage more conversation and find out.

'You were lucky,' Mimosa told her, an evil look in her eye. 'That could have been a very nasty bump.' She knocked back some more champagne and took a handful of crisps, then said deliberately, 'And you must have got to know the roads around here so well . . .'

Kirsty glanced at her, surprised that Mimosa would say something so barbed. But Mimosa immediately dropped to her knees to throw the last log on the fire. Still, a blotching red flush was spreading up from her neck.

Oh, so I do bother you, do I? Kirsty thought wearily, her head and back and ribs aching even more. I'm not surprised. It's horrible having me in your new house, is it? Well, actually, it's horrible being here too. And as soon as I can I'll be on my way.

'No,' Kirsty reassured her, 'not much time to get to know the roads. I was hardly ever here.'

It wasn't the truth. Kirsty had driven or been driven around there all her life, and in the brief time with Simon had had many opportunities to practise the turn into his drive. But while she decided that she didn't much like Mimosa, she didn't hate her for feeling competitive. If anything, Kirsty felt sorry for her. Kirsty was angry with herself for losing Simon and she wanted him back, but she wasn't going to get any relief from hurting Mimosa.

'I hope nobody drives into him,' Kirsty said, changing the subject. She rubbed her neck, wondering if she had whiplash.

'You don't need to worry about that!' Mimosa told her readily, now glad to move on to safer ground. 'And if anyone does, Simon will come off best. You may be surprised to know that tractors have excellent headlights.'

No, I won't be surprised, Kirsty thought irritably. I know that. I grew up on a farm.

'Although why they need them I can't imagine. Have you ever seen a farmer working at night?'

And don't say that either.

'Yes, of course,' Kirsty replied, 'all the time.'

'Pooh,' said Mimosa. 'They're too busy filling out their subsidy forms.'

What was that? Taken aback, Kirsty felt that at last things were looking up. Mimosa had definitely said 'pooh', and her last comment was rather unpleasant. Kirsty was relieved that there were now some good grounds for disliking her. She followed Mimosa into the kitchen, staring after her hopefully.

'I adore the countryside,' Mimosa told her melodramatically. 'And around here is as good as it gets. I could never live in a city again.'

Oh hurrah! Kirsty thought grimly.

'Which is lucky,' Mimosa went on, back to her old self, 'because Dad's offered to buy us some land. He's dying for me to put down some roots – literally! And we'll be able to show everyone how it should be done. I want to provide all the meat and veg for the Little Goose. Simon doesn't know about it yet, so don't say anything.'

Noticing the expression on Kirsty's face, Mimosa pulled a chair out from the kitchen table for her to sit down on. 'Look how pale you are! You need some Nurofen.' She now seemed genuinely concerned. 'I should have got them for you ages ago.'

Kirsty shook her head. 'Honestly, I don't have a headache, I'm fine.'

'I'm going to have a horse, too,' she told Kirsty, looking as if she was going to burst with enthusiasm for her wonderful new life.

It gets better and better, Kirsty thought. 'But do you know anything about horses?' she asked. 'Or farming?'

'Not much,' Mimosa admitted, opening a drawer. 'We'll be organic, of course. And I'm willing to learn. You're going to have to give me lots of tips.' She was sounding much brighter, as if she'd assessed Kirsty, and was pleased to find that she was no threat after all.

'I don't think so.'

'Oh yes, you must,' Mimosa insisted. She walked over and put a glass of water and two Nurofen into Kirsty's hand. 'Plough the fields and scatter. You're quite the local hero, aren't you,' she said, smiling down at her, an irresistible little dig that was out before she'd thought about it.

'What do you mean?'

At the tone of Kirsty's voice, Mimosa looked uneasy. 'I was talking about your job,' she insisted quickly. 'And about how much everyone seems to love you.'

Kirsty knew it wasn't true but she hadn't the energy to retaliate. She felt suddenly very vulnerable, bruised and bumped and unable to cope with the undercurrents and barbs being thrown at her. She longed to be away.

'Come into the Warehouse some time,' Kirsty suggested, 'not that I know the first thing about the important stuff. You'll have to get a farm manager to help you with that.'

Mimosa laughed in relief. 'God, yes! Of course I will. Don't think it'll be me wading through the cow shit or biting the balls off the young lambs.'

Just don't push your luck, Little Miss Chirpy, Kirsty thought. Or I might still find the energy to strangle you.

Mimosa glanced at her and didn't like what she saw. She moved to the other end of the kitchen. 'Feeling better now?'

'Much better, thank you,' Kirsty replied politely. 'I don't think I've done any permanent damage.' She rotated her head to the left and then the right, massaging her neck with one hand. 'I should call my friends and tell them where I am. Do you mind?' She dug into her bag and found her mobile.

'No, not at all. Give Simon a chance to bring back your car and I'm sure he'll drop you home.'

Kirsty called her friends and her parents, then sat back to wait for Simon. She even accepted Mimosa's offer of another glass of champagne.

Mimosa took her back through to the fire and they sat opposite each other in the throne-like armchairs and sipped champagne and stared into the flames.

'So, when do you think the farmers around here will wake up and smell the coffee?' Mimosa asked Kirsty, making a last attempt at conversation, still under the impression that this was a subject Kirsty would enjoy chewing over with her.

'What do you mean?'

'Realize that they have to stop waiting for someone else – us – to bail them out. Doesn't it annoy you?'

Kirsty didn't respond.

'Well, it annoys *me*! We've paid out a complete fortune for foot and mouth, and they're still exactly the same. Moaning, moaning, moaning. If BSE didn't ruin them, foot and mouth did, or the strong pound, or whatever else they can come up with to complain about. They forget that no one's making them do it!' Her eyes were wide and indignant-looking. 'They should find something more profitable if they can't afford to farm. Open a golf-course, or breed llamas or something. Don't you think?'

She was so far away from Kirsty then, that Kirsty knew

it was hardly worth arguing with her, and yet Mimosa was so appallingly ignorant and lacking in compassion that Kirsty found she couldn't keep quiet.

'If you let me take you to visit a few of the farms around here, you would never say something like that again. You have absolutely no idea what you're talking about.'

Mimosa was momentarily thrown, taken aback by the warning in Kirsty's voice, and the real emotion in her eyes. She looked back at her defiantly, but then turned and left the room.

Why did I bother, Kirsty asked herself. Why bother to explain to someone who didn't understand, and who wasn't interested anyway, that golf-courses depended on hundreds of people to come and play on them and that they cost hundreds of thousands of unattainable pounds to set up. That it wasn't llamas that could eat the short wiry grass but sheep. And that the farmers who'd battled through the soul destroying foot and mouth epidemic were fighting against the odds for their survival. That while everyone still wanted lamb and pork and beef on their tables, kept potatoes and carrots in their cupboards, needed sugar in their tea, and bread in the bread bins, there was now barely a role for farmers, as once there had been. How hard it was to understand that if they continued to care for their animals and cultivate the crops, it wouldn't be possible for them to be paid enough to survive on. Enough to have hope for the future and to stem the tide of suicides and bankruptcies and end the prospect of much of the countryside becoming a scrubby, deserted landscape, marked just occasionally by a groomed, green golf-course.

How had Simon managed to avoid hearing all this, Kirsty wondered? Or perhaps she'd got him wrong and he couldn't care less as long as he carried on getting hold of the produce he wanted for the Little Goose. Perhaps he would agree with Mimosa? Especially when he found out that Daddy was buying them land. Maybe it made Mimosa adorable? No. She couldn't pretend she didn't know Simon well enough to know he'd surely never think like that.

As if she had summoned him by thinking about him, Simon lifted the heavy iron latch and came in through the front door. The cold night air and the exertion had left him with a wild, windblown, Heathcliffian look. Simon must have known that she was waiting for him on the other side, and yet Kirsty caught a startled look that said he still hadn't prepared himself for seeing her there beside the fire. Kirsty smiled at him and he immediately disappeared into the kitchen.

'You okay, babes?' Mimosa called.

'Yes, of course.' Simon stood in the doorway with what Kirsty guessed was a Jack Daniels in his hand. He seemed to have got himself under better control now and even managed the briefest of smiles at them both.

He came and sat down on the rug at Mimosa's feet, leaned back against her legs and looked up at Kirsty. 'How are you doing?'

'She's fine,' said Mimosa.

'I think I'm fine.' Kirsty gazed at him. 'How's my car?'

'It'll cost more than it's worth to have the dents knocked out. At least fifty quid.' He smiled at her until she swallowed and looked away.

It was so hard, so bloody hard, to see him sitting there like that with Mimosa.

Behind him Mimosa started rubbing the back of his neck with her foot. He caught it in one hand, holding it still in its pale green angora sock while she wiggled her toes in delight.

Kirsty wondered how much Mimosa knew about her and Simon. She doubted that Mimosa would be sitting there quite so comfortably if she knew that Simon had once run naked out of the room where the three of them were sitting now, up to his bedroom to fetch the duvet and pillows off his bed, and had made him and Kirsty a nest in front of the fire, on the big square rug now acting as No Man's Land between her and Mimosa. He'd lifted Kirsty up in his arms, then dropped her gently into the goose-down before leaning over to kiss her in the fire-light's soft glow. And that it had been their first time together, and perfect enough for her to think that she would never let him go.

Looking at him, she was sure he was remembering too.

'You shouldn't drive something so flimsy,' Mimosa told Kirsty quietly, obviously emboldened by Simon's touch. 'You had absolutely no protection.'

Simon started to smile at the sight of Kirsty's angry face.

'Yes, I think Mimosa's right,' he told her seriously. 'Perhaps you should get a Land Rover? Something more robust.'

Kirsty glared at him.

'Or a tractor?' Mimosa giggled.

Kirsty had had enough. 'Will you take me home now, Simon?' She stood up abruptly. 'They'll be waiting for me. Thanks, Mimosa,' she added, 'it was good to meet you.'

Mimosa took hold of Kirsty's hand. 'All I can say is, thank God it happened outside our front door.' She shook her head. 'And thank God you're all right. I am so glad we were here to help and that I had the chance to meet you. And I hope you feel better in the morning.'

'I feel fine now,' Kirsty told her, removing her hand. 'Much better. But I want to go home.'

Kirsty slipped on her coat and walked slowly outside ahead of Simon, grateful for the dark. Simon followed her out and Mimosa waved him goodbye at the front door, then closed it, leaving them alone.

Simon's car was parked in an old stable building just a hundred feet or so from Pond House and they walked there slowly, side by side, their hands occasionally brushing together. There was an unbearable intimacy about him being so close. Heightened awareness meant she could feel the hairs on her arm nearest to his rising in excitement. Her heart thumped in pointless anticipation and she felt as if the dark night, the stars, the moon, were there only as a backdrop to her and Simon.

But all too soon they'd reached his car and nothing had

happened, nothing had been said, and there were only seconds left before the noisy engine and bright headlights broke the intensity of the moment.

She grabbed for his hand, surprising herself as much as him. It was a strong warm hand and at the touch a great flood of longing poured through her.

His hand stayed resolutely unresponsive in hers, but at least he didn't pull away and that gave her hope. Slowly she threaded each of her fingers through each of his and held on to him, and waited, and after what felt like forever, his hand sprang shut around hers. It was the most charged, erotic moment she had ever known.

In the darkness she moved to face him, saw him open his mouth to say something, his white teeth bright in the moonlight, the last glimpses of anger and vulnerability disappearing from his face, and desire growing in his eyes.

Before he could change his mind, she turned to him, pressing his hand between both of hers, but he pulled himself free and grabbed her roughly towards him, his hands touching her thick dark hair, kissing her so hard that their teeth clashed against each other.

She shoved her hips against him, feeling him hard against her, and his hands slipped down her back to cup her buttocks, holding her there. She wanted to sink to the ground with him there and then, to pull him down on top of her, guide his fingers through the zip on her jeans to pull aside her pants, to feel the ground cold against her back.

But almost before he'd started Simon stopped again.

Even though he still had his arms wrapped tightly around her, he lifted his head and rested his chin on the top of her head and she knew that she'd lost him.

'I'm sorry, darling Kirsty, but I can't do this again.'

He gently pushed her away from him, holding her at arm's length for a moment before letting her go. This was rejection. Kirsty had never been turned down at such a critical point before, never been turned down at all before.

'Why?' she almost cried.

'Because,' he said, 'you and I, for whatever reason, didn't work out. Whatever caused it to go wrong the first time hasn't gone away. It's probably not the coolest thing to say but I don't want to get hurt by you again.'

'Oh, Simon!' Kirsty said desperately, looking up at him. 'You can't say that! I don't know why I didn't come running after you but I know now it was the stupidest thing ever. Please!' she begged, 'can't you give me another chance?'

'No,' Simon shook his head. 'I'm not saying it because I want to play games. You know that's not my style. And I don't want to hurt you.' He looked down at her and smiled sadly. 'Even though you completely gutted me. But I don't believe it would work any better second time around than it did the first.'

'It would.'

'No, it wouldn't,' Simon said gently.

'It would.'

He didn't say anything.

'You're being so stubborn.' She looked pleadingly up at him. 'But I suppose there's Mimosa now. Of course,' she added bitterly when he didn't answer, 'let's not forget Mimosa.'

Simon nodded. 'Let's not forget Mimosa.'

She turned away from him then and opened the car door, so disappointed she couldn't speak. Once sitting beside her, Simon accelerated away so fast that gravel was flung wildly against the house.

'Slower, please,' she snapped. 'I've already had one accident tonight.'

He nodded and slowed down but there was still an urgency to the way he drove, an obvious eagerness to get her home.

I can't ever try again, Kirsty vowed, watching his profile as he concentrated on the road and wanting him more than ever. Or think about him any more. I will get over him and on with my life. And I'll meet someone else, and be just as happy.

'Has Mimosa moved in?' she asked despite herself, throwing Simon a quick sidelong glance.

'Yup.'

'That was quick.'

'Not especially.'

She tried to catch the expression on his face but he wasn't giving anything away.

'I didn't like her.'

'Well, how grown up of you.'

Kirsty smiled despite herself. 'Forget you and me. She's a Nazi bitch and I can't believe you've let her stay three days, let alone three weeks.'

Simon didn't answer.

'Okay, I'm sorry,' Kirsty said. 'You're right, I'm being childish.' She bit her lip. 'But I still don't like her. And tell me you two haven't slept beside the fire, like we did.'

'Not yet, but thanks for reminding me.' He turned to her. 'Don't play games, Kirsty,' he said sharply. 'You told me what you wanted and you got it. I've done only what you asked me to do. You can't get jealous when I meet someone else.'

'I know I can't but I have! And don't act like you don't understand what I'm talking about!' Kirsty told him angrily. 'You had your tongue down my throat less than ten minutes ago!'

'I know I did!' He looked at her and grinned. 'But I still don't want another relationship with you.'

'Okay,' Kirsty said with a sigh, 'just the sex, then.'

She made him laugh, restoring a little of her pride, but still she felt utterly miserable. Thank God they were nearly at Little Venus Farm and she could leap out of the car and get away from him.

He pulled up outside her parents' house and unclipped her seat belt.

'I didn't think you'd be like this.' He said it as a question, as if he was surprised that he could be hurting her. 'You seemed so sure.'

There was nothing else to do. Without replying, she opened her door and slipped out of the car, kept her head down and walked away.

You kissed me like you meant it, she thought stubbornly, booting open the front door. Now you're telling me you can walk away, but you're pretending that it meant nothing. Because, for a few moments there, I know I had you back. You can drive away from me but I don't believe you really want to go.

In answer, Simon's black Porsche swung past her in a fast circle and then left her alone.

13

Afterwards it seemed to Kirsty that she saw Mimosa all the time. Kirsty could never be sure if it was deliberate or not. Mimosa never showed any sign of noticing her, and yet she was always coming out of shops as Kirsty went in to them, or passing her on the street or in her car when Kirsty drove to work, and Kirsty couldn't quite believe that Mimosa didn't once register her presence. She wondered again what it was that had brought Mimosa to Welshpool in the first place. Asking around, she learned that Mimosa worked for an antique dealer somewhere in the south of England and that she was supposed to be recceing her way through Shropshire and mid-Wales, sniffing out bargains.

Whenever she was asked, Mimosa was always completely open about the fact that she wasn't very interested in antiques. She'd found herself falling into the job because she didn't know what else to do and because she fancied her boss – a friend of her father's – and because she liked the idea of telling people she was an antique dealer. Preoccupied with making money, and highly competitive, she was really motivated by the buzz of finding the bargains ahead of someone else, picking things up for a fraction of their value. And although bargains were no longer easily found, it was in the country houses, antique shops and auctions of Wales and the North of England where she found most of the little gems she could sell in the south for ten times more than she'd paid.

This time, she had been concentrating her efforts on Hope Castle, a tiny, perfect, russet-red castle dating back to the 1300s, built to withstand the murderous Welsh, and now to be converted into a luxury hotel. During the afternoon on the day she'd met Simon, and after painstaking spadework, she'd managed to wangle a private view with the frail Lord Hope, who, with no children to pass the castle on to, had sold his castle and was now disposing of its contents after living there for all his eighty-seven years. What had particularly caught the interest of Mimosa, and a good many other dealers too, was the fact that Hopes had lived at Hope Castle for four hundred years and had never before sold anything of value. Until the contents were listed and catalogued, nobody had any idea of what might be inside. Mimosa had won the chance of an invaluable private view – but then she'd met Simon and hadn't turned up.

Standing in the rain in the Safeway car-park, watching Simon working at her wheel with his coat off and his jersey pulled up to the elbows, her first thought had been, what a waste. What a waste that she'd found such a man here, because in her dismissive way that meant he was either an impoverished antiquarian bookseller or a struggling market gardener who had downsized because he hadn't been able to cope with real life. But then there had been that wonderful moment of surprise, as they had talked in the Little Goose and she had realized he wasn't the hopeless yokel she'd had him down for. She'd found herself thinking how attractive he was, and then he'd said something that made her realize that she knew him already, that he was the same impressively cool Simon Campion she'd known briefly at school. But the best moment had been when she'd peeped through the heavy velvet curtain that divided the restaurant from the pub, and watched Simon go over to talk to the manager on duty that night, and she had finally clicked that he was dynamic and stylish and booming with energy and that the dynamic and stylish Little Goose was all his.

She was thirty-four and tired of her single-girl's life-style in London. Tired of her little flat and of sleeping with her greying, fifty-five-year-old boss. The day after meeting Simon, she'd rung Lord Hope to be told that there was no possibility at all of rearranging her meeting. Where once she would have cried at the lost opportunity, now she didn't care at all. And a week after meeting Simon she'd rung her boss to tell him that she wasn't coming back.

One of the few things she worried about was Kirsty. Even before she had met her, she had realized from one or two idle lines of Simon's that she should classify Kirsty in the danger category, and the look on Simon's face when he'd realized whose car had hit the bank outside his house only confirmed what she'd already guessed. But, even worse, there was something powerfully alluring about Kirsty herself that nobody needed to tell her about. Something in the way she moved, something in the way she spoke, whatever it was, it had the power to make men buckle at the knees. What was strange for Mimosa was that more often than not she'd had that same effect on men and had never, until now, had to battle it out with someone like herself. Girls had often been far more beautiful than her but she'd always been the one to get the man she wanted. And although she must have come up against other Kirstys before, this was the first time that it had really mattered, that she'd been made to feel hopelessly vulnerable.

And so, just as Kirsty had stalked Pond House in the hope of catching sight of Mimosa, now Mimosa found herself watching out for Kirsty.

The morning after the accident, Mimosa came into the Warehouse, ostensibly to check that Kirsty was feeling better.

'Yes, thank you very much,' said Kirsty briskly, wanting the chat over and done with, aware of two other customers in the shop whose ears were already pricking up expectantly.

Mimosa didn't appear to notice. She played for time, looking behind Kirsty at the shelves of goods.

'I'm sorry,' Kirsty told her after one or two more inane attempts at conversation on Mimosa's part, 'I really have to get on here.'

'Oh well, maybe we can have a drink some time.'

Kirsty ignored the offer and Mimosa reluctantly left.

*

All the time, Kirsty missed Lily miserably. They'd spoken only once since she'd gone to London, following Lily's conversation with Amber, but after that there'd been the car accident and meeting Mimosa and the excruciating time with Simon, and Kirsty hadn't yet had a chance to tell Lily any of it.

In the days since Lily had gone, Kirsty had been to see Owl Cottage in Montgomery twice more, and had registered her serious, serious interest, feeling that if she put down roots for both of them she could ensure that Lily stayed. But even if Lily didn't stay, Kirsty knew that she herself was finally leaving home. On her salary she could just afford the rent on her own, and although there was another cheaper cottage that she was due to see that evening, she'd set her heart on moving to Owl Cottage.

Every third Saturday, Kirsty had to work at the Warehouse, and with Lily due back the next day, working this particular Saturday was a welcome distraction. That said, it was so quiet that by eleven nobody had been in to see her. Then, in the late morning, one of her farmers came in, Fred Gittins, an old man who'd decided after their first meeting that Kirsty was the most wonderful creature he'd ever laid eyes on and had made regular visits to the Warehouse every week since.

He came hesitantly through the door, glanced around the shop and rubbed his hands with satisfaction when he saw that she was alone.

'Hello, Fred,' Kirsty said, delighted to have some company, getting up to greet him and knowing from the look on his face that he had something to tell her.

Fred waved her to sit down again and then gave all his

attention to getting over to her desk, forcing his bandy, arthritic legs to move a great deal faster than they were used to. When he arrived, he put both hands on her desk in relief and leaned towards her.

'You've not been looking after yourself,' he told her gruffly, studying her face with watery blue eyes.

'No. You heard I bumped my car?'

'Arr,' he nodded, 'and hit your head.'

He took his time, looking over her face, and then when he was satisfied there was nothing seriously wrong, came and lowered himself slowly down in the chair beside her.

She waited, enjoying the fact that there weren't going to be any words of sympathy. Happy in the knowledge that he would do anything he could for her, at any time.

'You've come to tell me something, haven't you?'

'Arr,' Fred agreed, not giving any more away for the moment.

Kirsty waited. This was part of the Fred routine.

'You know that new filly over at Pond House?' he said eventually, looking down at his boots.

'Oh, he hasn't got her one already?' Kirsty burst out with disgust. 'Mimosa was telling me about it.'

When Mimosa had told Kirsty she was getting a horse, she must have had a horse in mind, Kirsty realized. She and Simon must have picked it up already.

'Bugger!' Kirsty told Fred. Simon must be keener than she'd realized. 'So where's Simon going to stable her?'

'In the house, I should hope!' Fred said, a delighted smile stretching across his face.

Kirsty looked at him blankly and then she laughed. 'So

229

you're talking about Mimosa, are you, Fred?' she checked. 'There isn't a new horse?'

'Mi-moh-sar,' Fred said slowly, repeating her name. 'Arr. That's her name. That's the one I'm talking about, Kirsty.' He fished a handkerchief out of his trouser pocket and coughed deeply. 'I'm not going to say that it should be you there.' He folded up his handkerchief and stuffed it back in his trousers, then leaned forward conspiratorially. 'But what I've got to tell you just might make you feel a little bit better about all that.' He nodded again, eyes watering, relishing what he was about to say.

'Mi-moh-sar,' he told her with glee, 'is being stabled in the spare bedroom.'

Kirsty sat back, wanting to pretend that this news didn't matter either way, but at the same time a warm trickle of hope began to flow through her veins.

'That's right,' Fred told her, puffed up with pleasure at her reaction, noticing everything. 'Simon agreed to put her up for a few nights around the time when she had that meeting arranged at Hope Castle. And he's never managed to get her out again.'

'But how do you know this?' Before she really believed it, Kirsty wanted to hear that the news was on good authority.

Fred thought about it. 'I wouldn't know how I know,' he told her slowly and earnestly, 'but I expect it was Beth Linden told Mary.'

Now Kirsty could see it might all be true. Mary was Fred's wife, and Mrs Linden cleaned Pond House for

Simon. It was Mrs Linden who'd first set the tongues wagging when she'd encountered Kirsty slinking down the stairs one morning, trying to avoid her, and her beady eyes would definitely take in evidence of Mimosa sleeping in the spare bed rather than Simon's.

'And so we were thinking, Mary and me, that you should let your Simon know that you're still soft on him. Otherwise you might find Mi-moh-sar never leaves. You can do that, now as you know you're not stepping on any toes.'

Not that that ever bothered me, Kirsty thought. But I don't mind you thinking it did.

Mimosa had been the evidence and proof that Simon had moved on and away from her. Now, if what Fred said was true, there was reason to hope again after all. But imagining baring her soul to him once more, putting herself again in the firing line, she thought that she couldn't bear to do it. That if anything ever did happen again, it would have to be because he made the running.

*

After Fred had left the shop she tried to settle down to clear some invoicing, but she couldn't concentrate and time and again she found herself at the window, imagining that if she waited long enough she would see Simon pulling up outside.

So Mimosa was a fraud, she thought with gleeful pleasure. She should have guessed. She remembered Simon catching Mimosa's foot as the three of them sat beside the fire and wondered if he'd done it deliberately to punish Kirsty? Or had it been a spontaneous gesture of affection, to someone who was perhaps a true old friend?

It was a pearl-grey day, the air hard and cold, and Kirsty had to search the sky to find the pale light of the sun. It was going to snow, she realized, looking up at the laden, low clouds. How lovely would that be? A childish rush of hope and excitement gripped her and she felt she had to get away from the Warehouse. She wanted to go for a walk, to climb high up to the ruins of Montgomery Castle and watch the snow arrive.

But she couldn't leave. Although customers were thin on the ground this morning, she couldn't close the shop until four. She continued to gaze out of the window, occasionally stretching her back and neck, trying to relieve the stiffness she'd felt since the accident and thinking obsessively about Simon. Thinking again and again about how he'd kissed her, convincing herself that she was going to get him back, particularly now that she knew he hadn't promptly fallen in love with somebody else. That even if he told himself he didn't want to get involved, he wouldn't be able to resist her, and that gradually she would wear him down, persuade him to trust her again. And Mimosa? Mimosa could now be cast aside. She didn't deserve him.

The stiffness in her back was bad and with her all the time, and with her legs straight she let her arms swing towards her toes, feeling the muscles in her back burning and then gradually starting to loosen up. Despite the aches and pains, she knew it had been only a relatively gentle bump, and apart from a round bruise on her forehead and a longer, deeper one just below her collarbone there was little to show for it. She swung her arms backwards and forwards a few times more, then stood up again and checked her watch, yawned and looked back out of the window. Then shut her mouth again in shock. Jogging towards her, in white lycra running shorts with a minidisk attached to her belt and a baseball cap on her head, was Mimosa.

Oh, not again, Kirsty thought, ducking away from the window. Who did she least want to see that day?

She raced to the door, flipped the Open sign to Closed, and swept the desk clear of her bits. Just off the main room of the Warehouse was a tiny annexe, more a cupboard than another room, housing three metal feed-bins. She lifted the lid off the first and climbed clumsily inside, dropping the lid gently down over her head. Only a day ago it had been three-quarters full of Flash Nuts for Show Ponies and she thanked the competitive, Sloaney mother who had cleaned it out the evening before.

She heard footsteps outside the shop and pictured Mimosa coming panting up to the glass door, taking in the sign, peering in and seeing nobody there, turning and jogging away again. How long should I give her, Kirsty wondered? The last thing she wanted was to be caught climbing out of a feedbin. But then, just as she thought she might risk a quick look, she heard the shop door opening.

Didn't you read the sign? Kirsty thought, incensed. The sign that said, quite clearly, Closed. She heard the door quietly closing, then silence. Are you in here now? Kirsty wondered.

'Kirsty?' Mimosa called, answering her. 'Are you in the back?' And then, 'Are you there?' Footsteps passed the bin and made their way cautiously through the Warehouse. 'Kir-sty,' Mimosa called again.

Kirsty crouched, prepared to wait it out, trying to gauge how far Mimosa had got by the sound of her footsteps. Then, just as she could hear Mimosa approaching, there was the sound of a car coming slowly down the lane beside the Warehouse. It changed down a gear and turned in and she knew that she was about to have a second customer to contend with. She heard the engine die, then the sound of a slamming door and more footsteps. She prayed that whoever was arriving now would see the sign and not Mimosa, and leave. But it was not to be. She heard the door open again and she sank down in the bin with her hands covering her mouth, fighting back the urge to start giggling.

'Hi there,' she heard a woman's voice say, 'any sign of Kirsty?'

'No. Nowhere!' Mimosa replied. 'I'm a bit worried about her, actually. She hit the bank outside our house in her car a couple of days ago and I thought I'd see how she was doing. It's strange she's left the place unmanned!'

'I thought she left every place unmanned,' the other girl said dryly.

Oh, you bitch, Kirsty thought, in surprise. Whoever you are.

Mimosa laughed. 'You know her, do you?' Kirsty could hear the interest in her voice.

'Not really. She's a good friend of my sister's.' There was a pause. 'I'm Grace Somerville.'

Kirsty immediately recognized Grace's voice. Great! Now she had both her best friends – *not* – in her shop together, and she was stuck in a feedbin and couldn't welcome them in.

'Mimosa McAlpine.'

Kirsty couldn't resist taking a chance. She popped her head around the door and looked out. They were standing just around the corner from her, a few feet away, both with their backs to her, Grace with a small black and white puppy quivering at her feet. As she watched, it began to piddle on the concrete floor. That's okay, she told it. Do some more. It might mean she has to take you outside.

'I'd better watch what I say about her then,' Mimosa laughed.

'No, no, just say it quietly, she's probably in the storeroom listening.'

'There's her scarf on the chair. She can't have gone for long.'

Kirsty crouched down again in her feedbin, holding the lid open just enough to squint through. She watched as Mimosa walked down to the other end of the shop, looking for her. Under the tight white shorts she was wearing only a G-string, and her surprisingly large bottom wriggled and jiggled with each thud of her feet. Not a pretty sight, Kirsty thought with satisfaction.

'*Kirsty*,' Mimosa boomed from the other end. She waited a few seconds. 'No, she's not there,' she said to Grace, striding back, hands on hips. 'She must have left the scarf behind when she went. We can say what we like.'

Why don't you, Kirsty thought, bracing herself.

'Actually, I quite like her,' Grace said to Kirsty's surprise. 'She makes me laugh.'

Kirsty couldn't quite imagine Grace laughing but still she was touched.

'Oh, me too,' Mimosa insisted, immediately. 'We've only met briefly but she seemed so nice.'

'I hope she's okay. I was bringing Hodge to meet her.' Grace bent down to pick up her dog and realized with horror that she was standing in a large pool of pee. 'Oh Lord. Look what he's done. I'd better clear it up.'

There was a pause as they both studied the floor then high-stepped away. Don't worry about it, Kirsty thought insistently. I'll do it. Go now, she willed them both. I'll mop it up.

Then Kirsty heard another car pulling into the yard outside. She couldn't believe it. She wondered whether to cut her losses and jump out of her hiding-place shouting, 'Here I am!' She pictured the wonderful look on their faces as she popped out of the feedbin like a jack-in-the-box.

'That'll be Simon,' Mimosa said. Kirsty sighed deeply and crouched lower into the bin.

'I got him to come and pick me up.' Mimosa moved to the window and waved. 'I always get knackered half-way around and this way it saves me one last bastard of a hill.'

But why meet here? Kirsty thought, despairingly. Of all places.

The door opened.

'Hullo babes,' Mimosa welcomed him in. 'Thirsty Kirsty's not here. Isn't it strange?'

'No,' Simon told her. 'Not if you see the big Closed sign on the door.'

'Oh! Is there?' Mimosa moved around the door to check. 'I wonder where she's gone? And why didn't she lock up?'

Why are you always so keen to see me? Kirsty wanted to ask her.

Mimosa shut the door again and draped herself around Simon's neck. 'Thanks for coming to get me.'

'Well, hello again,' Simon said to Grace, disentangling himself from Mimosa. He grinned. 'Do you come here often?'

Grace laughed nervously. 'No, actually! This is only my second time.'

'And both times I've been here too.'

Mimosa took Simon's arm proprietorially. 'Sorry to interrupt, babes, but as Kirsty's not here, it'd be great to get home. I'm dying for a shower.'

Kirsty watched Grace immediately back off. 'Of course,' she said, turning to Mimosa, 'don't let me hold you two up.'

Simon shrugged and went over to the door, opening it to let them both through. Mimosa and Grace stepped outside together.

'On second thoughts,' Simon said suddenly from the

doorway, 'you go home.' He threw Mimosa the car keys. 'I'm going to hang around a bit and see if she comes back. I don't like leaving the place unlocked.'

'But it's not your problem,' Mimosa snapped at him.

'I know,' he said calmly. 'And I won't stay longer than five minutes and then I'll walk home. You go on and have your shower. I'll see you soon.'

Mimosa nodded, obviously disappointed, and a little while later Kirsty heard first one and then another engine start, and then both cars pulled away.

Simon wandered over to the window and watched the cars go. Kirsty felt as if she shouldn't breathe in case he heard her. How long would she have to wait like this? Would it be hours more? She had to hope that five minutes was all he really did have in mind. She watched him leave the window and move over to her desk and chair and sit down, and she felt uncomfortable watching him, as if she was intruding. She hoped he wouldn't do anything that she'd rather not see, imagining how she'd feel if he farted or picked his nose while he waited. Instead he took her diary off the shelf beside the desk, placed it in front of him and flicked carefully through the pages. But that was okay, Kirsty thought – presumably he was checking if she had had anything planned that would have taken her away from the Warehouse.

When he had looked through several pages, he snapped it shut again and got up and slowly walked the length of the room, peering into corners, lifting lids, obviously looking for her, or for signs of her. He didn't seem unduly worried and yet she could tell he was puzzled by her absence and didn't want to let it go. She loved him for wondering, for showing concern for her.

When he came back again, he stood right in front of her bin. He looked at his watch and seemed to make up his mind to go, but then, just as he was moving towards the door, he turned and sat down heavily at her desk again. He felt behind him for her long red scarf, dragged it off the back of the chair and slowly wound it around his neck. Then he leaned back, looking more comfortable and comforted, and swivelled, lazily, around and around in her chair.

Watching him, Kirsty's heart squeezed with tenderness. More than anything, she wanted to climb out of the bin and into his arms, but she knew that it absolutely wasn't one of her options.

Eventually he'd had enough and came to a stop with his back to her. She watched him, fascinated, hardly daring even to blink in case she missed something. Then he turned towards her and dramatically pulled the scarf off his neck and buried his face in its folds.

'Drive me crazy,' she heard him say into the scarf.

'Hi!' she said loudly, unable to stop herself, rising out of the feedbin in front of him.

Simon jumped at least a foot. He looked at her, speechless for a few seconds. Then he banged his forehead down on the desk and covered his head with his arms.

She laughed at his reaction.

'*What-are-you-doing?*' he said, looking up at her again.

'Hiding from Mimosa!'

She looked at him sitting there, so shocked, and started

to laugh again, making him laugh too, until both of them were doubled up and Kirsty had to collapse back into her bin. When she could finally breathe again, she stood up and looked pleadingly across at him. 'Stop! Come and give me a hand getting out. Please.'

'How long were you planning to stay in there?' he asked, coming around from the desk. 'Do you have some food?'

'A few pony nuts. Enough to keep me going! But I don't think I can get out.'

'So you want me to lift you out, do you?' he asked, coming up to her and shaking his head. 'I don't think so.'

'Please,' she repeated. 'Come on. I've been in here too long already.'

'But I like you there. It makes me feel safe.'

As soon as he came into range, she clasped her arms around his neck.

'Pull me out, Mr Gorgeous,' she ordered, looking up at him through her eyelashes and thinking how perfect it would be if he kissed her now.

Simon put his hands around her waist and she leaned into him and climbed slowly out. Once free, she took her time regaining her balance, then reluctantly unhooked her arms.

'So what were you doing with my scarf?'

'Nothing,' he said, smiling, slowly letting her go.

'You were nuzzling it.'

'No, I was blowing my nose,' he said, still standing close to her. 'I've got this terrible cold.'

'Oh, right,' she said.

His face was very, very close to hers now. I think he wants me, she thought, feeling faint with longing and relief.

*

'Fancy a coffee?' Mimosa asked as she and Grace left the Warehouse.

'Sure!' Grace answered, wanting to talk to her some more, even if she could hardly bear the thought that this girl was not only going out with Simon but living with him too.

Mimosa was asking her at just the right time. In the past weeks it had struck Grace repeatedly that she had no friends, never had anyone to do anything with, and until she found a job she would love to have a girlfriend to share some of her time. Even in her moments of deepest despair, she had watched Lily and Kirsty together and had imagined how good it would be to have a Kirsty of her own. Now, feeling better, she felt pathetically grateful for Mimosa's offer of company, even if it did mean that she would have to bear the constant reminder of Simon.

'Come back to Pond House.'

Grace frowned. 'Sorry?'

'Oh.' Mimosa was surprised, used to everybody knowing the house. 'I'll lead, you follow.'

They left Welshpool and ten or so minutes later turned in through the gates and pulled up outside Pond House.

Looking at the house, Grace was caught by a surge of jealousy of Mimosa that almost prevented her from getting out of the car. Not because she particularly wanted Pond

House, but because it seemed that Mimosa had every aspect of her life perfectly in place. She could summon her beautiful man to meet her at the end of her no-doubt effortless run through the Montgomeryshire countryside, to pick her up and take her back to this beautiful, beautiful house.

She made herself get out, and walked around the car to let out Hodge.

'It's absolutely gorgeous,' she breathed to Mimosa, standing back to take it in properly. Hodge, nose to the ground, immediately zig-zagged away from her, running through a great arch cut out of a yew hedge and out of sight.

'He'll be okay. He can't go anywhere,' Mimosa told Grace. 'Come on, I'll show you around.'

Pond House was a small Elizabethan manor house, built of old red brick, warmed and weathered and faded over the years. Now at times it was more pale rose than red, and it sat secure and low against the ground. Today the uneven roof was white and glittering with frost and it hung protectively over the upper windows, almost like a thatch, or a low brimmed hat, seeming to push the house down even more securely into the ground.

'I didn't know it was here,' Grace said in wonder.

'Let me show you the garden.'

They followed Hodge through the archway, and there was the garden. It was on three levels, dropping down and down, each time linked by a gentle flight of stone steps. Today, set against the pale grey sky, with the grass frosted white and the heavy dark yew trees slipping in and out of the mist, it was magical, so still and white that Grace felt as if she'd stepped into a garden from Narnia. The yew hedge ran all the way down one side of the garden, once clipped into a dramatic row of globes and spires but now growing wild. In the centre of the first level there was a formal garden of box and thyme and lavender, planted out in formerly neat geometric patterns, but again the box had bushed out and the thyme and lavender had combined at some stage to overflow their beds and had never been cut back, and now their bare winter stalks trailed in all directions, spilling over on to the frost-patterned brick pathways that divided them.

'Garden,' Mimosa said after a moment, sweeping her arm to encompass it all. Then she turned back through the yew hedge and Grace followed her. She pointed at a range of buildings to the left of the house.

'Sheds, garages, log stores, kennels.'

Then she pointed to the right. 'Stables, more sheds and below that, orchard and a couple of paddocks.'

Grace smiled at her. 'Not much but it's home.'

'Anyway, come inside,' Mimosa told her briskly, leading the way in.

And inside was stunning too. Grace wondered whether it was Mimosa who had chosen the colour of the ochre walls, vivid against the ancient dark beams, and the thick mulberry curtains and wonderful rugs. She pictured Mimosa and Simon discovering Pond House together and slowly, lovingly, putting it back in order again.

'Have you lived here long?' Grace asked, in awe of it all.

'This is our first spring.'

'Gosh, so not long. To have made it so beautiful.'

Mimosa shrugged. 'Actually the place is falling down. The whole of the back wall is crumbling away. We're going to have to do some major rebuilding once the weather improves.'

She led the way into the kitchen and started to make coffee for them both. She always hated it when people went over the top about Pond House because she had had no part in making it as beautiful as it was. Mimosa liked to think of herself as someone with an excellent professional eye, and a good deal of creative flair, and it infuriated her that Pond House had already been done so well without her.

The fact that her father would definitely buy her some nearby land if she asked him to – and a house too if she wanted it – filled her with relief, because it would all come from her. She imagined the hills around Pond House filled with her sheep and horses, hers not Simon's, and she knew it would make her feel more secure. But she wouldn't be thinking like this if Simon would only give her a sign that he was falling in love with her.

Mimosa hadn't started out to mislead everybody about her relationship with Simon, but as most people thought she was his girlfriend anyway, and as she was so certain that he would, eventually be hers, she had started to gloss over the fact that it hadn't happened yet, at times even convincing herself. They got on so well together, were such a brilliant couple, he was always so affectionate and charming and thoughtful, that she told herself he was only being cautious and that it was just a matter of time. The odd comments he made about her needing to find a place of her own, she took with a pinch of salt. She was not about to move out. She needed to work on him and she needed to keep him in her line of vision, especially with Kirsty around.

*

Grace and Mimosa sat and chatted for half an hour about nothing in particular, neither of them wanting to lead the other towards dangerous ground by revealing anything very detailed about themselves. And then, just as Grace was thinking she should find Hodge and leave before she outstayed her welcome, Simon came bursting through the front door obviously in a wonderfully good mood.

'No sign of her, then?' Mimosa said.

'Actually, yes,' he grinned. 'She turned up just as I was leaving.'

'Where the hell had she been?'

'In a feedbin.'

'God, I don't know how she does that terrible job,' Mimosa told Grace. 'She must be permanently filthy.'

Simon caught Grace's eye and smothered a smile.

'I'm glad you found her,' she told him. 'I was wondering what had happened to her.'

Simon nodded, moving over to the coffee jug. 'I haven't even said hello to you properly,' he said turning back to her. 'I'm Simon Campion.' He held out a hand.

'Grace Somerville,' she said, taking it.

'And you live round here too, do you?'

There was a distracted look in his eyes, Grace thought. He was polite enough to seem interested in the answer and yet she could sense a suppressed energy in him that told her his mind was somewhere else.

'In Welshpool. On Green Lane.'

Simon nodded. 'Well, good to meet you!' He turned to Mimosa. 'I've got five minutes and then I'll have to go over to the Little Goose.' He drained his coffee mug. 'And by the way, I think you should call Nutt and Bower's again. There's a great little house in their window.'

'Oh, don't tell me you're leaving this beautiful place!' Grace cried.

Simon laughed. 'No, not me. But Mimosa is having the most terrible time finding somewhere to rent. You wouldn't think it would be so hard.'

Mimosa blinked in surprise. 'Oh goody, goody,' she said evenly, moving over to pick up his mug. She took it with her to the sink and bent her head low as she rinsed it out. 'Thanks. I'll ring them up and go and see it today.'

You poor thing, thought Grace, hearing the thickness of defeat in Mimosa's voice, at the same time riveted by what was going on. You didn't expect that to happen, did you?

Simon looked from Mimosa to Grace then back again. Then he went over to Mimosa and squeezed her shoulder. 'Got to go,' he told her ambiguously.

Mimosa continued rinsing out the mug. She would have to go, she realized. There was no point hoping for anything different.

Simon ran up the stairs and then they heard him striding across the room over their heads.

'He's going to the Little Goose,' Mimosa said awkwardly. 'Did you know it was his?' Grace looked blank. 'The one on Vincent Street,' she said shortly, avoiding Grace's eye.

Grace nodded. 'I've never been in.'

'And yes,' Mimosa added flatly. 'I'm finding a place to live.'

'Do you mind me asking? Are you two splitting up?'

'Good God! There was never any of that going on,' Mimosa laughed bitterly. 'We're just old friends. Simon offered to put me up for a bit. But obviously he's now got other plans.'

Is that so? Grace was unable to summon up real sympathy for Mimosa. If Simon wanted Mimosa out, who was Grace to argue? And then just as she was saying goodbye to Mimosa and slipping on her coat, she heard Simon thundering back down the stairs. He came into the kitchen and joined her at the back door, leaning past her to open it for the two of them.

They left the house together.

Thank God she'd started to make more effort to look good when she went out, she thought. She'd put on some mascara that morning and although she was only in old jeans and a black polo-neck jumper she knew she didn't look too bad. She gave Simon a quick sideways glance and tucked her hair behind her ears.

'I don't know you, do I?' he asked her, narrowing his eyes and considering her.

'No, you don't.'

'But I do remember that I met you that morning in Kirsty's shop. And you and Kirsty were definitely not getting on.'

Grace laughed awkwardly. 'You could say that. But I hope that's all over and done with now.' She wondered distractedly where Hodge had got to.

'Good,' he told her. Unexpectedly, his face broke into a wonderful, gleeful smile.

What did I say? thought Grace. Did I say something funny?

'And how's the dog bed? Or I should say, how's the dog?'

'What a memory!' Grace was pleased that he'd remembered. 'He's around here somewhere. God knows where. And he's lovely. Lots of work, like having a toddler apparently – although I wouldn't know about that – but worth every minute.'

She looked at him, not knowing what else to say, and at that moment Hodge reappeared, slinking up to join her, sliding around her legs guiltily, then, when he knew he'd been forgiven, bounding over to inspect Simon, licking his hands slavishly before tearing off around the yard at a hundred miles an hour.

Simon laughed as he watched him go. 'I do want a dog,' he said longingly.

Grace remembered a magazine article identifying the four most attractive types of men. They were supposed to be Scottish men, men with babies, men with fast cars and men with dogs. Simon liking *her* dog was good enough.

Getting into his fast car and driving away was not so good.

'So you run the Little Goose?' she said.

'Yes,' he smiled at her, humour twinkling in his eyes, as if she'd again said the funniest thing in the world, 'and I'm late so there will be nothing to give anyone to eat. I have to go.' He opened her car door for her.

Was there a note of regret in his voice? Grace couldn't tell. And, once he'd said goodbye, he'd almost run away from her to his car, revving up and shooting off at great speed, so she had to suppose he had other things on his mind than her. She opened the back of the car for Hodge and shut it again gently, surprised by how little the thought hurt. *Men – who needs them*, she thought, making a face at Hodge through the window.

14

If Lily could have planned the day, she would have woken at nine thirty, and would then have run herself a bath. She would have unhurriedly wiped all last night's make-up off her face and would have got into the bath with a piece of toast and a cup of coffee, where she would have soaked, letting the water slowly wash away last night's grime. Then she would have got dressed and would have opened the front door, not to a head-splitting dazzle but to a soft, misty morning. She would have strolled over the bridge and made her way to Starbucks in King Street where she would have slowly revived, drinking more coffee and reading the paper.

Instead, she was forced up through the layers of sleep into a pitch-dark and silent room. Deep in her warm pillows someone still smiled and beckoned her to him, but he was growing weaker by the second, the magic of her dream broken by her need to head for the bathroom. Lily took as short a time as possible but once back in bed her cold feet and beating heart put paid to any chance of slipping back to sleep and finding him again.

Eventually she gave up, sat up and looked with heavy-lidded eyes around the shadowy room. Her head wasn't quite as bad as it should have been, she thought, gingerly moving it from side to side. And she could still have the bath and the toast. She looked at her bedside clock. It was seven thirty. She shut her eyes again and dozed.

Later she went back to the bathroom and ran the hot tap, feeling the water pass between her fingers, nearly hot, slightly hot, warm, slightly warm, getting cooler, cooler, cold. So she would have to do without the bath. She washed sparingly, shoved deodorant under her arms and jumped straight into her clothes.

But, she thought, resolutely optimistic, Starbucks have surely not gone bust, and I didn't hear Hammersmith Bridge being bombed in the night. She could, at least, count on her coffee. That was the moment that she remembered her text message. What linked the two, she didn't know, but the coffee shop was momentarily put on hold.

Despite the condition she had been in when she read it, she could still remember each word. *If you are interested in my side of the story call me tomorrow.* Could it have been from Amber? Somehow Lily knew that it wasn't her. The conversation of the night before had had a definite ring of finality. She couldn't imagine Amber wanting to say anything more. Not Grace. Not Kirsty. Not likely to be one of her King's Cross friends. Who else? Who else with a story they might want to tell? Perhaps it was the awful man at her interview?

Or it was Josh. It made sense to think it could have been from him. He could have heard she was in London, and he had a story, one he had good reason to believe she might still be interested in hearing. And yet it somehow didn't fit with the Josh she thought she knew. From all she'd seen him do, he wouldn't care what people – what she – thought of him.

Perhaps that one brief kiss outside the Little Goose had seduced him, changed his life, got so under his skin he was going mad and needed an excuse, any excuse, to see her again? Unlikely as she knew it was, her stomach gave a great flip like a fish leaping out of water. It couldn't be Josh, she thought, because if Josh had been even the tiniest bit interested in her he'd have called her up before now. He wasn't the sort to need excuses, he would call a girl whenever it suited him. She was sure of it.

She got ready to leave the house. Somehow the horrible humiliating phone call with Amber's friend had changed everything. It had been the final straw, and all she wanted to do now was put them all behind her. She'd been embroiled in Hal's life for too long. She wanted to get on with her own. There was the date with Hal that she couldn't break and then she would have no need for anything more to do with any of them.

She knew that if Kirsty were here she would have told Lily she was being wet, would have grabbed the mobile off her and keyed 'reply'. She would have argued that the only reason Lily didn't want to call the number was because she was too scared it might be Josh at the other end. But Kirsty wasn't there and without her Lily could get away with it. And so, before she could change her mind, Lily deleted the message from her phone.

It was now nearly ten, with none of the glorious blue sky of the day before. She walked over the bridge heading towards Hammersmith and Starbucks feeling more and more hung over and listless, and realized halfway across that Starbucks too had lost its appeal. She didn't want to sit watching London through a window, it was too much of a waste when she was here so rarely, and yet she felt too fragile and too broke to do much else. Everyone she knew was working, so there was nobody to see. She didn't fancy window-shopping, and she certainly didn't feel up to stretching her legs and walking anywhere far. She wanted somewhere safe, yet distracting, somewhere to go that wasn't wasting her time, where she could kill a few hours.

She made her way towards the Victoria & Albert Museum. There was something wonderful if rather dusty and tame about it, perfect for the way she was feeling that morning. She was sure there were several collections there that it would be important for her to see, and she remembered Tippoo's Tiger, a mechanical man-eating tiger that had terrified her as a child, and wondered if it was still there. Once she had got off the tube and had made her way through the Exhibition Road entrance she began to feel uplifted at the thought of wandering among it all with the time to take as long as she wanted. This wasn't an over-indulgent hangover cure, she told herself. If she was going to work at the Registry this would surely be the first of many visits she'd make in order to undertake serious research.

There was so much that she'd forgotten about, or had never known was here – collections in the basements, dresses and seventeenth-century masks, modern British ceramics and china dolls – and looking confusedly at her map she didn't know where to start.

She chucked her map in a bin and strolled up two steps, deciding to wander, and there in front of her was the tiger, not quite as impressive as he'd been when she was a little girl but still gory enough. She remembered how she and Grace had stood where she was now, side by side, transfixed by his long fangs piercing the soldier's body. And then, in the hush, her mobile began to ring.

Around her people flinched and then stared at her accusingly. What a terrible *faux pas*, she thought, thinking how pompous they looked in their outrage. A mobile phone in the Victoria and Albert! So much worse than in the Tate Modern.

'Hi,' said a voice, and she stood still among them. She knew immediately who it was.

'Hello.'

'It's Josh here.' She could hear him smiling down the phone. 'Do you remember me?'

What a voice, she thought. I can't resist such a sexy voice.

One of the museum attendants was making his way towards her, a finger over his lips.

'Did you get my message? I sent you one last night.'

'How did you get my number?'

'I borrowed Hal's mobile . . .'

'And why are you calling me?' Lily asked, dropping her voice and turning her back on the attendant.

'Because I heard you were in London,' Josh whispered back, 'and I wanted to take you out while you're here. Put you straight about a few things.'

Lily walked away from the guide towards the café at the main entrance. 'Put me straight about what?' she asked. She stopped beside a small, exquisitely beautiful carving of the Madonna and child and absent-mindedly stroked her under the chin with one finger.

The museum attendant looked as if he was going to explode with outrage and Lily suddenly felt terribly embarrassed. How awful that she'd touched the Madonna like that. She was nearly a thousand years old.

She found a chair tucked behind a column and sat down.

'I've got to go. I can't talk to you now and anyway all that's over and done with.'

'Not quite all over, actually,' Josh told her, 'but that's not why I've called. You probably think it's ridiculous, but I care that you're walking around thinking I'm a son of Satan. I wanted to meet you while you were here, to talk about it.'

'Don't flatter yourself! I haven't thought about you for weeks.'

Josh laughed. 'You've seen a bit of Hal. I imagine my name might have come up once or twice. And I wanted to explain to you why I did what I did.'

'You don't need to explain to me,' she muttered, looking away as the attendant caught her eye again. 'You thought you were right. I thought you weren't. But I don't hold it against you. You don't need to explain. It's nothing to do with me any more. It's between you and Hal. And I can't talk now.'

'Yes you can. Please, Lily. Talk now,' he begged, laughing at her.

Get this man off the phone, Lily told herself, aware that she was now smiling inanely at the attendant, who had started walking, grim-faced, towards her. Get off the phone, and off the scene, for good. She knew the score, that he saw her as unfinished business. That if she said yes to a drink, the next thing she knew she'd be jumping into bed with him, and yet she couldn't bring herself to cut short the conversation in a way Josh would take seriously.

'Is there any point suggesting supper tonight?'

'No, there isn't.'

'Or lunch tomorrow?'

She took the phone away from her ear and looked beseechingly at the attendant.

'Two seconds,' he told her firmly, but disarmed a little by her smile. 'You know it's not allowed.'

The attendant turned his back on her and walked away.

'No,' she told Josh quickly, turning back to him, wishing she were a different sort of girl, someone who could cope with a guy like him, use him to have some fun and then forget all about him – because she didn't doubt that it would be fun.

'Lily, you don't have to sound so determined not to see me. It's not a problem. Get back to Welshpool. And forget about us all. It's probably for the best.'

There was a long pause.

'Thanks for calling, though.' Lily couldn't help herself.

'Where are you now?' Josh said.

'In the Victoria & Albert Museum.'

'Of course you are. Why haven't you got a job? How come you can wander around the V & A in the middle of a Friday morning?'

'What makes you think I'm wandering? I'm doing some research.'

'And I work just around the corner,' Josh said as if the two statements neatly coincided. 'So you can meet me for a cup of coffee. I'll come to the V & A so you don't need to waste any valuable research time.'

'Okay, I could manage that,' she said, relieved that she hadn't got rid of him after all. 'I'll wait for you in the café by the main entrance.'

She waited, burning her mouth on a coffee she bought to have something to do with her hands. She wouldn't be too frosty, she told herself, but at the first sign of any smouldering, at any whiff of a seduction routine, she'd get away from him. And she wasn't going to fancy him. She wouldn't give him the pleasure. It would do him good to see that not every woman tripped over herself in the rush to flirt with him.

But then, as she thought it all through, it was as if she could suddenly see herself, sitting there, one foot tucked tightly behind an aluminium table leg, her lips pursed, about to take a prim sip of coffee, thinking her tangle of suspicious thoughts about Josh and wondering how quickly she should get rid of him. And with awful self-recognition, she realized that she didn't like what she saw, and hadn't for a long while. She wondered what a stranger would make of her now, sitting there at the café table. Attractive, perhaps, but she didn't much care about that. She wanted warm and vibrant and interesting, she wanted to be someone who looked like they were good company, someone passionate, a lover of life. She wanted to be more of a Kirsty: exuberant and carefree. And she knew she didn't look like that at all.

She glanced self-consciously around the room but no one was watching her. In a few minutes Josh was coming and suddenly the thought of sitting next to him and behaving as she'd planned made her feel unutterably depressed.

Guys like Josh had always been out of bounds. The ones she had always warned herself off. She'd always played so safe, congratulated herself on being somebody who never got hurt, who always chose the decent, dependable Hals instead of the devil-may-care bastards like Josh. She had never had a fling, never allowed herself a relationship that was volatile or insecure – but, maybe, all the more exciting for being so. She'd never been hurt but she'd never been swept off her feet either. Both her long-term relationships had been with dull, boring guys and had been ended, of course, by her. She had been so careful not to hop into bed with somebody disreputable that she'd ended up hardly hopping in with anyone at all. Never with anyone who had the upper hand, and definitely never with anyone remotely as attractive as Josh. She'd looked at Grace, at the way she threw herself into every relationship she began, blind to everything, and had felt terribly superior. Perhaps it was that which Grace had hated so much.

And now, Lily wanted to be different. She wanted Josh. She wanted to throw caution to the wind and let herself go, just once, with Josh. Have some fun without worrying about the other girlfriends, or how little she could trust him. Take him on on his own terms, just to find out what it was like. If she didn't get involved, then she wouldn't get hurt.

A ripple of excitement rolled through her because there was nothing to stop her. And yet at the same time she was panic-stricken at the thought of changing the habits of a lifetime, especially where someone like Josh was concerned.

Why had it happened now? she wondered. Something to do with both Kirsty and Josie choosing almost the exact same moment to hint that she was missing out, that she was too strait-laced, even a bit of a killjoy. When they'd said it, she'd flinched but had then batted both of them away without a second thought. Now, with Josh's arrival imminent, it was as if she was hearing them again, and listening for the first time. She wished she could tell them what she was thinking now, and could have them to talk to, to tell her what she should do.

Josh arrived as he had said he would, just five minutes later. He strode around the corner of the coffee area without spotting her straight away, allowing her a few fist-clenching moments to watch him unaware. He was wearing a beautifully cut charcoal-grey suit with a pale pink shirt open at the throat, and he looked wonderful, a potent combination of rumpled sexiness and detached high-flying glamour.

When he finally caught her eye he raised a hand and smiled a loose, easy smile, and all the other women in the café swung round to look at Lily to see if she deserved him.

Oh Josh, Lily thought, breathing him in as she stood up and leaned slowly towards him, brushing her lips against his cheek. The problem with you is I know I couldn't walk away again.

He put a hand on her shoulder and kissed her cheek.

'I'll get us some coffee.'

In the queue she watched him make a quick quiet phone call and never once try to catch her eye.

Who are you ringing? she thought suspiciously, convinced it was a girl. Then she told herself sharply to stop it. She was not going to be that person.

He came and sat down opposite her and they started to talk. He made her laugh straight away, which she hadn't expected, and then listened more than he talked, which she hadn't expected either, so that gradually she found herself relaxing and almost forgetting the role she'd had him down to play. He was gentle in a way Lily had never imagined he would be and it took her aback, the flashes of sensitivity and compassion far more seductive than any chat-up line. They talked, inevitably, about Hal, and then she found herself telling him about Grace, about their childhood, and their parents, about her interview at the Registry and perhaps coming back to live in London.

Occasionally, she'd stop herself and think *I'm talking too much*. And yet, all the time, she knew that it was all right. That he wasn't sitting there thinking *how do I make this girl shut up?* But was enjoying being with her. And she was aware of every tiny part of him, of every movement that he made. Of the soft rise and fall of his pink shirt and how the muscles in his strong tanned throat contracted as he swallowed each sip of coffee.

She could remember every detail of the evening in the Little Goose, squashed up against him, thigh to thigh. The hand that was now lying so still on the table in front of her was the hand that had caressed her cheek, stroked her back. And the beautiful sensitive mouth now speaking about Hal was the one that had kissed her gently at the end of the evening with lust glittering in his eyes.

But Lily had to admit, as one coffee became two, that this time there was no sign that Josh had anything but the very best of intentions where she was concerned. Far from tumbling her into his bed, there was not a single attempt at a lingering look, not one flirtatious *double entendre* or anything else that she could have taken as a sign.

'Think about it,' he was saying.

She nodded. She was. She was imagining him standing up, crashing through the clutter of aluminium chairs to catch her in a Rodin-like kiss among the café tables.

'Hal is so innocent – you know that – he doesn't understand that women like Amber exist, let alone that they're going to make a beeline for him. And he does get these mad infatuations. He goes from nothing to passionately in love in a matter of days. He always has.

There've been so many others he might have married. But Amber was the clever one. And she grabbed him while she could.'

'What did you do to the others, then?' Lily asked suspiciously. 'Did they find themselves with faulty brakes on high mountainous roads? Or were they prodded with poison-tipped umbrellas as they walked down the Kings Road?'

'Nothing! I did nothing!' Josh insisted, laughing.

'Amber is very beautiful,' Lily said. 'Everyone says so. Hal must have thought he was in heaven. Especially after all those Sloaney-ponies he'd been out with before.'

Josh smiled and stretched both his arms up above his head, the smile turning into a long yawn. He rubbed his eyes and dislodged an eyelash which stuck out at a right-angle from all the others. She couldn't help herself leaning forwards to brush it gently away. At her touch Josh raised his eyebrows, but didn't say anything.

'Amber's very pretty,' he agreed. 'From a distance. Up close, there's definite wear and tear. You can't behave like her and not get a few cracks and chips along the way.'

'Those cracks and chips that miraculously don't show up on you anywhere.' She paused, considering him. 'If you're going to knock Amber, I think you should at least acknowledge that you're just the same as she is.'

Josh said quietly, 'You're right. But I wasn't quite as bloke-ish as you think I was. I didn't know the details of what was going on with Hal for a start, or I'd never have got involved.'

Lily was surprised by the sadness in his voice. She'd

not imagined he could sound so vulnerable. She looked back at him and he shrugged, then yawned again and stretched back in his chair.

'...had one too many late nights – at the office,' ...a good night's sleep.'

'Seriously. What would you have done if one of those other girls had tried to lead him up the aisle?' she asked, clicking the bedroom door shut on the thought. 'You can't have imagined Hal would have been any happier with them? Would you have stepped in then too? Done the same to one of them?'

'No.'

'Why not? If you choose to judge Amber, why not judge all of them? Give them all scores between nought and ten. Amber scored a nought for being such a bitch. But would another have got a nought for looking like a dog? And another perhaps only a two because of her rugby player's thighs, or her obsession with dust? Or just, perhaps, because she was boring? And what was the pass rate?' Lily went on, warming to her point. 'What if someone scored a four? Would that be good enough to win the wedding day? Perhaps only a ten-out-of-ten girl was ever going to be good enough for you?'

'No! Of course not,' Josh protested. 'But I do think he'd have been happier with any one of those other girls. I don't hate Amber. She's quite endearing at times. But she would have made Hal miserable.'

'But that was for Hal to find out! And he may have done in years to come, but isn't that the risk anyone takes when they get married? He still thinks she's a ten-out-of-ten girl,' Lily said, 'he really does. Even now. And it isn't your scoring that matters, it's his.'

'Yes,' Josh looked steadily back at her, 'of course you're right. But if we're talking score cards, on hers in a little time. But he wasn't going to get that time without us finding it for him. So we dashed in. Took him away. Got him out before it was too late.'

'You dashed in, did you?' said Lily. 'I knew it! You thought you were in the Rolf Harris song. You wanted to be like those two little boys!'

'Oh no, do you think so?' Josh said mortified, laughing.

'Yes,' Lily said smartly. 'But it wasn't ever going to work because Hal is still hell bent on running straight back into her arms.' She asked curiously, 'What are you going to do about that?'

'Do about it? Do you think I'd tell *you*? No, I don't need to do anything. This time around Amber's doing it all for me.'

'What do you mean? How do you know what she's up to?' Lily was intrigued.

Josh shrugged non-committally.

'Don't they both have a bit of a problem with you at the moment?'

'No, actually,' he said. 'Hal was pissed off with me, but even he is coming around now. And Amber . . .' Did she imagine it, or did Josh look rather uncomfortable? 'When I went to talk to Amber that morning she kissed me and smiled and said thank you very much and was off on that aeroplane before I'd finished the first sentence,' Josh told Lily.

Without you, please. Let it be that she went on her own.

'I was her new best friend,' Josh went on. 'Don't you see, Lily? It was exactly what she wanted to hear.'

'Why?'

'Because she'd got cold feet too. She didn't ever really want Hal. He was what she thought she should want. And I was gently letting her off the hook. If you'd met her, even once, you wouldn't be asking me this. Reliable is not one of Amber's middle names.'

From what she'd learned from the phone call with Amber's friend, Lily thought Screwed and Up probably were.

'You know,' he said, 'you're the first person who's ever challenged me about all this. Apart from Hal and Charlie, I haven't talked to anyone else about what we did.'

'So?'

'So, when you talk about it, of course it's impossible to justify. There's no getting away from it.'

'No,' Lily looked mortified. 'Don't say that. I'm just beginning to be convinced.' She laughed at herself. 'I don't believe I said that! 'Let's have more coffee?' She jumped up. 'It's my turn.' She wanted to ensure he wasn't about to say he had to go. She had little idea of the time, whether they were still talking in minutes since Josh had sat down opposite her, or if whole hours had gone by.

Later on she found herself telling him more about Grace, wanting him to know how she'd been through the same dilemma, how she still felt that she'd let Grace down. In the mood she was in now she wanted to tell him everything about everyone she'd ever known.

'You couldn't win that one,' he said, seeing how much it still bothered her. 'However you said it.'

'I barely said a thing,' Lily said defensively. 'Nothing like you!'

'Either you lie, tell them nothing at all apart from what a lovely couple they make, or stick your neck out and be damned.'

'Perhaps I should have done what you did.'

'I can't see you masterminding a successful kidnapping.'

'It's taken Grace two whole years to realize Jeremy's a bastard. I suppose I'd have had to hold on to her for a very long time. Someone might have come to rescue her.'

'Yes. People might have wondered where she'd gone. I can't see you doing anything like we did. You're too considered. Too measured.'

'Oh, please, don't you start. Not you too!' Lily groaned.

'Why do you say that?' Josh was amused. 'It's not a bad thing. I'm just saying you're not one to do something impulsive.'

As he said it he held her look, and the suggestion was suddenly there.

'It's not true,' Lily blurted out. 'I am.'

'That's very good news.' Josh smiled at her.

'I jumped out of a plane, once.'

'But I bet you had a parachute on.'

'Of course I bloody did!'

'Then I'm not sure that counts.'

'I don't care! I want nothing to do with your challenges. Not with your track record.'

Neither of them seemed able to look away. He caught hold of one of her hands.

'Please cancel it,' he said, suddenly very serious, 'whatever it is you're doing tonight,'

She looked in wonder at her hand in his, feeling it wouldn't now move if she wanted it to.

'I could take the rest of the day off. And spend it with you . . . it's Friday, I can do that . . .'

'Okay,' she agreed.

'Don't look like that,' he laughed. 'It'll be fun.'

15

As Josh and Lily moved to cross Exhibition Road he took her hand and kept it. They walked for about fifteen minutes, striding fast, hardly speaking, with little idea where they were heading for, and then, because it was lunchtime, and they were passing by, Josh stopped her outside an Italian restaurant just off the King's Road.

They ordered *pappardelle al cinghiale* and a bottle of wine, but when the food arrived Lily found she couldn't bring herself to swallow a single mouthful. She looked across at Josh and saw that he wasn't touching the food either.

'Have a cigarette if you want one,' she suggested. 'Don't mind me.'

'Don't tempt me. I gave up a few weeks ago.' Then he said, 'Let's go. Do you mind? It's ridiculous being here if we can't eat anything.'

She nodded and he jumped up immediately and pulled her to her feet, called over the bill and hurried Lily outside. As she came out of the restaurant after him, she tripped down the little step out on to the street and Josh reached out and just managed to catch her. Once she was in his arms he didn't let her go.

'Got you,' he said, his mouth instantly against hers.

He kissed her lightly and gently and yet immediately

a tidal wave of lust and excitement rose inside her, the warmth spreading through her, up through the soles of her feet, taking her over completely. She'd always been self-conscious about kissing in public, but standing on the pavement in Langton Street with Josh, Lily could have been standing there stark naked and she wouldn't have cared as long as he didn't stop.

She slipped her hands through his thick hair, stroking the nape of his neck where his hair was soft and clipped close like bristling velvet, touching the expensive wool of his suit and his well-muscled back beneath the thin material, then down again to touch his bottom, making him grab her harder and let out an involuntary groan in her ear, feeling his narrow hips and long lean thighs beneath her hands.

'What did you say?'

'That you were driving me mad.' Josh stopped and wrapped his arms around her, his cheek against her hair. 'And I want to kiss you again and again and again. You know, I've been going mad for quite a long time now. You have no idea.'

She felt her heart do a great trampolining somersault of delight.

'Since when?'

'Since I saw you in the Little Goose. How could you kiss me like that and then leave me to stew for four weeks?'

'You should have got in touch sooner.'

Even in the light-hearted laughter of the moment she wished she hadn't said that. Because it sounded as if she'd been waiting for his call when she hadn't. And if she knew one thing, it was that Josh would be bored by girls waiting for his call.

But Josh brushed it aside, slipping his arm around her shoulders and they walked down the street, back on to the King's Road.

'So what shall we do now?' he asked her, pulling her close against him. 'We can't eat. And I doubt that you'll come to bed with me. What have you never done before? Have you been on the Millennium Wheel?'

'I don't think I'd get to see much of London, would I?'

He kissed her cheek. 'It might qualify us for the mile-high club.'

'I meant because of the weather.'

Josh looked doubtfully at the sky. 'Then would you like to come back to my flat?'

They walked some more and she didn't answer and then he paused and looked at his watch and then across at her.

'If you're not coming back with me, Lily, I might as well head back to the office, if you don't mind. You know where you are, don't you?'

Lily stared at him gobsmacked. She couldn't believe it.

'Lily!' Josh laughed at her. 'Who do you think I am? I'm joking. Really, I'm joking! I want to spend the day with you, outside. And with as many other people as possible.'

'Bastard,' she laughed.

'Millennium Wheel,' Josh said. 'Tate Modern. Or the Wetland Centre?'

'You must be joking.'

'I'm serious. It's a great place.'

'Don't we need swimming costumes?'

'No, Lily,' Josh told her patiently, 'it's not a waterslide park, it's a nature reserve. It's in Barnes. Where you're staying.'

'Oh,' Lily said cautiously. 'I don't know.'

'I thought you'd appreciate it, coming from all that rain. I'm trying to think of somewhere you'd feel at home.'

Lily shook her head. 'I've just got away from it,' she said. 'Definitely the Millennium Wheel.'

*

The mist hadn't lifted properly and only a few people were queuing to get on the Wheel. They picked up their tickets straight away, bore the obligatory photograph and were joined by less than six others in a pod. They stood close together, looking out at the wonderful stretching view, but aware of nothing much but each other, lacing their fingers but otherwise not touching. 'I'll come back one day with my grandfather,' Josh told her. 'I can't take it in properly with you beside me.'

Then he leaned in close to her. 'So where next?' he said. 'I suppose you want the Tate Modern?'

'No,' said Lily, thinking of his flat. 'Nowhere else.'

Afterwards they walked slowly to the river and stood looking out at the Thames, Josh standing behind her with his arms around her, a light drizzle wetting her face, barely anybody else in sight, and Lily thought how it had to be the most romantic day of her life.

'Who'd have thought it?' she said to him, leaning back against him. 'That I'd be here today, doing this with you.'

Josh didn't answer but tightened his arms around her.

'Shall we come back again tomorrow?'

'No,' he said, 'we don't get another day like today.'

Lily turned in his arms. 'Don't say that!'

'I didn't mean it like that,' he said, kissing her gently on each fine blonde eyebrow, thinking how lovely she looked with her huge eyes and her pink cold cheeks. 'We'll have other days together, and they'll be even better.'

They got a taxi back to Josie's flat.

Once inside, Lily left him for a moment in the sitting-room and went through to the kitchen. Toast, she thought. I'll make some toast and tea. She cut a couple of slices of bread, wanting something to do to dilute some of the potency between them, and give herself a chance to think straight. How had it got like this? This wasn't how it was meant to be. Josh was so different that she couldn't think straight. Couldn't remember how she was supposed to be behaving. And yet she couldn't bear to be away from him, she thought, spreading the butter as quickly as she could. What was it that she hadn't anticipated, that was sending her spiralling away from how she'd planned to be? She felt in love. Already. Just like that.

She took the tea and toast through to the sitting-room and found him stretched out on the sofa, waiting for her. She put the plate down on the table and realized that she still couldn't imagine eating anything herself. Instead, she took a piece to Josh and leaned over him, holding it to his mouth. With three bites it had gone and he held her hand and licked the butter off her fingers.

'Come here,' he told her, putting down his tea and holding out his arms.

She climbed on top of him, sitting with her knees on either side of his body, and felt as if she was diving down into his sea-green eyes. He lifted a hand and carefully stroked back her hair and she collapsed on to his chest. They lay close together, two blond heads, his arms wrapped around her and her face buried in his neck.

Oh, Josh, she wanted to sigh. I wasn't meant to feel like this. I meant to have some fun, take advantage of you and then forget all about you, but I know now that I want to stay. That I like being here too much. She pushed herself up on her elbows and looked down into his face, running her fingers across his cheekbones and down across his lips. Stay with me, please. I don't want this to be just a fling.

He reached up for her and kissed her again. Everything was changing now, all the emotion and desire building up fast in both of them, as this time they both knew that they were going to see it through. She kissed him passionately back, hungrily, desperately, leaving cautious Lily far behind, clutching quick, urgent instructions that whatever happened next, she must never ever forget how wonderful, magical, utterly right this moment felt.

And then came the sound of a key turning in the front door lock of Josie's flat and a girl's voice calling out *hello*.

Lily saw her own disbelief mirrored on Josh's face,

remembering at the same time Josie's warning her that her little sister might be using the flat.

'So this happens in real life, too,' Josh said flatly.

'Is that you, Beth?' Lily called, still lying spread out on Josh but managing to sound quite normal.

'I'll get rid of her,' she whispered to him.

'Oh, Lily, great! I wasn't sure if you'd be in,' came the cheerful voice back again, followed by a heavy thud. 'Hang on a minute and I'll come and join you. It's a bit mad out here.'

'Yes, come and join us, why not?' Josh called and Lily covered his mouth with her hand.

'Who is she?' Josh whispered.

'She's a pain,' Lily hissed back. 'I can't believe this has happened.'

The door banged shut again.

'She's obviously your guardian angel.'

Lily glowered. 'A guardian angel wouldn't do this to me.'

She stood up and Josh got off the sofa and stood up behind her. When there was no further sound, she turned back to him but then they heard the front door slam again.

Lily immediately slipped out of the sitting-room and closed the door between Beth and Josh. She couldn't face the polite introductions straight away.

'Hi,' Lily breathed, covering the door. Beth was Josie's younger sister, just eighteen and someone she'd known since she was a child. She was standing in the hall in a sarong, a T-shirt and a pair of pink flip-flops.

'Hi you too!' Beth grinned back, then took in the

dishevelled hair, the bright eyes and stubble-burned chin. 'Oh no,' she said in horror, 'I'm interrupting, aren't I? I *thought* I heard a man's voice!'

'No, it's fine! Josie mentioned that you might be coming.'

Beth's face had flushed a bright crimson. 'I'm so sorry!' She sounded completely mortified.

'Beth,' Lily insisted, laughing despite herself, 'stop it!'

Beth made a face at the sitting-room door. 'I'll go out again. I'm going. Right this second.'

'It doesn't matter,' Lily lied, wanting to make it easy for her. 'We weren't doing anything.'

Beth was having none of it. 'My friends are having a drink on the other side of the bridge,' she gabbled, almost tripping over her sarong in her haste to get back out of the door. 'They're in one of the pubs on the river. And they're dying for me to join them. After tonight I'm not going to see them for ages,' she said, only adding the slightest of embellishments to what was, essentially, completely true. She rubbed her jangling bangled arms in agitation, and grabbed at a moth-eaten canvas bag, glancing again at the closed sitting-room door. 'I'll come back later?' She raised her eyebrows meaningfully. 'In about an hour? Is that long enough?'

'I'm in tonight,' Lily told her laughing. 'Are you? Can we catch up then?'

'Yes,' Beth said, desperate to be off as soon as she could. 'I'll show you my photos from India!'

'Can't wait.'

Before she could say another word, Beth was gone.

Lily opened the door, ran into the room and launched herself into Josh's arms.

'You can't get rid of me so easily,' she told him.

'Thank you, Beth, for your hour, whoever you are!' He pushed the door shut with his foot.

'She's sweet. And she was so embarrassed. And she was wearing a T-shirt and flip-flops. It's going to snow!'

'Don't talk about her any more.'

With Lily still in his arms he led her over to the sofa and dropped her gently down. She caught him by the lapels of his suit and pulled him on top of her.

'How long were you gone for, do you think?' he asked her, kissing her collarbone.

'About a minute? Definitely less than two.'

'That's the foreplay done then, don't you think?'

She laughed. 'Not on your life.'

*

Afterwards he propped himself up on an elbow and looked down at her.

'Lovely Lily. I can never let you go.'

They were lying on the floor, half covered with a cotton throw that usually lay along the back of Josie's sofa, which had at some point been dragged with them to the floor. Josh ran a finger gently down her cheekbone. 'I always want to be with you.'

Lily nodded, thinking am I mad to believe you're serious?

He kissed her again and she breathed in his warmth and sighed lazily and closed her eyes.

'But Lily,' he said and this time his tone of voice told her he was about to say something she wouldn't like. 'I'm going to have to go.'

'Why? Where?'

He winced. 'Can you believe I'm meant to be going to another stag night tonight?'

Lily sat up and looked at him disbelievingly.

'I know. Do you think I want to go? Do you think I want to leave you now?'

She reached for her jumper. *Maybe*, she thought.

'It's all right. You can't help it,' she said, feeling in a strange way unsurprised.

He leaned over to her, but he was already starting to get up. 'I'm so sorry. But it's something I can't miss.'

She nodded.

'I didn't know this was going to happen to us,' he said, stepping into his boxer shorts. 'I'd have got out of it.'

'Cancelled the stag night,' she managed to smile. 'Presuming you're the best man.'

'No, no one's ever going to want me for that job again.'

She got up and came close to him, surprising herself by how calm she was, how she almost didn't mind him going because she wanted some time to think about him.

'Shall we do something tomorrow? I'm leaving for home on Sunday.'

Josh didn't react.

'No. You have plans for tomorrow,' Lily answered the question herself, feeling sadness slip over her as doubt crept into her mind.

'Tomorrow and Sunday. Can you believe I'm escorting

a client on to the set of a film? I have to be in Brighton for the whole of tomorrow, home for the evening, and then back to Brighton for the whole of Sunday too.'

'A client?'

'A neurotic screenwriter who can't be let out on his own. Even at the weekend. But I could see you tomorrow night.'

'You know I'm seeing Hal. I told you.' She looked away, wondering if it would be so bad to cancel Hal for Josh. 'And I can't cancel him,' she said. Josh nodded. 'We've had this set up for ages. I feel I must see him. And I wouldn't have been able to see you on Sunday anyway because I'm leaving. I'm getting the train back in the morning.'

'Oh, Lily!'

'Shall we get together again in about six months?' She tried to sound light-hearted.

Josh shook his head. 'You won't get rid of me that easily. Hal's asked me to come back to the Little Goose for Easter.'

'What? Why?'

'He says it's important to him.' Josh shrugged. 'I was going to try to get out of it.'

Oh, Lily thought. Were you just?

'I didn't see the point.' At her face he stopped. 'Of course I wanted to see you again, but I didn't think you'd want to see me. I imagined going there with Hal – lots of long walks in the fresh air and endless conversation about Amber – and I have to say I can think of better ways to spend my time. But now, of course I want to come. That is, if you're still going to be there?'

Lily nodded.

'Then it's the only place I want to be.'

'Why do you think Hal wants you to go back?' she asked.

'He cares a lot that we patch things up. And I think he has a twisted sense of humour.'

'He's very forgiving.'

'Isn't he? He wants to stay in the Little Goose and try to see you two again.'

'You'll have to tell him about me. Otherwise we'll never get any time away from him.'

'I will, but I have to be careful!'

'Because he'll be worried for me?'

'No. Because he fancies you himself.'

Lily laughed. 'Hal! I don't think he's up to fancying anybody but Amber. Not yet.'

It was nearly an hour since Beth had gone and Lily guessed she'd soon be back. And knowing that Josh had to go, Lily realized that she wanted him out of the house quickly, needing a little time alone before Beth returned.

'I'll call you.' He hugged her hard but she could feel he was thinking about his stag night, ready to go.

She turned away from him and dressed quickly, but even as she was going through the sitting-room door, Lily heard the slap of Beth's flip-flops as she approached the front door again. Damn, she thought, as the key moved in the lock.

'I'll leave you both to it. Be friendly,' Josh instructed her. He gave her a last swift kiss goodbye.

Lily opened the front door for her.

When Beth saw Lily she jumped nervously.

'Has he gone now?' she asked, making it sound as if Josh was a dangerous animal, and then jumped again in alarm as Josh appeared behind Lily.

'Hi,' she mumbled, looking away, her face colouring again.

'This is Josh,' Lily told her, grinning at her reaction, 'and Josh's just leaving.'

*

'Isn't he lovely,' Beth said passionately, her pink and white complexion still more pink than white at the thought of him.

Lily turned back to her and smiled and the warmth inside spilled out through her face and Beth immediately caught her arm.

'You are a lucky cow,' she hissed, leading her back up the hall. 'Has Josie met him yet?'

'She knows about him but she hasn't met him. *I* hardly know him.'

She walked back into the sitting-room and Beth stood in the doorway and looked after her thoughtfully, taking in the throw still lying on the floor.

'But better than you did before I left, perhaps!'

Beth's confidence was obviously growing now that the reality of Josh had gone through the front door.

'Respect, please! You're far too young to talk to me like that.'

'If I wasn't so sad and single myself, I'd be very pleased for you.'

Beth went back out into the hall and dragged in a bright blue nylon rucksack, then opened a zip and pulled out a long string of dirty T-shirts and paisley cotton pyjama bottoms.

'Beth!' Lily exclaimed. 'You're not eligible for sad and single when you're only eighteen. It's the privilege of the twenties and thirties.'

Beth laughed, scrabbling deeper into her bag. 'I'm looking for something,' she explained. 'Josie said I can leave my stuff here. I'm going to Peru for six months on Monday.'

Lily looked at the mountain of moccasins and flip-flops and tie-dyed sarongs, at the cameras and jumpers and toe-rings and beaded photo frames that now engulfed Josie's tidy hall and spilled into the sitting-room, and wondered just how much of Beth Josie was expecting.

From deep in one of the bags, Beth unearthed a leather beaded necklace and matching bracelet and handed them both to Lily with a smile. 'Here,' she said. 'They're skitti beads – trust and love. Have them.'

'Thanks,' said Lily.

*

Josh didn't call Lily the next day. She told herself not to mind but still she did. Would it have been so impossible to call her from his mobile? She didn't think so, and a tiny bit of her took stock of the fact that he hadn't, and worried at it.

And then evening came and it was time to get ready to go out with Hal. As she put on her make-up she chatted to Beth, enjoying the distraction after a day spent trying not to think about Josh. And yet, as she chose what to wear, he was still with her. She wished that it was Josh she was dressing to meet, wished that she'd been able to see him again after their one wonderful day together, to reassure her that he had cared, that she wasn't mad to think the day had meant something to him too. A day without him, and with no word from him, had released the demons in her head and they were already whispering to her that she was being taken in, like so many others had been taken in before her. Telling her that he'd only got in touch because he'd already agreed to go to Welshpool with Hal and wanted to set himself up with a little distraction for while he was there.

But still she couldn't imagine changing anything. Already she was dying to see him again, willing away the days between now and Easter, and she didn't doubt that he wanted to see her again too, that at that moment she was as interesting to him as he was to her. But what she had to remember was not to hope it would last.

She was not going to let on to Hal what had happened between her and Josh, she decided, sitting on her bed in a pale pink satin camisole and painting pearly pink varnish on her fingernails. She waved dry her hands and considered them. If she told Hal, she thought, shaking the bottle again before adding a second coat, he'd be bound to be annoyed with her. He'd feel betrayed and upset, and would warn her away from him. And she didn't want to hear it.

To go with the camisole she had a beautiful vintage

fifties lace skirt that she'd found the year before in the Portobello Road, and she stood up and lifted it carefully out of Josie's cupboard and put it on. She added boots and a diamanté bracelet and was ready. She collected up her keys, shouted goodbye to Beth and left the house.

Across the room of the restaurant she saw him watching her and she caught his eye and waved, surprised by how good it was to see him waiting for her there. She handed away her coat and walked quickly over to him, and he stood up and put his arm around her shoulders and gave her a great warm smacker of a kiss.

'You're in a good mood,' she laughed.

'Who wouldn't be if they were waiting for you?'

'You smoothie!'

She sat down and he ordered them both a glass of champagne.

'Okay, let's get it out of the way,' he said determinedly, the moment the waiter had left their table, 'and then we can talk about something else.'

'What do you mean?' she said, looking down at her napkin, visions of her and Josh tumbling naked off the sofa filling her mind.

'Amber?' Hal helped her. 'Remember her? You were going to make a call for me.' He sighed, 'Oh, Lily, do I take it you still haven't managed to sort out my life?'

She looked up at him, hoping that she had heard a trace of humour in his voice.

'Hal, I'm sorry. I did call but it didn't go well.'

He tipped back his chair, considering her.

'I'm not surprised.'

'You're not?'

'No,' he said bringing his chair straight again. 'And don't worry. I think I'll survive.'

'It's been a long time now, Hal. Can you start to forget her?'

'I know I should,' he shrugged, 'and pretty soon I will, I'm sure I will. I'm still hurt but I'm used to that and I'm certainly not devastated any more.' He took a heavy breath. 'I can almost call her a silly bitch but not quite,' he sighed. 'But I still want to know what she said.' He said the last bit firmly, but there was a distinctly brave look in his eye.

'No you don't. She didn't say anything that would make you feel better. In fact, *she* didn't say anything at all. I spoke to a friend.'

'Barbie,' Hal nodded knowingly. 'Poor you.'

'What?' said Lily, surprised. 'How did you know?'

'They're always doing that, pretending to be each other. They've lived together for ages and they've got it down to a fine art. In fact, that's one good thing to come out of all this! I will never have Barbie's face peering around the bathroom door at me ever again!'

Lily laughed. 'Barbie as in the doll?'

'They could be sisters! And if it was her you spoke to, I'm not interested in hearing what she said.'

Lily nodded. 'Only her.'

'I knew nothing good was going to come out of it, but I was hoping that you'd somehow persuade Amber to get in touch with me.' He sighed heavily again. 'I know, I know, that's not going to happen now. But all I wanted was to apologize to her,' he said.

Lily raised her eyebrows. It was on the tip of her tongue to tell Hal what Josh had said about Amber practically dancing on the ceiling with relief at the news that her wedding was off.

'But that's it,' he said with finality. 'No more talking about Amber. I am going to get on with my life!'

'Good! Drink to that!' She clunked her glass with his.

'It's not as if we were together for years. Three, four months ago, I didn't even know her.'

'No more talk about Amber,' Lily echoed him.

He smiled and finished his champagne in two long swallows.

'I'm even starting to think . . .' he paused, 'that I was a bit of an arse to get so involved in the first place.'

Lily laughed.

'See. I'm not doing such a bad job of being normal, am I?' he demanded. 'I'm making you laugh, I'm taking you out, holding down my job – for a little while longer. *And* I'm bringing Josh with me to stay at the Little Goose over Easter. To patch things up with him.'

Lily felt herself reddening. 'Hey! You *are* forgiving!'

'Well, if I'm going to move on, I have to be. He's a good friend. And he was right, Amber didn't love me. I'd have been miserable.'

Lily shook her head. 'You're willing to forget what Josh did to you?'

'Probably. One day. Aren't I a pushover?'

A waiter appeared at their table, Hal ordered more champagne and the waiter passed her a menu.

'What about those other guys? Charlie and Richard and Alex?' she asked. 'Are you forgiving them too?'

Hal shrugged. 'Richard and Alex haven't been in touch since that weekend. Can you believe it! I've known them since we were seven . . .'

'I'm sorry,' Lily said.

'But Charlie and I will get together some day. It's just taking longer than it is with Josh. He's more ashamed about it all.'

'I understand.'

She picked up her menu.

'Lily, I wouldn't be in such good shape now, if it wasn't for you.'

She glanced up. Hal was looking at her earnestly and Lily thought what a fool Amber had been. Not to see what she'd got, and to hold on to him and to look after him properly.

'It wasn't me,' she told him.

'Yes it was. I was talking to you – and your sister – when I couldn't talk to anyone else.'

'But it didn't get you anywhere.'

'How do you know?'

'I don't believe you, but thank you for saying so.'

If Hal had been about to say more, he changed his mind.

'After Easter, I'm going away,' he told her. 'I've handed in my notice and I'm going travelling.'

'How fantastic. Where?'

'West Indies? Galapagos Islands? Wherever takes my fancy. I'll go for about six months.'

'That's brilliant. You are so lucky that you can do that. It sounds amazing,' said Lily wistfully. 'My plans are Welshpool, bit of London, Welshpool, bit of London, Welshpool.'

Hal laughed. 'Come with me, then?'

Lily raised her eyebrows at him. 'Seriously?'

He nodded.

'No, of course I can't,' she said.

There was something in his expression that meant she had to look away.

'Have you ever been away? I mean far away?' he asked her then.

'Portugal and Spain and France, but never outside Europe. Never to a sugar white beach with palm trees and turquoise water.'

'Then come with me!' Hal insisted.

'Okay, tell me when and I'll be there,' she joked, then looked at him again and wished she hadn't. Back off! She wanted to tell him, wrong-footed by the new look in his eyes, and by a sudden awareness of Hal as someone more than just the jilted bridegroom. You're messed up and vulnerable, she wanted to say. Don't even think of turning your attentions on me.

'When are you going away?'

'After Easter. And you will be in Welshpool over Easter, won't you? If Josh and I come down? You and Kirsty, and Grace too. Can we all have supper, in the Little

Goose over the weekend?' Hal said it eagerly. 'Would Friday night be okay? Good Friday?'

'We might be in our new cottage by then, Kirsty and I. But of course we'll come!'

At least if Josh and Hal were friends again, she thought, it wouldn't be so awkward when Hal realized what was going on between Josh and her.

'And we'll drink a toast to Amber for getting us all together. You never met her, did you?'

'I met her sister, but never her.'

'If you had, I think you'd have understood why I was so deranged,' he laughed bitterly.

'I understand now.' Lily reached out and touched his sleeve. 'Don't blame yourself for falling for her.'

It was still early when they left. Hal found her a taxi and helped her inside, then insisted on covering the cab fare home.

'I'll see you soon,' he said, leaning in through the open window and reaching for her hand.

'Thanks for tonight. It was lovely.'

He looked at her wistfully and then kissed her hand. 'Get home,' he said and turned away.

16

She was out of the door by eight the next morning. As she closed it quietly so as not to wake Beth her mobile rang, piercing in the silence of the sleeping street. She looked at the number and saw that it was Josh.

'Hello,' she said cautiously. Longing for him enveloped her. 'How was the film set?'

'Bloody awful.'

'And the client?'

'Spent the whole day in tears.'

'Oh no,' Lily laughed. 'Why?'

'Because they're messing with his script. What are you doing now, right now? Where are you?'

'Leaving the house, shutting the front door.' Lily did as she said and set off down the street. 'Walking down Lonsdale Road.'

'I thought you would be. Why don't you stay another day and wait for me. I could see you tonight.'

'I have to go back. I want to. I've things I have to decide . . .'

'Like what?'

'Like what I'm going to do. Where I'm going to live. Little things like that.'

'Where else would you live?'

'London, I suppose,' she said cautiously. 'If I get the

job at the Registry it would make sense if I moved nearer to it.' She couldn't say that what had happened between them made it hard not to think of moving to London just to be nearer to him.

As she talked, she turned left out of Lonsdale Road, heading towards the bridge.

'What are you doing now?' she asked Josh.

'Talking to you. Getting ready to pick up the dreadful Mr Barnsley for a second day of mental torture.'

'Why do you have to do it all over again?'

'Because he wants me to. And he's an important client.'

'Oh, I see,' she teased. 'So it's all about money.'

'Absolutely.'

She'd reached the bridge now. Sunday morning and it was empty. She liked it like that. She could see people jogging along the towpath below her and just one other person crossing the bridge from the other side.

'So have you missed me at all?' she asked, suddenly brave, not wanting the entire conversation to be one that he could have been having with his sister.

He was silent for a moment, thinking about it. 'Yes,' he said quietly.

'How much would that be?'

'Truly, madly, deeply. Masses and masses,' he laughed. 'More than I miss cigarettes.'

She laughed. 'Oh, thank you!'

'And I'd do anything, *anything*, to see you now.'

'Oh, right.' That's why you've cancelled your client, Lily thought.

'But you're going home and I'm going to Brighton. Will Kirsty be there to meet you at the station?'

The person walking towards her was very close now, she thought. If he didn't lift his head up and look where he was going he was going to walk straight into her.

'Why are you smiling?' Lily demanded.

'I'm not!'

'Yes, you are, I can hear it in your voice . . .' Josh didn't reply, but she was sure she'd been right. 'Josh,' she said again, 'are you there?'

'Where?' Josh said, standing there in front of her on the bridge and grinning at her. She felt her stomach do a great leap of shock and outrage as she struggled to take it in.

'I took a chance that you'd walk rather than get a cab,' he said, reaching for her, laughing delightedly because he'd managed to make it all the way up to her without her realizing it was him.

She was so surprised that she felt completely disorientated, dumbstruck. It was Josh, there, right in front of her. She stood back from him for a moment, then started to laugh with him, because now that she could see him all her old fears and insecurities vanished. The Josh she didn't trust, the cold-hearted seducer, was banished by the reality of the Josh who was obviously so pleased to see her now. In the quiet early morning, freshly shaved but with his hair still showing signs of having been slept on, he looked more endearing, more gorgeous than ever. Lost for words, she threw her arms around his neck and kissed him.

'You taste of peppermint,' she told him.

'Lily, I couldn't stay away. Mr Barnsley will have to wait.'

'You're crazy,' she laughed.

'No I'm not.' He shook his head. 'When are you going to take us seriously?'

She didn't reply but pulled him close to her and kissed him again.

'Oh baby,' he groaned, running his hands up her back. 'Can't we go back to your flat?'

'One-track mind,' She said, deep in his arms, thinking how nice that would be.

'Is that a yes?'

'What about Mr Barnsley? Won't he get tired of waiting?'

'I don't care.'

She looked up at him. 'I don't care about my train either.'

He took her hand and they ran back over the bridge together, back to Josie's flat. Distracted by Josh's phone call, Lily had forgotten to post her key back through the letter-box so she was able to let them both in. With Lily's bag still in his hand, Josh started to kiss her the moment the front door was open, turning her so that they stepped slowly backwards together to close it again. With their combined weight the door moved much too fast and then shut with such a loud clunk that it echoed through the flat, and for a second they stopped, certain that Beth was going to appear at the sitting-room door and spoil everything for the second time. But there was no sound. Josh dropped her bag to the floor.

'Where's the bedroom?'

'Behind me.'

He pushed her in and kicked the door shut. 'She can't disturb us now.'

'At this rate, I might still make the train,' Lily laughed as she fell backwards on to the bed.

*

Her train arrived at teatime and Kirsty was there at the station to meet her.

'I couldn't wait to see you,' she told Lily elatedly, taking her bag, beaming at Lily, at the station supervisor and at almost every other passenger that happened to be in range. 'So much has happened since you left!'

'Too right,' Lily nodded, but Kirsty didn't hear her. She took Lily's arm and steered her away from the platform and down the station steps to the car-park.

She unlocked the car and opened the door for Lily, slinging her bags into the boot. Then she drove them both quickly away, squeezing through a set of red traffic lights in her impatience to leave the station and reach a bit of clear road so that she could concentrate on Lily rather than the driving.

Before Kirsty could start, Lily turned to her. 'Actually, I've got a few things to tell you too.'

Kirsty raised her eyebrows.

'But I'm not going to tell you yet, because first *you're* going to tell *me* what's happened with Simon.'

'Oh, Lily!' Kirsty said in frustration.

'I know, I shouldn't have said anything. But you have to tell me first. You've got together again, haven't you?'

'But I want to know what's happened to *you*.'

Kirsty looked at her mutinously but she knew she wasn't going to win. And so she began to tell Lily what had happened, starting with the visit from Fred, and then Mimosa and Grace, and then, finally Simon.

'Poor Simon,' Lily said, 'you must be driving him insane. No wonder he's determined to stay away from you! Tell me what happened afterwards? After they'd all gone. After he'd helped you out of the feedbin. Tell me!'

Kirsty had been determined to make Simon kiss her. Every ounce of experience, all her powers of seduction, had gone into those few seconds where she had him again in her grasp. But he had known what to expect and he had broken free, laughing. She'd joined him at the window and they'd looked out together at the leaves spiralling around the yard in the wind.

'It's going to snow,' Kirsty said.

'Do you think so? Isn't it nearly summer?'

'No! And we don't often get summer up here, not in these parts.' She smiled up at him. 'It'll snow tonight, I'm sure.'

'Are *you* sure, country girl, or is Michael Fish sure?'

Kirsty turned to him. 'Look at the cattle,' she ordered, pointing across to a nearby field. 'When one puts its tail in the air like that, it always means snow.'

'Yeah, right!'

Kirsty nodded.

'Really?' He said, believing her. 'How funny!'

She looked up at the ceiling, trying to keep a straight face.

'I am such a mug.'

'Come for a walk with me tomorrow afternoon, after you leave the Little Goose,' she said impulsively. 'If it snows it will be wonderful. We could go up the Long Mountain. I bet you haven't ever seen it in the snow.'

'Why?' he asked her softly, but there was a soft, smitten look in his eyes that told her she was right to hope, that she was still on his mind.

Kirsty shrugged.

'I'll come and pick you up,' he'd said, 'and you can show me the way.'

'And so,' Kirsty said now, glancing gleefully over to Lily, 'we're going up there this afternoon.'

Lily looked out of the window. 'There's still time for it to snow.'

*

On the way home Kirsty made a detour via Montgomery.

Of all the places that Lily had grown to know so well, Montgomery was her favourite. And of all the places that could most tempt her to stay on there, it was Montgomery, with its pretty Georgian square, pink and olive and pastel blue houses and lovely gallery and shops. Kirsty had taken Lily there soon after she had arrived, knowing that she would fall for the little town and the old ruined castle sitting high above it. Lily had looked up at it from the square, listening as Kirsty had told her how it had been built in the early twelve hundreds and had been fought over for the next four hundred years until it had been won from the royalists in the Civil War and orders had been put through for its demolition in 1649. Lily had looked up at it, seeing it not as a ruin but as imperious and secure again, with horses and soldiers galloping under its arches, flags held high, ready to defend the town below.

Kirsty took Lily straight through the square and down a little lane that Lily had never noticed before, and stopped and pointed out Owl Cottage backed up against the craggy rock of the steep hillside at the end of a little path.

'What do you think?'

Lily looked at the cottage. It was hidden behind wildly overgrown creepers and ivy and a tangle of a garden, but was still incredibly pretty. Chocolate-box pretty if it were ever done up too neatly, with the old roof reaching half-way down the house and the stream running through the bottom of the garden. The wide borders were already full of promise, daffodils and tulips just starting to bud in readiness for the spring. For the size of the cottage, there was lots of garden, some of it hidden behind old apple trees and a yew hedge, and more spreading out in front of the cottage, divided in half by a pretty herringbone brick path that led away from the porched front door. In any other mood, at any other time, Lily would have fallen for it straight away, but now Josh had messed up everything. She didn't want to be anywhere he wasn't. And he was in London.

'Isn't it sweet!' she said, unable to feel anything at all. 'But I don't know what I'm going to be doing this summer . . .' She tailed off, knowing how awful it would be sounding to Kirsty.

'I do understand, you know,' Kirsty interrupted. 'I knew the minute you went that you'd come back feeling differently. When or if you decide it's time to move away from here, I'll still rent it – on my own. And you'll still be allowed to come and stay,' she went on. 'For a small fee. And if you've already decided and you need to tell me you're moving away, you mustn't feel guilty,' Kirsty told her, avoiding her eye. 'But you should let me know.'

Lily turned away. 'I'm sorry, I'm sorry. And I haven't decided anything. I think it would be lovely to live here with you. Forgive me? Please. When I tell you what happened in London you'll understand. But at the moment I promise you I have no plans to leave.' She shrugged. 'I have no plans.'

'There's only four weeks' notice in the contract so it's not as if I'm making a lifelong commitment. And if you can come too, then come. But if you don't it doesn't matter because I think it's perfect for me and I'm moving in. If you're thinking about your job and you need to wait and see what they say, do that. They may not want you. And if they do, then perhaps it *would* be better for you to move nearer to London. What did we agree?' Kirsty reminded her. 'That we'd take it for the summer and then we'd think again. Either way, I am doing that. What ever happens with me and Simon. With you or without you. I have to leave home. Big deal!' she laughed. 'Five whole miles away from my parents.'

'It's great that you get on with them so well,' Lily said, taken aback by how easy Kirsty was making it all. 'Look at Grace and me. As far away from ours as possible.'

They got out of the car and leaned side by side over the little wooden gate at the bottom of the path that led up to the cottage.

'Come on,' Kirsty said. 'Nobody lives there now. Let me at least show you around.'

Lily, panicking that some hidden owner might leap out and shout at them, ran lightly up the path after Kirsty.

She peered in through the kitchen window at the low-beamed ceilings and made out an old-fashioned Rayburn and a terracotta-tiled floor. And, despite what she thought she'd feel, something turned over inside her and shook itself out, a determination not to put her life on hold just for Josh, whom she hardly knew. She'd been happier here than she'd been anywhere else. And Kirsty and she had planned to move in together. Whatever she felt for Josh, she'd known him for just a few days. There was no hurry. She would move in as planned.

She would give herself the summer here, she thought, looking away from the cottage and down to the studio at the bottom of the garden. Where else was she going to go? And she'd still have Kirsty for some of the time, even if she was about to get it together with Simon.

She visualized herself and Kirsty out in the garden in bikinis, sunbathing and having barbecues, splashing in the stream when it was hot enough. Saw herself coming out of the studio, her hands caked in clay, having produced her first pieces for the Registry.

'I do want to live here,' she said to Kirsty as they opened the gate again and left the cottage. 'I definitely do. When do you want to move in?'

'Pheww!' Kirsty grinned in relief. 'We'll have a laugh, Lily, I promise you.' She paused and fixed Lily with a determined eye. 'And now you are going to tell me what's been going on.'

How should I put it, Lily thought? 'When I said I didn't know where I wanted to be, I wasn't only thinking about my job,' she started tentatively.

Kirsty listened, transfixed.

'I saw Josh again.'

'How did you manage that?'

As they drove away from the cottage and Montgomery, Lily told her about the wonderful, perfect day with Josh. How quickly and intensely she had felt for him. And then how he'd met her on the bridge, how it was the most romantic thing that had ever happened to her. And how now that she was home again, back in Welshpool, she felt as if she'd fallen in love and she had to keep reminding herself that she couldn't have done, mustn't have done, not with Josh.

'If I wish I was in London again, it's only because of him. Because I want to see some more of him, find out if he is as I think he is. You don't mind me saying that?'

'I don't. I understand what you're saying,' Kirsty insisted immediately. 'But Lily . . .'

She looks frightened for me, Lily thought in surprise, and disappointment rose up inside her, making her bite her lip and turn away.

'Don't hate me,' Kirsty begged, leaning around her to look at her face. 'I know it's not what you want me to say. But I have to say it!'

Lily nodded, not trusting herself to speak.

'Don't take him too seriously, Lily, that's all. Please,' Kirsty continued, 'have some fun with him but don't let him get to you. He could hurt you so badly.'

Lily gave a curt little nod.

'Don't get me wrong. I'm excited for you,' Kirsty said, desperate to make amends. 'I think it's fantastic that you've met someone.'

'But you don't trust Josh.' Lily nodded slowly. 'I don't think you'd say that if you'd seen him with me. I know how he seemed when we saw him here but he wasn't like that at all in London.'

'That's great.' Kirsty shrugged, thinking *never again* will I put myself in this position. Next time I will be dishonest. I will not risk my friendship. I will not alienate myself from her. Better that I'm there at her side when he dumps her than not at her side at all.

'I wanted you to tell me it was all going to be okay.'

'It probably is,' Kirsty said. 'All I'm saying is I think you're right to be wary. That he's used to having lots of fun, with lots of girls. Maybe you're the one to change that,' she shrugged. 'Why not? But I don't think you can know that yet.'

'He's coming down for Easter with Hal,' Lily said, feeling better. 'They want us to have supper with them! They want to stay at the Little Goose.'

'Oh, do they now!' Kirsty laughed.

'Who are you, getting all proprietorial already? Business is business. Simon will be pleased.'

'And then you will know,' Kirsty said simply. 'You'll have proper time together. And how fantastic if Hal is coming back again too,' Kirsty smiled. 'It makes it even better.'

*

Ten minutes before Simon was due at Little Venus Farm Kirsty set out to meet him, walking rather than driving because the snow had finally arrived, coming down slowly, in fat, fluffy flakes. Wearing jeans and a jumper, wellingtons and a brown oilskin with a hood, she set off along the long, twisting lane that led away from Little Venus Farm. The snow was already creaking under her boots, high in the hills she knew it would be deep. She wondered whether Mimosa had realized who Simon was going walking with, wondered how desperate she was under the steam-rolling exterior and whether she might try to stop him.

With the snow's arrival, the wind had stopped, but still the air was icy cold and Kirsty shivered inside her coat, wishing that she'd brought some gloves and a scarf. She wondered how far she would have to walk before she met Simon's car, hoping it wouldn't be all the way to Pond House. She'd set off impulsively, almost to ensure that he had to come out to meet her, to avoid the possibility of him phoning her to say, for whatever reason, that he wasn't able to come.

As she walked she listened for the sound of his car, following the lane as it twisted sharply left and right, and after what felt like ages she saw him slowly making his way towards her, struggling on the slippery narrow road, his lights on and the windscreen wipers on full too. She walked faster to meet him, sliding rather than walking, until she was level with the car. He stopped and opened his door.

'Want a lift?' he called.

She nodded and came around to the passenger side and got in beside him.

'This car hates the snow,' he told her, turning up the heater. 'It's already tried to take me over one precipice on the way here.' He gingerly let off the handbrake and the car started to slide forwards. 'Are you cold? How long have you been walking for?'

'Not long,' she said, on edge now that she was with him again.

He drove on for a moment longer and then suddenly said, 'So where are we going, Kirsty, you and me?'

'What?' she exclaimed, not expecting him to get so heavy so soon.

'There's no way we'll make it up on to the Long Mountain. Watch.' He touched the foot brake and the car didn't react at all, gliding slowly on down the road in a perfect straight line.

Kirsty's eyes widened. 'Are you serious? Can you really not stop?'

'No. But it's okay, isn't it?' He carefully took her hand

and looked at her and laughed. 'Because we're together again.'

'Don't do that! Keep them on the steering-wheel,' she said, thinking, damn him for joking about it.

'Don't worry,' he said reassuringly. 'The hedges will stop us falling over the edge. That's what they're there for.'

'Does your steering-wheel work? Can you turn the wheel?'

'A little.'

'I can't be in another accident. I've only just got over the last one! Turn into the hedge before we go any faster.'

'No way!' Simon protested. 'It'll scratch the car. It was your idea to come out.'

'I hadn't realized how bad it was.'

'We'll be fine. Watch me.'

He lifted his hands off the steering-wheel again and the car responded by slowly turning off the road and into a gateway. It bumped carefully over the raised verge and came to a gentle halt.

'It's always better if you let them find their own way.' Simon turned off the engine.

'Good car. Thank you, car,' Kirsty said shakily, patting the dashboard.

'I'm sorry if you were scared,' he said after a moment's silence. 'Are you okay?'

Kirsty nodded, not looking at him.

The falling snow had moved up a gear now, coming down in a swirling mass, and for a while they both looked out at it. Then Simon turned to Kirsty questioningly, and she looked back at him, waiting for him to speak, but he didn't say anything and so they sat silently together, cocooned in the car, still not talking.

Why didn't he talk? Or at least make some effort with her? Why had he come? Perhaps he didn't realize what she wanted. Perhaps he didn't want anything to happen between them? Now it was awkward and awful and she wished she hadn't assumed it was all going to be wonderful, because the disappointment was gut-wrenchingly horrible. She wondered if he was laughing at her for bringing him out like this.

She glanced sideways at him, willing him to make a move, but he continued to stare impassively through the windscreen.

'I'm off then,' she said irritably.

She opened her door and stepped outside and snowflakes immediately bombarded her, settling in her eyelashes and on her cheeks and hair.

She shut the door hard behind her and wiped the snow away and then, when there was no sign that Simon was following her, she strode away down the lane, turning a corner and quickly disappearing from his sight.

She heard a click and a slam in the distance but she didn't turn around, and then at last he came up alongside her and slid his arm around her shoulders.

'What's the matter with you?' he said.

Kirsty turned on him. 'I didn't want it to be like this!' she retorted, making Simon jump back with alarm. 'I don't want to have to feel that it's all up to me. For fuck's sake.

What did I do? Nothing so terrible.' She started walking faster. 'And I've said sorry, and tried to explain, not that there's a lot of explaining to do. And I've told you how I feel – which is horrible, by the way.' She turned to him, furiously. 'And yet you're still punishing me. You kiss me and then you tell me, actually no. You wait in the Warehouse for me and then walk away the minute you find me. Do you want to be with me or not? Because if you do, I think it's *your* turn to show *me* now. Horrible man,' she added.

'Why do I always forget what a bolshie pain in the arse you are?' Kirsty looked away to hide her grin. 'It's always the same. You go away, and all I can think about is my adorable, scrumptious Kirsty, with her little turned-up nose,' he paused, 'and her lovely blue eyes, and her beautiful, sweet lips. And then I see you, and you swear and shout and stomp around me, and I think: remember this next time, stupid man! Remember what she's really like. Stay away from her!'

'And then?' Kirsty said, slowing down.

'And then,' he said, putting out his arms to stop her, 'I can't do it. I never could.'

Kirsty felt relief wash through her.

'And if it's okay, I'm not even going to try any more. Because I'm not very happy if I'm not with you.' He put his arms over her shoulders and looked down at her. 'And I'm very happy if I am.' He paused. 'You know why I had to try to be without you for a while? For my pride, and for you to have a chance to sort yourself out, and to realize what you were missing out on.'

She moved closer to him and slid her arms around his waist. 'Don't tell me you deliberately got hold of Mimosa to make me jealous?'

'What?' he sounded amazed. 'But of course!'

Kirsty laughed and shoved him backwards. 'Poor Mimosa.'

'I know. But I think she's got the message now. Even if she hasn't, she's not my problem and I don't want to think about her. I want to think about you. And me.' He held her still.

They stood there in the middle of the lane, oblivious to everything else but each other. She lifted her face to his and he kissed her with all the hungry passion that Kirsty could ever have hoped for, with the snow falling fast and silently on their heads, on Simon's shoulders and Kirsty's black wellington boots, and piling up around them.

For a long time neither of them moved, until finally Kirsty looked down at her feet, and laughed to see how much snow had fallen around them. She turned in Simon's arms, sliding one of hers around his waist.

'Look at us,' she said softly. 'Another ten minutes and we'd have been buried alive.' She kicked the snow off her boots.

'I can think of worse things.'

Slowly they walked over to a gap in the hedge and stood together, Simon pulling her close, and they looked out at the snow, spreading soft and silently across the hills. After a while, Kirsty turned to watch him instead. He was standing so close and yet she could see that he was far away from her. She watched him as he looked

out across the rolling, snow-covered hills and was transfixed. It had been like that all along, she thought, he had
always been like that. But here, in the silence and the
peace of the moment, it was intensified. There was a
stillness, a wonderful calmness, about him that she loved.
That didn't make him detached or solitary, but was a
sign of his strength. However much he needed her and
wanted her, she thought, he would always have that
about him. He was always going to be independent of
her too.

From the start he'd had the strength of character not to
need to play games with her but to tell her straight away
that he'd fallen for her. What she'd mistaken for over-
dependence was actually his confidence, a willingness to
be open about what he felt for her. But before she'd
realized how good that was, she'd run away.

She'd always seemed to attract needy men, those who
would latch on to her and who made her feel as if they
were dragging her down, holding her back. And at first
she'd thought Simon was like that too. But she'd been
wrong. She stretched up and kissed him gently on his
cheek and then again on the corner of his mouth, making
his lips twitch into a smile.

'Back to the car now?' he said, turning to her. 'Shall we
go home?'

She nodded and started to walk away from him,
moving ahead and out of sight as she turned the corner
and he followed her slowly, wondering why she hadn't
waited for him. When a snowball hit him on his shoulder
he shouted in surprise.

'It's romantic,' she laughed. 'It's what people like us are meant to do.'

'And this, are we meant to do this too?' He took a handful of snow and bit into it, then ran after Kirsty down the lane towards the car, and grabbed her and kissed her again, bending her backwards over the bonnet, making her gasp with shock, but his mouth was already over hers and no sound came out. The cold snow and his hot tongue sent waves of desire throbbing through her as the snow melted, turning their lips slippery and wet, and Kirsty felt as if she was going to collapse with longing for him.

'I love you,' he told her, still leaning over her.

Her eyes widened. 'Surely not.'

'And I've loved you for as long as I've known you.'

She bit her lip, feeling her eyes burn with tears at the look in his eyes. 'I love you too.'

She couldn't believe it was happening, this miraculous, perfect moment she'd never dared to hope would happen to her.

'And I'm taking you home.'

'What about Mimosa?'

They got into the car and slid their way carefully back to Pond House.

'Don't worry about Mimosa,' Simon told her as they pulled to a halt. 'I'm sure she said she was going out.'

The front door was locked. Simon found the key and opened it for them and together they walked into the kitchen. There on the table was a note for Simon.

'What did I say? It's from Mimosa,' he told her. 'I knew something was up.' He read it out loud.

Simon, I'll admit I didn't want to go! He looked up at Kirsty and grinned at that. *But I know now that I've definitely outstayed my welcome.*

'Oh, you haven't!' said Kirsty.

Don't worry, Kirsty, I won't be moving in on your doorstep! And Simon, thanks a million for putting up with me for as long as you did. I'll keep in touch, love, Mimosa.

'Why's she talking to me?'

'Because she's a thoughtful considerate person. I suppose she guessed you might be coming back with me after our walk.'

She kissed him gently. 'So you told her who you were meeting, did you?'

'Yes, I did. I don't think she was surprised. Once she'd realized it was never going to happen between me and her, she didn't want to hang around to watch.'

Kirsty stood in front of Simon. 'Nothing ever happened between the two of you?'

'No, of course it didn't.'

'She never said, "Take me to bed or lose me for ever"?'

'No, she didn't,' he said seriously, coming towards her. 'Who did?'

'Kelly McGillis in *Top Gun*!'

He smiled. 'Say it again?'

17

The snow didn't settle, and almost as soon as it disappeared it felt like spring. In the week before Easter, the air turned softer and primroses and violets started to appear through the grass in the verges. There were pussy-willow and hawthorn in the hedges, and lambs in the fields. On good days, when the sun was out, Lily walked around feeling as if she was in a production of *The Darling Buds of May*, but with no part for herself. The longer she went without seeing Josh, the more she worried that there was no future for them. If she mentioned how she felt to Kirsty, hoping for some reassurance, Kirsty only nodded gravely, making Lily feel even more convinced that all her fears were well founded and that she should write off any hope of a future with Josh. And then, after he'd called her on the telephone, she told herself that she was being hysterical and ridiculous, that there was nothing wrong that seeing him again wouldn't cure. Around her everyone and everything seemed suddenly full of the joys of spring, and everyone and everything was joyfully pairing off, from Kirsty and Simon to the wood pigeons canoodling in the trees. Even the blackbirds who lived in the ceanothus bush next to her studio were passing her window at half height, their beaks stuffed with grasses and bits of twig.

Only a few days after Lily returned from London, she

and Kirsty moved in to Owl Cottage. For Kirsty it was a huge step, both practically and emotionally, and necessitated borrowing a van from a neighbour to transport all her things. For Lily it felt very casual and involved only the packing of a couple of bags and fetching her pots and portable kiln from Grace's. And somehow, even as they moved in together, both of them were acknowledging that their time together might be short-lived, that, however much they denied it, everything was changing for both of them. Much as Kirsty loved Lily and being with Lily, she was now happiest when she was with Simon.

For the first time since she'd arrived in Welshpool, there was no pressure on Lily to stay there. She and Kirsty had committed themselves to spending the summer together, which she was happy to honour, but the summer was only three more months and from the day she moved in the restlessness started to build inside her again. In this part of Wales, she'd found people and a place she would always know and love, but not somewhere she could live in permanently like Grace and Kirsty could.

Alone for so much of the day, Lily found herself working far harder than she'd ever done before. Using her pottery to divert her attention from herself and Josh and their future, she produced better work than ever.

Then, almost as a reward for her good behaviour, the Registry finally got in touch and offered her the job. Now there was a real reason to feel that her time here was ending. She felt that she was only marking time in Montgomery, that she had no roots anywhere any more, nothing to help her to stay.

As the days passed and Good Friday drew closer, she found she was spending up to twelve hours at a time in the studio. At the thought of seeing Josh again, she was tied into knots of anticipation and excitement and panic. She veered between thinking that she hardly knew him and that she couldn't expect anything from him at all, to feeling that something wonderful and special had happened between the two of them and that as soon as she saw him again everything was going to be all right.

He had called her every day since she'd left London, oblivious to all the heart-searching going on, and she had to admit that on the telephone he had said all the right things, that he missed her desperately and that he couldn't work or eat or sleep until he saw her again. And for a little while after the phone calls, she'd feel that it was all going to be fine, that Josh hadn't simply been making the words up.

Hal called her too, sounding bright and happy again. Thank God he's not with Amber, she found herself thinking every time she put the phone down. He's so much too nice for Amber. She wanted to see him again, and she recognized, before she dashed the thought away, that if Josh hadn't taken away her ability to fancy anybody else, perhaps something might have started to kindle between the two of them. As far as she knew, Josh had still not told Hal about her, and she wished that he would because she felt that she owed it to Hal not to mislead him. Hal's openness with her was not being reciprocated and she hated lying to him about anything, however much he'd understand. She imagined the moment when he found out, when he realized, yet again, that his best friend had not been straight with him, and she knew, even if he understood, that he would be hurt.

The night before Josh and Hal were due to arrive, Kirsty told Lily that Simon wanted to cook for them all at Pond House rather than at the Little Goose.

'If Simon thinks it's a good idea,' Lily agreed cautiously, thinking that actually she preferred the idea of the anonymity and noise of the Little Goose.

'Because, of course, then it *is* a good idea, isn't it?' Kirsty joked. 'He is, after all, always right in your book, isn't he? Simon says this is how to do it, Simon says that's a good idea. You're as bad as my mother.'

Lily laughed. 'It's true!'

She called Hal and told him about Simon's offer and gave him directions to Pond House.

'How's Josh?' she asked then, in a moment of weakness, before Hal put down the phone. 'Have you spoken to him recently?'

'He's great. Charlie thinks he's met someone.'

'Really!'

'I'll believe it when I see it.'

'You haven't met her then?'

'No,' Hal said. 'Charlie says she lives in New York. He's been over there a lot recently. And if she was a London girl I think we'd have met her.'

'Maybe she lives outside London?' Lily dared, sick at heart.

'Perhaps,' Hal laughed. 'I don't think she exists at all. Josh doesn't believe in keeping still where his women are concerned.'

'Doesn't he?'

'No, Lily,' Hal said rather sharply, 'he doesn't. We're not talking about girls like you. We're talking about the kind of girls Josh goes after. Anyway,' he changed the subject firmly. 'We're driving up together tomorrow. Josh wanted to leave early in the morning but I have to do some work. So we'll come straight to Pond House if that's okay with you?'

*

Next morning her first thought was *He's coming tonight.* She lay in bed, wondering if he was awake, imagining him and Hal packing the car, filling up with petrol and leaving London.

As the hours moved by, and she walked across the garden to her studio, she imagined their journey up the motorways. She saw them on the M25, travelled with them the hour on the M40, then the M54 and through Shrewsbury. She imagined them getting nearer and nearer, until she felt she couldn't bear to wait any longer to see him again.

After lunch Kirsty rang her from Pond House, guessing how she was and insisting that she went around to keep her company while Simon prepared the supper.

'But I don't want to. Josh might come around here to see me first.'

'Then don't be there.'

'I thought you said not to play games.'

'If you don't come, I'll send Chukka around to fetch you. You shouldn't sit around waiting for him. Do what you'd normally do. And Josh isn't the sort of guy that would expect you to hang around. He won't appreciate it.'

'I'll go out with Grace. I feel like a walk.' She felt she needed someone more soothing than Kirsty promised to be at that moment, and she owed it to Grace to tell her what was going on before she met Josh that evening.

'What's Simon cooking for us?' she asked. 'Is he preparing a feast?'

'I suggested he did something from Jamie Oliver.' Lily laughed.

'You didn't.'

'I didn't think he'd be so touchy.'

She walked through the wet grass to the studio, snapping off some branches of cherry blossom to stick in a vase. She let herself in, filled a vase with water for the blossom and then went over to the cup she'd been working on the day before. It was a loving cup, something she'd always meant to make but had never found the right reason to start before. She'd finished building it the day before and now she unwrapped it carefully from the polythene that she'd put on to prevent it from drying out. It was going to be beautiful. The traditional double handles were already in place and she held it up, looking at it critically, turning it around to check it from every angle, seeing if there was anything wrong with it that she hadn't noticed the day before. Then she sprayed it with a mist of water to soften the clay. Today she was going to paint it, first with a white slip and then, when that was dry, starting work on the spring flowers that she wanted to decorate it with. Some in relief and some two dimensional. She was going to wind them into the handles, cowslips and daisies and violets, and carry one or two of them and their stems down into the inside of the cup. When she'd finished inscribing it, decorating and painting it, she would biscuit fire it, then dip it into the glaze and leave it to dry again, rubbing it down to get rid of any tiny little blemishes in the glaze. Finally, it would be ready to glaze fire. And then she could give it to Kirsty.

Loving cups could be big business, she realized as she began work on it again. The Registry would definitely fall for them. They didn't take too long to make and she could picture them, filling up an alcove on the ground floor for Valentine's Day, each one unique. Then her mind grew full of Josh again and she saw him dumping his bag on the bed in the Little Goose, utterly carefree, leaning out of the window to stare down into the street, hurrying Hal up so that they could get down to the bar for a beer.

Would he call her straight away? Would it feel strange for him to be back here again? Wasn't it strange that he'd ever come? That he'd chosen this little place to spirit Hal away to? And strange that she'd ever come too. If she hadn't followed Grace here. If Grace hadn't got ditched, hadn't found her way to Welshpool in the first place . . .

Grace, she thought in agitation, her mind leaping on again. She really did want to go and see Grace. She wanted to be with her and to tell her all about Josh. In the old days Grace would have been the first person Lily would have turned to. Why hadn't she now? Since she'd come back from London, Lily had hardly seen her and had spoken to her only once on the phone. She felt horribly guilty and hoped that Grace hadn't been too hurt by the silence. Lily ran back to the house and rang her number, and Grace picked up the phone.

'Can we take Hodge out? Can I come with you for a walk?'

Grace agreed immediately, delighted at the need for her that she could hear in Lily's voice. She was back in the driving seat, literally, as she jumped into her car, turned it around in Green Lane and headed towards Montgomery.

Outside Lily's cottage she hooted and then waited, watching Lily come out through the front door, lock it and run down the path. Lily didn't ask where Grace was taking her, and Grace, apart from saying she knew a good place to walk, didn't elaborate. After ten or so minutes of driving extremely fast up tiny lanes that Lily had never noticed before, she parked the car in an unused gateway and turned off the engine.

They had stopped in the entrance to an old forestry track that wound, wide and inviting, into the hills, long since spread over with pine-needles and springing soft grass.

'Let's walk from here.' She turned to Lily and smiled. 'You haven't been here before, have you?' Lily shook her head, picturing the scene. Grace setting off alone up the track in her orange coat.

They got out of the car and climbed, one after the other,

over the old gate. Hodge was immediately off, jumping into an overgrown ditch, his tail waving ecstatically, and then he streaked away through the trees.

For about ten minutes Lily and Grace walked in silence, up the track that led them slowly higher and higher, winding them around the side of the hill. All that could be heard were the softly snapping twigs beneath their feet and then gradually, as Lily relaxed and concentrated on walking, her breath began to come hard as she and Grace started to fight it out between the two of them to be the fastest. Eventually Lily started to laugh, at the same time conceding defeat.

'Stop! Okay. You're much, much fitter than me!' she gasped, doubled over to get back her breath. 'I've got to have a rest.' She collapsed on to the grass at the side of the track, then pulled off her sweatshirt and pushed it underneath her.

'It's Hodge,' Grace said. 'If I didn't have to walk him I wouldn't be so fit.'

As soon as she'd caught her breath, Lily stood up again and looked around her. On her right the woods spread on above her, tall and dense and dark. But to her left, there was a gap in the trees. She walked slowly towards it, and looked, and there suddenly were the sky and the sun, and Housman's blue remembered hills.

'It's absolutely beautiful,' she called back to Grace. 'I'm so glad you've brought me here.'

'Wait until you see it from the top,' Grace said, taking off her coat and coming to stand and look at Lily's side. 'But let's have a breather here first.'

She went back to her coat and scrambled in her deep pockets.

'We have two classy plastic cups,' she said then, making Lily turn in surprise. She passed them both over to her.

'Two slices of lemon,' she pulled out a little sandwich bag with two pieces of lemon and dropped one in each of the cups, and Lily started to smile.

'And two cans of Vodka and Tonic, ready mixed.' She brought them out from the other pocket and twisted back the ring pulls, as calmly as if she carried such things around with her every day. 'Cold,' she said, holding the can against her red hot cheek. 'But sadly, no ice.'

She poured and both of the cups fizzed up and immediately overflowed. 'I got the impression you needed one.'

'You're wonderful,' Lily smiled.

'It's medicinal,' said Grace, taking a glass from Lily and catching the spill on her tongue, quickly drinking it down to a level that would stay in the cup. 'Drink it.'

'Thanks!' Lily said.

She drank far too quickly because she was so thirsty, and when she had finished she lay down, putting the cup on the grass beside her, and turned over on to her back.

'Now I'm pissed, Grace,' she said indignantly, staring up at the sky. 'It must be the altitude.'

'Or that you haven't eaten anything for God knows how long,' Grace said, looking at Lily's concave stomach and jutting hipbones exposed to the cold air.

They lay there silently for a moment longer.

'Give us a cigarette then,' Lily said.

Grace moved back to her coat pockets. She brought out a packet and lit and handed one to Lily and then sat back against a tree, watching the smoke curl from Lily's lips and drift upwards into the sky.

Slowly Lily started to tell her about Josh.

'I keep thinking how lucky I am to have found someone. Finally feel all those things I'm meant to feel,' Lily said, speaking so quietly that Grace could hardly hear her. 'You said things about me once. And you were right.' She looked over to Grace. 'Those things about me not feeling anything. You were right. I never had.'

'I shouldn't have said that.'

'No, you were right,' Lily insisted. 'And that was why it was fantastic to meet Josh, and finally feel it. I've felt what it's like now.' She stopped again.

'And?' Grace said, aware of a tightening in her chest, because Lily was finally talking to her like she'd always wanted her too, giving ground, conceding weaknesses and admitting a vulnerable side, giving Grace the opportunity to help her.

'Now I can't believe I'll be able to keep him.'

'I think that's part of the deal. Until you know him better. If you care about someone, a part of you is always going to imagine how much it would hurt to lose them. I think everybody does that.'

Neither of them spoke for a while and Lily eventually stubbed out her cigarette and dropped the butt in her empty can and stood up again.

'Why do you think you're going to lose him?' Grace asked looking up at her.

Lily didn't answer at first. 'Because he's a massive flirt,' she said, walking away a little. 'And I've seen it first hand. He did it to me when he was here. I was fun, a distraction. I know I didn't mean anything to him.'

'And then I saw him with another girl, just a few weeks ago. And she looked just like I think I would look – gazing up at him like she couldn't believe her luck. And I can't help wondering what happened to her, and whether I'm destined to be that girl too. I'm scared that there must have been at least another hundred and fifty girls like her. And another hundred and fifty to come.'

'But you didn't think that when you were with him?'

'No,' Lily agreed with a sigh. 'When I was with him, I couldn't think of anything apart from how wonderful he was. And I think he guessed how I'd doubt him now. He even warned me about it. Told me not to doubt him. Not to do exactly what I'm doing now. But I can't help it. I still think he's a serial seducer.'

'Oh, don't, Lily,' Grace told her emphatically. 'You'll do your head in. Don't think. Don't worry. You're seeing him again today, just get on with it!'

'But it's not that simple! I can't just say, yes Grace, you are absolutely right! I'm sure you are. But it doesn't work like that.'

'I know. But what's your choice?'

Lily bit her lip and shrugged. 'I have no choice. Even if I knew, absolutely *knew* that he was bad news, there's no way I'd get out first.'

'Lily!' Grace said impatiently. 'Stop it! I can't believe you're talking about getting out. Nothing has gone wrong!'

'I know,' Lily winced. 'Don't shout. I thought you of all people would think I should get away, but you're right. I'm being pathetic. Once I see him again it'll all be fine.' She fell silent again and then sat back against a rock and closed her eyes.

For all her common-sense talk, Grace's first thought had been that Lily should get away. That nothing and no one was worth the risk of being hurt like she had been. But before she'd said anything out loud she had managed to clamp down on herself, because she knew that Lily had no alternative but to see it through just like she had. The thought of Lily with someone who might mess with her just a tiny bit turned Grace's stomach. In the bad times, she'd even wished it upon Lily, thought that if Lily could only experience one tiny bit of what she was going through herself, she would be a better, more compassionate person because of it. Lily had seemed so strong, so insulated from pain that she'd wanted to puncture her. But now she felt ashamed that she could have imagined such a thing, wanting to protect her and yet knowing that only Lily could take the decision to get out, and that the likelihood of her doing so was zero. Because who in Lily's position had ever chosen to do that?

'I know it's nothing like what you went through with Jeremy,' Lily ventured, her eyes still closed. The words hung in the air. She hadn't raised the subject of Jeremy for a long while.

'Of course it's not. I never once doubted Jeremy. I wish I had,' Grace said. Lily smiled up at her. 'Well, if I did doubt him I pushed the doubt away again, because I thought married to Jeremy and miserable was better than not married to Jeremy and miserable.' Grace stopped for a moment. 'It was different. People were telling me to keep away from him. Nobody's saying that to you.' She looked down at her again. 'And now that you've mentioned Jeremy, I'm going to ask you something, Lily,' she said, coming to sit down beside her. 'And you've got to tell me the truth.' She took her time. 'Did something once happen between you two, something that you haven't told me about?'

Colour immediately flooded Lily's cheeks and she couldn't help herself looking away.

Oh my God! Grace thought in horror. I didn't mean an affair. In all this time I never thought *that*.

'Yes, in a way,' Lily said heavily. Then she saw the look on Grace's face. 'Not that! Not an affair!' Lily said, outraged, seeing the question on Grace's face. 'For God's sake, Grace! I'm your sister!' She moved away from Grace and rolled over on to her stomach.

'What then?' Grace asked, calming down.

'I told him what I'd said to you,' Lily said hesitantly. 'That I didn't think he loved you enough.'

'And?'

'And I told him I thought he should leave you alone . . .'

Grace's eyes widened. 'Did you? And what did he say?'

323

'That he wanted the pleasure of marrying you first.'

Grace sharply drew in her breath. Then she said in a quiet, sad voice, 'And then what did he say?'

'I'm so sorry, Grace.' Lily came and sat next to her and put her arm around her, seeing that she was starting to cry. 'I said that he couldn't do that to you. You know, I remember thinking at the time that he didn't mean it. That he said it because he knew I didn't like him, and it made him really hate me, and he wanted to hurt me. It wasn't anything to do with what he felt for you.' She touched Grace's arm, trying to reassure her. 'But then, he didn't show up, so God, I've always felt that perhaps he did it because of what I said.'

'That's what I've always felt too. I blamed you for frightening him off somehow. The fact that he was so spineless, so despicable that he could be frightened off, didn't matter. I'd rather he'd stayed. I really loved him . . .' Tears filled Lily's eyes too. 'What did I do to deserve him?' Grace smiled. 'I'm fine. Honestly. I'm not crying because I'm sad about him. Not any more. I'm crying because it took me so long to get over him, and I hate myself for it.' She sniffed. 'He means nothing to me now. I promise you. I can't even remember what it was like to be in bed with him.' She laughed, and wiped her nose and eyes with her sleeve.

'The vodka doesn't help!'

Grace nodded. 'Now I want to be strong. I don't want this hanging over me any more. I mean it, Lily. I was over him long before I was over what happened to me. It was the humiliation and the rejection and envying everyone else who seemed to be leading normal lives. But I needed to know. I needed to ask you.'

Lily nodded.

'It couldn't happen to me again because I'm so much stronger now. I don't need a man to make me happy. And you've got to be the same. Strong and confident. Go there for dinner thinking he's mad about you because he will be. Make him need you more than you need him.'

18

Lily had half hoped, half expected Josh to come and find her at Owl Cottage before dinner, but then at about six he rang from the car to say that the traffic was awful and that he and Hal would meet them at Pond House.

The previous afternoon, in her favourite shop in Welshpool, she'd found a 1940s lace and velvet top, fitted and very sexy, with a low scooped neck and tiny jet buttons at the cuffs. Not wanting to dress it up too much, she was going to wear it with her jeans.

Kirsty came into her bedroom while Lily was getting ready, and watched as she put some sparkle stick on her eyelids. She smiled at Lily's reflection, thinking how wonderful Lily always looked, with her own personal mix of modern and old, as always wearing her clothes with the cool they required.

'Josh won't know what's hit him! You look amazing.'

'Do you think?' Lily grinned happily back at her, moving on to the mascara.

'How's Grace going to cope tonight?' Kirsty asked, trying on the sparkle stick in the mirror over Lily's shoulder.

'I think she'll enjoy herself. As long as you don't give her a hard time.'

'Have I ever!'

Lily laughed uncomfortably.

'No, of course I won't. Grace and I understand each other now.' Kirsty smiled at Lily. 'And I was never horrible to her face, just behind her back. She never knew.'

'She's a different person now. And she needs you to be *very* nice.'

'I know. And I'm pleased she's coming. But when I said how was she going to cope,' Kirsty said, 'I was thinking of you and Josh. It won't be easy for her, seeing you with him. Won't it remind her of everything and make her worry about you?'

'We talked about it this afternoon. I think she'll be okay.'

Kirsty caught Lily's eye in the mirror and held it. 'She's got a lot to thank you for. Don't let her get in the way of you and Josh.'

'She wasn't ever going to! She's happy for me.'

Kirsty added some of Lily's lipstick, then turned to her for approval.

Lily nodded. 'Why is it, whenever I think about him I feel sick?' She fell back on the bed.

'You know you were so much more fun before you met him.'

Lily laughed. 'Really?'

'Really.'

'Come on. We'll be late.' Lily sat up again on the bed.

'No, Lily! It's half past six! But we can go now if you want to. Simon will be pleased to see us early.'

'To see you.'

'And you.'

'And we could give him a hand, couldn't we? Peel some vegetables or something.'

'Have you ever tried? He goes crazy if anyone gives him a hand. Carving knife crazy.'

'Well, let's go and sit with him in the kitchen and have a drink until they arrive. Grace will be there soon. She's early for everything.'

'We could have a little sherry together.'

'Stop teasing me.'

Kirsty was driving and was going to stay the night with Simon afterwards, and Lily was either going back to the Little Goose with Josh or would stay at Pond House with Kirsty and Simon if the disaster that she insisted she could now feel in her bones materialized. She felt that if she planned to stay with Josh she was tempting fate, but if she at least pretended that she was going to stay at Pond House, then it would turn out all right.

Simon had some lethal raspberry cocktails ready for them when they arrived, and as soon as she saw him and them, Lily felt better. She and Kirsty took up positions at the other end of the kitchen away from Simon, and watched him preparing supper.

'Don't you think it's odd,' Kirsty asked Lily in a low voice when Simon took a sip of something off a wooden spoon, 'how cooking is so sexy?'

'How can I answer that?' Lily demanded. 'You'll wonder about me if I say yes, and kill me if I say no.'

Kirsty drummed her fingers on the kitchen table and looked at Lily. 'They'll be here soon.'

'Really?' Lily said sarcastically.

'Stop winding her up, Kirsty,' Simon said, walking back to the other end of the room where two fat plucked ducks were sitting in a pan. He brought a bowl out of the fridge.

'What is that?' Lily asked, interested.

'Butter, zest of an orange, a little honey, some pancetta.' He began sliding the mixture expertly under the ducks' skin with his fingers.

Kirsty grimaced and looked away. 'Tell Lily what we're having,' she told him.

'I'm not hurt by that look, Kirsty,' Simon replied. He turned to Lily. 'Remember, when it comes to food, she knows nothing.'

'We're having roast duck,' Kirsty said bitterly. 'Two roast ducks, and I knew them both well. And it's not funny,' she snapped at Simon, noticing him catch Lily's eye. She turned back to Lily and said plaintively. 'I knew them when they quacked.'

Lily nodded, looking solemn. 'And now they've croaked.'

Grace arrived. She was led through into the kitchen by Kirsty and she looked thin and pretty in a little black top and dark red stretchy skirt.

'What happened to Mimosa?' she whispered later to Lily when Kirsty was out of earshot.

'She's gone,' Lily told her. 'Gone for good.'

Lily led Grace through into the hall and they sat down together in front of the fire and Lily told her what had happened – about Kirsty and Simon's walk, and how Mimosa had packed and left before their return – and there was nothing in Grace's face that gave her away. Nothing that could have given Lily any idea of the lovely lighting up inside when she heard that Mimosa had gone, and then, just seconds later, the horrible realization that Simon was now with Kirsty.

'There was something sad about Mimosa,' Grace said instead. 'I'm sorry for her, but Simon is better off with Kirsty.'

She wasn't going to let on to Lily what it took to say that. How when she'd first told Lily that she didn't need a man, secretly she'd still thought she might have Simon, because the more Lily talked about Kirsty and Simon, there was less and less for Grace to say. Hearing it all, she saw that, of course, Simon had been Kirsty's all along. Grace remembered the first time she'd seen him, there in Kirsty's Warehouse, and when she thought about it, how obvious it had been, even then, that Kirsty was the only girl he could see, the only one he was aware of. And somehow, realizing that she'd never had a chance made it easier to deal with now. She looked across at Kirsty, who was standing just through the doorway in the kitchen talking to him, and thought how again Kirsty was closest to the one person Grace wanted for herself. First Lily, now Simon. But she could give in this time. Could even look over at Kirsty and think how she was going to use this evening to get to know her, to get on with her, and do away with all the tension that had so dominated every moment each had spent in the other's company.

Once, soon after Lily had moved in with Grace, Lily had invited Kirsty around for supper, no doubt hoping it would jolly Grace up a little. Grace had refused supper and had instead left the table and stretched out on the sofa where she'd stayed, glaring at the television and feeling humiliated, while Kirsty and Lily had sat across the room, laughing and eating and ignoring her. But even then she'd wished that Kirsty was someone she could get to know. Known that if only Grace could have grabbed hold of her, Kirsty would have been good for her. That evening Grace had finally left the room and crept defeated up the stairs to her bedroom, with each step feeling as if she was sinking. Going down, slowly and invisibly.

But this evening, as she walked into Pond House, she knew straight away that Kirsty had been watching for her. When she'd knocked on the door, it had been Kirsty who had let her in, who had kissed her and squeezed her shoulder, told her how great it was to see her, put a drink into her hand and led her through to find Simon and Lily.

When there was a second loud knocking at the door, Lily's heart immediately started to do the same. She came out into the hall, wanting to hide behind Kirsty.

Simon opened the front door to Josh and Hal, and Grace immediately joined Lily and stood protectively at her side, narrowing her eyes suspiciously as she waited for first sight of Josh.

Vaguely Lily was aware that Hal was there in the house, and talking excitedly in her right ear, but she wasn't taking him in and she felt him move away, to envelop Grace in a great hug and then turn to Kirsty. She could hear him telling her how much he'd been looking forward to seeing her again. But all the time, she was standing still and looking for Josh, and he was there, looking back at her. He came over to her slowly, savouring the moment, staring at her with such unashamed delight that she collapsed inside, wondering why she had ever felt she needed to doubt him.

'Hello, my darling,' he said, pulling her against him, and kissed her long enough for nobody to misunderstand the situation.

'I've missed you so much,' she said, looking up at him.

He hugged her tighter. 'Tell me just one tenth as much as I've missed you.'

'I can't believe you're here.'

'We nearly weren't. I am never letting Hal drive me around these lanes again. And tell me we don't have to sit through a dinner party. Not now. Not when I haven't seen you for so long.'

Lily smiled at him. 'It's only Hal who'd call it that. It's just supper. I thought it would be good fun. And with Hal here and everything . . .'

'I don't mind! I'm still with you, aren't I? I'll just have to look forward to being on my own with you afterwards. In a big bed in the Little Goose.'

Lily looked around to see they had been left alone. She wondered what Hal had made of seeing them together, but when they walked back into the kitchen there was no sign of him. Before the evening was up, she decided, Josh or she was going to have to talk to him.

Supper seemed to cook itself while Simon sat, relaxing on the arm of Kirsty's armchair, chatting and laughing with Grace and Hal, only getting up once to make another jug of cocktail. And then, just as everybody was becoming aware of how hungry they were, he told them it was time to eat.

Lily got up with the others and noticed how Hal immediately came over to take Josh's arm and lead him purposefully out of the room. He *had* seen Josh kiss her, Lily guessed. She let them go ahead, wanting to give Josh the chance to talk to Hal. At the same time, she could hear Simon calling her to come through and she knew she couldn't leave it too long. She walked quietly out into the hall and caught them standing in the shadows. Hal didn't see her go by and as she passed he raised his glass to Josh.

'You're pinching someone from me yet again, Josh,' she heard Hal whisper. 'Congratulatons!'

What? Lily thought, as Josh glanced worriedly in her direction. She kept on walking. She was unable to tell from his voice whether or not he was joking. Could it be true? Could Hal really be thinking of her like that?

She found herself in the kitchen, where Grace was sitting alone at a round table waiting for the others, and she pulled out a chair and sat down opposite her. Very quickly Hal and Josh joined her. Josh immediately caught her eye and nodded his head gently, directing his look across to Hal. Then he gave her a tiny smile as if to say that all was well. Hal must have been joking, Lily decided. He couldn't have been thinking of her like that.

Looking across to Hal, Lily could see no sign at all that he was upset with Josh. And if Josh was happy that surely must mean that Hal was pleased for them. He wouldn't have started to think of her like that, she told herself again. Not so soon after Amber.

Josh came to sit next to her on her left-hand side. To her right there was an empty place waiting for Simon. Seconds later he appeared, carrying two succulent, crispy, perfectly roasted ducks, Kirsty behind him with bowls of vegetables and bubbling dauphinoise potatoes.

All through supper, as they picked over the last pieces of duck, licking their fingers and talking and laughing, Lily watched Hal carefully, and knew by the end there was nothing on his mind, nothing for her to worry about. Then, later on, Josh caught her eye and whispered quickly, *I've told him*, and she grinned back, relieved that it had all been so straightforward.

Sitting next to Josh and looking across the table to Grace, watching her as she started to giggle at something Hal was whispering to her, Lily felt suddenly aware that this was one of those precious moments, one that she would remember, like a photograph, for the rest of her life. That whatever was to happen later, in days, months, years to come, at that moment everything was perfect, a fleeting flash of true happiness. Josh must have seen something in her face because she felt his hand reach for hers, and she thought how different it was to be sitting next to him this time, how lovely it was to allow her fingers to entwine with his in a secret delight at what they had together.

A crème brûlée and a gooseberry tart later, Hal decided it was time to stand up and propose a toast.

Sweet, Lily thought, catching Kirsty's eye. I wonder what he's going to say.

'Simon,' Hal began, raising his glass, 'I should start with you, because that was the most delicious supper. You deserve a star, a Michelin Star.' He paused. 'Then Lily, for being so utterly sweet, but I've told you that already so I'm not going to say it again.' He moved on. 'Kirsty and Grace,' he said, 'thank you both for all your efforts to sort me out.' Then he turned to Josh and slowly raised his glass. 'Without whom I wouldn't be here today,' he said staring at him. 'And I'm glad I am. Very, very glad.' He relaxed and smiled. 'You might be dangerously self-opinionated, extraordinarily arrogant, and sickeningly attractive to women, but thank you. I mean it, I'm truly grateful. Finally,' Hal said, 'I think we should toast Amber. The girl who got us all together. But who isn't here tonight.'

He put down his wine and pulled his jacket off the back of his chair, fumbling slowly in its pockets. Then he brought out his wallet, opened it, and prised out a photograph.

'I haven't shown you this before, have I?' he asked Lily, who was sitting opposite him.

Lily shook her head.

Hal held the little photograph in one hand and then picked up a fork with the other. Everybody watched silently as he slid the photograph carefully in between its prongs so that the photo was held in place.

'I need a prop,' he said and looked around for what he wanted. On a side table was a bowl of fruit and Hal went over to it, picked it up and carried it carefully back to the middle of the table. He chose an orange from the bowl, cut a neat hole in it with his knife and pushed the handle of the fork straight into it so that the fork stood up out of the orange like a sword in a stone. Then he replaced the orange in the bowl and placed the bowl in the centre of the table.

'Hello, everybody,' Hal said, moving the bowl from side to side and making them all smile. 'I'm Amber, your new table decoration. Everyone raise your glass to me.'

Lily waited until the photograph was there in front of her and then she looked curiously at it. The girl was smiling straight at the camera, undeniably beautiful, with long smooth dark brown hair and full cherry red lips. But she was also, undeniably, the girl who'd been with Josh that day on the Fulham Road. The girl he had walked with, arm in arm, straight past her. The girl Josh had put his arms around and kissed just ten feet away from her. It was Amber, Amber, Amber, all along.

She controlled herself beautifully. 'Oh, she is gorgeous, Hal!' Lily said, disentangling her hand from Josh's grasp under the table.

On no account was she going to let Hal notice anything was wrong. She was not going to add to the pain that his bastard of a friend had put him through already and was no doubt going to put him through again.

She turned the fruit bowl away again. 'You don't need to see her in the flesh to tell that.'

Josh and Amber would have been carrying on together ever since the aborted wedding day, she thought dully.

He must have flown off with her on honeymoon, just as Amber's sister had suspected. And he must still be seeing her, stringing Lily along at the same time. Why, *why* bother with me too? she thought miserably. Unless it was simply because he could. Because she, Lily, had made it so easy for him to do just that. After the day they'd spent together, he'd probably gone straight from Lily to Amber. And she couldn't believe that she could be so stupid as to let this happen.

Hal looked at the photograph and talked as if she was the only person in the room.

'I'm not carrying your photo around because I think I can make things better. Not any more,' he said quietly. 'But it feels a bit like taking off a wedding ring, throwing you away. Even though I know it's over, it's a big step.'

'I would,' Lily told him, bitterly, breaking the silence. 'I'd throw it away. Tear it into little pieces and get on with your life.'

She picked up her glass of wine, drained it, then reached across the table for Hal's cigarettes and lit one.

You bastard, she thought, still looking anywhere but Josh.

Hal was staring at her, eyebrows raised.

'Just every now and again,' she told him. 'When I get desperate. I'll smoke it by the fire.' She stood up and quickly left the room, aware of the immediate resumption of laughter and conversation that told her the rest of them had noticed nothing wrong.

So, she thought bitterly, staring into the flames. The cracks and chips have shown up on Josh after all. How

desperate he must be to do that to Hal! But perhaps he
and Amber were so in love they couldn't do anything else.
The thought that Hal had forgiven Josh and was now
starting to put everything to do with Amber behind him,
and was about to get hurt all over again made her angrier
for Hal than for herself. She wanted Hal to know what a
devious, gutless man he had for a friend. And yet she
knew she couldn't do it to him.

She imagined them all sitting around the table unaware
of what was going on inside her, and she wanted to go
home. And never see Josh again. But she sat instead close
to the fire, not feeling strong enough to stand up and leave,
and pretty soon Josh came through the door and over to
her chair, taking in the look on her face, concern growing
in his eyes.

He crouched down in front of her. 'Are you okay?'

'Fuck off,' she hissed.

For a moment he looked as if she had knocked all the
breath out of him. He dropped her hand but seemed not
to know what else to do and continued to crouch there at
her feet, speechless.

'I mean right now.'

His face went hard and he got up and turned away
and left her.

Then the others realized that something was up and
came through to join her. Only Hal seemed oblivious. He
came and sat down in the armchair opposite Lily, with
Amber's orange in his hand, and started to peel it, then
offered it around. When nobody took him up on the offer

he started to eat it messily, the juice trickling down his chin and on to his trousers.

Then Josh reappeared again in the doorway. Without looking at Lily, he announced to the room that he was going back to the Little Goose.

'But what about me?' Hal called. 'I don't want to go yet!' He looked at his watch. 'Come off it, Josh!'

To shut Hal up Grace offered to drop him off on her way home. Then she left her chair and came over to Lily, full of worry.

'Come outside. Please tell me what's wrong,' she begged her.

But Josh, his face angry and hurt, had turned his back on all of them and was starting to make his way out to the front door. That it was the end between them, Lily knew with terrible certainty. But still the thought of him leaving, and her never speaking to him again, was too awful to imagine. She couldn't let him go, and she got up and ran out of the room after him.

'Is there more?' Josh asked as she met him on the other side of the front door.

She stared back at him, still feeling as if she might burst with fury at him for being so stupid.

'Explain to me, please, why you said that,' he said quietly. 'I should know what's going on.'

'You and Amber are going on.' She watched him flinch and knew that, of course, she'd been right, and any last vestige of hope had to go. 'And I've only just realized.' Josh looked at her sharply. 'You must have thought I would never find out,' she went on. 'Or perhaps you wouldn't have cared if I had? And I suppose Hal doesn't know either. Even if you could do it to me, how could you do that to Hal? Your friend. How dare you do it to either of us?'

He walked away from her and looked up at the stars.

'I thought you knew. Something you said made me think you already knew . . . It never occurred to me that it was such a big deal. I wouldn't have kept it back from you either. It had nothing to do with you and me.'

'You thought I wouldn't mind! That it didn't matter? Of course it did.'

'Lily,' he looked back at her. 'It didn't.'

'But how can you say that? How can you not see that I'm not like all your other girls!' she cried. 'And I always knew what you were like! I was so stupid to get involved with you.'

'Really? You were so stupid why? What am I like?'

'Faithless, unfaithful . . .' Lily ventured.

'Anything else?'

'Shallow, unreliable.'

'No wonder you want to get away. But all I've wanted to do,' he said, 'from the moment I first saw you, is be loyal to you, faithful to you, to love you, to look after you. Only you!' He laughed bitterly. 'Do I deserve this? Is that why this is happening now? A punishment for never having felt anything like this before? I finally get to see what it's all about and then, instantly, it's taken away from me again?'

'How can you ask me that?' she spat out.

He waited for a moment, as if he still couldn't quite believe it. That if he waited long enough, she was going to apologize, or tell him that it was all one hugely unfunny joke at his expense. But she didn't, and eventually he turned his back on her and walked towards his car.

'No, don't go!' she called then. 'I deserve more than that.'

He turned back again.

'*You* deserve more than that? *I* deserve more than that! Amber has absolutely nothing to do with you and me and if you weren't programmed to be *quite* so suspicious of me, *quite* so sure that I'm so *faithless*, and *unfaithful*, we wouldn't even be having this conversation.'

'Oh really,' Lily said sarcastically. 'What would Hal say?'

'Hal knows. Amber told him months ago.'

'Told him what? That you took his place on the honeymoon?'

'I did not do that!' Josh said enunciating each word extremely clearly. 'That is ridiculous.'

'Josh!' Lily said, heart beating faster. 'I know that you're still having an affair with her.' She felt a grim thrill at the words because, horrible as it was, she knew she'd got him.

'No, Lily. I am not. Nothing has happened between Amber and me for months.'

'But I saw you kissing her on the street,' Lily blurted out. 'Just last week. I saw you both on the Fulham Road.'

'Oh, you did? What do you think you saw?' he said contemptuously. 'The most you saw was someone happy

341

again. She's been let off the hook! She's enjoying herself! So she wants to kiss me! Big deal! What's wrong with that? You should be having this conversation with Amber, Lily. Not with me.'

'You were kissing her, too,' Lily insisted, wanting to hang on to the certainty, unable to face the awfulness of everything that she'd said to him if it wasn't true. 'It was obvious that you were more than just friends.'

'Oh, for Christ's sake Lily! Listen to yourself.'

All at once it was the last thing she wanted to do.

'You don't understand.'

She wanted to say that she'd seen Amber looking at Josh with love practically pouring out of her ears, that anyone would have thought like she had done. But she'd presumed everything from it, and already said so much that she couldn't bring herself to say anything else. She knew that she'd ruined all the chances for her and Josh. That the one day, that beautiful golden day, was all that they'd have. He was still angry with her. She could see it in the turn of his shoulders against her as he moved towards his car.

'You should have trusted me,' he said, opening the door.

'I know I should.'

She walked over to him and stood close by him and for a while neither of them spoke.

'If I said please forgive me. That I'll go crazy if I lose you. That I'm sorry. Would it make a difference?'

'*If* you said that? Or you *are* saying that?'

'I *am* saying that.'

He got into his car and looked at her through the open window. 'Then forgiveness could be in order.'

'When? Now? Tomorrow? Next month?' She couldn't believe that he was still prepared to drive away from her. 'Don't go yet.'

'I've things to do. It's late.'

'Josh! Wait!' she said aghast. She bent down and looked in through the window. 'When am I forgiven?'

'Lily,' he told her wearily. 'I forgive you now. How could I not? I completely adore you.'

'You haven't told me that before.'

'Well, I'm telling you now.'

'Then get out of the car,' she insisted. 'Let me tell you how much I adore you too. You've got to.'

'No. I haven't got to. This time you've got to trust me. Start practising!' He kissed her quickly on the cheek. 'I've got to go.'

Without saying anything more, or even looking at her again, he started the engine.

'But aren't you even going to say goodbye?' she called after him as the car shot forwards out of the drive.

When Lily walked back into the house, Kirsty and Grace looked at her anxiously but it was obvious that whatever had happened outside the house was an improvement on whatever had happened inside and that Lily was feeling better.

'I'll tell you later,' Lily mouthed to them both, nodding slightly at Hal, who was still sitting in front of the fire, eyes half closed.

Later, as she and Grace cleared up together, she caught

sight of Kirsty and Simon in the kitchen, kissing under a tea towel, and she turned away, busying herself with finding all the dirty glasses left in the hall. Josh and I could be like that, she thought. Why had he gone? How could he have said that to her and then disappeared? But she knew why. That after such a conversation, leaving her was the best thing to do. She'd have done the same.

Hal had obviously decided the best thing to do was to avoid the subject of her and Josh completely. Instead he talked to her about his holiday, which was scheduled to start almost as soon as he returned to London from Welshpool. Lily listened to his itinerary half-heartedly, her mind on Josh.

'I can't believe you've never travelled outside Europe,' Hal said.

'I don't think it's a problem,' she told him tiredly.

'But it is,' Hal insisted, 'it's a terrible gap in your education.'

She smiled. 'If you say so.'

'And I feel it is my duty to fill such a gap.'

'Really, Hal,' she laughed.

'Would you let me?'

Anything I say to you now, you'll forget in the morning, she thought, looking at his sweet face and his slightly bleary eyes. And anything you say to me you'll have forgotten too. 'Sort it out then,' she said in a moment of irresponsibility.

Hal smiled and nodded with satisfaction and leaned back for his jacket, now draped across his armchair. Again he reached for the inner pocket.

No more horrors, please, Lily thought as he pulled out

an organizer. He keyed something in that she couldn't read and then looked back at her with satisfaction.

'Done. Now I won't forget you in the morning,' he told her.

Suddenly, she couldn't bear it any longer. She wanted to bury her head in a cushion and sleep.

'Do you want me to take you home?' asked Grace, immediately standing up and coming over from the other side of the room.

'No, I think I'll stay the night here.'

Lily turned back to Hal. 'I have to go to bed. Do you mind?' She called through the door to Kirsty and Simon. 'If that's okay with you. Do you mind if I stay here?'

'Of course not,' Simon said.

'I'll dump Hal at the Little Goose,' Grace said.

'Dumping me at the Little Goose would be most kind,' Hal told her from his chair.

Lily leaned over to him and kissed him goodbye. He cupped her face in his large hands and looked carefully into her face. 'Don't worry,' he said. 'It's going to be okay.'

After Grace and Hal had left, Simon insisted that Kirsty take Lily up to bed and leave him to clear up the last things.

'It was absolutely awful,' Lily told Kirsty later in the bedroom. 'It was terrible. I was so horrible to Josh.'

'It wasn't your fault if you got the wrong end of the stick.'

'It was! I should have trusted him.'

'I didn't. I understand exactly why you said what you said.'

345

'But I'm supposed to know him better than you do!'

'I saw him in the Little Goose! You weren't so wrong.'

Lily sat down on the bed. 'What I'm saying, seriously, is that he was never like that. Not really. Not once I got to know him, and he got to know me. But I couldn't trust it. I was so scared I was going to be taken in.'

'But I don't think you've blown it. I think you've got another chance.'

'I think so too.' Lily smiled up at Kirsty.

'Give him tonight to get over it, then see him tomorrow.' Lily nodded.

Kirsty smothered a long yawn. 'Sorry!'

'Go to sleep. I'm sorry. I'll shut up.'

'It's okay. We can talk all night if it helps. But I don't think there's anything we can say. You'll see him tomorrow and talk it all though and everything will be fine. I don't think there's any doubt.'

'Thanks. Go to bed.'

'I'll drive you home as soon as you wake up. And then you can go and see Josh.'

*

Lily woke up the next morning to Kirsty shouting up to her from the bottom of the stairs.

'No thanks,' she called back, even though she couldn't hear a word, deciding this was the best way to shut her up.

It seemed to work. Peace returned to her bedroom. Lily waited for a few seconds then pushed her head deep into the soft white pillow and closed her eyes again, wondering if it had really worked, and how long she would be left alone, and then what it was that she'd turned down. She drifted, half awake, half asleep, aware of the breeze tickling the edges of her bedroom curtain, and listening to the gentle, musical woodwind of the doves cooing in the trees outside her window, and thought what a lovely house it was to wake up in, even if Kirsty did always have to do it so raucously.

Then came the sound of Kirsty's feet, heavy and purposeful on the wooden stairs, and Lily braced herself. As Kirsty came in she pushed herself upright in the bed.

'What do you mean *no thanks*?' Kirsty asked, indignantly, breathing hard, and she tossed a thick white envelope on to Lily's lap.

Lily picked it up in surprise, and turned it over in her hand.

'It's addressed to you, but why has it been sent *here*?'

Kirsty came and sat down on the bed beside Lily. 'What might it be?'

Lily looked down at her name neatly typed on the front and shrugged and suddenly was completely awake. She opened the envelope and pulled out a folded piece of paper and glanced quickly up at Kirsty before opening it. Inside, there was a sheet of Little Goose writing paper with a short scrawled message.

> Go home and get packing.
> We're going on holiday.

'I don't believe it,' Lily cried in astonishment.

Kirsty took it from her and read it and looked over to her silently for a few seconds. 'Best get off home!' she said then. 'Get packing!'

'Don't go all flippant on me. What's going on?' Lily pleaded. 'When? What holiday?' She swung the duvet off her legs. 'Where on holiday?' But she was starting to smile as she said it, because the thought of a holiday with Josh was fantastic, wonderful. She leaped out of bed. 'I can't believe it. Isn't this what you dream about?' She looked at Kirsty then turned around in the room. 'I need to find my jeans!' she panicked. 'I've got to get home.'

It's as if her speed setting's been turned up, Kirsty thought, sitting on the bed and watching Lily run around the room gathering up her things and stuffing them into her bag, then seconds later pulling everything out again as she searched for deodorant and a clean jumper.

'What if it's from Hal?' Kirsty said casually from the bed. 'He was definitely very keen on you last night.'

'What?' Lily said. She stopped what she was doing and looked up, a pair of knickers dangling from one finger.

'How do you know it's definitely from Josh?' Kirsty asked. 'It might be from Hal.'

Lily's face sagged. 'It can't be from Hal!'

Kirsty looked back at her. 'Why? And would it be so bad? Hal's a really nice guy. A really nice, rich guy. You'd have a great time.'

'Kirsty! What are you saying! I don't want to go on holiday with Hal! I'm not going on holiday with Hal,' she insisted. 'It was Josh who sent this letter to me.'

'Okay. Forget I said it. 'It's Josh. Definitely Josh.'

Lily stared back at her. 'But you're right. Hal did keep asking me to go away with him. And he put me in his bloody organizer.'

Kirsty got off the bed. 'I'm sorry I said anything. Give me five minutes and I'll drive you home.'

Lily went on downstairs and sat in the kitchen waiting for Kirsty. She wondered whether she was right to think that Kirsty still didn't like Josh. She unzipped her bag and found her mobile and called Grace, needing somebody else to tell about the note, someone more on Josh's side. The phone rang for a long time.

'Hmm?' Grace said eventually, not sounding like Grace at all. Grace usually answered as if she just might be being judged on her phone-answering skills.

'Have you got your mouth full?'

'Hello Lily.'

'I'm sorry. Have I woken you up?'

'No.'

'I wanted to talk to you.'

'Okay,' Grace said sounding cagey. 'About what?'

'I've had this weird note,' Lily started, already wishing she hadn't. There were things in Grace's voice telling her that Grace was not on for a chat. 'I think it must be from Josh. He says that he wants to take me away on holiday. I wondered what you thought . . .' Lily tailed off.

'That's great. Go for it.'

'Is that all?'

'What else?'

'Kirsty thought it might have been from Hal.'

'Oh no,' Grace said immediately. 'I doubt it would have been Hal.' And as she spoke the words, there was a cough. A distinctly male cough in the background.

'Grace!' Lily cried. 'You were meant to take him back to the Little Goose! Not take him home and shag him!'

'Lily,' Grace exploded back. 'I did not do that!'

Lily started to laugh. 'Yes you did.'

'He's here. Okay. But he's just arrived. Do you want to ask him yourself?'

'No!' She wanted to get off the phone and leave them to it. 'If Hal's with you, it's answered my question.'

She was thrilled for both of them. Completely delighted that Hal was with Grace. She hoped he had stayed the night. That he would stay the next night too, and the one after.

'I'll call you soon.'

'Lily, Hal arrived ten minutes ago. He really did.'

'Of course he did. Have fun!' Lily put down the phone, just as Kirsty walked in through the door.

'Guess what,' Lily said.

*

'But maybe he had just arrived for coffee,' Kirsty said when they were in the car driving back towards Owl Cottage. 'It doesn't mean he didn't send you the note.'

'Why do you keep doing this to me? Of course he didn't. Why can't you just accept that Josh wants to take me on holiday. You've got Simon. Why can't I have Josh?'

'I want you to have Josh,' Kirsty said, looking at her.

'Don't think I don't. Of course I do. But I can't help saying these things. They're on my mind.'

'Well, they're not on mine. Not until you put them there anyway . . .'

'Honestly, Lily. It's nothing to do with what I think about Josh. I like him. I really, really like him and I can't think of anyone better for you. But I'm worried that he didn't send you that note. Why don't you call him now and ask him?'

'But then I'd spoil it. Wouldn't I? He's wanting me to trust him. That's the whole point. He won't want me to check it all out with him first.'

They'd arrived back at the cottage.

'Are you coming in?'

'What do you think? That I'd leave you on your own?'

They unlocked the door and walked tentatively into the cottage together, almost as if they were expecting Josh to jump out at them, or at the very least to find another white envelope lying on the mat. There was nothing there.

'Don't stay,' Lily told her then. 'You don't have to, and I know you promised Simon you'd be around this morning.'

Kirsty was obviously torn.

'Honestly. I promise I'm fine,' Lily insisted. 'What do I need you here for anyway? If anything happens you'll be the first to know. But I'm not going to start packing. Not without an idea of whether this is some joke.'

Kirsty took her arm, seeing in her face that Lily was losing her earlier certainty. 'Don't worry. It's not some joke.'

As she said that the letter-box rattled behind them and they both jumped around. In a flash Kirsty raced to the window.

'It's okay. It's just the postman,' she said turning back. But Lily was already standing in front of her, another envelope in her hand.

'He's a bit too clever by half,' Lily said, trying to sound unfazed. 'There's no postmark on this. One more of these and he'll start to give me the creeps.' She pulled open the envelope.

'He must have got the postman to drop it off. Why couldn't he just give it to you himself?' Kirsty asked her impatiently. 'No, I know,' she said immediately. 'It's kind of more fun this way.'

Lily hadn't replied. Seeing the dazed look on her face, Kirsty took the letter out of her hands and read it.

'Have you seen *when* you're going?' Kirsty asked at last.

Lily took it back again. 'What's today, Saturday? Oh, not today! He's mad. What if I couldn't? And how did he manage to sort it all out so fast?'

'It's possible. If you find the right sort of travel agent.'

'But I have to get ready. Packed. I have to find my passport!' Lily looked frantically around the room. 'And I have to get to the airport. Where am I meant to be flying from?'

'Birmingham International. I'd say we should leave in the next couple of hours. You should call Grace and say goodbye.'

'Oh Kirsty!' Lily shook her head. 'I had no idea. I thought he was talking about Devon, or the Lake District.'

'Shame! If only you'd known you could have got your legs waxed.'

'St Lucia,' Lily said, starting to laugh too. 'I don't *know* anyone who's been there. Will you really take me to the airport?'

Kirsty left her in Owl Cottage getting ready, promising to come and pick her up again within the hour. And once she'd gone Lily started circling the cottage, throwing together her things. She had no bikini, no sun tan lotion. Just a few grubby T-shirts and an old sarong. But she didn't care. Alone in the house, running around, up and down the stairs in her bare feet, she felt as if she could fly, full of anticipation and happiness and wild excitement.

She was ready for Kirsty when she returned to pick her up and then, almost before she'd settled down to the journey, they had arrived at the airport, pushing their way in together and making their way over to International Departures.

There was no sign of Josh. Twenty minutes later and there was nothing left to do but for Lily to leave Kirsty on the other side of passport control and make her way towards the plane.

'I just can't bear it!' Kirsty cried. 'I want to know so badly.'

'You do know. We both know it's him.'

Lily hugged her tightly and whispered goodbye. She left Kirsty then, not wanting to look back at her, and disappeared into passport control, and Kirsty waited another moment more and then turned back, out through the doors, willing Lily to remember to find a moment to call her and to tell her that it really had been Josh waiting for her on the other side, and that the whole thing hadn't been some terrible joke.

Lily moved hesitantly on towards the X-ray machines, thinking all the time that she could see him. But there was still nobody there that she recognized. She slid her handbag on to the checks, and then picked it up again the other side, still looking around her, nervously, still not finding him.

And then she did see something. Someone. A golden head, a foot taller than nearly everybody else, turning instinctively towards her. And it was Josh. When she caught his eye she started to laugh because he looked so delighted, and so relieved that she was there, and then she ran towards him.

'What are you doing here?' she said into his neck. 'I'm waiting for Hal.'

'Give up, Lily.' He bent to kiss her lips. 'You've been waiting for me.'

She looked up at him. 'Yes,' she said. 'It's true.'

Arms around each other, they started to walk away from passport control and on into the departure lounge. It was still half an hour before their flight was to be called, and Lily could see a tiny boutique out of the corner of her eye. She could see that they had sunglasses for sale, and some perfect Burberry bikinis.

Epilogue

They walked along a gently twisting path towards the hotel's reception, past tiny waterfalls and fantastic flowers and under great canopies of scented blossom. As they drew near a waiter came out to join them, with a silver tray and two long glasses of fruit punch.

'Welcome to La Mouskia – Mr Fairfax and Miss Somerville – we hope you will have a wonderful stay.'

At the hotel's reception their arrival caused a sudden burst of activity. What's the problem, Lily wondered, waiting patiently next to Josh. Eventually the hurried conversation stopped and the manager looked up, beamed at them both and came over.

'We would like to move you to another room,' he explained.

'Oh!' said Lily. 'Why?'

The manager paused, for a brief moment torn between professional discretion and an acute desire to spill the beans. 'Our honeymoon suite has unexpectedly become available.'

He looked at them both and sadly shook his head. 'It appears that the bride has decided not to marry her groom after all.'

Lily thought it was better if she didn't catch Josh's eye.

'We would be delighted if you would take the suite instead.'

Josh took a firm grasp of Lily's hand.

'That would be perfect,' he said.

Acknowledgements

Of course Kirsty is wrong and there are lots of good-looking men in Welshpool and I hope she hasn't offended male residents of Welshpool or anyone else. I owe my thanks to many of them for helping me with the book, especially Liz Wait, Sharon Sheppard and Heather Pugh. Thanks too to my family, particularly to Josie for swapping tea for vodka, to Hez for the details about Montgomery and to Charlotte Bevan who was such a brilliant sounding board, and also to friends who helped in so many ways, especially Edla Griffiths, Antonia Brooks and Louise Voss. Thank you to Clifford Evans of the Shropshire Rural Stress Support Network who provides an invaluable service and whose advice I greatly value. Thanks to everyone at Pan for their great ideas and hard work, especially my wonderfully supportive editor, Imogen Taylor. And to Jo Frank, a better agent and friend would be hard to find. And, most of all, thanks to dearest Ant. As he says himself, greater love hath no man than he who lives with a writer.